C8 000 0

KU-074-180

FROM
London
With Love

With Love
COLLECTION

February 2017   February 2017   February 2017

March 2017   March 2017   March 2017

FROM
London
With Love

SARAH
MALLORY

LYN
STONE

MILLS &
BOON

All rights reserved including the right of reproduction in whole or in part in any form. This edition is published by arrangement with Harlequin Books S.A.

This is a work of fiction. Names, characters, places, locations and incidents are purely fictional and bear no relationship to any real life individuals, living or dead, or to any actual places, business establishments, locations, events or incidents. Any resemblance is entirely coincidental.

This book is sold subject to the condition that it shall not, by way of trade or otherwise, be lent, resold, hired out or otherwise circulated without the prior consent of the publisher in any form of binding or cover other than that in which it is published and without a similar condition including this condition being imposed on the subsequent purchaser.

® and TM are trademarks owned and used by the trademark owner and/or its licensee. Trademarks marked with ® are registered with the United Kingdom Patent Office and/or the Office for Harmonisation in the Internal Market and in other countries.

First Published in Great Britain 2017
By Mills & Boon, an imprint of HarperCollins*Publishers*
1 London Bridge Street, London, SE1 9GF

FROM LONDON WITH LOVE © 2017 Harlequin Books S.A.

Disgrace and Desire © 2010 Sarah Mallory
The Captain and the Wallflower © 2012 Lynda Stone

ISBN: 978-0-263-92762-7

09-0317

Our policy is to use papers that are natural, renewable and recyclable products and made from wood grown in sustainable forests.
The logging and manufacturing processes conform to the legal environmental regulations of the country of origin.

Printed and bound in Spain
by CPI, Barcelona

DISGRACE
AND DESIRE

SARAH MALLORY

For Dave, Roger and Norman,
my very first heroes!

Sarah Mallory was born in the West Country and now lives on the beautiful Yorkshire moors. She has been writing for more than three decades—mainly historical romances set in the Georgian and Regency period. She has won several awards for her writing, most recently the Romantic Novelists' Association RoNA Rose Award in 2012 (*The Dangerous Lord Darrington*) and 2013 (*Beneath the Major's Scars*).

Prologue

Major Jack Clifton dragged one grimy sleeve across his brow. The battle had been raging all day near the little village of Waterloo. The tall fields of rye grass had been trampled into the ground as wave after wave of cavalry charged the British squares between bouts of deadly artillery fire. A smoky grey cloud hung over the battlefield and the bright colours of the uniforms were muted by a thick film of dust and mud.

'Look,' said his sergeant, pointing to the far ridge. 'That's Bonaparte up there!'

A nervous murmur ran through the square.

'Aye,' Jack countered cheerfully. 'And Wellington's behind us, watching our every move.'

'So 'e is,' grinned the sergeant. 'Well, then, let's show the Duke we ain't afraid of those Frenchies.'

Another cavalry charge came thundering towards them, only to fall back in a welter of mud, blood and confusion. Jack rallied his men, knowing that as long as he stayed calm the square would hold. A sudden flurry of activity caught his attention and a party of soldiers approached him, carrying someone in a blanket.

'Lord Allyngham, Major,' called one of the men as they laid their burden on the ground. 'Took a cannonball in his shoulder. He was asking for you.'

The bloodied figure on the blanket raised his hand.

'Clifton. Is he here?'

Jack dropped on one knee beside him. He averted his eyes from the shattered shoulder.

'I'm here, my lord.'

'Can't—see—you.'

Jack took the raised hand.

'I'm here, Tony.'

His calm words seemed to reassure Lord Allyngham.

'Letters,' he muttered. 'In my jacket. Will you see they are sent back to England, Jack? One for my wife, one for Mortimer, my…neighbour. Important…that they get them.'

'Of course. I'll make sure they are sent tonight with the despatches.'

'Thank you.'

Jack glanced up at the sergeant.

'Take him back, Robert, and get a surgeon—'

'No.' The grip on his hand suddenly tightened. 'No point: I know I'm done for.'

'Nonsense,' growled Jack. 'We'll have the sawbones patch you up—'

The glazed eyes seemed to clear and gain focus as he looked at Jack.

'Not enough left to patch,' he gasped. 'No, Jack, listen to me! One more thing—do I still have my hand?'

Jack glanced at the mangled mess of blood and bone that was his left side.

'Aye, you do.'

'Good. Can you take my ring? And the locket—on a ribbon about my neck. Take 'em back to my wife, will you? In person,

Jack. I'll not trust these damned carriers with anything so dear. Take 'em now, my friend.' He gritted his teeth against the pain as he struggled to pull a silk ribbon from beneath his jacket.

'Be assured, Tony, I'll deliver them in person,' said Jack quietly, easing the ring from the bloodied little finger.

Allyngham nodded.

'I'm obliged to you.' He closed his eyes. 'Good woman, Eloise. Very loyal. Deserved better. Tell her—' He broke off, wincing. He clutched at Jack's hand again. 'Tell her to be happy.'

Jack dropped the locket and the ring into his pocket and carefully buttoned the flap.

'I will, you have my word. And if there is anything I can do to help Lady Allyngham, be sure I shall do it.'

'Thank you. Mortimer will look after her while she is in mourning but after that, keep an eye on her for me, Jack. She's such an innocent little thing.'

A sudden shout went up. Jack looked up. For the past few moments he had been oblivious of the noise of the battle raging around him. Allyngham opened his eyes.

'What is it, why are they shouting?'

All around them the men were beginning to cheer.

'The French are in retreat,' said Jack, his voice not quite steady.

Allyngham nodded, his cracked lips stretching into a smile.

'Damnation, I knew the Duke would do it.' He waved his hand. 'Go now, Major. Go and do your duty. My men will look after me here.'

An ensign at his side nodded.

'Aye, we'll take care of him, sir,' he said, tears in his eyes. 'You may be sure we won't leave him.'

Jack looked down at the pain-racked face. Lord Allyngham gave a strained smile and said, 'Off you go, my friend.'

Jack rose and followed his men down the hill in pursuit of the French, who were now in full flight.

'Steady, lads,' he called, drawing his sword. 'We'll chase 'em all the way to Paris!'

In the drawing room of Allyngham Park, Eloise stood by one of the long windows, gazing out across the park, but the fine view swam before her eyes. There were two sheets of paper clutched in her hand and she glanced down at them before placing them upon the console table beside her. It would be useless to try to read while her eyes were so full of tears. She took out her handkerchief. It was already damp and of little use in drying her cheeks.

'Mr Mortimer, my lady.'

At the butler's solemn pronouncement she turned to see Alex Mortimer standing in the doorway. His naturally fair countenance was paler than ever and there was a stricken look in his eyes.

'You have heard?' She forced the words out.

'Yes.' He pulled a letter from his pocket. 'I came over as soon as this arrived. I am so very sorry.'

With a cry she flew across the room and threw herself upon his chest.

'Oh Alex, he is d-dead,' she sobbed. 'What are we going to do?'

She felt a shudder run through him. For a long while they sat on the sofa with their arms around each other. The shadows lengthened in the room and at last Eloise gently released herself.

'It says he d-died at the end of the day, and…and he knew

that the battle was won.' She dabbed at her eyes with the edge of the fine linen fichu that covered her shoulders.

'Then at least he knew he had not died in vain.' Alex had turned away but she knew he, too, was wiping away the tears. 'I had the news from a Major Clifton. He enclosed Tony's last message to me.'

Eloise rose and took a deep breath, striving for some semblance of normality. She walked over to pick up the papers.

'Yes, that is the name here, too. He says Tony gave him our letters to send on.' She swallowed painfully. 'Tony knew what danger he was facing. He…he wrote to say goodbye to us.'

Alex nodded. 'He bids me look after you, until you marry again.'

'Oh.' Eloise put her hands over her face. 'I shall never marry again,' she said at last.

Alex put his hands on her shoulders.

'Elle, you do not know that.'

'Oh, I do,' she sobbed, 'I doubt there is another man in the world as good, and kind, and generous as Tony Allyngham.'

'How can I disagree with that?' He gave her a sad little smile. 'And yet you are young, too young to bury yourself away here at Allyngham.'

She held up Tony's last letter.

'He has asked me to ensure that our plans for the foundling hospital go ahead. You will remember we discussed it just before he left for Brussels.' She sighed. 'How typical that when he was facing such danger Tony should think of others.'

He took her hand, saying gently, 'My dear, you will be able to do nothing until the formalities are complete. You will need to summon your man of business, and notify everyone.'

'Yes, yes.' She clutched his fingers. 'You will help me, will you not, Alex? You won't leave me?'

He patted her hand.

'No, I won't leave. How could I, when my heart is here?'

Chapter One

It was more than a year after the decisive battle at Waterloo that Jack Clifton returned to England. As he rode away from his comrades and the army, which had been his life for more than a decade, there were two commissions that he had assigned himself before he could attend to his own affairs. One was to return Allyngham's ring and locket to his widow, but first he would make a trip to a small country churchyard in Berkshire.

The little village outside Thatcham was deserted and there was no one to see the dusty traveller tie his horse to the gatepost of the churchyard. Jack shrugged off his greatcoat and threw it over the saddle. The rain that had accompanied him all the way from the coast had eased and now a hot September sun blazed overhead. He strode purposefully between the graves until he came to a small plot in one corner, shaded by the overhanging beech trees. The grave was marked only by a headstone. There were no flowers on the grassy mound and he was momentarily surprised, then his lip curled.

'Who is there but me to mourn your passing?' he muttered.

He knelt beside the grave, gently placing a bunch of white roses against the headstone.

'For you, Clara. I pray you are at peace now.'

He rose, removed his hat and stood, bareheaded in the sun for a few moments then, squaring his shoulders, he turned away from the grave and set his mind towards London.

Eloise clutched at her escort's arm as they entered Lady Parham's crowded reception rooms.

'I am glad you are with me, Alex, to give me courage.'

'You have never wanted courage, Elle.'

She managed one speaking look at him before she turned to greet her hostess, who was sweeping towards her, beaming.

'My dear Lady Allyngham! I am delighted to see you here. And honoured, too, that you should attend my little ball when everyone is quite *desperate* for your company! Some expected to see you in the summer, but depend upon it, I said, we will not see Lady Allyngham until the Little Season. She will not come to town until the full twelve months' mourning is done. As the widow of a hero of Waterloo we should not expect anything less. And Mr Mortimer, too. Welcome, sir.'

Lady Parham's sharp little eyes flickered over Alex. Eloise knew exactly the thoughts running through her hostess's mind and felt a little kick of anger. Everyone in town thought Alex was her lover. Nothing she could say would convince them otherwise, so she did not make the attempt. Besides, it suited her purposes to have the world think she was Alex's mistress. She had seen too many virtuous women hounded by rakes and roués until their resolve crumbled away. At least while the gentlemen thought she was living under Alex's protection they might flirt with her but they would not encroach upon another man's territory. Yet occasionally it galled her, when she saw that knowing look in the eyes of hostesses such as Lady Parham.

Twelve months of mourning had done much to assuage the feelings of grief and loss that had overwhelmed Eloise when she had learned of Tony's death. Through those lonely early weeks Alex had always been there to support her and to share her suffering. He was a true friend: they had grown up together and she loved him as a brother. She did not want the world to think him a deceitful womaniser who would steal his best friend's husband, but Alex assured her he was happy to be thought of as her *cicisbeo*.

'If it satisfies their curiosity then we should let it be,' he told her, adding with a rueful smile, 'Much less dangerous than the truth, Elle.'

And Eloise was forced to admit it kept the wolves at bay. Now she fixed her smile as she regarded her hostess, determined no one should think her anything less than happy.

'Mr Mortimer was kind enough to escort me this evening.'

'La, but you need no escort to my parties, dear ma'am. I am sure you will find only friends here.'

'Yes, the sort of friends who smile and simper and cannot wait to tear my character to shreds behind my back,' muttered Eloise, when her hostess had turned her attention to another arrival. Angrily she shook out the apricot skirts of her high-waisted gown.

'They are jealous because you cast them all into the shade,' remarked Alex.

'I did not think it would be so difficult,' sighed Eloise, 'coming back into society again.'

'We could always go back to Allyngham.'

'If I were not so determined to get on with fulfilling Tony's last wish to build a foundling hospital I would leave now!'

muttered Eloise angrily. After a moment she squeezed Alex's arm and gave a rueful little smile. 'No, in truth, I would not. I have no wish to be an outcast and live all my life in the country. I am no recluse, Alex. I want to be able to come to London and—and *dance*, or visit the theatre, or join a debating society. But I could do none of these things if you were not with me, my friend.'

'You could, if you would only hire yourself a respectable companion.'

She pulled a face.

'That might give me respectability, but I would still be vulnerable. Even worse, it might make people think I was on the catch for another husband.'

'And is there anything wrong with that?'

'Everything,' she retorted. 'I have been my own mistress for far too long to want to change my situation.'

'But you might fall in love, you know.'

She glanced up at him and found herself responding to his smile.

'I might, of course, but it is unlikely.' She squeezed his arm. 'I have some experience of a sincere, deep devotion, Alex. Only a true meeting of minds could persuade me to contemplate another marriage. But such a partnership is very rare, I think.'

'It is,' said Alex solemnly. 'To love someone in that way, and to know that you are loved in return, it is the greatest blessing imaginable.'

Eloise was silent for a moment, considering his words.

'And I could settle for nothing less,' she said softly. She looked up and smiled. 'But these are grave thoughts, and unsuitable for a party! Suffice it to say, my friend, that I am very happy to have you as my protector.'

'Then you must also accept the gossip,' he told her. 'It is no different from when Tony was in the Peninsula and I escorted you to town.'

'But it *is*, Alex. Somehow, the talk seems so much more salacious when one is a widow.'

He patted her arm.

'You will grow accustomed, I am sure. But never mind that now.' He looked around the room. 'I cannot see Berrow here.'

'No, I thought if he was going to be anywhere this evening it would be here, for Lord Parham is an old friend. Oh, devil take the man, why is he so elusive?'

'You could write to him.'

'My lawyer has been writing to him for these past six months to no avail,' she replied bitterly. 'That is why I want to see him for myself.'

'To charm him into giving you what you want?' asked Alex, smiling.

'Well, yes. But to do that I need to find him. Still, the night is young; he may yet arrive.'

'And until then you are free to enjoy yourself,' said Alex. 'Do you intend to dance this evening, my lady?'

'You know I do, Alex. I have been longing to dance again for the past several months.'

He made her a flourishing bow.

'Then will my lady honour me with the next two dances?'

Alex Mortimer was an excellent dancer and Eloise enjoyed standing up with him. She would not waltz, of course: that would invite censure. She wondered bitterly why she worried so about it. Waltzing was a small misdemeanour compared to the gossip that was spreading about her after only a few weeks in London—already she was being called the Wanton

Widow, a title she hated but would endure, if it protected those she loved. Eight years ago, when Lord Anthony Allyngham had first introduced his beautiful wife to society everyone agreed he was a very lucky man: his lady was a treasure and he guarded her well. During his years fighting in the Peninsula he had asked Alex to accompany Eloise to town, but it was only now that she realised the full meaning of the knowing looks they had received and the sly comments. It angered her that anyone should think her capable of betraying her marriage vows, even more that they should think ill of Alex, but since the truth was even more shocking, she and Alex had agreed to keep up the pretence.

The arrival of the beautiful Lady Allyngham at Parham House had been eagerly awaited and Eloise soon had a group of gentlemen around her. She spread her favours evenly amongst them, giving one gentleman a roguish look over the top of her fan while a second whispered fulsome compliments in her ear and a third hovered very close, quizzing glass raised, with the avowed intention of studying the flowers of her corsage.

She smiled at them all, using her elegant wit to prevent any man from becoming too familiar, all the time comfortable in the knowledge that Alex was in the background, watching out for her. She was surprised to find, at five-and-twenty, that the gentlemen considered her as beautiful and alluring as ever and they were falling over themselves to win a friendly glance from the widow's entrancing blue eyes. The ladies might look askance at her behaviour but the gentlemen adored her. And even while they were shaking their heads and commiserating with her over the loss of her husband, each one secretly hoped to be the lucky recipient of her favours. Eloise did her best to discourage any young man who might develop a serious *tendre* for her—she had no desire to marry again and wanted no broken hearts at her feet—but she was willing to indulge any gentlemen in a flirtation, secure in the knowledge that Alex would ensure it did not get out of hand.

It could not be denied that such attention was intoxicating. Eloise danced and laughed her way through the evening and when Alex suggested they should go down to supper she almost ran ahead of him out of the ballroom, fanning herself vigorously.

'Dear me, I had forgotten how much I enjoy parties, but I am quite out of practice! And perhaps I should not have had a third glass of—oh!'

She broke off as she collided with someone in the doorway.

Eloise found herself staring at a solid wall of dark blue. She blinked and realised it was the front of a gentleman's fine woollen evening coat. She thought that he must be very big, for she had always considered herself to be tall and yet her eyes were only level with the broad shoulder to which this particular coat was moulded. Her eyes travelled across to the snow-white neckcloth, tied in exquisite folds, and moved up until they reached the strong chin and mobile mouth. For a long time she felt herself unable to look beyond those finely sculpted lips with the faint laughter lines etched at each side. It was quite the most beautiful mouth she had ever seen. A feeling she had never before experienced thrummed through her. With a shock she realised what it was. Desire.

Summoning all her resources, she moved her glance upwards to meet a pair of deep brown eyes set beneath straight black brows. Almost immediately she saw a gleam of amusement creep into those dark eyes.

'I beg your pardon, madam.'

He spoke slowly but did not drawl, his voice deep and rich and it wrapped around Eloise like a warm cloak, sending a tiny *frisson* of excitement running down her spine. Really, she must pull herself together!

'Pray think nothing of it, sir…'

'But I must, Lady Allyngham.'

She had been enjoying the sound of his voice, running over her like honey, but at the use of her name she gave a little start.

'You know who I am?'

He gave her a slow smile. Eloise wondered if she had taken too much wine, for all at once she felt a little dizzy.

'You were described to me as the most beautiful woman in the room.'

She had thought herself immune to flattery, but she was inordinately pleased by his words. She did not know whether to be glad or sorry when she felt Alex's hand under her elbow.

'Shall we get on, my lady?'

'Yes,' she said, her eyes still fixed upon the smiling stranger. 'Yes, I suppose we must.'

Really, she felt quite light-headed. Just how many glasses of wine had she taken?

The stranger was standing aside. The candlelight gleamed on his black hair and one glossy raven's lock fell forwards as he bowed to her. Eloise quelled an impulse to reach out and smooth it back from his temple.

Alex firmly propelled her through the doorway and across the hall to the supper room.

'Who is he?' she hissed, glancing back over her shoulder. The stranger was still watching her, a dark, unfathomable look in his eyes.

'I have no idea,' said Alex, guiding her to a table. 'But you should be careful, Elle. I saw the way he looked at you. It was pure, predatory lust.'

She sighed. 'That is true of so many men.'

'Which is why I am here,' replied Alex. 'To protect you.'

She reached for his hand.

'Dear Alex. Do you never tire of looking after me?'

'It is what Tony would have wished,' he said simply, adding with a rueful grin, 'besides, if you had not dragged me to London, I should be alone in Norfolk, pining away.'

'And that would never do.' She smiled and squeezed his hand. 'Thank you, my friend.'

When supper was over, Eloise sent Alex away.

'Try if you can to discover if Lord Berrow plans to attend,' she begged him. 'If he does not, then we need not stay much beyond midnight. Although I think you must do the pretty and dance with some of the other ladies in the room.'

'I must?'

His pained look drew a laugh from her.

'Yes, you must, Alex. You cannot sit in my pocket all night. Several of the young ladies are already looking daggers at me for keeping you by my side for half the evening. You need not be anxious about me; I have seen several acquaintances I wish to talk to.'

When he had gone, Eloise moved around the room, bestowing her smiles freely but never stopping, nor would she promise to dance with any of the gentlemen who begged for that honour. Her eyes constantly ranged over the room, but it was not an acquaintance she was seeking. It was a dark-haired stranger she had seen but once.

Suddenly he was beside her.

'Will you dance, my lady?'

She hesitated.

'Sir, we have not been introduced.'

'Does that matter?'

A little bubble of laughter welled up. All at once she felt quite reckless. She held out her hand.

'No, it does not matter one jot.'

He led her to join the set that was forming.

'I thought you would never escape your guard dog.'

'Mr Mortimer is my very good friend. He defends me from unwelcome attentions.'

'Oh? Am I to understand, then, that my attentions are not unwelcome?'

Eloise hesitated. This encounter was moving a little too fast and for once she was not in control. She said cautiously, 'I think you would be presumptuous to infer so much.'

His smile grew and he leaned a little closer.

'Yet you refused to stand up with the last four gentlemen who solicited your hand.'

'Ah, but I have danced with them all before. I like the novelty of a new partner.' She smiled as the dance parted them, pleased to see the gleam of interest in his eyes.

'And does my dancing please you, my lady?' he asked as soon as they joined hands again.

'For the moment,' she responded airily.

'I agree,' he said, his eyes glinting. 'I can think of much more pleasant things to do for the remainder of the evening.'

She blushed hotly and was relieved that they parted again and she was not obliged to answer.

Eloise began to wonder if she had been wise to dance with this stranger: she was disturbed by his effect upon her. Goodness, he had only to smile and she found herself behaving like a giddy schoolgirl! She must end this now, before the intoxication became too great. When the music drew to a close she gave a little curtsy and stepped away. Her partner followed.

'I know I have not been in town for a while,' he said, 'but it is still customary to stand up for two dances, I believe.'

She put up her chin.

'I will not pander to your vanity, sir. One dance is sufficient for you, until we have been introduced.'

She flicked open her fan and with a little smile she walked away from him.

Alex was waiting for her.

'Our host tells me Lord Berrow has sent his apologies for tonight. He is gone out of town. However, Parham expects to see him at the Renwicks' soirée tomorrow.'

'How very tiresome,' said Eloise. 'If we had known we need not have come.' She tucked her hand in his arm. 'Let us go now.'

'Are you sure? You will disappoint any number of gentlemen if you leave now: they all hope to stand up with you at least once.'

Eloise shrugged. If she could not dance with her dark stranger she did not want to dance with anyone.

'There will be other nights.'

She concentrated on disposing her diaphanous stole across her shoulders rather than meet Alex's intent gaze.

'What has occurred, Elle? I mislike that glitter in your eyes. Did your last partner say anything to upset you?'

She dismissed his concern with a wave of one gloved hand.

'No, no, nothing like that. He was a diversion, nothing more.'

'He was very taken with you.'

'Did you think so?' she asked him, a little too eagerly.

Alex frowned.

'Does it matter to you that he should?'

Eloise looked away,

'No, of course not. But it is very flattering.' She tried for a lighter note. 'He was very amusing.'

Alex looked back across the room to where the tall stranger was standing against the wall, watching them.

'I think,' he said slowly, 'that he could be very dangerous.'

'Hell and damnation!'

Jack watched Lady Allyngham walk away on Mortimer's arm.

It would not have taken much to have Parham present him to the lady. That had been his design when he had first arrived, but the sight of Eloise Allyngham had wiped all intentions, good or bad, from his mind.

He had carried Allyngham's locket with him for the past year and was well acquainted with the tiny portrait inside, but he had been taken aback when he saw the lady herself. The painting only hinted at the glorious abundance of guinea-gold curls that framed her face. It had not prepared him for her dazzling smile, nor the look of humour and intelligence he observed in her deep blue eyes.

He had intended to find the lady, to hand over the bequests and retire gracefully, but then Lady Allyngham had collided with him and when she had turned her laughing face to his, every sensible thought had flown out of his head. He had prowled the room until she returned from the supper room and by then his host was nowhere to be seen, so Jack seized the moment and asked her to dance. He should have told her why he was there, but he could not resist the temptation to flirt with her, to bring that delicious flush to her cheeks and to see the elusive dimple peeping beside her generous mouth.

He pulled himself together. It had been a very pleasant

interlude but he had a duty to perform. He sought out his hostess.

'Lady Allyngham?' She looked a little bemused when he made his request. 'My dear Major, I would happily introduce you to her, if it were in my power, but she is gone.'

'Gone!'

'Why, yes, she took her leave of me a few minutes ago. Mr Mortimer was escorting her back to Dover Street.' She gave him a knowing smile. 'He is a *very* attentive escort.'

Disappointment seared through Jack. He tried to convince himself that it was because he wanted to hand over Tony's ring and locket and get out of London, but he knew in his heart that it was because he wanted to see Eloise Allyngham again.

Jack took his leave and made his way to St James's Street, where he was admitted into an imposing white stone building by a liveried servant. White's was very busy and he paused for a while to watch a lively game of Hazard, refusing more than one invitation to join in. Later he wandered through to the card room where he soon spotted a number of familiar faces, some of whom he had seen in Lady Parham's ballroom earlier that evening. A group of gentlemen were engaged in a game of bassett. One looked up and waved to him.

'Had enough of the dancing, Clifton?'

Jack smiled. 'Something like that, Renwick.'

He looked at the little group: Charles Renwick was an old friend and he recognised another, slightly older man, Edward Graham, who had been a friend of his father, but the others were strangers to him—with one exception, the dealer, a stocky man with a heavily pock-marked face and pomaded hair. Sir Ronald Deforge. A tremor of revulsion ran through Jack. At that moment the dealer looked up at him from beneath his heavy-lidded eyes. Jack saw the recognition in his glance and observed the contemptuous curl of the man's thick lips. As he hesitated a gentleman with a florid face and bushy red side-whiskers shifted his chair to make room for him.

'Doing battle in the ballroom can be as hellish as a full-scale siege, eh, Major? Well, never mind that now. Sit you down, sir, and we'll deal you in.'

'Aye, we are here to commiserate with each other,' declared Mr Graham. 'Come along, Deforge, deal those cards!'

'Oh?' Jack signalled to the waiter to fill his glass.

'Aye. There was no point in staying at Parham House once Lady Allyngham had left.' Edward Graham paused, frowning over his cards. 'Hoped to persuade her to stand up with me later, but then found she had slipped away.'

Jack schooled his features to show no more than mild interest. Sir Ronald cast a fleeting glance at him.

'It seems Major Clifton was the only one of us to be favoured with a dance.'

The whiskery gentleman dug Jack in the ribs.

'Aye, Sir Ronald is right, Major. You lucky dog! How did you do it, man? Are you well acquainted with her?'

'Not at all,' Jack replied, picking up his cards and trying to give them his attention. 'I know very little about the lady.'

'Ah, the Glorious Allyngham.' Jack's neighbour raised his glass. 'The whole of London is at her feet. She would be a cosy armful, for the man that can catch her! We are all her slaves, but she spreads her favours equally: a dance here, a carriage ride there—keeps us all on the lightest of reins—even Sir Ronald there is enthralled, ain't that right, Deforge?'

A shadow flitted across the dealer's face but he replied indifferently, 'She is undoubtedly a diamond.'

'Rumour has it she is on the catch for a royal duke.' A gentleman in a puce waistcoat chuckled. 'Ladies don't like it, of course, to see their husbands drooling over another woman. They've christened her the Wanton Widow!'

'So they have.' Mr Graham sighed. 'But I wish she were a little more wanton, then I might stand a chance!'

Ribald laughter filled the air, replaced by good-natured oaths and curses as Sir Ronald Deforge displayed his winning cards and scooped up the little pile of rouleaux in the centre of the table. There was a pause while a fresh hand was dealt and the waiters leapt forwards to refill the glasses.

'Where did Allyngham find her?' asked Jack, intrigued in spite of himself.

'She was some sort of poor relation, I believe,' said Graham. 'Caused quite a stir when Allyngham married her—family expected him to make a brilliant match.'

'Caused quite a stir when he brought her to town, too,' remarked Renwick, pushing another pile of rouleaux into the centre of the table. 'We were all in raptures over her, but Allyngham was careful. He made sure no one became over-familiar with his new bride.'

'Except Alex Mortimer, of course,' remarked one of the players.

'Nothing surprising in that.' Edward Graham grimaced as he studied his hand. With a sigh of resignation he threw one card down. 'He is a neighbour and close friend of Allyngham. Escorted the lady to town while her husband was in the Peninsula.'

'While the cat's away,' said Sir Ronald said softly. 'And now the cat is dead do you think Mortimer plans to jump into his shoes?'

'Shouldn't be surprised if he's got his eye on the widow,' said Charles Renwick. 'Apart from the title, which died with Allyngham, his lady inherits everything, I hear.'

'In trust, I suppose?' said Deforge, dropping his own tokens on to the growing pile of rouleaux in the centre of the table.

'No,' declared Mr Graham. 'I heard she has full control of the property.'

'Making her even more desirable, eh, Deforge?' murmured Jack.

The dealer grew still.

'What the devil do you mean by that, Clifton?'

There was a tension around the table. Jack met Deforge's hard eyes with a steady gaze.

'I think you might be looking to replenish your fortune.'

Deforge shrugged.

'No sensible man takes a penniless bride.'

'Your first wife was not penniless,' remarked Jack, a hard edge to his voice. 'I hear that there is nothing left of her fortune now, save the house in Berkshire, and you would sell that if it were not mortgaged to the hilt.'

An unpleasant smile curled Sir Ronald's thick lips. He said softly, 'Your allegations have all the marks of a disappointed suitor, Clifton.'

'Gentlemen, gentlemen, this is all history,' declared the whiskery gentleman sitting beside Jack. 'If you wish to quarrel then take yourselves off somewhere and let the rest of us get on with our game!'

'Aye, let us play,' added Charles Renwick hastily. 'Deal the cards, Deforge, if you please.'

Jack spread his hands, signifying his acceptance and after a final, angry glare Deforge turned his attention back to the game. It did not last long. Luck was running with the dealer and as soon as the last card was played Sir Ronald scooped up his winnings and left.

Charles Renwick called for a fresh pack of cards.

'You caught him on the raw there,' he remarked, watching

Deforge stalk out of the room. 'Damnation, Jack, why did you have to mention his dead wife?'

'Because I don't believe her death was an accident.'

Charles Renwick leaned over and placed his hand on Jack's sleeve. He said, 'Let be, my friend. It was years ago. It can do no good for you to dwell on it now.'

Jack's hands clenched into fists, the knuckles showing white against the green baize of the table. How could he be thankful that the girl he had wanted to marry, the love of his life, was dead?

They subsided into silence as the next game of bassett began. Jack played mechanically, his thoughts still on Deforge. He hated the man because he had stolen the woman he loved, but was that rational? Clara had been free to make her own choice. He had no proof that she had not been happy in her marriage, only a feeling in his gut. He gave himself a mental shake. Clara was dead. There was nothing he could do about that now. It was time to forget the past.

'I did hear Deforge is running low on funds.'

The remark by one of the players broke into Jack's thoughts.

'As long as he can pay his gambling debts, I don't care,' laughed Edward Graham.

'If he marries the Glorious Allyngham his worries will be over,' said the gentleman with the red side-whiskers.

'She won't have him,' said Jack emphatically.

'Oho, what do you know, Clifton?'

Jack shook his head. The thought of that beautiful, golden creature marrying Sir Ronald Deforge turned his stomach. He schooled his face into a look of careful indifference.

'If the lady is as rich and independent as you say she has no need to marry a man like Deforge.'

'Perhaps you think she might prefer a handsome soldier,' chuckled Graham, giving a broad wink to his companions.

Charles Renwick cocked an eyebrow.

'Fancy a touch at the widow yourself, Clifton? Well, I wish you luck.'

'I need more than that,' grinned Jack. 'We have not yet been introduced.'

The red side-whiskers shook as their owner guffawed loudly.

'What, and you stole a dance with the widow? Impudent young dog!'

'If you want an introduction, my boy, my wife is giving a little party tomorrow. A soirée, she calls it,' said Renwick. 'Come along and she'll present you to the Glorious Allyngham.'

'Thank you, I will.'

'I'll wager Mortimer won't let you breach that particular citadel,' declared Mr Graham. 'I think Renwick has the right of it and Alex Mortimer's looking to wed her himself. His principal estate marches with the Allyngham lands: I'd wager a monkey he would very much like to combine the two.'

Jack took another card and studied his hand. He did not like the conversation but knew that any remonstrance on his part would only fuel the speculation.

'That might be *his* intention, but what about the lady?' remarked Renwick, flicking a smile towards Jack. 'Our mutual acquaintances in Paris tell me the Major has gained quite a reputation over there with the fairer sex, to say nothing of the havoc he wreaked with the beauties of Spain and Portugal.'

'Ah, but the Glorious Allyngham's different: you might say Mortimer is already in residence,' chuckled Graham. 'He will protect his own interests, I'm sure.'

Jack threw down his hand.

'Deuce and a pair of fives. I am done, gentlemen.'

Mr Graham gave a snort.

'Well you know what they say, Clifton, unlucky at cards...
I'll wager Lady Allyngham will be married before the year
is out. Any takers, gentlemen?'

Jack smiled but made no reply to that. With a nod he took
his leave of them and as he walked away he heard the man
with the red side-whiskers calling for the betting book.

Jack made his way to his lodgings in King Street, where
his valet was waiting up for him, dozing in a chair. He jerked
awake and jumped up as Jack came in.

'You's early, Major,' he said, rubbing his eyes. 'Didn't think
to see you for an hour or so yet.'

'I have an appointment with my man of business tomorrow
morning.'

Jack allowed himself to be eased out of his coat and waistcoat but then waved his man away.

'Thank you, Robert. I can manage now. Wake me at eight,
if you please.'

When he was alone, Jack delved into the bottom of his
trunk, searching for the ring and the locket that he had carried
with him since Waterloo. They were safe, tucked into a small
leather pouch at one side of the trunk. On impulse he pulled
out the locket and carried it to the bed, where he opened it and
turned it towards the flickering light of his bedside candle.
Two faces stared out at him, the colours jewel-bright. Lord
Allyngham's likeness was very much as Jack remembered
him, curling brown hair and a cheerfully confident smile.
The other face was but a pale imitation of the original. He
frowned. Tony Allyngham's image of his quiet, loyal, loving
wife was sadly at odds with the glorious creature that now
had all of London at her feet.

* * *

The Renwicks' narrow town house was full to overflowing by the time Eloise arrived.

'What a squeeze,' muttered Alex as he escorted her upstairs. 'I do not know how you expect to find anyone in this crush!'

'You are too pessimistic, my friend. If Lord Berrow is here I shall find him.' She swept ahead of him to greet their hostess, and moments later they were pushing their way through the crowded rooms. There was to be no dancing, just a little music provided by those proficient at the pianoforte and the harp, and Mrs Renwick had hired an Italian singer for their entertainment.

Eloise left Alex talking to an old acquaintance and made her way to the music room in search of her quarry. A young lady was playing the harp and while it could not be said that her audience was universally enraptured, the crowd was a great deal quieter than in the other rooms. It did not take Eloise long to realise that Lord Berrow was not in the music room and she turned to make her way back to the main salon.

'Ah, Lady Allyngham!' A silk-coated gentleman approached her. His wizened, painted face looked unnaturally white in the candlelight and it made his crooked teeth look even more yellow. She forced herself to smile, not to flinch as he took her hand and bowed over it. 'My dear madam, you are looking lovelier than ever tonight.'

She inclined her head, wishing she had not dismissed Alex quite so quickly.

'And shall we hear you sing, this evening, ma'am?'

She shook her head.

'No, sir. Tonight I am a mere spectator.'

His yellow smile widened and he leaned towards her.

'You could never be a *mere* anything, my lady! Shall we find a quiet corner where we may be private?'

'Alas, sir, that will never do,' she said archly, treating him to a flutter of her dark lashes. 'I must not keep you all to myself when there are so many ladies here waiting to talk to you—I see Lady Bressington even now doing her best to attract your attention.'

The old man straightened, his narrow chest puffing out and with a murmured excuse and a flash of her lovely smile Eloise moved away, barely suppressing a shudder. How had she come to this, she wondered miserably, to have every rake and roué hounding her?

You know very well it is your own fault.

The words clattered through her head as clearly as if she had said them aloud. Her spirit sank a little lower. Yes, it *was* her own doing. When she had first come to town with her husband he had not objected to her flirting with other gentlemen. Indeed, Tony had been happy to encourage it. It had amused him to see his beautiful new bride the object of such admiration, but Tony had always been there in the background to ensure that the flirtations were not carried too far. Eloise's return to town as a beautiful young widow had aroused a great amount of interest and it had suited her plans to allow herself to be drawn once more into that heady world of flirtation, but now she wondered perhaps if she had taken the game a little too far. Respectable hostesses were beginning to look askance at her and she was for ever fending off unwanted amorous attentions. She could only be thankful that Mrs Renwick had taken her under her wing and still treated her kindly. Eloise bit back a sigh. Once she had concluded her business with Lord Berrow she would retire to Allyngham and live quietly there until the world had forgotten the Wanton Widow.

She heard her hostess calling to her.

'My dear Lady Allyngham, I have a gentleman here most eager to make your acquaintance.'

Eloise turned, schooling her face into a polite smile which changed to one of genuine pleasure when she recognised the man beside Mrs Renwick as her dancing partner of the previous evening. There was no smile on the gentleman's face, however, but a faint look of frowning disapproval. She lifted her chin. No doubt he had seen her encounter with the old roué.

'May I introduce Major Clifton, madam? He is new to town, having only recently returned to England—he was with the Army of Occupation in Paris.'

'So you are a soldier, sir?' She held out her hand.

'I was, ma'am. I have sold out.'

Major Clifton took her fingers in a firm clasp. She was not prepared for the tiny flutter of excitement she experienced at his touch. Glancing up she saw the startled look in his eyes. Was he, too, shocked by this sudden, unexpected connection? Eloise withdrew her hand and struggled to speak calmly.

'And what will you do now, sir?'

'Oh, this and that. Become a gentleman farmer, perhaps.'

His response was cool, distant. If she had not seen that look of surprise and confusion in his face she would have thought him nothing more than a polite stranger. Inconsequential thoughts chased through her head: how dark his eyes were, fringed by long black lashes. She liked the way his hair curled about his ears. She wondered how it would feel to run her fingers through those glossy black locks, to stroke his lean cheek… The major was still speaking and Eloise had to drag her mind back to concentrate on his words.

'I knew your late husband, my lady. We served together in the Peninsula and at Waterloo.'

'Ah, yes.' She gave her head a tiny shake as his words put

her frivolous thoughts to flight. She must be serious now. 'Of course—you wrote to me. I am sorry; I did not recognise your name at first. You were with him when he died.' Her pleasure drained away. Instead of the laughter and chatter of a London drawing room she imagined the battlefield as Tony had described it to her, the pounding thunder of artillery, the shouts and screams of the soldiers. So much pain and violence.

'My lady? I beg your pardon, I did not mean to arouse unpleasant memories.'

'It would be unpardonable for any of us to forget, sir.' She fixed her eyes upon him. 'Why did you not tell me this last night?'

The major hesitated, then gave a rueful grin, dispelling his rather disapproving look and making him look suddenly much younger.

'Last night I was taken by surprise. Our encounter was... unusual. I did not want to ruin the moment.'

So she had not dreamed it! He had felt it, too. Eloise found herself unable to look away as she recalled her dance with a stranger. Yes, it had been special, and slightly alarming. She had never felt such an attraction before. But she must be on her guard, she could not afford to lose her head. The major was speaking again and she twisted her hands together, trying to concentrate.

'Your husband gave me a commission, to deliver to you certain items. I would like your permission to call, if I may?'

'What? Oh, yes, yes, of course, Major.'

'Thank you. Shall we say tomorrow morning, at ten, or is that too early?' She gazed up at him, fascinated by the laughter lines around his mouth, the way his eyes crinkled when he smiled. He was smiling at her now and she thought how wonderful it would be to stand with him thus all evening,

letting his voice drift over her like a soft summer breeze…
'So, madam, shall we say ten?'

She blinked. 'Um…yes. I mean, ten o'clock tomorrow
morning. You have my direction—Dover Street.' She swallowed. What was happening to her? She was not at all sure
that she liked being so out of control. He was very striking,
to be sure, but she had met many gentlemen equally good
looking, so she did not think it could be his lean, handsome
face that caused her emotions to riot. She needed to put a little
distance between them so that she could consider these new
and alarming sensations dispassionately.

Eloise dragged her mind back to what she had been doing
before Mrs Renwick had brought the major to meet her. Oh,
yes. She had come in search of Lord Berrow. It was important;
she must put duty before pleasure.

'Now the formalities are over,' Major Clifton was saying,
'may I—?'

She interrupted him as she spotted her quarry.

'I beg your pardon, but I cannot talk now.'

'Of course.' He stood back. 'Perhaps later…?'

'Yes, perhaps.' She summoned up her dazzling society
smile but directed it at his neckcloth, afraid that if she met
his eyes again her resolve would weaken. 'Excuse me.'

She forced herself to walk away from him, hoping that
his magnetism would fade if she put some space between
them. Resolutely she fixed her eyes on the jovial-looking
gentleman in a grey wig making his way towards the music
room.

'Good evening, Lord Berrow.'

The Earl turned his pale, slightly protuberant eyes towards
her.

'Lady Allyngham!' he smiled and took her hand. 'My dear,
you are looking positively radiant!' He hesitated. 'But you

have been in mourning. My lady wife sent you our condolences, did she not?'

She thought of the neat little letter she had received after Tony's death, so obviously composed and written by a clerk.

'You did, my lord, thank you. I was touched by your concern.'

He harrumphed and nodded.

'Yes, well, least we could do, m'dear! Sad business. We lost so many fine men at Waterloo, did we not? But that's all in the past now, and here you are, looking more beautiful than ever!'

'I have been hoping to meet up with you, my lord.'

'Have you now?' He beamed at her. 'Been very busy—government business.' He puffed out his chest, swelling with self-importance. 'Member of the Cabinet, you know.'

'Yes, of course,' said Eloise. 'I wanted to talk to you—that is, my lawyer has written several times now, about the land at Ainsley Wood.'

'Has he? Well, no need to worry ourselves about that, m'dear. My steward is an excellent man. He will deal with everything.'

'Actually, he will not,' she replied, determined not to be put off. 'He writes that he has no authority to sell...'

Lord Berrow waved his hand.

'Yes, yes, we can discuss that later.' He took her arm. 'Come and sit with me, my dear, and we can listen to the soprano our hostess has brought in. She's not quite Catalini, but I understand she is very good.'

Eloise realised it would be useless to press her case further at that moment. With a smile she allowed the Earl to guide her to the gilded chairs set out for the guests. Having found Lord Berrow, she was determined she would not leave him now until she had explained to him why she needed to purchase Ainsley Wood.

* * *

Jack leaned against the wall and watched Lady Allyngham. The tug of attraction was just as strong as it had been the night before. She felt it too, he was sure, but she had not tried to flirt with him. Quite the contrary, she had seemed eager to get away. He observed her now as she took Lord Berrow's arm, smiling, turning her head to listen to the man as if he were the most interesting person she had ever met. No wonder all the gentlemen were enraptured. Alex Mortimer was on the far side of the room. He, too, was watching Lady Allyngham as she walked off with the Earl and did not seem the least perturbed. If he really was her lover then he must feel very sure of himself to allow her such freedom. Jack frowned. It demeaned Allyngham's memory to have his widow flaunting herself in town in this way. But she had been discomposed when Jack had mentioned her husband, so perhaps she did have a conscience after all. He gave himself a mental shake. Enough of this: it was no business of his how Tony's widow behaved.

Suddenly the noise and the chatter was grating on his nerves and he decided to leave. Once he had called at Dover Street tomorrow morning his mission would be complete and he need not see Eloise Allyngham again.

Chapter Two

Eloise sipped at her morning chocolate. Last night had not gone quite as planned. Lord Berrow had resolutely refused to discuss selling the land at Ainsley Wood. Despite all her efforts to charm the Earl the best she had achieved was his promise that he would talk to her when he was not quite so busy. She had had to be content with that, and when she left the Earl she had fallen into the clutches of Sir Ronald Deforge. She felt a certain sympathy for Sir Ronald. She knew him to be a widower and she thought perhaps he was lonely, but Sir Ronald with his pomaded hair and oily manner was all smug complacency, and less than twenty minutes in his company had her yawning behind her fan. Thankfully Alex rescued her and carried her off to supper before she had grown too desperate. And she had suffered another disappointment: Major Clifton had left early. Not that that mattered, she told herself, for he was calling upon her at ten o'clock.

It was her habit to breakfast early, no matter how late she had been out. While she nibbled at her freshly baked bread she looked through the morning's post, putting aside the numerous invitations and letters to be answered and reading carefully

the daily report from her steward at Allyngham. This morning
there was one note at the bottom of the pile that caught her
attention. She did not recognise the writing, and there was
no hint of the sender. She put down her coffee cup and broke
the seal.

The single sheet crackled as it unfolded, and as her eyes
scanned the untidy black writing her cheeks grew pale. She
summoned her butler.

'Noyes, send a runner to Mr Mortimer. Ask him to join
me, immediately, if you please!'

Alone again, she pushed her plate away, her appetite
gone.

She hoped Alex would appear soon. He had taken a house
only a few doors away but for all she knew he might still be
sleeping. Thankfully it was only a matter of minutes before
she heard the bell jangling in the hall. Carefully folding the
letter and putting it in her pocket, she made her way to the
morning room.

Alex was waiting for her. His brows snapped together when
she entered.

'What is it, Elle? You are very pale—what has happened?'

Silently she pulled the letter from her pocket and held it
out to him. He scanned it quickly and looked up.

'Is this all there is?'

She nodded. He looked again at the letter.

'I know your secret,' he read. 'Very cryptic.'

'What should I do?'

'Nothing.'

'Do you...do you think someone knows, about us?'

Alex smiled.

'No names, no clues—someone is trying to frighten you,
Elle. Some jealous wife or mistress, perhaps. Your return to
town has put many noses out of joint.'

She spread her hands.

'Why should anyone be jealous of me? I have not stolen any of their lovers.'

'Not intentionally, but the gentlemen are singing your praises and laying their hearts at your feet.'

Her lip curled.

'I do not give the snap of my fingers for any of them. Idle coxcombs!'

Alex laughed.

'That is part of your attraction.'

She indicated the letter.

'So what do you think it means?'

'I have no idea.' He turned the letter over. 'There was nothing to say who sent it?'

'No. Noyes told me one of the footmen found it on the floor of the hall this morning and put it with the post. Who would do this?'

'Some idle prankster.' Alex screwed the letter into a ball and threw it into the fire. 'You should forget about it. I am sure it is nothing to worry about.'

She eyed him doubtfully and he took her hands, smiling down at her.

'Truly, it is nothing.'

'Major Clifton, my lady.'

Jack followed the footman into the morning room. Lady Allyngham turned to greet him, but not before he had seen Mortimer holding her hands. Damnation, what was the fellow doing here so early in the morning, did he live here?'

Setting his jaw, Jack made a stiff bow. Unperturbed, Alex Mortimer nodded to him before addressing Lady Allyngham.

'I must go. I am going out of town this afternoon: I have business with my land agent in Hertfordshire which will take me a few days, I think.' He lifted her hand to his lips. 'Send a note if you need me, Elle. I can be here in a few hours.'

Jack watched the little scene, his countenance, he hoped, impassive, and waited silently until Alex Mortimer had left the room. There was no doubt that Mortimer and the lady were on the very best of terms. He had to remind himself it was none of his business.

'What is it you wished to say to me, Major Clifton?'

Lady Allyngham's softly musical voice recalled his wandering attention. She disposed herself gracefully into a chair and invited him to sit down.

'Thank you, no,' he said curtly. 'This will only take a moment.'

'Oh. I had hoped you might be able to tell me something of my husband.'

She sounded genuinely disappointed. He reached into his pocket.

'Before he died, Lord Allyngham gave me these, and asked me to see that they were returned to you.' He dropped the ring and locket into her hands. 'I apologise that it has taken so long but I was in Paris until the summer, with the Army of Occupation, and I had given Lord Allyngham my word that I would bring them in person.'

She looked down at them silently.

Jack cleared his throat.

'He asked me to tell you…to be happy.'

'Thank you,' she whispered.

She placed the ring on her right hand. Jack remembered it had been a tight fit for Lord Allyngham: it had been a struggle to remove it, but now the signet ring looked big and cumbersome on the lady's dainty finger. He watched her open the locket and stare for a long time at the tiny portraits. At last she said, 'I had this painted for Tony when we first married.

He would not let me accompany him when he went off to war, so I thought he might like it…' Her voice tailed off and she hunted for her handkerchief.

Jack sat down.

'He was a very courageous soldier,' he said quietly. 'We fought together in the Peninsula: he saved my life at Talavera.'

She looked up and he saw that her eyes were shining with unshed tears.

'You knew him well, Major Clifton?'

He shrugged.

'As well as anyone, I think. We drank together, fought together—he spoke very fondly of you, madam, and of Allyngham. I think he missed his home.'

'His letters to me were very brief; he mentioned few of his fellow officers by name.'

'He kept very much to himself,' replied Jack.

She nodded, twisting her hands together in her lap.

'He was a very private man.' She blinked rapidly. 'Forgive me, Major Clifton. I know it is more than a year since Waterloo, but still…' She drew a steadying breath. 'How…how did he die?'

Jack hesitated. There was no easy way to explain.

'Artillery fire,' he said shortly. 'A cannon ball hit him in the chest. It was very quick.'

Her blue eyes rebuked him.

'How could that be? You said he had time to ask you to bring these things to me.'

He held her gaze steadily.

'He was past any pain by then.' He saw her eyes widen. The colour fled from her cheeks and she swayed slightly in her chair. He said quickly, 'I beg your pardon, madam, I should not have told you—'

She put up her hand.

'No, I wanted to know the truth.' She closed the locket and placed it on the table beside her, then rose and held out her hand, dismissing him. 'Thank you, Major. I am very grateful to you.'

Jack bowed over her fingers. He hesitated and found she was watching him, a question in her eyes.

'Forgive me, ma'am, but…' How the devil was he to phrase this?

'What is it you wish to say to me, Major Clifton?'

'I beg your pardon, my lady. Lord Allyngham having given me this commission, I feel an obligation to him. To his memory.'

'What sort of obligation, Major?'

He shot a look at her from under his brows.

'You know what people are saying, about you and Mortimer?'

She recoiled a little.

'I neither know nor care,' she retorted.

'I would not have you dishonour your husband's name, madam.'

Her eyes darkened angrily.

'How dare you suggest I would do that!'

He frowned, annoyed by her disingenuous answer. Did she think him a fool?

'But you will not deny that Mortimer is your lover—it is the talk of London!'

She glared at him, angry colour flooding her cheeks.

'Oh, and gossip must always be true, I suppose!'

Her eyes darted fire and she moved forwards as if to engage with him. Jack could not look away: his gaze was locked with hers and he felt as if he was drowning in the blue depths of her eyes. She was so close that her perfume filled his head, suspending reason. A sudden, fierce desire coursed through him. He reached out and grabbed her, pulling her close and as her lips parted to object he captured them with his own. He felt her tremble in his arms, then she was still, her mouth yielding and compliant beneath the onslaught of his kiss. For a heady, dizzying instant he felt the connection. The shock of it sent him reeling with much the same effect as being too close to the big guns on the battlefield, but it lasted only for a moment. The next she was fighting against him and as sanity returned he let her go. She pushed away from him and brought her hand up to deal him a ringing slap across his cheek.

He flinched.

'Madam, I beg your pardon.'

She stepped aside, clinging to the back of a chair as she stared at him, outraged.

'Get out,' she ordered him, her voice shaking with fury. 'Get out now before I have you thrown out!'

'Let me explain—' Jack had an insane desire to laugh as he uttered the words. How could he explain the madness that had come over him, the all-encompassing, uncontrollable desire. Dear heaven, how could he have been so crass?

Eloise was frantically tugging at the bell-pull, her face as white as the lace around her shoulders.

'Have no fear, my lady, I am leaving.' With a stiff little bow he turned on his heel and walked out of the room, but as he closed the door behind him he had the impression of the lady collapsing on to the sofa and heard her first anguished sob.

Eloise cried unrestrainedly for several minutes, but such violence could not be sustained. Yet even when her tears had abated the feeling of outrage remained. She left the sofa and began to stride to and fro about the room.

How dare he abuse her in such a way! He had insinuated

himself into her house and she had treated him with courtesy. How had he repaid her? First he had accused her of having a lover, then he had molested her as if she had been a common strumpet! She stopped her pacing and clenched her fists, giving a little scream of anger and frustration.

'Such behaviour may be acceptable in Paris, Major Clifton, but it is *not* how a gentleman behaves in London!'

She resumed her pacing, jerking her handkerchief between her fingers. Rage welled up again, like steam in a pot, and with an unladylike oath she scooped up a little Sèvres dish from the table and hurled it into the fireplace, where it shattered with a most satisfying smash. The noise brought her butler hurrying into the room.

'Madam, I beg your pardon, but I heard…'

The anxiety in his usually calm voice brought Eloise to her senses. She turned away and drew a deep breath before replying.

'Yes, Noyes, I have broken a dish. You had best send the maid to clear it up: but tell her to be careful, the edges are sharp, and I would not like anyone to cut themselves because of my carelessness.'

When the butler had withdrawn Eloise returned to her chair. Her rage had subsided, but the outpouring of emotion had left her feeling drained and depressed. She could not deny that Major Clifton had some excuse for thinking that Alex was her lover. They had never made any attempt to deny the rumours and Eloise had been content with the situation. Until now.

She was shocked to realise how much Major Clifton's disapproval had wounded her, and he had had the audacity to compound her distress by attacking her in that disgusting way. She bit her lip. No, she had to be honest: it was not his actions that had distressed her, but the shocking realisation that she had *wanted* him to kiss her. Even when her anger was at its height, some barely acknowledged instinct had made her move closer and for one brief, giddy moment when he had pulled her into his arms, she had blazed with a desire so strong that all other thoughts had been banished from her mind. Only the knowledge of her own inadequacy made her push him away.

She hung her head, wondering if Jack Clifton could tell from that one, brief contact that the Wanton Widow had never before been kissed?

Jack strode quickly out of Dover Street and back to his own lodgings, his mind in turmoil. Whatever had possessed him to behave in that way towards Eloise Allyngham? He might disapprove of her liaison with Mortimer but he had hardly acted as a gentleman himself. Scowling, Jack ran up the stairs and into his sitting room, throwing his cane and his hat down on to a chair.

'Oho, who's ruffled your feathers?' demanded his valet, coming in.

Jack bit back a sharp retort. Bob had served with him as his sergeant throughout the war and was more than capable of giving him his own again. He contented himself by being icily civil.

'Fetch me pen and ink, if you please, Robert, and some paper. And be quick about it!'

'We are in a bad skin,' grinned Bob. 'Was the widow disagreeable?'

'Damn your eyes, don't be so impertinent!' He rubbed his chin, scowling. 'If you must know I forgot myself. I need to write an apology to the lady, and quickly.'

Jack rapidly penned his missive, sealed it and despatched Robert to deliver it to Dover Street.

* * *

The valet returned some twenty minutes later and handed him back his letter, neatly torn in two.

'She wouldn't accept it, Major.'

'Damnation, I didn't ask you to wait for a reply!'

'No, sir, but I arrived at the house just as my lady was coming out, so she heard me tell that sour-faced butler of hers who the letter was from. She didn't even bother to open it. Just took it from me and ripped it in half. Said if you thought she was the sort to accept a *carte blanche* you was very much mistaken.' He grinned. 'Seems you upset her right and proper.'

With an oath Jack crumpled the torn paper and hurled it into the fireplace. He would have to talk to her. Whatever her own morals—or lack of them—he was damned if he would have her think him anything less than a gentleman.

A few hours attending to her correspondence and a brisk walk did much to restore Eloise's composure. She had derived no small satisfaction from being able to tear up Major Clifton's letter and send it back to him. She thought it might be an apology, but she was determined not to accept it. The man would have to grovel before she would deign to notice him again! However, she could not quite forget his words and when she prepared to attend a party at Clevedon House that evening she decided upon a robe of dark blue satin worn over a gold slip and wore a tiny cap of fluted blue satin that nestled amongst her curls. She added a collar of sapphires and matching eardrops to lend a little lustre to the rather severe lines of the gown, but even so, she considered her appearance very suitable for a widow, and once she had fastened a gold lace fichu over her shoulders no one—not even a certain disagreeable major whom she was determined never to think about—could mistake her for anything other than a respectable widow.

She was a little nervous walking into Clevedon House without Alex by her side, but she hid her anxiety behind a smile as she sought out Lord Berrow. He gave her a quizzical look as she approached.

'If you are come to talk to me about selling my land again, my dear, then you are wasting your time.'

Eloise laughed and tucked her hand in his arm.

'Allow me at least to tell you why I want the land, sir.'

'Very well.' He gave her an avuncular smile. 'No harm in my being seen with a pretty woman, eh? Come along, then. We will sit in this little alcove over here, out of the way. Now, what is it you want to say to me, ma'am?'

She conjured up her most winning smile.

'I want to found a charitable institution as a memorial to my husband. You knew Anthony, Lord Berrow; you will remember how kind-hearted he was.'

'Aye, a very generous man, and a good neighbour, too,' nodded the Earl. 'And he left no children.' He shook his head. 'Pity the Allyngham name will die out now.'

'Yes, and the title, too, is lost.'

'But everything else comes to you?'

'Yes.' Eloise sighed and gazed down at her lap. She put her left hand over the right, feeling the hard outline of her Tony's ring upon her finger beneath the satin glove. 'Being a soldier, my husband knew there was a strong possibility that he might die before me, and he saw to it that there would be no difficulties there. And we discussed doing something to help those less fortunate. It has given me something to think about during the past twelve months. I have spoken to the mayor of Allyngham and he has agreed my plans. We have set up a trust and I am giving a parcel of land for the building itself. However, when we came to look at the map there is a narrow stretch of your own land, sir, at Ainsley Wood, that cuts between the town and the proposed site. It is less than half a mile wide but without a road through it we will need to make a journey of several miles around the boundary.'

'But the woodland is very profitable for me.'

Lord Berrow's response convinced her that he had at least been giving her proposal some thought.

'Of course it is, sir, and we would give you a fair price. The wood could provide timber for the building and of course firewood. However, if the trust cannot buy it then perhaps you would allow us to put in a road, my lord. The project is not viable unless we have access to the town.'

'Well, we shall see, we shall see.' He smiled down at her. 'And just what is this project you are planning?'

Eloise clasped her hands.

'A foundling hospital, my lord. As you know, the plight of the poor is so much worse since the war ended—'

'A foundling hospital?' he exclaimed, horrified. 'No, no, no, that will never do.'

'My lord, I assure you—'

'No, no, madam. Out of the question.' He shifted away from her, shaking his head. 'I cannot support such a scheme.'

Eloise was shocked.

'But my lord, I thought you would be in favour of it! After all, you are a great friend of Wilberforce and his Evangelical set, and I read your speeches to the House, in favour of reform…'

'Yes, yes, but that is different. A foundling hospital would bring the very worst sort of women to Allyngham, and I spend a great deal of time in Norfolk. I could not countenance having such an institution in the area.' Lord Berrow stood up. 'I am sorry, my dear, but I think you should consider some other plan to honour your husband.'

With a little bow he walked off, leaving Eloise wondering

what to do next. She had not expected such strong opposition from the Earl. She wondered if he would perhaps be more amenable once he had had time to think about the idea. She hoped so, and decided to renew her argument again in a few days.

Eloise noticed that several of the gentlemen were looking in her direction and she realised that to be sitting alone in the alcove might be construed as an invitation. Even as the thought occurred to her she saw one fashionably dressed gentleman excusing himself from a little group and making his way towards her. Recognising Sir Ronald Deforge, she quickly slipped out of the alcove and lost herself in the crowd.

'Lady Allyngham.'

Eloise whipped round to find Jack Clifton behind her.

'What are you doing here?'

'I came to find you.'

She hunched one shoulder at him.

'Then you have wasted your time, Major Clifton,' she said coldly. 'I will not talk to you.'

He grabbed her wrist as she turned away, saying urgently, 'I want to apologise.'

'I do not care what you want!' she hissed at him, wrenching her hand free.

Quickly she pushed her way through the crowds, never pausing until she reached the ante-room. There she glanced around and was obliged to stifle a tiny pang of disappointment when she discovered the major had not followed her. She saw Mrs Renwick coming out of the card-room and went to join her, hoping to avoid any further unwelcome attentions by staying close to the lady and her friends. The ploy worked very well, and she was just beginning to think that she might soon be able to make her excuses and leave without arousing too much speculation when a footman approached and held out a silver tray.

Eloise looked doubtfully at the folded note resting on the tray.

'What is this?' she asked, suspicion making her voice sharp.

A flicker of surprise disturbed the servant's wooden features.

'I do not know, my lady. The under-footman brought it into the ballroom and requested that I deliver it to you.'

One of Mrs Renwick's companions leaned closer.

'Ah, an admirer, my dear!'

The arch tone grated upon Eloise, but she merely smiled. Carefully, she picked up the note.

'Thank you; that will be all.'

She dismissed the footman and stepped away from the little group of ladies. They were all regarding her with varying degrees of curiosity. She hoped her own countenance was impassive as she opened the note and read it.

Go into the garden and look under Apollo's heel.

Eloise stared at the words, trying to work out their meaning. She realised one of the ladies was stepping towards her and hurriedly folded the note.

'So, Lady Allyngham, is it an admirer?'

She looked into the woman's bright, blatantly curious face and forced herself to laugh.

'What else?' she said lightly. 'One is pursued everywhere. Excuse me.'

Her mind was racing. Apollo. A statue, perhaps. She remembered that the long windows of the grand salon had been thrown open, recalled seeing the ink-black sky beyond. She did not know what lay beyond the windows: she had no choice but to find out.

Eloise returned to the salon. The noise and chatter of the room was deafening and she began to make her way around the edge of the room until she reached the first of the long windows. Looking out, she could see a narrow terrace with a flight of steps at each end. Eloise took a quick look around to make sure no one was watching her and slipped out on to the terrace. From her elevated position she could see the dark outlines of the garden and in the far distance, at the perimeter of the grounds, a series of lanterns glowed between several pale figures: marble statues.

In seconds she had descended the steps and was running along the path, the gravel digging painfully into the thin soles of her blue kid slippers. The moon had not yet risen and the gardens were dark, the path only discernible as a grey ribbon. She thought she heard a noise behind her and turned, her heart beating hard against her ribs. She could see nothing behind her except the black wall of the house rearing up, pierced by the four blocks of light from the long windows.

She hurried on, past the rose garden where the late-summer blooms were still perfuming the air, and on through a tree-lined walk. The path led between two rows of clipped yews and was in almost total darkness but at the far end she could see the garden wall and hanging from it the first of the lanterns. Emerging from the yew walk, she saw the statue of a woman ahead of her, the marble gleaming ghostlike in the lamplight. She approached the statue and noted that the path turned to the right and ran past five more statues, each one illuminated by a lamp. She put her hand to her throat: the third statue was clearly male, and holding a lyre in his arms. She stepped forward: yes, it could be Apollo. She moved closer, peering at the base of the statue. One marble heel was slightly raised and tucked beneath it was a small square of folded paper.

Eloise bent to pick it up. She unfolded it, turning the writing towards the golden glow of the lantern. Her heart, thudding so heavily a moment earlier, now stopped. She had expected to find another note but this was obviously a page torn from a book. A journal, judging by the dates in the margin. It was covered with a fine, neat hand that was all too familiar. As she read the page she put a hand to her mouth, her eyes widening with horror. The sentiments, the explicit nature of the words—innermost thoughts that would cause a scandal if they were made public. A scandal that could destroy both her and Alex.

For a sickening moment Eloise thought she might faint. Then, as her brain started to work again, she quickly refolded the paper and thrust it into the bosom of her gown. Her spine began to tingle, and she had the uneasy feeling that she was being watched. She backed away from the statue, straining her eyes and ears against the surrounding darkness. The air was very still and the only sound to reach her was the faint chatter of the guests gathered in the house. Suddenly she wanted nothing more than to be standing safely in that overheated, overcrowded salon. She picked up her skirts and began to run back along the path, trying not to think of who or what might be hiding in the darkness around her. The steps to the terrace were within sight when a figure stepped out and blocked her path. She screamed and tried to turn away. Strong hands reached out and grabbed her, preventing her from falling.

'Easy, my lady. There is no need to be afraid.'

Recognising Jack Clifton's deep warm voice did nothing to calm her. The noise coming from the open windows above was such that she felt sure no one had heard her scream and no one would hear her now, if she called out for assistance. Fighting down her panic, she shrugged off his hands.

'You persist in tormenting me,' she said in a low, shaking voice.

She heard him laugh and gritted her teeth against her anger.

'You wrong me, madam. I saw you slip away, so I came outside to wait for you. I thought, perhaps, when you came back from your assignation, I might speak with you.' His teeth gleamed in the dim light. 'I did not expect you to return as if the hounds of hell were snapping at your heels.'

She peered at him, trying to read his face, but it was impossible in the gloom.

'You know why I went into the garden?'

She sensed rather than saw him shrug.

'I presumed it was to meet a gentleman.' On this occasion his opinion of her character did not arouse her anger. 'So now will you accept an apology for my behaviour this morning, madam?'

She said cautiously, 'I might do so.'

'Then I humbly beg your pardon. My conduct was not that of a gentleman.'

He was so close, so reassuringly solid, but could she trust him? She glanced nervously over her shoulder. If Major Clifton had not sent her that note, then who could it be? She looked up at him. 'Did you see anyone else in the gardens, Major?'

'No. What is it, Lady Allyngham, did not your lover keep the assignation?'

His coldly mocking tone banished all thoughts of seeking his help. She gave a little hiss of anger.

'You are quite despicable!'

'And you are hiding something.'

She drew herself up.

'That,' she said icily, 'is none of your business!'

Jack did not move as the lady turned and ran quickly up the steps and into the house. There was a mystery here: she had seemed genuinely frightened when she came running up to him. If it had been any other woman he would have done his best to reassure her, but Lady Allyngham had made it abundantly clear what she thought of him. And she could take care of herself, could she not? He thought back to that morning, when he had held her in his arms before she wrathfully fought him off. He toyed with the idea of following her and persuading her to confide in him. Then he shrugged. As the lady had said, it was none of his business.

Jack decided to leave. He had come to Clevedon House in search of Lady Allyngham, determined to deliver his apology and he had done so. There was now no reason for him to stay: he took no pleasure in being part of the laughing, chattering crush of guests gathered in the elegant salon. A discreet enquiry at the door elicited the information that Lady Allyngham had already departed and since there was no other amusement to be had, he made his way directly to his rooms in King Street. He decided not to call in at White's. He had business to conclude in the morning and needed to have a clear head. After that, he thought, he would be glad to quit London and forget the bewitching, contradictory Lady Allyngham.

Chapter Three

The following morning Jack took a cab into the City. His first meeting with his lawyer had convinced him that he was right to sell out and take charge of his inheritance, or what was left of it. Now he quickly scanned the papers that were put before him.

'Once the property in Leicestershire is sold that will give me capital to invest in the Staffordshire estates,' he decided.

His lawyer's brows went up.

'The Leicestershire estate was your father's pride and joy: he always said the hunting there was second to none.'

'I shall have precious little time for hunting for the next few years,' muttered Jack, looking at the figures the lawyer had written out for him. He pushed the papers back across the desk. 'You say you have a buyer?'

The lawyer steepled his fingers, trying to keep the note of excitement out of his voice. Years of dealing with old Mr Clifton had made him cautious.

'The owner of the neighbouring property, a Mr Tomlinson, has indicated he is interested in purchasing the house and the land. He is eager to have the matter settled. He is a manufacturer, but a very gentlemanly man.'

'As long as he can pay the price I don't care who he is.' Jack rose. 'Very well. Have the papers drawn up for me to sign tomorrow, and I'll leave the rest to you.'

Ten minutes later Jack walked out into the street, feeling that a weight had lifted from his shoulders. He had always preferred Henchard, the house in Staffordshire. It had been his mother's favourite, but sadly neglected after her death, his father preferring to live in London or Leicestershire. He had died there following a short illness eighteen months ago, but with Bonaparte gathering his army and Wellington demanding that every able soldier join him in Brussels, Jack had not had time to do more than to send to Henchard any personal effects he wanted to keep before rejoining his regiment. Now he planned to settle down. He would be able to refurbish Henchard, and in time the land might even be profitable again. Settling his hat on his head, he decided to walk back to King Street. He had reached the Strand and was approaching Coutts's bank when a heavily veiled woman stepped out of the door, escorted by a very attentive bank clerk. Despite the thick veil there was something familiar about the tall, fashionably dressed figure, her purposeful tread, the way her hands twisted together. As she pulled on her gloves he caught sight of the heavy gold ring on her right hand. Even from a distance he recognised Allyngham's signet ring. Jack smiled to himself, wondering what the lady would say if he approached her. Would she give him a cold, frosty greeting, or perhaps she might simply refuse to acknowledge him? Even as he considered the matter she swept across to a waiting cab and climbed in. Instantly the door was closed and the carriage pulled away.

* * *

'Well, Miss Elle? Is your business ended, can we go home now?'

Eloise put up her veil and gave her maid a strained smile.

'Yes, Alice, we are going back to Dover Street now.'

The maid gave a little sniff. 'I do not see why we couldn't use your own carriage, if you was only coming to the bank. It may be unusual for ladies to visit their bankers, but if they are widows, like yourself, I don't see what else is to be done.'

Eloise did not reply. Leaning back in one corner, she clutched her reticule nervously. It rested heavily on her knees but she would not put it away from her. She had never been inside a bank before, but the manager himself had taken charge once he realised her identity, and the whole process had been conducted with the utmost ease. When she had said she needed to draw a substantial amount to distribute to her staff he had given her a look which combined sympathy with mild disapproval: no doubt he thought that she really required the money for some much more trivial reason, such as to buy new gowns or to pay off her gambling debts.

She pulled a paper from her bag and unfolded it: the scrawling black letters might have been live serpents for the way they made her skin crawl. When the letter had arrived that morning and she had read it for the first time, she had felt very alone. Her first thought had been to send for Alex, but she had soon dismissed the idea. Alex was a dear friend, but he could be rash, and this matter required discretion. No, she must deal with this herself. She scanned the letter again, chewing at her lip. Her biggest problem now was how to get through the rest of the day?

Mrs Renwick was a little surprised when Eloise appeared at her card party that evening.

'I know I had sent my apologies,' said Eloise, giving her hostess a bright smile, 'but I was not in humour for dancing tonight and thought you would not object…'

'Not in the least, my dear, you are most welcome here. Come in, come in and join our little party.' Mrs Renwick drew her towards a quiet room filled with small tables, where ladies and gentleman were gathered, staring at their cards in hushed concentration. Bathed in the glow of the candles, it looked like a room full of golden statues. 'This is turning out to be an evening of pleasant surprises. Major Clifton, too, made an unexpected appearance. It seems his business in town will not now be concluded until tomorrow so we have the pleasure of his company, too—'

Eloise drew back quickly. She had spotted Jack Clifton on the far side of the room.

'No! I—I was hoping for something a little…less serious, ma'am.'

Her hostess laughed softly. 'Well if you would like to come into the morning room, some of our friends are playing looe for penny points: nothing too alarming in that, now is there?'

Resigning herself to an hour or so of tedious play, Eloise smiled and took her place between a bouncing, bubbly young lady fresh from the schoolroom and an emaciated dowager in heavy black bombazine. Concentrating on the cards proved a surprisingly effective distraction for Eloise and when the little group split up to go in search of refreshment she was relieved to note that her evening was nearly over.

She made her way downstairs to the dining room where a long table was loaded with a sumptuous array of food and drink. A little supper might help to settle the nervous anticipation that was beginning to build within her. A group of gentlemen were helping themselves to delicacies from an assortment of silver dishes. She noted that both Major Clifton and Sir Ronald Deforge were amongst their number so she avoided them and made her way to the far end of the table. She kept her eyes lowered, determined to concentrate on the food displayed before her but the gentlemen's light-hearted banter intruded and she could not help but listen. The conversation turned to gambling and she found her attention caught when she heard the major's voice.

'You know I play the occasional game at White's but the high stakes are not for me,' he was saying. 'You will think me very dull, I dare say, but I prefer my funds to be invested in my land, rather than lining some other fellow's pockets.'

'Very different from Sir Ronald, then,' laughed Edward Graham. 'You never refuse a game of chance, ain't that right, sir?'

'If it is cards, certainly,' Sir Ronald replied cheerfully. 'I have something of a passion for cards. I played young Franklyn 'til dawn last week.'

'Then you have more energy for the pastime than I do,' returned the major coolly, turning away.

'I hear that playing 'til dawn is a common occurrence with you, Deforge,' remarked Mr Renwick. 'By Gad, sir, your servants must be falling asleep at their posts if they have to wait up for you every night.'

Sir Ronald laughed.

'No, no, Renwick, I am not so cruel an employer. My household retires at a Christian hour. Only my valet waits up for me, and he snoozes in a chair in the hall until I give him the knock to let me in.'

'The pleasures of being a bachelor,' declared his host. 'A wife would certainly curtail your nocturnal activities, Deforge!'

'Oho, when have I ever prevented you doing exactly as you

wish?' demanded Mrs Renwick, walking by at that moment. 'My husband would have you think his life very restricted.' She tapped the straining front of Mr Renwick's waistcoat with her fan. 'Well, gentlemen? Does he look as if he is wasting away?'

Eloise gave a little chuckle as her hostess came towards her.

'I am sure we will all find something to tempt our appetite here,' she smiled. 'A truly magnificent supper, ma'am.'

'Thank you, Lady Allyngham. Are you enjoying yourself?'

'Yes, thank you. It is a most delightful evening.'

'But, my dear, you are very quiet this evening, and a trifle pale, I think.' Mrs Renwick came closer. 'I hope you are not ill?'

'No, ma'am, a little tired, perhaps.'

Mrs Renwick gave her a warm, sympathetic smile.

'Too many engagements, ma'am?'

'I think perhaps I have had enough of town life.'

Overhearing, Mr Graham turned quickly towards her.

'My dear Lady Allyngham, you will not desert us!'

'Of course she will not,' put in Lady Parham, coming up. 'Not when there are so many diversions to be enjoyed.'

Eloise forced herself to smile. Suddenly she was tired of play-acting.

'I think I may well go back to Allyngham.'

'Ah,' nodded Lady Parham. 'Perhaps that is why you were in the Strand this morning, settling your affairs with your bankers.'

Eloise stiffened. 'No, I had no business there today.'

'Oh, I was so sure it was you!' Lady Parham gave a tinkling little laugh, glancing around at her friends. 'I had gone to Ackerman's, to look at their new prints—so amusing!—and

I saw a lady coming out of Coutts's bank. But she was veiled, so perhaps I was mistaken.'

'It must have been someone else,' said Eloise firmly. 'I was not in the Strand this morning.'

She selected a little pastry and turned away, only to find Jack Clifton regarding her with a little frown in his eyes.

Now what the devil is she about?

Jack had been watching Lady Allyngham for some time. He had noted that she was nervous, her eyes constantly straying to the clock, and her vehement denial of visiting the bank aroused his suspicions. She caught his eye and moved away so fast he abandoned any thought of speaking to her, but when, a short time later, Eloise made her excuses and left the party, he followed.

The press of traffic in the streets made it an easy task for Jack to follow her carriage on foot, and when they arrived at Dover Street he was close enough to hear the lady's instructions to the coachman to come back in an hour.

Jack grinned. So she *was* up to something! He dashed back to King Street, quelling the little voice in his head that objected to the idea of spying on a lady. After all, Tony Allyngham had been a good friend and had asked him to look after his widow—well, perhaps not in so many words, but Jack was not going to admit, even to himself, that he had any personal interest in Eloise Allyngham.

Just over half an hour later he was back in Dover Street, his evening coat replaced by a dark riding jacket and with a muffler covering his snowy neckcloth. Hidden out of sight in Dover Yard, Bob was looking after his horse and in all probability, Jack thought, animadverting bitterly on the ways of the Quality. He positioned himself opposite Lady

Allyngham's door and settled down to wait. As with many of the streets in this area of London, Dover Street housed a variety of residents, from members of the *ton* to ladies who, while they would never receive an invitation from the great society hostesses, were very well known to their husbands. Courtesans such as Kitty Williams who, it was rumoured, could boast of having a royal duke amongst her many admirers. Jack was not one of their number, but Kitty's residence had been pointed out to him by his friends, and he watched with interest as an elegant town carriage pulled up at the door. A portly gentleman climbed out and was immediately admitted, as if the doorman had been looking out for him. So Lord Berrow was one of Kitty's customers. Jack grinned: the Earl professed himself to be one of Wilberforce's saints—the old hypocrite!

The sounds of another coach clattering into Dover Street caused Jack to step back further into the shadows. He nodded with satisfaction as it drew up outside Lady Allyngham's house. He saw Eloise come out, wrapped now in a dark cloak, and step up into the carriage. It drew away immediately and Jack turned and ran for his horse.

'I still think I should come with you,' grumbled Robert as Jack scrambled into the saddle.

'No, you go back now and wait for me.' Jack patted his pocket. He had a pistol, should he need it, and besides, he forced himself to face the thought, if this should prove nothing more than a sordid little assignation with a lover, the less people who knew of it the better.

Keeping a discreet distance, Jack followed the coach as it bowled through the darkened streets. They headed north through Tottenham Court Road and soon the town was left behind and they were bowling along between open fields. It was a clear night, the rising moon giving sufficient light for the carriage to set a swift pace. The coach slowed as it climbed through the village of Hampstead. When they reached the open heath Jack drew rein and as the carriage came to a halt he guided his horse off the road into the cover of the stunted trees. He watched Eloise climb out. Silently he dismounted, secured his horse to a branch and followed her.

Eloise hesitated, glancing back at the coach drawn up behind her. The carriage lamps twinkled encouragingly and the solid shape of her coachman sitting up on the box was reassuring. She had also taken the precaution of asking Perkins to come with her. He had been her groom since she was a child and she was confident of his loyalty and discretion. Turning again to face the dark open heath, she took a deep breath and stepped forwards. She suspected it was not the autumnal chill in the night air that made her shiver as she moved along the narrow path. She felt dreadfully alone and had to remind herself that Perkins was discreetly following her. For perhaps the twentieth time since setting out she went over in her mind the instructions she had received in the letter that morning. The carriage had stopped at the fork in the road, as directed, and the path to the right between a boulder and small pond was easily found. She counted silently, thankful that the letter had stated the number of steps she would need to take rather than asking her to judge a half a mile: in her present nervous state she felt as if she had walked at least three miles already. There was sufficient light to see the path, but the trees and bushes on either side were menacingly black, and she had to force herself not to think how many malevolent creatures might be watching her from the shadows.

At one point she saw a black square on her left; a shepherd's hut, she guessed, although there were no sheep or cattle visible on the heath. Then, ahead of her, she could make out the path splitting on either side of a fallen tree. She stopped and glanced about her. Everything was silent. Shivering, she stepped up and placed a package under the exposed roots of the tree.

There, it was done. She was just heaving a sigh of relief when she heard a scuffle and crashing in the bushes behind her. She turned in time to see Perkins dragging something large and heavy out from the bushes.

'I got 'im, m'lady,' he wheezed, 'I've got yer villain!'

Eloise ran back and gazed down at the unconscious figure lying at the groom's feet.

It was Major Jack Clifton.

Chapter Four

Anger, revulsion and disappointment churned in her stomach. The major might be an odious man but she had not wanted him proved a scoundrel.

'Check his pockets,' she said crisply.

'What exactly is you looking for, m'lady?'

'A book—a small, leather-bound journal.'

'Nope,' muttered Perkins, 'Nothin' like that. But there is this!'

He pulled out a pistol and held it up so that the moonlight glinted wickedly on the barrel.

'Heavens,' exclaimed Eloise, eyeing the weapon nervously. She straightened her shoulders. 'We must tie his hands,' she declared. 'I'll not risk him getting away.'

Perkins nudged the still body with the toe of his boot.

'He's not going anywhere, m'lady.'

'Well, we cannot remain out here all night,' she retorted. 'We must take him back to town with us.'

Perkins spat.

'And just 'ow do you propose we do that? The carriage is a good half a mile hence.'

'We will carry him,' she announced. 'And don't you dare
to argue with me, Perkins!'

Her groom scratched his head.

'Well, I ain't arguing, m'lady, but he's no lightweight. I'd
suggest you'd be best takin' his legs but that ain't seemly…'

'Never mind seemly,' she replied, gazing dubiously at the
major's unconscious form. Suddenly he seemed so much larger
than she remembered. 'You cannot carry him alone, so I must
help you.'

Eloise had never carried a body before. She had never even
considered how it should be done. When Perkins had lifted
the shoulders she took a firm grip of Jack's booted ankles and
heaved. Half-carrying, half-dragging, they staggered back
along the path with their burden, but they had not gone many
yards before she was forced to call a halt.

'We will never carry him all the way back to the carriage,'
she gasped.

'Well, I could always run back and fetch Coachman
Herries.'

A cold wind had sprung up and it tugged at her cloak.

'I do not want to be standing out here any longer than
necessary.' She looked around. 'There is a hut of some sort
over there. Perhaps we could put him in there until he comes
around.' She sensed the groom's hesitation and stamped her
foot. 'For heaven's sake, Perkins, do you think we should let
him perish out here?'

'Aw, 'tedn't that cold, madam, and besides I don't see why
you should worry, if he's such a villain.'

'*He* may be a villain but I am not,' declared Eloise angrily.
'Now take his shoulders again and help me get him into that
shelter!'

It was a struggle but eventually they managed to get their
unwieldy burden into the shepherd's hut. Perkins spotted an

oil lamp hanging from the roof and pulled out his tinder box to light it. Eloise, very warm after her exertions, threw off her cloak before picking up a piece of twine to bind the major's hands behind his back. Not a moment too soon, for even as she finished tying the knot Jack groaned.

'Quickly, now, help me to sit him up.'

'If I was you I'd leave him on the floor, where 'e belongs,' opined Perkins, but she overruled him: she did not like to think of any creature bound and helpless at her feet.

They propped him up against a pile of sacks in one corner and Eloise stood back, watching as the major slowly raised his head.

'Where am I?'

'There is no point in struggling,' she said, trying to sound fierce. 'You are my prisoner.'

'The devil I am!'

'You keep a civil tongue when speakin' to my lady,' growled the groom.

'That is enough, Perkins.' Eloise turned back to Jack. 'Where is the journal?'

'What journal?'

'The diary. Where is it?'

'I have no idea what you mean.'

Her eyes narrowed.

'What were you doing on the heath?'

Jack looked up at her from under his black brows. The feeble lamplight threw dark shadows across his face and she could not see his eyes.

'I was following you. What were *you* doing?'

'That is nothing to do with you. I—' She stopped, her eyes widening. She turned to her groom, saying urgently, 'The package! Run back to the tree, quickly, and collect it.'

Perkins hesitated.

'I don't like to leave you alone with 'im, m'lady.'

'His hands are bound, he cannot hurt me. But leave me the pistol, if you like, only go and collect that package!'

As the groom let himself out of the hut she weighed the pistol in her hand.

'If that is mine I would advise you to keep your fingers away from the trigger, it is very light.' She glanced up to find Jack watching her. 'I would guess you had never used one of those.'

She shrugged.

'It should not be difficult, at this range.'

'Not at all, if you think you can kill a man.'

She glared at him.

'I can and will, if you give me cause!'

A derisive smile curved his mouth and she looked away.

'Who tied my hands?'

'I did.'

'And how did I get in here?'

'We carried you.'

'We?'

'Yes.' She flushed, saying angrily, 'It is you who should be answering questions, not I.'

'Then you had best ask me something.'

She was silent, and after a moment he said wearily, 'I wish you would sit down. Since I cannot stand it is very impolite of you to put me at such a disadvantage.'

Eloise was suspicious, but she could read nothing from his countenance, save a certain irritation. She glanced around. There was a small stool in one corner and she pulled it forwards, dusted it off and sat down. He smiled.

'Thank you. Now, what did you want to ask me?'

'Why were you following me?'

He leaned back, wincing a little as his head touched the sacking piled behind him.

'I saw you coming out of Coutts's this morning. When you denied it so fiercely at the Renwicks' party I became suspicious.'

'Oh? And just what did you suspect?'

'I don't know: that you had run out of money, perhaps.'

'I am not so irresponsible!' she flashed, annoyed.

He ignored her interruption.

'I followed you through Hampstead,' he continued, watching her carefully. 'It occurred to me that perhaps someone has a hold on you. This journal that you talked of: are you trying to buy it back?'

'That is none of your business!'

'I have a cracked skull that says it is my business,' he retorted. 'By the bye, is my head bleeding?'

She looked up, alarmed.

'I don't know—does it hurt you very much?'

'Like the devil.' He winced. 'Perhaps you would take a look at it.'

Eloise slid off the stool to kneel beside him. Absently she brushed his hair out of his eyes before gently pulling his head towards her, eyes anxiously scanning the back of his head.

'Oh heavens, yes, there is blood—oh!'

Even as she realised that he had somehow freed his hands he reached out and seized her. The next moment she was imprisoned in his powerful grasp and he had twisted her around so that it was she who was pinioned against the sacks, with Jack kneeling over her.

'Some day I'll teach you how to tie knots, my lady,' he muttered, taking the pistol from her hand.

'What are you going to do to me?'

She eyed him warily. Despite the shadows she felt his eyes burning into her.

'What would you suggest? After all, you have done your best to murder me.'

'That is quite your own fault!' She struggled against him. 'You had no right to be following me, dressed all in black like a common thief! Anyone might have mistaken you!'

She glared up at him, breathing heavily. She became aware of a subtle change in the atmosphere. Everything was still, but the air was charged with energy, like the calm before a thunderstorm. Her breathing was still ragged, but not through anger. He was straddling her, kneeling on her skirts and effectively pinning her down while his hands held her wrists. She stopped struggling and lay passively beneath him, staring at his shadowed face. He released one hand and drew a finger gently along her cheek.

'I think we may have mistaken each other, Lady Allyngham.'

His voice deepened, the words wrapped about her like velvet. She did not move as he turned his hand and ran the back of his fingers over her throat. Eloise closed her eyes. His body was very close to her own and her nerves tingled. Her senses were heightened, she was aware of every movement, every noise in the small dark hut. She could smell him, a mixture of leather and wool and spices, she could feel his warm breath on her face. Eloise lifted her chin, but whether it was in defiance or whether she was inviting his lips to join hers she could not be sure. Her breasts tensed, her wayward body yearned for his touch.

It never came.

The spell was broken as the door burst open and Perkins's aggrieved voice preceded him into the hut.

'Dang me but I couldn't find it, m'lady. Looked everywhere

for that danged package but it'd gone, and nothing in its place! I think it—*what the devil*!'

The groom pulled up in the doorway, his eyes popping. As he looked around for some sort of weapon Jack eased himself away from Eloise and waved the pistol.

'Perkins, isn't it? I beg you will not try to overpower me again,' he said pleasantly. 'You would not succeed, you know.'

Eloise struggled to her feet.

'I did *not* untie him,' she said, feeling the groom's accusing eyes upon her. 'But he is not our villain. The fact that the package is gone confirms it.'

'He might have an accomplice,' said Perkins, unconvinced.

'Believe me, I mean your mistress no harm,' said Jack, standing up and dropping the pistol back into his pocket. 'I want to help, but to do that I need to know just what is going on.'

He drew out his handkerchief and pressed it cautiously to the back of his head. Eloise saw the dark stain as he took it away again. She said quickly, 'Yes, but not now. First we must clean up that wound.'

'My man will do that for me when I get back to town.'

'Then let us waste no more time.'

She clutched at his sleeve and led him outside, leaving Perkins to put out the lamp and shut the door.

'Can you walk?' she asked. 'Do you need my groom to support you?'

'No, I will manage very well with you beside me.' She felt his weight on her arm. 'I am not too heavy for you?'

'I helped carry you,' she retorted. 'You were much heavier then.'

She heard him laugh and looked away so he would not see

her own smile. She was not yet ready to admit to a truce. They continued in silence and soon the carriage lights were visible in the distance.

'Did you ride here?' asked Eloise.

'Yes. My horse is tethered to a bush, close to your carriage.'

'Give Perkins your direction and he will ride it back to the stable.'

'And just how is *he* to get back?' demanded the groom.

'He will travel back with me in the carriage.' Eloise bit her lip. 'I think I owe Major Clifton an explanation.'

Jack followed Eloise into the carriage and settled himself into the corner, resting the undamaged side of his head against the thickly padded squabs. The coachman had orders to go carefully, but the carriage still rocked and jolted alarmingly as they made their way back towards town. He peered through the darkness at his fellow passenger.

'Are you going to tell me the truth now, madam?'

There was silence. He thought he detected a faint sigh.

'This morning I received a letter,' she said at last, 'asking me to put one hundred guineas under the roots of a fallen tree on Hampstead Heath. The instructions were quite explicit.'

'And what did you expect to get for your money?'

'The—the return of a diary. When I went into the Clevedons' garden last night it was because I had received a note, instructing me to do so. At the base of Apollo I found a piece of paper. It was a page torn from a… a very personal diary.' There was a pause. 'I discovered it was missing last year, but with all the grief and confusion over Allyngham's death, I thought it had been destroyed.'

'I see. I take it you do not wish the contents of this journal to become public?'

'That is correct.' The words were barely audible.

'And what is it you wish to keep secret, madam?'

There was an infinitesimal pause before she said coldly, 'That you do not need to know.'

'I do if I am to help you to recover the book.'

'If you had not interfered tonight I might already have it back! Who knows but your untimely appearance frightened off the wretch?'

'He was not too frightened to take your money,' Jack retorted.

'Well…mayhap he will return the book to me tomorrow.'

'You are air-dreaming, Lady Allyngham. In my experience this type of rogue will keep on demanding money until he has bled you dry.'

'No!'

'Yes.' He leaned forwards, saying urgently, 'The only way to stop this man is to catch him.'

'Perhaps.'

'There is no perhaps about it.' The carriage slowed and began to turn.

'King Street,' she said, peering out of the window. 'We have arrived at your rooms, Major. Would you like my footman to accompany you to the door?'

'No, thank you, I can manage that short distance.' He stepped carefully down on to the flagway.

'Major Clifton!'

Jack turned back to the darkened carriage. Eloise was leaning forwards, her face pale and beautiful in the dim light.

'I am sorry you were injured,' she said. 'And I thank you, truly, for your concern.'

He grasped her outstretched hands, felt the slight pressure of her fingers against his own before she gently pulled free, the carriage door was closed and the carriage rolled off into the night.

* * *

Eloise stirred restlessly. *Such* dreams had disturbed her
sleep: menacing letters, walking alone across a lonely heath,
bags of guineas. An encounter with Major Jack Clifton. She
sat up. *That* was no dream. As the reality crowded in upon
her she put her hands to her head. She had left a packet containing a hundred guineas on Hampstead Heath. The money
had gone, and the diary had not been returned. She gave a
little shiver as she thought of the damage that could be done
if ever its contents were made known. On top of all that she
had been obliged to explain something of her plight to Jack
Clifton. For a moment she forgot her own worries to wonder
if his head was hurting him this morning—perhaps he had
forgotten the night's events. The thought occurred only to be
dismissed. Jack Clifton had not been that badly injured; witness the way he had overpowered her.

Eloise allowed herself to dwell on that scene in the shepherd's hut, Jack sitting on the floor, looking up at her with a
devilish grin on his handsome face. And when she had knelt
before him, fooled into concern for the cut on his head, he had
not hesitated to seize her. She could still remember the sensation of being at his mercy, the shiver that had run through her
when she looked up and saw the devils dancing in his eyes.
It had not been fear, but excitement that had coursed through
her veins, the thought of pitting herself against him, her wits
against his strength. Angrily she gave herself a little shake.

'Enough,' she muttered, scrambling out of bed and tugging at the bell-pull. 'He never thought highly of you, and
after last night he thinks even less. You had best forget Major
Clifton.'

But it seemed that was easier said than done. As she par-
took of her solitary breakfast she tried to put him out of her

mind but it was almost as if she had conjured him up when Noyes came to announce that she had a visitor.

'Major Clifton is here to see you, my lady. He is waiting for you in the morning room.'

For a single heartbeat she considered telling Noyes to deny her, but decided against it. After all, it was her servant who had attacked the major: the least she could do was to show a little concern.

'Thank you, I will go to him directly.' She rose, putting a hand up to her curls, and it took a conscious effort not to stop at the mirror to check her appearance before entering the morning room.

Major Clifton was standing by the window, staring out into the street. He seemed to fill the room, his tall figure and broad shoulders blocking the light, and when he turned she was disturbed to find she could not read the expression on his shadowed face. He bowed.

'Lady Allyngham.'

She hovered by the door, wishing she had asked the butler to leave it open.

'Good morning, Major. How is your head?'

'Sore, but no lasting damage, I hope.'

'I hope so, too.' She gave him a tentative smile. 'Won't you sit down, sir?'

She indicated a chair and chose for herself a sofa on the far side of the room. To her consternation the major followed and sat down beside her. Heavens, would the man never do as he was bid? She sat bolt upright and stared straight ahead of her, intensely aware of him beside her, his thigh only inches away from her own. Her heightened senses detected the scent of citrus and spice: a scent she was beginning to associate with this man. She made a conscious effort to keep still: she thought wildly it would have been more comfortable sitting next to a wolf!

'M-may I ask why you are here?' she enquired, amazed that her voice sounded quite so normal.

'I want to help you catch whoever is persecuting you.'

Her head came round at that.

'Thank you, sir, but I do not need your help.'

'Oh, I think you do. Who else is there to assist you? I presume the journal is your property, so perhaps you intend to enlist the services of a Bow Street Runner to retrieve it?'

'That is impossible.' She glared at him. 'If you had not interfered last night the matter might well have been concluded.'

'I doubt it. However, I do acknowledge that I am in some small way embroiled in this affair now...'

'Nonsense! This is nothing to do with you.'

'I would not call having my head split open nothing.'

'I should have thought *that* would be a warning to you to stay away!'

His slow smile appeared, curving his lips and warming his eyes, so that she was obliged to stand up and move away or risk falling under the spell of his charm.

'My friends would tell you that I can never resist a challenge, madam.'

'And *my* friends would tell you that I am perfectly capable of looking after myself.'

'Quite clearly that is not true, for you are in serious trouble now, are you not?' When she did not reply he said softly, 'Perhaps you intend to enlist the help of Alex Mortimer—'

'No! Mr Mortimer must know nothing of this.'

'And why not? I thought he was a close friend of yours. A very *close* friend.'

His meaning unmistakable, Eloise turned away, flushing.

She said in a low voice, 'You know nothing about this. You do not understand.'

'Oh, I understand only too well, madam,' he said coldly. 'This—journal you are so concerned about: I have no doubt it contains details of your affairs. Details that you do not wish even Mortimer to know.'

She gave a brittle laugh.

'You are very wide of the mark, Major.'

'Am I? Tell me, then, what it is in this book that is so terrible?' She looked at him. There was no smile in his eyes now, only a stony determination. As if sensing her inner turmoil the hard look left his eyes. He said gently, 'Will you not trust me?'

Eloise bit her lip. She wanted to trust him. She thought at that moment she would trust him with her life, but the secrets in the journal involved others, and she could not betray them. And if he should discover the truth, she thought miserably that he would look upon her with nothing but disgust. Unconsciously her fingers toyed with Tony's heavy signet ring that she had taken to wearing on her right hand.

'I cannot,' she whispered. 'Please do not ask it of me.'

She met his gaze, her heart sinking when she saw the stony look again on his face. It was no more than she expected, but it hurt her all the same.

Jack watched her in silence. The distress he saw in her every movement tore at him. He wanted to comfort her, but she was no innocent maid: she had told him quite plainly she did not need his protection. So why did he find it so difficult to leave her to her fate? He rose, disappointed, angry with himself for being so foolish. He had wanted her to confide in him, to tell him she was an innocent victim, but it was clear now that she could not do so. Better then to go now, to walk away and forget all about the woman.

'Very well, madam. If that is all…'

'I am very sorry,' she murmured.

'So, too, am I.'

A soft knock sounded upon the door and Noyes entered.

'I beg your pardon, madam, but you asked me to bring any messages to you.'

He held out the tray bearing a single letter: she reached for it, hesitating as she recognised the untidy black scrawl.

Jack made no move to leave the room. Eloise had grown very pale and she picked up the letter as if it might burn her fingers.

'Thank you,' she said, 'That will be all.'

'Well?' Jack waited until the butler had withdrawn before speaking. 'Is it another demand? What does he say?'

She handed it to him.

'You had best read it.'

Jack ran his eyes over the paper.

'So he wants to meet with you.'

'Yes, but at Vauxhall Gardens. That will be very different from Hampstead Heath.'

'But even more dangerous. Much easier for a villain to lose himself in a crowd than on a lonely heath.'

'He does not ask for more money,' she said hopefully. 'Perhaps he means to give me back the book.'

Jack frowned. 'I think it more likely that he has other demands to make of you.' He gave her the letter. 'He does not expect an answer: the fellow is very sure of himself, damn his eyes!' He began to pace about the room. All thoughts of abandoning Eloise had disappeared. 'We will need to use your carriage, ma'am, and I think it would be useful to have your groom and my man there. We could send them on ahead of us: they will not look out of place in the crowd; one sees all sorts at Vauxhall. We have a few days to prepare…'

'We?' She raised her brows at him. 'I told you I do not want your help, Major, and I thought we had agreed I do not deserve it!'

Jack stared at her, unwilling to admit even to himself why he was so determined not to leave her to her fate.

'Allyngham saved my life,' he said curtly. 'I owe it to his memory to help you and to protect his name.'

'Whatever you may think of me?'

'Whatever I may think of you!'

Chapter Five

Eloise looked around the crowded ballroom. The plans were laid: tonight, very publicly, she was to invite Jack Clifton to escort her to Vauxhall. She experienced a sudden spurt of anger towards the unknown letter-writer: if it were not for him it would not be necessary for her to attend another glittering party. Lord Berrow was adamant that he could not sell her Ainsley Wood, so there was no reason for her to remain in London, and with Alex away she would much rather have returned to Allyngham than be walking alone into a crowded ballroom, knowing that nearly every man present would be turning lustful eyes towards her. She shivered: any one of them could be her villain.

'My dear Lady Allyngham, you are looking charming this evening, quite charming!' Lord Berrow was at her side, beaming and offering her his arm. 'And no Mr Mortimer to escort you.'

'He is gone into Hertfordshire,' she responded. 'But I expect him back very soon.'

She tried to smile, but the idea that any one of her acquaintances could have the diary had taken hold of her mind and she could not relax.

'Excellent, then you must allow me to take his place: can't have such a pretty little thing unattended.' He held up his hand as she opened her mouth to protest. 'I know what you are thinking: Lady Berrow is happily engaged with our hostess for the moment, and I know she will not begrudge me a turn about the room with a pretty woman, eh?'

She felt a tiny flicker of amusement at the Earl's behaviour. He puffed out his chest and strutted beside her, showing her off to his friends as if she was a prize he had won. However, it was not long before she began to find his rather self-centred conversation quite tedious, and it was with relief that she spotted Major Clifton. He made no effort to approach and at length she excused herself prettily from Lord Berrow, who squeezed her arm and invited her to come back and join him whenever she wished.

Eloise moved off but immediately found her way blocked by a stocky figure in an amethyst-coloured coat and white knee-breeches.

'Lady Allyngham.' Sir Ronald Deforge bowed his pomaded, iron-grey curls over her hand. 'A delightful surprise: I was afraid you had left town.'

She gave him a smooth, practised answer.

'Why should I wish to do that, when so many friends remain?'

'But you said, the other night, that you were tired of town life.'

'Did I?' She managed a laugh. 'Let us ascribe that to low spirits, Sir Ronald. I am perfectly happy now, I assure you.'

She walked away, making for the refreshment table, where she observed Major Clifton filling a cup from one of the large silver punch-bowls.

'You cannot know the happiness it gives me to hear you say that,' declared Sir Ronald, following her.

Eloise paid him no heed: she was watching Jack as he continued to fill his cup: she was sure he had seen her, but unlike every other gentleman in the room, who would have been at her side at the slightest invitation, he was studiously avoiding her eye. Stifling her irritation, she approached the table. Sir Ronald sprang forwards.

'Let me help you to a cup of punch, ma'am.'

Jack looked around, as if aware of her presence for the first time.

'Good evening, Major Clifton.'

'My lady.'

His slight bow was almost dismissive. Her eyes narrowed.

Deforge handed her a cup. 'Your punch, Lady Allyngham.'

She thanked him but turned away almost immediately to make it plain she had no further need of his company. As Sir Ronald questioned one of the servants about the ingredients of the punchbowl, she moved a little closer to Jack.

'A delightful crush tonight, is it not, Major?' she said, smiling.

'Delightful.'

His response was polite but hardly encouraging. She reached past him to pick up the ladle and add a little more punch to her cup.

'Are you avoiding me, sir?' she asked him quietly. 'Perhaps you do not wish to continue with our plan?'

A smile tugged at the corners of his mobile mouth.

'Of course I do,' he murmured. He took the ladle from her hand, brushing her gloved fingers with his own. 'Allow me, my lady.'

She carried the refilled cup to her lips, watching him all

the time. His smile grew. He turned slightly so that no one else could hear him.

'Well, madam? You must invite me to go with you to Vauxhall.'

Indignation swelled within her as she noted the wicked glint in his eye: he was enjoying this!

She raised her voice a little. 'Have you thought any more about Vauxhall, sir? I should very much like to visit the gardens on Tuesday, if you will escort me.'

He seemed to consider the matter.

'Tuesday… I *think* I could be free that evening.'

Eloise seethed. Her smile became glacial.

'If it is too much trouble for you—!'

'Did you say Vauxhall, my lady?' Sir Ronald stepped up. 'I would be more than happy—'

'Thank you, sir, but having offered to go with Major Clifton, it would be very cruel of me now to deny him.' She gave Jack a glittering smile. 'Would it not, Major?'

Her heart missed a beat as he hesitated.

'It would, of course,' he said slowly, 'but if Sir Ronald is willing…'

There could be no mistaking the venomous look that passed between the men. Sir Ronald said coldly, 'If the major is not able to escort you, madam…'

Jack put up his hand.

'And yet I do not think that will be necessary. I have not been to Vauxhall for some time, ma'am. It will be amusing to visit the gardens with you.' His eyes laughed at her. 'Shall we go by water, or the road?'

'We will take my carriage, naturally,' she replied, her calm tone quite at odds with the fury inside her.

'Naturally,' he murmured. 'So much more…intimate.'

Eloise knew her smile did not reach her eyes. She sipped at her punch, determined not to make a hasty retort.

'Then you will not be requiring my services.' Sir Ronald's angry mutter recalled Eloise to her surroundings. She held out her hand to Sir Ronald and gave him a warm smile.

'Perhaps another time, sir.'

'Perhaps, my lady.' He bowed over her hand and walked away.

She and Jack were momentary alone at the table.

'And what was that little charade about?' she demanded icily.

'Just that, a charade.'

'You made me almost *beg* you to come with me!'

He laughed.

'You have the whole of London at your feet: there has to be some reason for the Glorious Allyngham to accept the escort of a mere major. Everyone will think I played my hand very cleverly and piqued your interest.'

She placed her cup back on the table with a little bang.

'I wish I had turned you down!'

'What, and accepted Deforge as your escort instead? You would find him a dead bore, I assure you.'

She ground her teeth in frustration.

'I do not need you! I could write to Alex: he could be back here tomorrow.'

Jack refilled her cup and handed it back to her.

'But you do not want him to know what you are about: what excuse would you give him, calling him away from his business just to escort you to Vauxhall?'

She eyed him resentfully, hating the fact that he was right. He laughed again.

'You may as well accept my help with a good grace, my

lady. Now drink your punch and we will let the world see that I have fallen under your spell!'

After a solitary dinner on Tuesday night, Eloise went up to her room to prepare for her trip to Vauxhall Gardens. She chose to wear an open robe of spangled gauze over a slip of celestial blue satin. Her cap was a delicate confection of lace, feathers and diamonds that sparkled atop her golden curls. Looking in the mirror, she was pardonably pleased with the result.

'You look elegant and very stylish,' she told her reflection, adding, as thoughts of a certain tall, dark soldier entered her mind, 'and you do not look in the least fast!'

With her domino of midnight-blue velvet thrown over her arm she made her way downstairs to wait for Major Clifton. Minutes later he was shown into the drawing room, attired in a dark blue coat that seemed moulded to his figure, as did the buff-coloured pantaloons that encased his legs and disappeared into a pair of gleaming, tasselled Hessians. She put up her chin a fraction as she was subjected to his swift, hard scrutiny.

'Well, Major, do I pass muster?'

Her spirits lifted a little when she saw a flicker of admiration in his face: she had seen that look too often to be mistaken.

'I have never questioned your beauty, my lady.'

'Only my morals!' she flashed.

He put up one hand.

'Shall we call a truce, ma'am? We will need to work together if we are to succeed this evening.'

'What do you mean by that?'

'We have no idea who is writing these letters, but you may be sure that they will be watching you tonight. We must make everyone believe that I am there purely as your escort, to be easily dropped while you slip off to…where is it?'

'The Druid's Walk.'

'Yes, the Druid's Walk for your assignation.'

A smile tugged at the corners of her mouth.

'Do you really think you can act the role of a mooncalf, Major?'

He grinned back at her.

'Oh, I think I can manage that, madam.' He held out his arm. 'Shall we go?'

The journey to Vauxhall was accomplished much more quickly than they had anticipated, the traffic over the bridge being very light, and they were soon part of the line of carriages making their way to the gardens. Despite her anxiety, Eloise enjoyed Major Clifton's company far more than she had anticipated. He said nothing contentious, and treated her with such courtesy and consideration that she soon relaxed.

Jack, too, was surprised. He had heard enough of the Glorious Allyngham to expect her to be a witty and entertaining companion but he was taken off guard by the generous, unaffected nature that shone through her conversation: she was as happy to discuss the government or the plight of the poor as she was Edmund Kean's latest performance. She had little interest in gossip and confessed that she was happier living quietly at Allyngham than being ogled in the ballrooms of London. Intrigued, Jack regarded her across the dim carriage.

'This is a very different picture of you, my lady. You are not at all the Wanton Widow you are named.'

'She does not exist.'

'That is not what I have heard.'

She shrugged.

'The *ton* must gossip about someone. It may as well be me.'

'And do they not have good reason to talk of you? You have captivated every gentleman in town, and in so doing you have made every lady jealous.'

'They have no need to be jealous of me: their menfolk may lust after me, they may talk of laying siege to the Glorious Allyngham—you see, Major, I know what is said of me!—but I have no interest in any of them.'

'If that is so, then why did you come to town?'

'Oh, for company. For the concerts, and the society.' She added pointedly, 'It is possible to enjoy a man's conversation without wanting to take him for a lover, Major.' She glanced out of the window. 'Goodness, we are at the entrance already. How fast time flies when one is talking.'

She turned to smile at him and Jack's senses reeled. The flames from the blazing torchères illuminated the interior of the carriage, glinting off the lady's lustrous curls and lighting up her countenance, giving her the appearance of a golden goddess. Desire wrenched at his gut. He wanted to reach out and pull the pins from her hair, to watch those curls tumble down her back in a glorious golden stream. He wanted to take her in his arms and lose himself

'Major? We must alight: we are holding up the traffic.'

There was a laugh in her soft voice. He snapped out of his reverie and jumped down. Damnation, he must be careful: he was enjoying her company but he had no intention of falling victim to her charms. Jack handed her out of the carriage and waited silently while she adjusted her domino, resisting the temptation to help, knowing if he did so his hands would linger on her shoulders. What was is she had said? *It is possible to enjoy a man's conversation without wanting to take him for a lover.* Perhaps that was true: all he knew was that he wanted nothing to mar the easy camaraderie that was growing between them.

'We have an hour to spare before supper,' he told her as they walked through the Grove, the sounds of the orchestra drifting through the air towards them. 'Shall we take a stroll about the gardens?'

'Yes, if you please. Perhaps we should find the Druid's Walk, so I know where I am to go later.'

Eloise was happy to accompany Major Clifton through the tree-lined avenues illuminated by thousands of twinkling lamps. At one intersection they spotted Perkins and Jack's man, Robert, but they exchanged no more than a glance. Until that moment Eloise had been able to forget the purpose of their visit to the gardens. Now the fear came flooding back and she stole anxious glances at each person they passed.

'It is very unnerving to think that any one of these people might be our villain,' she muttered.

'We will know soon enough. Until then let us try to pass the time without worrying. Perhaps you could tell me something of your history.'

She looked up at him, surprised.

'It is not very interesting. I have done little, and travelled less.'

'I understand there was some opposition to your marriage to Lord Allyngham?'

'Strong opposition,' she told him. 'My parents died when I was a baby and I was sent to Allyngham to be brought up with the family. Lady Allyngham had no daughter, you see, and she brought me up with the intention that I would be something in the nature of a companion to her.'

'Did they treat you well?'

'Yes, very well. Tony and I grew up together—and Alex,

of course, who lived on the neighbouring estate. We were all close friends, inseparable until the boys went away to school, and even then we were always together when they came home for the holidays.'

'If that was the case then the Allynghams might have expected Tony to fall in love with you.'

She sighed. 'I do not believe the thought occurred to them. He was their second son and it was expected that he would make an advantageous match. It is not surprising that they were mortified when he decided to marry me, a penniless orphan.'

'That must have been very unpleasant for you.'

'It was, a little. Oh, they did nothing so very bad; they loved Tony far too much to disinherit him or anything of that nature, but there was always a certain—coolness. It lasted until they died five years ago.'

'If you had given Allyngham an heir...'

She flinched a little at that.

'Perhaps that might have helped, but it was not to be.'

He glanced down at her, concerned, and she gave him a strained little smile.

'You are not to be thinking my life is empty, Major. I have plenty to occupy me, looking after the Allyngham estates.'

'That must be a heavy burden for you.'

'Not really, I enjoy it. I took charge initially because Tony was away in the army. He trusted me to look after everything for him and we have an excellent steward, too. And Alex is always there to advise me.'

'Ah, Mortimer.' She heard the harsh note creep into his voice. 'And was he also *always there* while your husband was away?'

She stopped. Suddenly it was important that she make him

understand. She turned towards him, fixing her eyes upon his face.

'Alex and I are very close, we share many of the same interests, but we have never been more than friends. Tony knew that: it gave him some comfort to know that when he was away we could look after each other.' Impulsively she put her hands on his chest. 'I may flirt a little, Major, but I have never played my husband false, and I never intend to do so. I want you to believe that.'

They stared at one another, oblivious of the raucous laughter and exclamations of the crowds around them. Jack's hand came up and covered her fingers.

'I do believe it,' he said slowly. 'The more I know of you, the more I am intrigued. I think you are more innocent that you would have me believe.'

Eloise stepped back. Warning bells were clamouring in her head: he was far too close to the truth! She gave a little laugh.

'Do not put me on a pedestal, Major, I pray you.' She tucked her hand in his arm. 'Shall we find our supper box now?'

However, when they were seated in their box, Eloise gave Jack a smiling apology.

'I am afraid my appetite has quite deserted me. We are so exposed here, with all the world and his wife walking by.'

'Then let us give them a performance,' murmured Jack, bringing his chair a little closer. 'You need to eat, so I shall feed you titbits.'

'No, I should not—'

He speared a tiny piece of the wafer-thin ham with his fork and held it out to her.

'Yes, you should.'

'But everyone is watching!'

'Exactly. If our man is out there he will be reassured. And

as for the rest, well, they will think I am the luckiest dog alive!'

Looking into his smiling eyes, Eloise capitulated. She opened her lips to take the proffered morsel. It was delicious, which seemed to heighten the decadence of the action, and she did not protest when Jack offered her another. She felt he was tempting her with so much more than a mouthful of food. Eloise put down her wine cup. The arrack punch was very strong and it was already making her senses swim.

'You are flirting with me, Major.'

'Very much so. And if I bring my head closer to yours while I pour the wine…'

'No more for me, thank you! I need to keep a clear head for later. Do you really think we are being watched?'

'I do. We must show him that I am truly enamoured of you.'

'Oh, how?'

He took her hand.

'Like this.'

Her toes tingled with excitement when she saw the wicked gleam in his eye. She watched as he slowly pulled off her glove, holding her hand like a delicate piece of porcelain. Gently he turned it over and lowered his head to press a kiss on the inside of her wrist. She gasped. He continued to drop kisses on the soft skin of her arm. Little arrows of fire were shooting through her; it was all she could do to keep still.

'I—um—I think we should stop now.'

He ran the tip of his tongue lightly across the hinge of her elbow. Unspeakably pleasurable sensations curled around inside her, so intense she was afraid she might slide off her chair. She gazed at his head as he bent over her: she wanted to reach out and caress the raven's gloss of his hair. She clenched her free hand to prevent herself from trying such a thing.

'Major. *Jack*!' She hissed his name, almost squirming now under his touch. 'People are staring.'

He raised his head, fixing her with a devilish grin.

'That is exactly what we want,' he murmured. 'It is almost time for you to keep your appointment in Druid's Walk.'

Immediately the pleasant lassitude she had been feeling disappeared. She swallowed nervously.

'It is?'

He nodded, slipping one arm around her waist.

'So I am going to try to kiss you, then you will slap my face and leave me. Can you do that?'

Swallowing again, she nodded. Smiling, Jack gently pulled her into his arms. It was like coming home. Eloise gazed up into his eyes, black and fathomless as night. His face was only inches from her own. Her lips parted instinctively, her eyelids drooped. She ached for him to kiss her but his mouth remained tantalizingly just out of reach.

'Now you have to slap me.' Jack's voice was no more than a croak. He said curtly, 'Do it!'

Eloise dragged her wandering thoughts back. She knew what was expected of her. Pulling herself out of his grasp, she slapped him with her bare hand. Then, snatching up her glove and her domino, she marched off.

The gardens were much more frightening for an unescorted lady. Eloise pulled the hood of her domino over her head and hurried along the paths, trying to ignore the rowdy laughter coming from the darker walks. She kept her head down. Someone knocked her shoulder.

'I beg yer pardon, lady.'

She heard Perkins's familiar voice and felt a rush of gratitude, glancing up in time to see him tugging at his forelock before he turned and sauntered away. It was reassuring to know she was not quite alone.

She had memorised the instructions. The second arbour off Druid's Walk. Now as she turned into the famous avenue she began to worry. What if someone was already there? What if the writer wanted to harm her? She shook her head and tried to think rationally. If her tormentor had the journal then most likely he would want some extortionate payment. She would pay it, too, if it was the only way to get the book back.

She reached the second arbour and slowed down. Cautiously she approached the dark space. A canopy of leaves blotted out almost all the light, but as her eyes adjusted to the darkness she could see an empty bench at the back of the enclosure. Her heart beating, she walked to the bench and sat down to wait. Almost immediately a voice sounded to her right.

'You keep good time, madam. I congratulate you.'

Eloise jumped up. A black shape detached itself from the shadows. It was a man, wrapped in a dull black cloak and hat, his face hidden beneath a black mask. As he moved forwards the light glittered eerily on the eyes peering through the slits in his mask. She cleared her throat.

'What do you want of me?'

He held out his hand and she saw the grey oblong held between his fingers. It was too dark to read it but she knew from its shape and size that it was another page from the diary. As her hand reached out he snatched it back.

'How much?'

He laughed.

'You are very sensible, ma'am. No tears, no hysterics.'

'Would they do me any good?'

'Not at all.'

'Then I will ask you again, how much?'

'This page I will give you in exchange for a kiss.'

'And the rest of the book?'

She heard him chuckle. It sent a shiver of revulsion running through her.

'That depends upon the kiss.'

He reached out and pulled her to him, pressing his lips hard against her mouth. She froze, fighting against an impulse to push him away.

When he let her go she gasped and instinctively dragged the back of her hand across her mouth.

'Who are you?'

'You will discover soon enough. Here.' He held out the grey oblong. 'Take it. I shall let you know the price for the rest.'

She twitched the paper from his fingers.

'How...how did you come by the book?'

'You do not need to know that.'

She put up her chin.

'It could be a forgery.'

He laughed softly in the darkness.

'And would you have left me a hundred guineas on Hampstead Heath if it had not been genuine?'

She bit her lip, regretting that first, rash action. She said, coldly, 'What if I refuse to continue with this?'

'But you won't.' His voice was low, just above a whisper, and it sent unpleasant shivers through her. 'Neither will you leave town. Do you think if you bury yourself in the country you can escape the scandal? You know that is not true.'

She put up her head.

'If you publish I shall go abroad—'

'And what of the Allyngham name? Such an illustrious history—are you content to see it tainted?'

Eloise peered into the darkness. It was impossible to tell

much about her tormentor: the hat and cloak concealed his body as effectively as he had disguised his voice.

'What is it you want from me?'

'You will continue with your engagements. I understand a party will be going to Renwick Hall at the end of the month. You will be invited.'

'How can you be so sure?'

'Mrs Renwick likes you. I have heard her say she would like you to be there.'

She turned away, shaking her head.

'No. I have had enough of your games—'

'If I publish that book your name will be disgraced.'

'Allyngham is dead,' she said dully. 'It will make no odds.'

'But others are very much alive, and they will suffer, will they not? Are you willing to risk their disgrace, perhaps even to risk their lives, Lady Allyngham?'

She stopped. He was right, of course. Slowly she turned back.

'How much do you want?' she asked again.

'I shall let you know that in due course. For now you will continue to adorn the London salons and ballrooms while you await my instructions.'

He stepped back into the shadows. There was a rustle of leaves, then silence. She could see nothing. She put her hands out and stepped towards the back of the arbour. Branches and leaves met her fingers; there was no sign of the cloaked man. Eloise backed away. As she moved closer to the main path she held up the paper, still clutched in her fingers. Even in the dim light she recognised the writing. It was another page from that damning journal. Turning the page to catch the best of the light spilling in from the walk, she read it quickly then, with a sob and a shudder, she turned and ran out on to the path.

Chapter Six

After the darkness of the arbour the lamps strung amongst the trees of the Druid's Walk were positively dazzling. Eloise looked around wildly. Perkins and Robert came running up as she emerged on to the path.

'Did you see him?' she cried. 'He was in there. Did you see him?'

'Wasn't no one in that nook when we got 'ere,' said Perkins. 'We've bin watching all the time and no one's appeared.'

Hasty footsteps scrunched on the gravel and she looked around as Jack approached. He went to put his arm about her but she held him off.

'Where were you?' she demanded. 'You said you would follow me.'

'I did. I set off shortly after you. I admit the crowds in the main walks impeded my progress but I was no more than five minutes behind you.'

Eloise shivered. Had she been in there such a short time?

Jack took her arm. 'You are trembling. Come away from here.'

'No, I must know how he got into the arbour and how he left it again without being seen. There must be a back way.'

Robert reached up and unhooked one of the lanterns from a nearby tree.

'Well, then, madam, perhaps we should take a look.'

With Jack beside her, she followed Robert and Perkins back into the arbour. The lamplight flickered over the closely woven branches that formed the walls. She pointed behind the bench.

'He disappeared through there.'

Robert moved closer, holding the lantern aloft.

'Aha.'

Jack's grip on her arm tightened. 'What is it, Bob?'

'Two of the uprights have been sawn through. A man could squeeze through there.'

Perkins stepped up.

'Shall I go after 'im, m'lady?'

'No,' said Jack. 'He will be long gone by now. We must take Lady Allyngham home. Run ahead, Perkins, and summon the carriage.' He looked down at her. 'What happened, did he demand more money?'

Beneath her cloak Eloise crumpled the paper in her hand and slipped it into her reticule. She was not about to let Jack read it.

'He said he will let me know his demands later.'

'And did you get a look at him, ma'am?' asked Robert. 'Was he taller than you, fatter—'

She shook her head.

'I could not see. It was very dark, and he was disguised.' She cast a quick glance up at Jack. 'I am sure it is someone who was at the Renwicks' party earlier this week—he knew I was thinking of leaving town. I wondered for a moment if it might *be* Mr Renwick, but he is such a short, round, jolly gentleman his size would have been difficult to disguise.'

'But why should you think of Charles?'

'Because the man said I would be invited to join the Renwicks at their house party, and I was to accept.'

'So our villain is not a stranger to society.' He put his hand over hers. 'I should not have let you meet with this man alone.'

Eloise said nothing. She found herself listening to his voice, trying to match it to the breathy tones of her tormentor. After all, Jack had been at the Renwicks' and standing near to her when she had said she might leave London. And he had been nowhere in sight when she had emerged from the arbour. Had he been discarding his disguise?

She tried to dismiss the idea as they walked back through the gardens. Her instinct was to trust him, but what did she know about this man? He was a soldier, but that might not make him any less a villain. Every nerve was stretched to breaking point and she could not relax, even when they were seated in her comfortable travelling chaise and on their way back to town. She was not at ease, being so close to Jack Clifton. She remembered that night on the Heath. Was he really as innocent as he claimed? He might well have had an accomplice, who had taken the money from the tree roots. She cast a swift, furtive glance at the black shadowed figure beside her. Had the man in the arbour been taller or shorter than Jack, had he been fat, or thin? It was so difficult to tell; the enveloping cloak and tall hat had been a very effective disguise. She thought perhaps he had been more her own height, but everything had happened so quickly she could not be sure.

She turned to stare out of the window at the dark, shadowy fields and the houses flying by. Jack had kissed her once. It should be possible to compare that to her experience in the arbour. Both kisses had been swift and rough, but could they have been from the same man? She tried to think back to Major Clifton's first visit to Dover Street. She remembered her surprise when he had pulled her into his arms, she could even recall the excitement that had flared within her, the dizzying pleasure that for a brief moment had kept her motionless in his arms. But she could not remember the *detail*.

The carriage jolted over the uneven road and she was briefly thrown against her companion. Instead of shrinking away, she held her position, her face only inches from his shoulder. She breathed in, trying to detect any scent that might remind her of the man in the arbour. She leaned closer, desperately searching her memory for any little point that might identify the man. It had been very dark in that leafy bower, and she had seen very little, but she had felt the man's hands gripping her arms—that certainly had been very similar to Jack's savage embrace!—and she had been aware of his mouth pressing her lips, and his rough cheek rubbing against hers. If it was the man sitting beside her in the carriage, there was one way to find out. Aware of her proximity, Jack turned towards her.

'What is it?' he asked her, concern in his voice. 'Madam, are you afraid still?'

Amazed at her own daring, Eloise edged a little closer.

'I vow I *am* a little nervous, sir.'

Jack put his arm about her shoulders.

'There is nothing to be nervous of now, Lady Allyngham. I shall not let anything happen to you.'

She leaned against him with a little sigh.

'You are very good,' she murmured, looking up towards the paler shadow that was his face. She felt his arm tighten around her. There was a momentary hesitation before he bent his head, blocking out the light. Her face upturned, Eloise closed her eyes and waited for his kiss.

The feel of his lips, soft and warm against her own, almost robbed her of her senses but she battled against the mind-numbing sensations he was arousing within her. She must remain calm and make her comparisons. The man in the arbour had smelled of leather and snuff and wine. Now her head was filled with much more refreshing aromas of citrus and spices. The rogue had been content to press his lips hard against hers but Jack's mobile mouth was working gently upon her lips, encouraging them to part. She almost swooned as his tongue explored her mouth, playing havoc with her already disordered senses. She had peeled off her gloves, now with a little moan her hand came up to his cheek. It was smooth and cool beneath her fingers, not rough and pitted. Suddenly it was all too clear; Major Jack Clifton was *not* the villain.

Having established this fact, Eloise knew she should now draw back, but her body would not obey her. Instead of press-ing her hands against his chest and pushing him off, they crept up around his neck. In one sudden, swift movement he caught her about the waist and dragged her on to his lap, all the time his mouth locked on hers and his tongue darting and teasing, robbing her of any ability to think.

At last he raised his head and gave a long, ragged sigh but he kept his arms tightly about her, and she could not find the strength to disengage herself from his hold. Instead her fingers clung to his jacket and she buried her face in his shoulder.

'Oh, what must you think of me?' she murmured into the folds of his beautifully starched neckcloth.

He rested his cheek on the top of her head.

'You were in need of comfort,' he murmured.

She could feel the words reverberating in his chest.

'I was, of course, but I should not have imposed upon you.'

His laugh rumbled against her cheek.

'That was no imposition, my dear, it was sheer delight. In fact, I think we should do it again.'

Eloise was filled with horror. She had behaved quite as wantonly as her reputation had led him to expect and suddenly it was very important that he should not think ill of her. She raised her head and tried to slide off his lap, but strong hands held her firm. She blushed in the darkness, aware of his body pressed against her. The heat from his powerful thighs seemed to be transmitting itself to her own limbs and she had to make a determined effort not to wriggle. She said quietly, 'Please, Major, let me go.'

Immediately he released her and she eased herself back on to the padded seat of the chaise.

'It—it is not as is seems,' she began. How much should she tell him? How much *could* she tell him?

They were rattling into London now and when she looked up the light from the streetlamps showed her that her companion was smiling.

'How is it, then?' he said. 'Tell me.'

Jack waited, watching as she clasped her hands in her lap, searching around in her mind for words to explain herself. She was such an intriguing mixture of shy innocence and searing passion. It was almost possible to believe she was a virtuous woman. Almost.

'I am afraid I have given you a very false impression, Major Clifton. I am nothing like the Wanton Widow society has christened me. In fact, I—'

She broke off as the carriage slowed. Jack glanced out of the window.

'Dover Street. You are home, my lady.' He opened the door

and jumped down, turning to hold out his hand to her. 'We will continue this conversation inside.'

'Oh, no!' She shrank back. 'No, I do not think we should to that. It is so very late…'

He grinned.

'After the events of the past few days I do not think we need to stand upon ceremony, ma'am. Come, we will be more comfortable inside. Besides, your nerves are still disordered and I want to see you take a cup of wine before I leave. It will help you to sleep.'

Jack helped her down from the carriage, but even as they trod up the steps into the house she was suggesting that they should continue their discussions on the morrow. Jack ignored her protests. He was reluctant to leave her: the anger he had felt when he realised the blackguard had escaped them was nothing compared to the cold, gut-wrenching fear he had experienced, knowing that Eloise had been alone with the villain. Lady Allyngham might consider herself a woman of the world, she might enjoy her flirtations with gentlemen of the *ton*, but for a brief time tonight she had been at the mercy of an unscrupulous villain, and Jack's blood ran cold when he thought of what might have happened to her. With one hand possessively around her waist he swept her into the house and guided her towards the morning room, where a thin strip of candlelight glowed beneath the door.

'Major Clifton, I assure you I am perfectly composed now.' She continued to protest as the wooden-faced lackey threw open the door of the morning room. 'There really is no need for you to stay.'

Jack opened his mouth to reply as he followed her into the room but the words remained unspoken. They were not alone. Alex Mortimer was sitting in a chair beside the fire, a glass of brandy on the table beside him and his booted legs stretched out towards the hearth.

'Alex!'

The lady's unfeigned pleasure at the sight of her visitor had Jack grinding his teeth. Mortimer, too, looked particularly at his ease. Damn him. He rose as Eloise went forwards, her hands held out towards him.

'I did not expect you back in town for days yet.'

'My business was concluded early.' Mortimer took her hands and planted a kiss on her cheek. 'Noyes told me you had gone to Vauxhall, so I thought I would wait for you.' He looked across at Jack and raised his brows. 'Am I *de trop*?'

'No, of course not,' said Eloise quickly. Jack noticed she had the grace to blush. 'You know Major Clifton?'

'We have met.' Alex nodded towards Jack, his eyes wary. 'Is it the usual practice to bring gentlemen home now, Elle?'

Jack's chin jutted belligerently. 'Is it the usual practice to treat a lady's house as if it was your own?'

Eloise stepped between them.

'Major Clifton escorted me back from Vauxhall.'

Alex's brows rose higher. 'I trust you had a pleasant evening.'

Jack was about to retort that pleasure had not been the object of attending the gardens when he realised Eloise was looking at him, such a look of entreaty in her blue eyes that he could not ignore it. He allowed himself a faint, mocking smile.

'How could it be otherwise,' he drawled, 'with Lady Allyngham at my side? And now that you are safely home, madam, and have no further need of my...services, I shall take my leave.'

There was some bitter satisfaction in the way her cheeks flamed at the inference. Mortimer frowned and took a step forwards. Jack braced himself for the challenge but it never came. Eloise put out her hand, palm down, saying coolly,

'Yes, thank you, Major, for escorting me tonight. I am very grateful.'

The shadow of reproach he saw in her eyes flayed his lacerated spirits. He cursed silently. They find Mortimer making himself at home in her house and she expects *him* to act like a gentleman. Clenching his jaw against further unwary comments, he gave a stiff little bow and retired, reminding himself that the widow's behaviour really was no concern of his. But this comforting thought did nothing to alleviate the black mood that enveloped him as he strode back to King Street.

Eloise watched the door close with a snap behind the major and let her breath go in a long and very audible sigh. She untied her cloak and threw it over a chair.

'I am sorry if I have frightened off your lover,' murmured Alex.

Eloise swung round.

'Major Clifton is *not* my lover!' she retorted, knowing the heat was flooding back into her cheeks.

'Well, I think he would like to be,' mused Alex, pressing her down into a chair. 'The look on his face when he saw me here was one of severe disappointment.'

'It was?' She looked up hopefully.

Alex grinned.

'Oh, yes. I think he could happily have murdered me. He looked most disapproving.'

'Well, that is no surprise,' she retorted. 'It was a shock for *me* to find you here at this time of night.'

'This time in the morning, actually,' Alex corrected her, sitting down. 'I was concerned about you. It is not like you to go off to Vauxhall with only Clifton for company.

Unless, of course, you have decided to live up to your wicked reputation.'

'I would never do that!' she retorted.

She clasped her hands tightly in her lap, thinking back over the events of the evening. She did not know what to do. About the journal. About Jack. He had been angry when he left, and with good reason. To find Alex waiting for them had been a shock. She was so accustomed to having Alex around that she had thought nothing of it, but a moment's reflection had shown her how it must look to Jack. It confirmed all the disgraceful things he had already heard about her. She gave an inward shrug. It was too late now to worry about that. She turned her mind instead to the problem of the missing journal. She glanced at Alex. Perhaps, after all, she should take him into her confidence. He had always been her friend and she knew she could trust him. Besides, this matter involved him. It was only right that he should know what was happening. She said slowly, 'You will remember, after Tony died, we searched for the journal and could not find it?'

'Yes, but I thought Tony had destroyed it.'

'No. It was stolen.' Eloise looked up. 'And now someone is using it against me.'

Alex sat up straight. 'The devil they are!'

Briefly, Eloise told him all that had happened since he had left town. When it came to explaining Major Clifton's role in the affair she said only that he wanted to keep Tony's name free from scandal and to help her to catch the culprit. When she had finished her recital she reached into her reticule and pulled out the crumpled paper. 'When I met with the villain he gave me this tonight.' She shuddered as she handed it to him. 'Burn it, please, once you have read it.'

Alex took it, rubbing his chin as he frowned over the writing.

'You will see that you are only mentioned there as "M",' she said, 'but if anyone begins to put together the dates and the places, your identity must be known.'

He looked up.

'Why did you not tell me?' he asked. 'Why did you not write to me? I would have come back to town immediately.'

She spread her hands, saying miserably, 'I thought I could deal with this myself. And then…and then Major Clifton became involved.'

Alex tossed the paper into the fire, a look of distaste marring his fair features. He said, 'Tony mentioned Clifton to me in one or two of his letters. Thought quite highly of him, so I suppose we can trust him.' He shot a glance at her. 'How much does he know, Elle?'

'Only that I am desperate to recover the diary.' A knot of unhappiness was twisting itself in her stomach. 'He knows nothing of its contents.'

She lowered her eyes, unwilling to meet Alex's keen glance.

'He thinks it is a scandalous record of your affairs,' he stated baldly.

Eloise shrugged. 'Better that than the truth.'

'And you don't mind that?'

'Of course not. Major Clifton is nothing to me!' She looked away from his searching gaze. 'And there is no need for you to look at me like that. You know I have no wish for another husband.' She managed a scornful laugh. 'Certainly not the major!'

Eloise did not think she sounded very convincing, but Alex seemed satisfied. He said, 'Well, I am here now, and I will help you recover that damned book. You can tell Major Clifton that we no longer require his help.'

Eloise could not understand herself: she had thought she

wanted nothing more than to be free for ever of Jack's disturbing presence, but Alex's words gave her pause.

'I am not sure he will be that easy to put off,' said Eloise slowly. 'He is very anxious to protect the Allyngham name.'

'Is that all he wishes to protect?'

Her cheeks grew warm again as she remembered her behaviour in the carriage. She stifled a sigh.

'He has no reason to think well of me.'

'No, it is most likely that Clifton thinks to take you for his mistress.'

'No!' cried Eloise, tears starting to her eyes. 'He must know I would never agree to that!'

'Are you sure? When you go off alone with him to Vauxhall, and invite him into your house in the middle of the night?'

Eloise bit her lip. She had been about to tell Jack the truth, but had he understood that, or had he thought she was offering to take him to her bed?

'Much as I hate to admit it, Jack Clifton could be useful to us,' mused Alex, rubbing his chin. 'After all, we cannot involve too many people in this affair. And if we are careful, there is no reason why he should ever discover that the journal is anything other than an account of the Wanton Widow's scandalous past, is there?'

Eloise stared into the fire. A short while ago she had been on the verge of telling the major everything. Now she must continue with her role, and abandon any hope of Jack Clifton ever regarding her with respect.

'No,' she said dully. 'No reason at all.'

Chapter Seven

Lady Chastleton's rout promised to be a huge success: the elegant salons were so full that it was impossible to move freely and even though the tall windows to the garden had been thrown open, the noise and heat had increased to an uncomfortable level.

Catching sight of her reflection in the gilded mirror, Eloise thought that no one watching the Glorious Allyngham would think her anything other than a wicked flirt.

She was in Lady Chastleton's elegant salon, at the centre of a group of attentive gentlemen. One young buck was gazing at her adoringly, another had taken her fan and was gently waving it to and fro; Sir Ronald Deforge was offering her a glass of champagne while a red-faced gentleman in a powdered wig was bending to take snuff from her upturned wrist.

Her eyes travelled to where Alex was standing, paying court to a shy ingénue who blushed prettily whenever he addressed her. She sighed. They were both playing out their charade and she knew Alex was as sick of it as she. If only they could retire again to their respective country acres. But it could not be, not yet. Not while the threat of exposure hung over them.

'You must take care not to allow the snuff to stain your fair skin, my lady.' Sir Ronald's voice broke into her reverie. 'Allow me to brush it off.'

He caught her hand and rubbed his thumb over her wrist. It was an effort for her not to pull her hand away with a little shudder of revulsion. Instead she gave him a roguish smile as he bent to touch his lips to the soft whiteness of her inner wrist. Some instinct made her look up at that moment and her smile slipped a little when she saw Major Clifton glowering at her from across the room. Her head went up and she hunched one white shoulder at him. She had heard nothing from him since Vauxhall and it did not matter what he thought, he was nothing to her. When she looked again he had disappeared into the crowd and Eloise tried to convince herself that she did not care, but her dissatisfaction with the evening was intensified.

With soft smiles and caressing words she retrieved her fan, disengaged herself from her entourage and moved away. Lord Berrow was smiling and nodding to her from across the room but she pretended she had not seen him: he might still be persuaded to sell her Ainsley Wood but she had laughed and flirted enough for one night. She would find Alex and ask him to take her home.

'You are frowning, madam. It does not become you.'

Major Clifton's voice at her shoulder brought her to a halt. She looked round to find him beside her. Glancing up, she saw no sympathy in his face, only a cool, considering look in his hard eyes.

'I have the headache,' she said shortly.

'A little air will revive you.' He held out his arm. 'Let me escort you outside.'

She hesitated but the sight of Sir Ronald Deforge standing

a short distance away decided her: if she turned from Major Clifton she knew Sir Ronald would be at her side, offering to escort her, enveloping her with his suffocating attentions. She laid her fingers on Jack's sleeve and allowed him to lead her to the nearest of the tall windows. His arm was reassuringly solid beneath the soft wool of his evening coat and it was tempting to lean upon him. It was very odd that she should feel so safe with Jack Clifton beside her, despite his obvious disapproval.

As they stepped outside the night air was cool on her face and the exposed skin of her arms. After the cloying heat of the salon it was refreshing. There were several couples already on the wide balcony, and Eloise made no protest as her partner led her away from them.

'I have not seen you since Vauxhall, Major,' she began. 'I wanted to thank you.'

'For what?' His voice was harsh. 'The kiss we shared in the carriage, or for not knocking Mortimer's teeth down his throat?'

'Neither! For escorting me to the Gardens. For your protection.'

'Little enough protection, since the rogue was able to approach you.'

'Nevertheless, I was very grateful that you were there.' Eloise released his arm and busied herself with arranging her fine lace shawl over her shoulders. 'After…after you had gone, the other night, I decided to tell Alex about the letters. He is involved, you see.'

'I had guessed as much. Well, he will be able to deal with this.'

She paused. She had promised Alex she would seek the major's assistance in recovering the journal. This was her opportunity. She drew a breath.

'Actually, I—*we* would appreciate your continued help, Major. This is a very delicate matter, and there is no one else we can confide in.'

He turned away from her, staring out across the vast expanse of Green Park that stretched away beyond the moonlit gardens. Eloise looked at him. There was something very reassuring about his strong, uncompromising profile, his upright bearing. He looked honourable, incorruptible. Suddenly it was very important to her to have his support. She reached out and touched his arm.

'Please, Major Clifton.'

'Give me one reason why I should help you.'

'You called Tony your friend. I thought you wanted to protect his good name.'

'I did, I do, but why should I concern myself with keeping the name of Allyngham free from scandal when *you* are so determined to sully it?'

Her hand dropped.

'Because I flirt a little—'

He swung round to face her, his countenance as hard as stone in the moonlight.

'A little? You are the talk of the town, madam. The betting books are filled with wagers about you!'

She stiffened.

'I allow no man to go beyond friendly dalliance.'

He gave a bark of mirthless laughter.

'Oh? I was watching you tonight, surrounded by your admirers! Why, you even allowed that fop to take his snuff from your hand!'

'But that is all. It goes no further than that!'

'Does it not?' *I* have kissed you twice, madam. Was that mere dalliance? And what of Mortimer? You consider it *friendly dalliance* to allow him into your house at all hours of the night?'

'No one but you knows he called upon me.'

'Oh, so as long as he visits you in secret it does not matter?'

She bit her lip.

'Alex is an old family friend, nothing more. I told you that.'

'Aye, you did, and I wanted to believe you, but the more I see and hear of you—' He shook his head and said bitterly '—I fear our standards are not the same. Standards—hah! I have known alley cats with better morals than you.'

'How dare you!' Eloise brought her hand up swiftly but he was even quicker. He caught her wrist, his fingers biting into her flesh.

Jack stared at the angry face turned up towards him. The moonlight glinted on her eyes, sending daggers of light towards him. She was radiating fury, her lips parted as if she was about to hiss and spit at him. And with good reason; he had been very uncivil—but what had he said that was not true? It angered him that he threw such accusations at her and she did nothing to deny them. He admitted to himself that he was jealous, too. Jealous that she should bestow her smiles and honeyed words on other men.

They were standing very close and as her breast rose indignantly the flowers of her corsage brushed his waistcoat and filled his senses with a heady perfume. It was distracting, intoxicating. His fingers tightened on her slender wrist, pulling her even closer. Suddenly he wanted to sweep her into his arms and kiss her, transforming her rage into the passion he sensed was just beneath the surface. He saw the anger leave her face. Her eyes widened, as though she was reading his thoughts. He could take her now, he knew it. They were standing breast to breast; he would only have to move a little to bring his mouth down to hers. It was like holding a taper close to a tinderbox, knowing that the slightest touch would ignite a blaze.

She swallowed hard and his eyes were drawn to the convulsive movement in the slender column of her throat. He would like to kiss her there, he thought distractedly. He would like to trail his mouth over her skin to the base of her throat where a pulse was beating so rapidly, and carry on until his lips reached the soft swell of her breasts. Then...

She gave a little sob.

'Let me go, you monster!'

His head jerked up and he came to his senses. She was struggling to free herself from his vice-like grip. Jack released her and she stepped away from him, her left hand cradling her wrist. He hardened himself against her look of anger and reproach to say coldly, 'I am not one of your fawning admirers, Lady Allyngham. You will not strike me for telling the truth.'

Eloise glared up at him, rubbing her sore wrist. She was still furious, but beneath her anger was a lurking fear for the disturbing emotions he aroused in her. The blaze she had seen in his eyes when they had been standing so close had very nearly overset her: she had wanted to throw herself at him, kicking, biting and scratching until he responded. For one dizzying moment she had imagined him pinning her against the wall, subduing her anger with a savage kiss before carrying her off to ravage her in ways that she had heard other women talk of, but had never experienced for herself. Even now, standing before this big, disturbing brute of a man, she did not know whether she was most glad or sorry that he had let her go. She struggled to regain some form of dignity and managed to say in glacial accents, 'We have nothing more to say to each other, Major Clifton. We will consider our acquaintance at an end.'

He clipped his heels together and made her a stiff little bow.

'As you wish, madam.'

She drew herself up, blinking away the tears that threatened to spill over.

'I *wish*,' she said in a low, trembling voice, 'that it was you and not Tony who had perished at Waterloo!'

Turning on her heel, she marched back into the ballroom and did not stop until she had found Alex.

He was playing cards, but as soon as he saw her he excused himself and came to meet her.

'Well, well,' he said, taking her arm, 'now what has occurred to ruffle your feathers?'

'Nothing. I merely want you to take me home.'

He grinned.

'Then I shall do so, of course, but you cannot storm into the card room with the colours flying in your cheeks and tell me nothing is wrong.'

She almost ground her teeth.

'Major Clifton has insulted me.'

Alex raised his brows.

'Oh? Do you want me to call him out?'

'Yes,' she said savagely. 'I want you to challenge him to a duel and then run him through. I want him to die very painfully!'

'Well, I would, of course, my dear, but Clifton is a soldier, so he is bound to be a much better swordsman than I. Then, of course, he might choose pistols, and you know what a terrible shot I am…'

Even through her rage she could not but laugh at his non-sense. Alex patted her arm.

'That's better. Come along then, I will take you home.'

They said nothing more until they were bowling along in the elegant Allyngham town chaise. As they rattled over the cobbles, Alex demanded to know just what had occurred.

'I was going to tell Major Clifton that I had received my invitation to Renwick Hall. I thought he might help us.' She rubbed her sore wrist.

'And what happened?'

'He told me I had the morals of an alley cat.' She hunted for her handkerchief. 'And I c-could not deny it, especially after he found you in my house when we got back from Vauxhall.'

'He hasn't spread that about, has he?'

'No, of course not.' She blew her nose defiantly. 'But he thinks me quite *sunk* in depravity.'

'As well he might,' remarked Alex with what she thought was heartless candour. 'I think he might be jealous.'

'No, he is not.' She wiped her eyes. 'He is merely the most odious man that ever lived. I hate him!'

'If that is the case, then why are you so upset?'

'Because I am quite *sick* of this charade! I hate everyone thinking ill of me.'

'You mean you hate Jack Clifton thinking ill of you.'

She stamped her foot on the carriage floor.

'That is not it at all,' she said crossly.

'If it's your reputation you are concerned for, I could always marry you.'

'Alex!'

'Well, it is one solution.'

'But you do not want to marry.'

'No, and I do not think it would make you happy, Elle. But if it puts paid to a scandal…'

She shook her head.

'It will not do that, we both know it.' She sighed. Putting away her handkerchief, she reached across the carriage to pat his hand. 'It is very good of you, Alex, but we neither of us want to marry. I am sorry; I should not have let the hateful Major Clifton upset me so. I think I must be very tired tonight.'

'I think so, too. It is not like you to be so disheartened. If you are truly worried about that journal, Elle, why not come abroad with me and forget about England? It matters little to me now where I live.'

'No, I am resolved not to run away because some, some insignificant little *worm* dares to threaten us!' She drew herself up, saying in a much stronger voice, 'But I am determined we will not ask for Major Clifton's help again. You and I will go to Renwick Hall, we will find a way to recover this wretched book and then I can go back to Allyngham, build my foundling hospital in Tony's memory and, and become a recluse!'

Eloise found herself looking forward to the Renwicks' house party. At least it would mean that she need no longer parade herself in the fashionable salons of the town. During her period of mourning she had missed the society, but the role she had set herself was proving to be very wearing. When Tony had introduced her to the *ton* she had enjoyed the parties and the company, but then the admiration of the gentlemen for Lord Allyngham's wife had always been tempered by her husband's protective presence. Even when Tony was fighting in the Peninsula and she had come to town with only Alex as her escort, somehow Lord Allyngham's shadow hovered over her and no man dared to go too far. However, all that was now changed. As a widow—and a rich one at that—she seemed to attract the predatory males of the town. They circled about her like a pack of wolves and it was only the fact that they considered her to be under Alex's protection that kept them from pouncing. She was aware of her precarious position: her wealth and status gave her entrée to all the grand houses of the *ton*, but if she allowed the flirtations to get out of hand, if she caused too much of a scandal, then society's hostesses would close their doors to her. She would be consigned to the ranks of the *demi-monde* and the proud name of Allyngham would no longer be revered. Her husband would no longer be remembered as a valiant soldier—she might even be obliged to remove the memorial stone from the wall of Allyngham church. That was why it was so important to recover the journal: if its contents ever became known, she and Alex would not only be ostracised by the *ton*, they would be obliged to fly the country.

These sobering thoughts occupied her mind as she journeyed to Renwick Hall. Eloise became even more acutely aware of how society viewed her when she joined her hostess in the drawing room before dinner that evening.

'My dear, how prompt you are,' declared Mrs Renwick, coming forwards to meet her. 'Everyone else is still at their *toilette*.'

'Oh dear, if I am too early…'

'By no means. I am glad of the company. Come and sit here beside the fire and tell me how you like your room.'

'It is very comfortable, ma'am, and has a lovely view of the lake,' said Eloise, disposing her skirts about her on the satin-covered sofa.

'I knew you would like the blue bedchamber,' smiled Mrs Renwick. 'I regret that we could not find an adjoining room for Mr Mortimer. He sent me word that he will be joining us in the morning. We have had to put him in the bachelor wing, on the far side of the house. With such a house full of guests, I am sure you will appreciate that we have to allocate all the bedchambers in the main building to our married guests.'

Looking into her hostess's kind face, Eloise's heart sank at this tacit acceptance that Alex was her lover. She took a deep breath.

'That is as it should be, ma'am. As a matter of fact, I wanted to ask your advice. I have been thinking for some time that I should have a companion when I am in London. I thought I might ask Allyngham's cousin, Margaret Cromer. We have lost touch a little in recent years but I hope she will consider my request. I have always been a little in awe of her, but I know she is a good friend of yours, ma'am, and wanted to ask you what you thought of the idea before I write to her: do I presume too much, do you think she would accept?'

'Meg Cromer? Oh. I had thought you preferred *not* to have a chaperon! That is, I mean…'

'A widow has a great deal more freedom than a single woman,' said Eloise, taking pity on her hostess's confusion. 'I am aware that there is already a great deal of talk about me, although I hope you will believe me when I say that it is all unfounded. And Mr Mortimer…Mr Mortimer is a good friend, but I have imposed upon him long enough. I think I should go on more comfortably now if I had some female company.'

'You do not think…' Her hostess looked down at her hands. 'Have you considered that marriage would give you a great deal more protection, Lady Allyngham? I am sure there can be no shortage of eligible suitors…'

Eloise shook her head.

'You are very kind to say so, but I have no wish to marry again.'

'No, of course,' replied Mrs Renwick quickly. 'It is very early days, and I believe Lord Allyngham to have been the very best of men. It would be difficult to find his equal.'

'I would not even attempt it,' replied Eloise. 'I am resigned to a single life, but that does not mean I need be bored or lonely. I have a large estate at Allyngham. That brings its own responsibilities, and I intend to travel, now the Continent is safe again, but for the present I need to make a life for myself, and that necessitates spending some little time in London and I find I am growing tired of being labelled the Wanton Widow.'

Mrs Renwick nodded.

'You are very right, Lady Allyngham, you would be subjected to much less comment if you had Meg as your companion. And you have no need to write to her because she is staying here with me at the moment. So, you may ask her as soon as you wish. She is a stickler for convention, of course: her reputation and character are of such high standing that I feel sure her presence would be an advantage to you.'

'That is why I thought I might invite Cousin Margaret to come with me when I leave here and return to London.'

'Very wise, my dear. Talk to her while you are here. As a widow of several years' standing she is a very independent person, but I am sure she would be happy to stay with you for a few months. But I hope that does not mean you intend to cut short your visit here. I am looking forward to such a happy time, for we have invited only close acquaintances on this occasion—and here is one of Mr Renwick's oldest friends, now. Major Clifton, you are in good time, sir!'

Chapter Eight

Eloise's head snapped around. She watched Jack Clifton walk
into the room, tall and elegant in his black swallow-tailed coat
and buff pantaloons. He looked relaxed and at his ease, and she
schooled her own features into a look of bland indifference as
she rose to her feet. More people were coming into the room
and Mrs Renwick hurried away to greet them, leaving Eloise
with the major.

'What are you doing here?' she demanded as he bowed to
her.

He raised his brows.

'Renwick invited me. Do you think I should remove
myself because you do not want me here? I am a guest,
madam, as you are. You will have to make the best of it.' He
bared his teeth. 'Smile, madam, we are in company; you do
not want anyone to suspect an intrigue, do you? Or perhaps,
considering your reputation, it is of no matter to you.'

'Your being here is no matter to me, Major,' Eloise flashed
back at him. She gave him a smile as false as his own and
swept away to meet the other guests.

* * *

With the exception of Alex Mortimer, the party was complete, and when Eloise sat down to dinner it was with the almost certain knowledge that her tormentor from Vauxhall Gardens was amongst the guests. She glanced around the table as the servants came in with the first course. She discounted Mr and Mrs Renwick from her list of suspects and, reluctantly, Major Clifton. Lord and Lady Parham were inveterate gossipmongers, but she did not think either of them capable of such subterfuge. Sitting near her were two other couples, both related to Mrs Renwick, plus Sir Ronald Deforge. Then there was a gentleman called Graham with an unfortunate taste in florid waistcoats and her late-husband's cousin, Mrs Margaret Cromer, an iron-haired lady whose forbidding countenance was relieved by a decided twinkle in her grey eyes. At the far end of the table was Mr Renwick's sister, her clergyman husband and two pretty daughters. Eloise knew them slightly, but since Mr Briggate and his family had travelled from Dorset to join the party at Renwick Hall she hoped she might discount them.

With a sigh she turned her attention to her dinner. In truth, she had no idea whom she should suspect. She must not relax, even for a moment. She pushed a piece of chicken across her plate, sadly aware that her appetite had disappeared.

After dinner the ladies withdrew to the long gallery, where fires blazed in the two fireplaces. They disposed themselves gracefully on the elegant sofas while they talked and gossiped, and during a lull in the conversation Eloise wandered off to look at the numerous pictures that covered the walls.

'We have some very fine paintings here, Lady Allyngham,' said Mr Renwick, leading the gentlemen into the room at that moment. 'However, they don't show to advantage in the candlelight: you are best looking at them during the day.'

'I should like to do so,' she replied.

'And I should be delighted to escort you,' replied her host, smiling. 'Or let Clifton be your guide; he knows as much as I about the pictures here at the Hall.'

'You flatter me, Charles,' said Jack. 'I do not claim to be an expert.'

'But you have an eye for a beautiful work of art,' returned Mr Renwick.

'And for a pretty woman,' added Mr Graham, walking by.

'And that,' Jack replied gravely.

He was about to turn away. Eloise said quickly, 'You consider yourself a connoisseur, perhaps?'

'Of art, madam, or women?'

'Oh, Clifton is decidedly a connoisseur of women!' laughed Mr Renwick, clapping his friend on the shoulder.

'I take leave to question that,' muttered Eloise, so quietly that only Jack could hear her. She found his dark, unsmiling gaze resting on her.

'I have enough experience to know when beauty is merely a sham, a bright veneer to cover a tarnished character.'

Colour flamed through Eloise's cheek. She turned away, furious with herself for challenging him. It was a game she could not win. She fixed her eyes on a large portrait, pretending to study it while she struggled to regain her composure.

'What—' Jack was standing at her shoulder, his words quiet in her ear, '—has the Glorious Allyngham no laughing riposte for me?'

She drew herself up and turned to him, masking her anger with a glittering smile.

'I am amazed, sir, that you claim any expertise at all when it comes to our sex. In my experience you show no aptitude at all and see only what you want to see!'

With no more than a small inclination of her head Eloise moved away, back to the relative safety of the crowd.

It was still early so it came as no surprise when one of the younger members of the group suggested dancing. The party moved to one end of the room where the fine pianoforte was situated and footmen were called to roll away the carpet. With her nerves at full stretch, Eloise could not share in the general high spirits so she stepped up to her hostess and offered to play for the dancers. Mr Graham, overhearing her, immediately cried out at this, saying with a laugh, 'Would you deprive us of the pleasure of watching you dance, Lady Allyngham?'

'Would you deprive us of the pleasure of partnering you?' added Sir Ronald Deforge.

She shook her head.

'Thank you, but I am very happy to play tonight.'

Mr Graham was inclined to argue.

'But, my lady—'

'Someone else may take a turn at the pianoforte later,' declared Mrs Renwick, the peacemaker. 'I know Lady Allyngham to be an excellent pianist and it would be an honour to have her play for our little party.'

Major Clifton carried a branched candlestick across to the pianoforte.

'Out of sorts, Lady Allyngham?'

She gave him a frosty look and turned her attention to leafing through the music piled on a nearby table.

'I am not always so flighty as you think me, Major.'

'Perhaps you are missing Alex Mortimer.'

'Oh, do go away!'

She ground her teeth as he sauntered off, laughing.

Seating herself at the instrument, Eloise began to play. Her fingers flew over the keys, her lively playing accompanied by the happy laughter of the dancers.

* * *

After an hour even the most energetic of the young people was glad to take a break and while they refreshed themselves with cups of wine, lemonade or ratafia, Mrs Renwick and her husband were persuaded to sing a duet. This was so successful that their audience clapped and cheered and demanded more. Mrs Renwick beckoned to Mrs Cromer.

'Meg, my dear, come and join us to sing the trio from *Così fan tutte*. Do you remember, we saw it together at the Haymarket in the year Eleven and immediately purchased the music so we could learn it.?

Margaret Cromer stepped up.

'I remember it well and will sing it, with pleasure, if Cousin Eloise can play it?'

'I can,' said Eloise, waving her hand towards the side-table. 'If I can find the music.'

Before she could get up Jack picked up a large book and carried it across to the piano.

'You will need someone to turn the pages for you, my lady.'

'That is not necessary, Major Clifton, I shall manage.'

'Do not be so stubborn,' he murmured, placing the music before her. 'Would you have the performance ruined because you will not accept a little help?'

Knowing he was right, she set her jaw and began to play. The soft, haunting notes soothed away her anger. *Soave sia il vento*, 'May the wind be gentle'. She knew the song well, a beautiful, sad farewell sung by two sisters to their soldier sweethearts. The ladies' voices blended beautifully, with Mr Renwick's rich baritone adding depth to the gentle, lilting melody. Eloise concentrated on the accompaniment, trying to ignore Jack standing so close, his arm stretching past her as he turned the pages. She was calmed by the music, and by the singers' sweeping cadences rising and falling, imitating the gentle breeze of the Italian lyrics. She was almost disappointed when the last notes died away and the applause began. While everyone was praising the singers for their splendid performance, Eloise remained very still, enjoying the sinful sensation of Jack Clifton's presence beside her, his lean body so close she could feel his heat. Energy emanated from him, making her skin tingle with anticipation. She jumped when he reached out to pick up the book.

'Mr Mozart's opera is clearly a favourite,' he remarked, flicking through the pages. 'Let me find you something…here it is.' He replaced the open book on the piano and she looked at the aria he had chosen. '"*Donne mie, la fate a tanti e tanti*",' he read the title. 'Perhaps you would like me to translate if for you: "my dear ladies, you deceive so many men…"'

Abruptly Eloise stood up.

'I can translate it very well for myself,' she muttered, turning away from him.

She forced her lips into a smile as Margaret Cromer approached her.

'You play most beautifully, Cousin, but you have a delightful singing voice, too. Will you not let us hear it?'

'Thank you Meg, but I do not think—'

'Oh, my dear ma'am, do say you will sing for us,' declared Lady Parham, beaming at her. 'Mrs Cromer has been telling me that you were used to sing regularly for the guests at Allyngham.'

Eloise tried to decline, but other guests came up, adding their persuasion. Mrs Renwick took her hand and led her back towards the pianoforte.

'Come along, my dear, you have played so well for us it is your turn now to shine—Mrs Cromer will accompany you, will you not, Meg?'

'Of course, I should be delighted to play for Eloise—such a beautiful voice you have, Cousin! Now, what will you sing for us, my dear?'

Eloise hesitated, looking around at the happy, expectant faces. To decline would be impolite. She smiled.

'Something else from Mr Mozart, I think. *The Marriage of Figaro.*'

'We have it!' cried Mrs Renwick, pulling another book from the pile.

Eloise nodded and looked at her cousin.

'Can you play "*Porgi, amor*," Meg?'

'Oh heavens, my favourite aria!' declared Lady Parham. 'Do be quiet, everyone, and listen!'

An expectant silence settled over the room as Mrs Cromer played the short introduction. Eloise ran her tongue over her dry lips and composed herself. Many of the guests had pulled their chairs into a semi-circle to watch. Her eyes strayed around the room, noticing tiny details such as Sir Ronald leaning forwards, hands on his knees, Mr Graham sitting at the back of the group, picking his teeth, Mr and Mrs Renwick sitting shoulder to shoulder. And Jack Clifton, standing a little apart, his face in shadow. She must forget them all.

Eloise began to sing the Countess's heartbreaking aria about the pain of losing her husband's love. She had chosen to sing the English translation, but it was still beautiful and she closed her eyes, allowing herself to be swept away by the evocative words and music.

Jack stood in the shadows and listened, entranced. He was familiar with the opera but it had never before had such power to move him. Eloise sang the countess's role with dignity and restraint, her full, rich voice filling the long gallery. There was such longing in her voice, such sadness in her blue eyes that he could almost believe her sincere. Almost. As the last, lingering notes died away he found himself swallowing hard to clear some constriction in his throat. There was a moment's silence, then the room erupted into cheers and applause. Lady Allyngham was blushing, accepting their praise with modestly downcast eyes. Jack scowled as Sir Ronald stepped up to take her hand and kiss it. Damnation, the woman had bewitched them all!

There was a few moments' stir and confusion. Renwick's young nieces came up for their turn to perform and the mood lightened considerably as they sang a selection of folk songs. Jack watched Eloise move away from the crowd and he stepped quickly up to her.

'So you identify yourself with the wronged countess, my lady.' His tone was harder than he had intended. She cast one brief look up at him and he was taken aback to see her eyes glistening with tears.

She hurried past him without speaking and slipped out of the room while the company's attention was fixed upon the young performers. In two strides Jack was at the door and following her along the cold stone corridor.

'Lady Allyngham—Eloise!'

She stopped at his words but did not turn.

'Will you not leave me alone?' she muttered as he came up to her. She was hunting for her handkerchief. Jack handed her his own.

'I beg your pardon. I did not mean to upset you.'

'Did you not? I think you delight in upsetting me.'

He heard the bitter note in her voice. There was a sudden upsurge of sound as the door to the long gallery opened again. Eloise looked up, startled. Jack caught her arm and pulled her to one side, into an unlit corridor. There was a half-glazed door at the far end, through which pale moonlight gleamed and fell in silvery squares upon the tiled floor of the passage. They stood silently in the semi-darkness, listening to the soft sound of footsteps hurrying past. When the silence settled again Eloise realised that he was still holding her arm and tried to shake him off.

'Let me go. We have nothing to say to each other!'

'I think we do.' Instead of obeying her demands, Jack caught her other arm. Her struggles to free herself were half-hearted. 'Will you not hear me, madam? Please.'

She grew still suddenly, but did not raise her eyes. Jack breathed out in a long sigh and looked up at the blackness above him. 'I don't know why it is, but you bring out the worst in me.'

'I have done nothing to warrant your cruel jibes.'

'That is just it! To have spent the whole evening in your company and received not one warm look, one real smile. I confess I wanted to provoke you, to make you respond to me, even if it was with anger.'

'Then it is better that we should not meet—'

'No! At least, you must allow me to apologise—to say how sorry I am that Allyngham is dead. Your words when we last parted—that you wish I had perished on the battlefield instead of Tony—I had never before considered what you have lost, what you must have suffered. Watching you in there, hearing you sing, I realised how much you miss him.' Jack looked at the still figure before him. She was trying very hard not to cry, her bottom lip caught between her teeth to stop it trembling. He said gently, 'I do not pretend to understand your behaviour, madam, and if I have misjudged you, I pray you will forgive me.'

Even in the dim light he could make out the long lashes fanned out on her pale cheeks. Now those lashes fluttered and lifted slightly. Jack put two fingers under her chin and gently pushed her head up. He said softly, 'My lady, will you not cry friends with me?'

She met his eyes for a moment, her own so dark and liquid he thought he might drown in them.

'Not friends,' she said quietly. 'Too many harsh words have been exchanged for that. But it would be better for our hosts if we were not always arguing,'

He smiled, his spirits lifting a little.

'A truce, then. And if I can help you discover who is sending those letters—'

'No.' She was withdrawing from him again. 'I would not have you concern yourself with that.'

Jack was tempted to argue but he resisted: if she was not willing to confide in him then he would not force her. With time and patience he would win her round, he was sure of it. His instinct was to protect her. He wanted to carry her off, to shelter her from every ill wind. She was, after all, the widow of a valued comrade. With a little nod he stepped back.

'Very well. But if you need my assistance, you only have to ask.' He lifted his head, listening to the quiet strains of the pianoforte drifting from the long gallery. 'They are dancing again. Do you wish to return?' She gave a little shake of her head and his mouth twisted into a rueful smile. 'No, nor I.' Jack held out his arm to her. 'Perhaps a stroll through the gardens, until you are more composed? There is a full moon tonight.'

Eloise opened her mouth to refuse, but it was as if someone else was controlling her voice.

'Thank you, I would like that.'

Moments earlier she had been wishing Jack Clifton at Jericho, now she was taking his arm and accompanying him outside. The passage door opened on to a small cobbled yard at the far side of which a narrow gate in the low wall led the way into the rose garden. The bushes were overgrown with only a few late-summer blooms hanging on, but even so it looked beautiful in the moonlight. The only sound was the occasional cry of a fox from the park and the soft crunch of the gravel beneath their feet. Eloise felt her tension draining away. Despite their differences, Jack Clifton was the one man at Renwick Hall she was sure she could trust.

'You seem to know your way about the house very well, Major.'

'Renwick and I are old friends. I have stayed here many times before when I have been on leave.'

'I understand you have quit the army now. What will you do?'

'Yes, I have sold out. I have no family, My father died just a year ago, leaving me a pretty little property in Staffordshire, Henchard. It needs some work but it is a snug little house and the land could be very profitable, I think. Did I not tell you I shall become a gentleman farmer?'

She smiled at that.

'Yes, I remember, but somehow I cannot imagine it!'

'Oh? How do you see me?'

She thought for a moment.

'As an adventurer.'

It was Jack's turn to laugh. Eloise liked the sound, it was deep and rich and dangerously attractive. Just like the man.

'I have had enough of adventure. It is time I settled down.'

She nodded. He was a man of means, it would be very sensible to settle down, marry and have children. Her head jerked up. The thought of Jack taking a wife hit her with such force she felt as if someone had thrown a bucket of cold water over her.

He stopped.

'Is something wrong? Are you cold, do you want to go indoors?'

'N-no, a sudden chill, nothing more,' she said quickly. 'Do let us continue, the gardens have a different kind of beauty in the moonlight.'

'Very well, but I cannot have you catching cold.'

He shrugged himself out of his coat and placed it around her, his hands resting on her shoulders for a moment. The action was so personal, so intimate that Eloise was obliged to set her jaw hard to stifle a gasp. The air, so calm a moment ago, now seemed charged with expectation. She knew a brief disappointment when he stepped back and waited for her to stroll on. She stole a glance at him. An exquisitely tailored waistcoat hugged his body, accentuating the broad shoulders. She was dazzled by the whiteness of his billowing shirtsleeves and the tumbling folds of his neckcloth. She found her eyes wandering down the tapering form. The slim hips and flat abdomen drew her attention, as did the strongly muscled thighs outlined by the pantaloons. Swallowing, she dragged her gaze back to his face, but the sight of his clean, chiselled jaw and raven-black hair gave her no relief from the sudden fire that was engulfing her. She realised Jack was watching her, a faint, glinting smile in his eyes. Heavens, had she considered him an adventurer? He was far more dangerous than that! She looked away and began to walk again, this time at a much quicker pace.

'We should not linger, sir, or it is you who might catch a chill. I see a balustrade directly ahead of us. Is that the end of the garden?'

'Yes, it runs along a high ridge. There is a fine view of the park from that point.'

Eloise walked on. The scrunch of the gravel beneath her firm step was reassuringly crisp and business-like. The major had fallen in beside her, his long legs allowing him to take a much more leisurely stride.

'I understand Mortimer will be joining us tomorrow.' His voice was perfectly calm. 'Renwick tells me you particularly asked that he should be invited.'

'Yes.' Had she told him the real reason for coming here? She could not recall. 'I did not wish to find myself here without any good friends to keep me company. Of course, I did not know then that *you* would be here.'

Eloise winced: that was just such a flirtatious remark as he might expect from her. She glanced up. Jack's smile had disappeared, and he was looking directly ahead, his lips pressed firmly together. She sighed and huddled beneath his coat. She turned her head to rub her cheek against the lapel. The fine wool was soft on her skin and she breathed in the faint slightly spicy scent that she now associated with Jack Clifton.

The balustrade was soon reached and she gazed out in genuine admiration at the park stretching out before her, bathed in moonlight. They were standing on a ridge with the land falling away on all sides. The full moon sailing high above cast a silvery sheen over the landscape.

'It is beautiful,' she breathed.

'Yes. Renwick's grandfather planned it all and planted the trees.' He pointed. 'Down there to the south, just beyond the lake, is the deer park.'

Eloise looked around. 'And what is that building on the promontory over there?'

'That is the Temple of Diana. The family used to hold dinner parties there, but now I think it is employed mainly by the ladies of the house for their sketching. The path between the temple and the house is thickly wooded, but the views on the other three sides are magnificent. Would you like to walk there now?'

The temptation to accept was very great, to prolong this magical time together, but she knew she must not. She shook her head.

'Thank you, but no. I think it is time we returned to the house. They will be serving tea soon.'

She took one final look at the little Temple of Diana with its elegant cupola outlined against the night sky. The shallow steps and graceful columns looked most romantic, and the idea of being there in the moonlight with Jack sent a little shiver of excitement down her spine. All the more reason to return to the safety of the house, she thought, setting off back along the path. Without a word Jack fell into step beside her and they walked in silence back through the gardens. She laughed to herself: if she had been alone with any other man he would have taken the opportunity to make love to her, at least to flirt—here she was in the moonlight with the most attractive man she had ever known and he was behaving with perfect propriety.

And she hated it.

They slipped back into the house by the little glazed door and Eloise handed Jack his coat.

'You will need this before you rejoin the others, Major.'

She helped him into it, telling herself it was necessary for her hands to smooth the coat over his broad shoulders, to brush a speck of dust from one lapel, but it was such an intimate gesture that her mouth went dry and her fingers trembled. Jack caught her hand and carried to his lips. She was immobilised by the tenderness of the gesture. She looked up and did not move as he lowered his head towards her.

'We…should…not…' she breathed, still looking up at him.

'Why not?' he murmured. 'Moonlight is the time for stolen kisses.'

'You cannot steal what I give you freely.'

A fierce gleam lit his eyes: elation, triumph, she could not be sure. She dropped her own gaze, and gave a remorseful little sigh.

'I should not be here with you. It was very wrong of me to go outside—what must you think of me?'

He pushed up her chin and gently brushed her lips with his own.

'I think you an enigma, but I hope one day you will explain yourself.'

'If only that were possible.'

'It *is* possible. You have only to trust me.'

For the space of a heartbeat she was tempted.

'If it was just my secret—'

'Yes?'

She gave her head a little shake, put her hands against his chest to hold him off.

'Perhaps, one day, I might be able to tell you more, but not yet.'

'Then I shall not press you. When you are ready, you may come to me and tell me everything.'

Eloise bit her lip and blinked to drive back the tears. The more she knew of Jack Clifton, the more honourable she thought him. And the more impossible it was that he would ever understand. She said, with a masterly effort to keep her voice from shaking, 'Mrs Renwick will be preparing tea soon. We should go back now, I think.'

'As you wish, my lady.' Jack pulled her hand on to his sleeve and walked her through the dark corridor.

They reached the hall just as the butler appeared, carrying the tea tray.

'I have no doubt our absence will have been noted,' murmured Jack as they followed him into the long gallery.

'Then it will be best if we move apart, Major Clifton.' She pulled her arm from his sleeve, saying nervously, 'Pray do not speak to me again tonight, sir. I fear we may set tongues wagging.'

'Not for the first time, Lady Allyngham,' he said drily.

A little tut of exasperation escaped her. 'I had hoped to repair my reputation with this visit.'

'There is time yet. And Mortimer will be here tomorrow: you will have your guard dog to protect you.'

With a last, fleeting smile he walked away and she joined the crowd around her hostess. It was only when she was preparing for bed that she realised Jack's handkerchief was still in her pocket. She took it out and held it for a moment, pressed against her mouth. She should of course give it to Alice to have it laundered and returned to the Major. Instead she turned and tucked it quickly under her pillow.

Chapter Nine

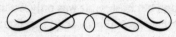

'So Mortimer is arrived. The Glorious Allyngham's lapdog.'

Jack heard Deforge's words as he walked into the library. Sir Ronald was standing by the window, gazing out at the post chaise and its four sweating horses that had just pulled up at the door of Renwick Hall.

'Ah, but has he lost his place as the lady's favourite?' Edward Graham threw down the newspaper he had been reading and grinned at Jack. 'Well, Clifton, you and the widow were missing for some considerable time last night: is she well and truly won?'

'Lady Allyngham required a little air. I accompanied her,' returned Jack evenly.

Sir Ronald shot a piercing look at him. 'So you obliged her with a stroll in the moonlight. Are you sure it was nothing more?'

Jack made an effort to keep his countenance impassive.

'Nothing.'

'Then you wasted your opportunity, Major.'

'I do not consider it so,' said Jack, shrugging. 'Forcing a woman is not *my* style, Deforge.'

Sir Ronald's heavy features darkened angrily.

'Are you saying it is mine?'

'I have heard so.' Jack's lip curled. 'I have heard that even your wife tried to run away from you.'

'Blast your eyes, Clifton, you will unsay that!'

'You will have to make me, Deforge.'

Jack met his look steadily, facing down the blustering challenge in the other man's eyes. At length Sir Ronald shrugged.

'Of course you would like to believe that, would you not, Major? It must be galling to know that pretty little Clara chose me over a penniless soldier. I can see how it would be some comfort to think she was unhappy, but she was not.' He stepped closer. 'I served her very well, Clifton, remember that when you are lying awake at night!'

Sir Ronald turned on his heel and walked away. He picked up the newspaper and carried it over to the far corner of the room. Mr Graham gave Jack a knowing look.

'Well,' he said, rising, 'I'm off to change for dinner. How about you, Clifton?'

The two men left the room together and as the door closed behind them Graham said softly, 'A word of warning, Major. Be wary of Deforge. He's a nasty piece of work.'

'I am aware,' muttered Jack grimly, 'but he won't call me out, no matter how hard I try.'

'Not his style,' Graham retorted. 'You are more likely to be found in a dark alley with a knife in your back.'

Jack gave an angry snort. 'I am surprised Renwick invited him.'

'No choice, old boy. It appears he's some sort of distant cousin to Mrs Renwick, and he almost invited himself. She of course is far too kind-hearted to turn anyone away, especially family—' He broke off as they reached the hall, where they found their host greeting Alex Mortimer, who was divesting himself of his greatcoat. 'Mortimer, how do you do! Good journey?'

Alex Mortimer looked up, a ready smile on his fair, handsome features.

'The last stage was tiresome. One of the wheelers was lame. Couldn't make any pace at all.'

'Well, you are in good time for dinner,' declared Mr Renwick. 'I'll have Grassington show you to your room—'

'No need,' cried Mr Graham, stepping forwards. 'He's in the room next to me, is he not? Clifton and I will take him up with us. Come along, Mortimer. Grassington can follow on with the bags!'

Linking arms with Jack and Alex, Edward Graham set off up the wide, shallow staircase, chatting merrily. Looking up, Jack realised that Mortimer was regarding him with a very thoughtful expression. No wonder, if Lady Allyngham had told him of their stormy meeting in London. Well, that was past now, and he hoped that after last night he and the lady could at least meet as friends. And once Eloise had explained matters to Mortimer, perhaps they could even work together to help the lady out of her predicament.

When the party gathered in the drawing room before dinner that evening, Eloise greeted Alex with unaffected pleasure, and she was happy to find that most of the party shared her delight. To have another handsome and eligible bachelor staying at Renwick Hall could not be considered anything other than an advantage, and she was amused to watch Mrs Briggate taking every opportunity to bring her daughters to his attention.

Seeing Lady Allyngham was alone, Jack crossed the room to join her. At first she did not notice him, for her eyes were on Alex Mortimer, who was standing on the far side of the room, surrounded by ladies.

'Mortimer is very patient,' he murmured. 'I was not half so polite when the Briggate woman forced her chits under my nose. He will find himself leg-shackled if he doesn't take care.'

She smiled.

'Not he! Alex is too good-natured to snub anyone, but he will not allow the situation to get out of hand. Nor will he let either of those silly girls lose their hearts to him. He is far too kind for that.'

'Perhaps his interests lie in another direction.'

She looked up at him, a startled look in her eyes.

'I—I don't understand you, Major.'

He gave her a rueful smile.

'I thought his heart lay at your feet.'

'Oh.' The colour rushed back into her cheeks. 'Oh, well, yes, I suppose that is true.'

He leaned a little closer.

'Perhaps, when you talk to him, you will tell him that I am no longer your enemy. He has behaved like a dog with his hackles up ever since he arrived here. You may also tell him, if you please, that I am no rival. He has nothing to fear from me.'

He turned on his heel and walked away. Eloise stared after him, but she had no time to consider his words, for no sooner had he moved off than Sir Ronald Deforge was at her side and she forced herself to listen to his pleasantries and respond with a smile. There was no opportunity to speak to Alex until they were going into dinner, when he offered her his arm as they processed from the drawing room across the hall and into the dining room.

'Well, my dear, you have all the men enchanted, as usual. And judging by the number of times I heard you laugh I suppose you must be enjoying yourself.'

'You are mistaken!' Eloise glanced around to make sure no one was close enough to overhear them. 'Until I know who has been writing those dreadful letters to me I cannot relax for a moment. Oh, Alex, it is so unsettling! With the exception of yourself and Mr Renwick, not one of the gentlemen can come near me without I have to suppress a shudder.'

'Not even Major Clifton? I thought we had agreed he was above suspicion.'

Eloise spread her hands.

'He is, but that does not mean I can bear to have him by me.' She was not going to admit to Alex that the shaking she experienced when Jack Clifton was near was for a very different reason. 'However, we are not enemies any more.'

'You are not?'

'No. We—um—we understand each other now.'

'Is that since he took you into the garden last night?' He grinned at her horrified look. 'Graham took great delight in telling me that Clifton had cut me out.'

They were entering the dining room and Eloise was obliged to swallow the infelicitous remark that rose to her lips.

'It was no such thing,' she hissed. 'We merely…talked, and he apologised for misjudging me.' After a brief pause she added, 'He said to tell you that he is not our enemy. And that he is not your rival.'

Alex handed her to her seat, saying, 'Generous of him to tell me he has no interest in you.'

'Yes,' she said bleakly. 'Isn't it?'

* * *

The following morning Mr Renwick took the gentlemen off shooting and the ladies were left to amuse themselves. The more energetic of the ladies, including Eloise, joined their hostess for a tour of the grounds, ending with refreshments served at the Temple of Diana. As they approached the pavilion, Eloise could see that it was a perfect cube with shallow steps on four sides leading to columned porticos. It was a bright, sunny day and Mrs Renwick had ordered the wide doors of the pavilion to be opened and the chairs moved out under the porticos so that the ladies could all sit and enjoy the magnificent views. The occasional gunshot could be heard, carried on the light breeze. Miss Briggate and her sister whiled away the time by staring at the woods on the far horizon, trying to spot the gentlemen. Eloise took a chair beside her cousin and they sat in companionable silence, gazing out across the park. The autumn colours were beginning to show themselves and Eloise could not help comparing the cheerful riot of green, red and gold with the silver-blue landscape she had seen the previous night.

'Such a sad sigh, Cousin,' remarked Mrs Cromer. 'I hope you are not unhappy?'

Eloise started.

'Did I sigh? Oh dear, I was not aware of it. I beg your pardon. How could one be unhappy in this beautiful place?'

'I could not, certainly, and when you were younger I remember how much you enjoyed being in the country,' returned Meg, smiling. 'But I have not seen you for a long time, Cousin, you may have changed. We have seen little of each other since you and Tony were married. Understandable, of course.'

'No, it was very remiss of me,' declared Eloise. 'I should have made more effort to invite you to stay—'

Meg threw up her hands and laughed at that.

'No, no, you young people were far too busy with your own concerns. Besides, I had my girls to look after, and they were a handful, always wanting to be gadding about the town.' She threw a smiling glance at Eloise. 'That is why I thought you might be missing the delights of London.'

Eloise quickly disclaimed, 'Not at all, Meg, why should you think that of me?'

'Gossip travels, my dear.'

'Ah.' Eloise turned in her chair to regard her cousin. 'Gossip about me, I suppose. I know some people think I am behaving disgracefully.'

Meg leaned across and took her hand. 'Cousin, it is only natural that you should want to enjoy yourself, after a year in mourning, but perhaps you have let your high spirits run away with you. And it is not only your behaviour in town: I am well aware that you and Major Clifton were missing for more than an hour last night. A reputation is far more easily lost than won, you know.'

Eloise bowed her head.

'I know it. Did—did anyone else notice?'

'I am sure they did! Mrs Renwick made some passing comment, but only to the effect that she was glad to see the major taking an interest in women again.'

'Oh.' Eloise began to rearrange her skirts, saying casually, 'Our hostess knows the major well?'

'Her husband does, certainly,' replied Meg, turning her face up to the sun. 'I understand Major Clifton suffered some disappointment in his youth. He was in love with a maid but she married someone else. Seems she was such a paragon that he has not looked at a woman since—not at women of his own class, that is,' she amended with a knowing smile. 'I have heard that he has had any number of mistresses.'

Eloise stared across the park in silence as she digested this. She could well imagine the upright, incorruptible Major Clifton falling in love with a model of propriety. In comparison, her own reputation would seem bad indeed, but he was clearly attracted to her. Perhaps he saw her only as mistress material. Suddenly the day did not seem quite so bright.

'I think perhaps I have been a little careless,' she said quietly. 'Some may even call me fast—but I intend to change that.' She paused. Everything depended upon her recovery of the journal, but she could not tell Meg that. She told herself fiercely that she would not countenance failure. She said decisively, 'When I leave here I have to return to London for a few weeks, to wind up my affairs before going back to Allyngham for the winter. Once in Norfolk the management of the estate will take up most of my time, but I wanted to ask if you would come back to town with me.'

'To lend you countenance?' asked Meg, giving her a quizzical look.

'Yes, if you like,' said Eloise, smiling. 'To make me respectable!'

'Oh, my dear, you know I would love to come with you, but my daughter is lying in next month and I must go to Shropshire to be with her. I am so sorry. But next Season, if you go to town, it would be my pleasure to come and live with you.'

'Yes, of course, Meg. Thank you.'

'And until then I am sure we can find some other respectable lady to keep you company in town—'

'No, no, I would not wish to take on a stranger for a mere few weeks.' Eloise shook her head. 'And once I retire to Allyngham, there is so much to do that I shall not have time to be lonely.' She smiled reassuringly at her cousin. 'I am sure I can manage to keep out of trouble for a few more weeks!'

'Then let us start with this evening,' retorted Meg, a twinkle in her sharp eyes. 'There must be no moonlight walks tonight, no matter how handsome the gentleman!'

No one could have been more decorous than Lady Allyngham at dinner that evening. She was gracious and charming, but she could not be persuaded to leave her hostess's side until the card tables were set up and even then she would only play a friendly game of whist. Jack observed it all. He made no move to approach her, and watched with a detached amusement as the other single gentlemen tried unsuccessfully to draw her away from the group. Mortimer, he noticed, was unconcerned, and he guessed that whatever game the widow was playing, her guard dog knew of it. He was even more convinced when Mortimer agreed to join him for a game of billiards.

'You would not rather play at cards with us, Mortimer?' cried Edward Graham, looking up.

Alex grinned and shook his head.

'If Sir Ronald has only half his usual luck I would be handing over my shirt to him. I shall enjoy a quiet game of billiards with Clifton instead.'

'On leave from your sentry duty?' Jack murmured as the two men made their way to the billiard room.

Alex did not pretend to misunderstand him.

'My lady has turned over a new leaf,' he replied evenly, selecting a cue from the rack. 'She wants her cousin to live with her, to protect her reputation.'

'That sounds very much like shutting the stable door after the horse has bolted.' Mortimer said nothing, but Jack observed the heavy frown that flitted across his face. He said, 'Have I offended you?'

Alex shrugged.

'Not at all. Shall we play?'

'I would rather you told me about Lady Allyngham.'

'What is there to tell?' Alex responded lightly. 'She is a beautiful woman.'

'And you have known her a long time?'

'Almost all my life. We grew up together, as neighbours. She is a very loyal friend.'

'Then perhaps you know what it is that she is hiding from me.'

Alex did not reply until he had made his first shot.

'All women have their secrets, Major Clifton.' His derisory grin flickered. 'As a man of the world you must know that. Now…' he nodded towards the billiard table '…I have made my play; it is time to see what you can do!'

By the time they returned to the drawing room the card tables were packed away and the party was gathered about the crackling fire, drinking tea. There was a burst of laughter as they entered: Mr Renwick was entertaining his guests with stories of his childhood at Renwick Hall.

'Always falling into some fix or another,' he chuckled, shaking his head. 'The woods were our favourite playground. The poor gamekeeper came pretty close to peppering us with shot on more than one occasion.'

'Ah, but boys will be boys,' murmured Mr Briggate, steepling his fingers.

'And not only boys,' put in Mrs Cromer with a laughing glance at Eloise, sitting beside her on the sofa. 'My cousin here was for ever in trouble with Lord and Lady Allyngham.'

'Meg, please, you will put me to blush!' Eloise protested laughingly.

'No, please, do go on, Mrs Cromer,' Sir Ronald begged. 'We can never hear enough of Lady Allyngham.'

'She and my cousin grew up together,' explained Meg.

'Anthony treated her more like a boy than a girl, and as often as not when I came to call they would be out together clambering over the rocks or climbing trees,' She nodded towards Alex. 'And that young man was usually with them. Three scamps they were, but inseparable, until the boys went off to school and Eloise was sent to Bath, where she learned to be a lady.'

'Ah, so your youthful companions were lost to you after that,' remarked the eldest Miss Briggate, sighing.

'Not at all,' replied Eloise, smiling. 'We were together in the holidays and once my schooling was over I returned to Allyngham and saw them often and often.'

'And you were all as wild as ever,' laughed Meg. 'The number of times I called and found that Eloise was in disgrace and had been confined to her room! My poor Aunt Allyngham was in despair, wondering how to deal with such a hoyden!'

'I think I must defend my lady,' put in Alex, smiling. 'She was loyal to a fault and often took the blame for our pranks.' He walked across and stood behind the sofa. 'Of the three of us, Lady Allyngham was the sensible one. She spent most of her time rescuing Tony and me from our more outlandish scrapes.'

There was general laughter, Mrs Renwick began to refill the teacups and Jack wondered if anyone else had noticed Alex's hand rest briefly on Eloise's white shoulder. His eyes made a quick sweep of the room. Most of the guests were chattering but Sir Ronald was silent, staring intently at Eloise, his fingers tapping on the arm of his chair and a sly smile on his face. Jack frowned. He misliked that smile. The man was dangerous, and if Lady Allyngham had somehow offended him, perhaps rejected his advances…

He broke off from his reflections as Miss Briggate brought

him a dish of tea, but even as he joined in the general conversation he made a mental note to keep an eye on Deforge.

It was gone midnight when the party broke up and Eloise accompanied her cousin up the stairs to the main guestrooms. She was very sleepy and was tempted to remark that remaining virtuous all day was extremely tiring, but she did not think Meg would appreciate the joke. They parted on the landing and Eloise retired to the cosy silence of her bedchamber. Several candles were burning and the draught as she shut her door set the shadows dancing on the painted panels of the room. There was no sign of her maid, and she tugged on the embroidered bell-pull, impatient now to get out of her gown. Something on the bed caught her eye, a small, pale square on the near-black of the covers. A letter.

A sudden chill swept through her bones. Her fingers were not quite steady as she picked up the paper and unfolded it. The heavy black writing danced before her eyes and she turned the paper towards the light, blinking until her vision cleared.

'I beg yer pardon, my lady, I wasn't expectin' you quite so soon.'

Eloise pressed the paper to her chest as Alice bounced into the room. She must think, and quickly.

'Alice, I need you to run an errand for me.'

'At this time o' night, m'lady?'

'Yes, I am afraid so.' She turned and tried to give her maid a confident smile. 'I need you to carry a message to Mr Mortimer for me.'

Alice's eyes grew round.

'Mr—but 'e's in the east wing, with all the gentlemen!'

'I know, Alice, and I am sorry to ask it of you but it is very important, and I cannot trust anyone else.' She added coaxingly, 'You have known me since we were little girls together at Allyngham: you know I would not ask if it was not very important.'

She could see the maid mentally girding her loins as she digested this.

'Very well, Miss Elle.' Alice drew herself up, looking very resolute. 'What is it you want me to do?'

Eloise stood by the little gate into the rose garden, clutching her cloak around her. She prayed that Alice had carried her message faithfully. A sudden movement to her left made her jump: someone was approaching. She relaxed a little as she recognised Alex's familiar form.

'Now, Elle, what is all this?' he whispered.

'He has written.' She held up the note. 'It is too dark for you to read it, but he wants me to meet him, tonight, at the Temple of Diana.'

'Does he, by thunder! Then I'll go back and fetch my pistol—'

She gripped his arm.

'No, no violence! But I want you to come with me, Alex, and hide in the woods. The letter says I am to come alone but I do not think I am brave enough to do that.'

'Of course I will come with you, I would not let you go unattended to meet the villain.'

'Good. We will set off now, if you please. I expect him to be watching out for me, so we must go separately. You must take the path through the woods, I will follow the lower track beside the lake.'

'It could be dangerous.' Alex caught her arm. 'You do not have to do this, Elle.'

'I do,' she replied softly. 'You know that until we destroy the journal we cannot be safe.'

'There is a way out of this that does not involve paying the blackguard!'

'Go abroad, you mean? The Allyngham name would still be tarnished, and I will not do that to Tony's memory.' She squeezed his arm. 'Wait for me in the woods, but be ready to come if I call.'

They hurried through the rose garden and Alex set off up the hill. Eloise watched him disappear into the trees and felt a slight moment of panic. Giving herself a mental shake, she pulled her cloak more tightly about her and set off along the lakeside path. Black clouds were scudding across the sky, occasionally blocking out the moon and making it difficult to see the ground in front of her. The sudden cry of a fox made her jump and at one point an owl flew silently overhead like a sinister dark angel. Eloise walked on, keeping her eyes fixed on the solid shape of the temple in the distance. A slight breeze blew across the lake, rippling its calm surface. The trees sighed and a tingle ran the length of her spine: unseen eyes were watching her, she knew it. She left the lakeside and made her way up the slope towards the temple. The steps and the portico gleamed white in the moonlight, but deep shadows filled the interior. Taking a deep breath, she climbed the steps and entered.

The square temple had a glazed door and large windows on each of the four sides, casting a silver-grey light into the centre. Eloise was immediately aware of a figure standing in one of the shadowed corners. His face was a ghostly pale disc against the blackness around him.

'I have come,' she said, steeling herself to keep still. 'What is it you want of me?'

'Well, that depends.' The grating whisper jarred on her stretched nerves. 'How badly do you want the return of that book?'

She shrugged. 'It is worth something to me, I admit, but not much. There are no names in it, after all.'

He laughed softly.

'Oh, come now, Lady Allyngham. A full year's reminiscences: dates, places. It would not take a vast intelligence to work out the identities of those mentioned. I have not yet decided if I should publish it in book form—look how popular Caro Lamb's *Glenarvon* has become in just a few months!—or perhaps I should release it to the newspapers, little by little…'

'How much do you want?' she interrupted him sharply.

'Everything.'

'Now you are ridiculous!'

'Am I? To prevent your ruin, and that of your friends?'

Anger surged through her.

'Step out of the shadows,' she challenged him. 'I am tired of talking to nothing. I want to see the villain who dares to threaten me!'

Again that soft laugh.

'Villain, madam? I am your most ardent admirer.'

He stepped forwards and as the cloak of darkness fell away she recognised Sir Ronald Deforge. Eloise knew a momentary insane desire to laugh. The fear, shock and horror she should have felt was outweighed by relief. Relief that it was not Jack Clifton. Despite everything she had been afraid her judgement had let her down where Major Clifton was concerned. She stared haughtily at Sir Ronald as he stood before her, one white hand resting negligently on his silver-topped cane. With his tight-waisted frockcoat and tasselled Hessians he looked as if he had just strolled in from Bond Street.

'An admirer who would stoop to threats,' she said, her lip curling. 'Tell me, how did you obtain the diary?'

'A stroke of great good fortune, nothing more. Some time

ago I was travelling back to town on the Great North Road and when we stopped to change horses a ragged wretch approached me. He wanted the fare to London and offered to sell me the journal.'

'So you bought it.'

'Of course not. I do not deal with thieves. He had no idea what it contained, I doubt if he could read well enough to know its true value. No, I had him flogged, and told him I would return the book to its rightful owner.' He grinned. 'Of course, I did not then know what a pleasant task that would be.' He moved closer. 'I admit when I first read that journal I thought only to sell it. After all, I guessed it must be worth something to protect the revered Allyngham name. But then you came to town and I was captivated. The more I see you, the more you inflame me.'

She suppressed a shudder and stepped away from him.

'And you disgust me.'

'Now that is a pity, my lady, because there is only one way I will give up the journal to you.' He waited until she had turned again to face him. 'You must marry me.'

Eloise laughed at that.

'The full moon has affected your wits, Sir Ronald! I would never do that.'

'Oh, I think you will, madam, when you consider the consequences of *not* becoming my wife. I can tell by your look that you are not convinced. Perhaps you think to wrest the book from me. You will not succeed. It is with my lawyer in London, in a sealed box. He has instructions to make its contents public if anything should happen to me. Anything at all,' he added softly, 'so you should pray no ill befalls me!' He moved towards her. It took all Eloise's will-power not to back away. He reached out to touch her face. 'Do not look so shocked, my dear, you might even enjoy being my wife.'

She brushed his hand aside.

'It astonishes me that you should wish to marry someone you do not know.'

He bared his teeth in a leering smile that made her feel physically sick.

'Oh, I know you, Lady Allyngham. I have seen you in the salons and ballrooms, throwing out lures to every man in the room. And remember I have read that journal. You are a woman of experience, not averse to the more…unusual demands of the male.' His hand shot out and grabbed her wrist as she began to back away.

With a cry she tried to pull free. A shadow fell upon them and she heard Alex's curt voice from the open doorway.

'Let her go, Deforge!'

Sir Ronald's brows rose.

'So you did not come alone as I instructed.'

'Did you think I would be that foolish?' she retorted, struggling against his grasp.

'I thought you had more concern for your friends.'

Even as Sir Ronald was speaking Alex launched himself forwards. Deforge released Eloise and leapt back, putting his hand to the top of his cane and unsheathing a lethal-looking blade.

'Alex, be careful, he has a sword-stick!'

Her warning came too late. Deforge lunged and the blade pierced Alex's shoulder. He staggered back. Eloise tried to grab Deforge's arm but he shook her off so violently that she fell to the floor. In horror she watched him advance upon Alex, who retreated to the door. Moonlight glinted on the sword as Deforge slashed Alex across the thigh and following up with a kick that sent him tumbling down the steps and on to the grass.

Eloise was still struggling to rise when another shadowy

figure flew past the window. She saw Sir Ronald turn but before he could defend himself his head was snapped back by a swift, hard punch to the jaw and he crashed to the ground.

'Attacking an unarmed man is not worthy of you, Deforge.'

Jack Clifton bent to pick up the sword-stick. For a moment a look of pure hatred transformed Sir Ronald's face.

'What are you doing here?'

'Taking a stroll in the moonlight. It appears to be a very popular pastime.' Jack stepped into the little room and held out his hand to Eloise. She allowed him to help her up, aware of the tension within him. Despite his casual words he was taught as a bowstring, alert and ready for action.

'So she has caught you in her web, too, Clifton.' Sir Ronald was climbing to his feet, one hand feeling his jaw.

'We will leave the lady out of this, if you please.'

Sir Ronald laughed.

'Your concern for the lady's reputation is touching, Major, but misplaced, believe me.'

With a growl of anger Jack stepped towards him, fists raised. Eloise gripped his arm.

'No, Major, please!

'She is right to stop you, Clifton. If you lay another finger on me I shall cause a scandal that will destroy what remains of Lady Allyngham's reputation, and that of her...friends.' He straightened his coat and made a play of smoothing out the creases of his sleeve. 'I am going back to bed. I leave you to explain it how you will, Major Clifton. You may try what you can to keep the lady's name out of this. Oh—my cane, if you please?'

Jack picked up the discarded cane and sheathed the wicked blade.

'Here.' He tossed it to Sir Ronald. 'You had best keep out of my way, Deforge. I would like nothing better than an excuse to kill you.'

Sir Ronald bared his teeth.

'Oh, I am well aware of that, Major. I rely upon Lady Allyngham to dissuade you from doing anything foolish.' He turned to Eloise. 'Consider my offer, madam. It is all that stands between you and disaster.' Then, with an airy salute of his cane, he walked down the steps and strolled away, walking past Alex's body without even a glance.

Chapter Ten

As if released from a spell, Eloise ran down the steps and fell to her knees beside Alex.

'He breathes,' she muttered thankfully.

Jack gently turned him on to his back and Eloise bit back a cry. One leg of his buff-coloured pantaloons was black and wet with blood and another dark stain was spreading over the left shoulder of his coat

'The first thing we must do is to stop the bleeding from his thigh,' said Jack, pulling off his neckcloth and wrapping it tightly around the wound. Alex groaned.

'Keep still,' muttered Eloise, her fingers scrabbling at his throat. 'I am going to use your cravat to staunch the blood from your shoulder wound.'

'Damned villain. If only you had let me bring a pistol—'

Eloise choked back a sob.

'I know, Alex, I am very sorry. It is all my fault—'

'Recriminations can come later,' Jack interrupted her. 'We must get you back to the house, Mortimer. If I help you to stand, do you think you can walk?'

Alex closed his eyes, his brow contracting.

'I do not know...'

'Well, we must try. I do not want to send to the house for assistance. The less people who know of this escapade the better.'

'I can help,' said Eloise. She blushed, knowing that Jack's eyes were upon her and added fiercely, 'I *can*. I carried you over the heath, and Alex is much slighter.'

'I am also conscious,' muttered Alex as Jack helped him to his feet. 'If you let me put my weight on you, Clifton, I think we can manage.'

With Alex's arm about his shoulders, Jack set off for the house, half-carrying, half-dragging the wounded man. Eloise walked along beside them, keeping the pad firmly pressed over the injured shoulder. It was clumsy and uncomfortable and her heart went out to Alex as he gritted his teeth to prevent himself crying out in pain.

'Hold on, my dear Alex,' she muttered, her voice breaking, 'hold on and we will soon have you safe.'

Jack heard the affection in her voice and blotted out any angry thoughts as he struggled back towards the house with his burden. He must think of Mortimer as a wounded colleague, not a rival, but it was hard to ignore the lady's concern as she kept pace with them, her whole attention locked upon Mortimer. Jack had left the house by a side door and he was relieved to find that it was still unlocked. By this time Alex had lost consciousness and it took Jack and Eloise's combined efforts to carry him up the stairs to his room.

When they struggled into the bedchamber Mortimer's valet fell back, a look of profound shock upon his face. Eloise gave him no time to ask questions.

'Your master has been wounded, Farrell. Pray run downstairs and fetch hot water and bandages while we get him into bed. Immediately, if you please.'

The valet dashed away. Jack carried Mortimer to the bed and laid him upon the patterned bedcover.

'You command and Farrell obeys.'

She did not look at him, but threw aside her cloak and made her way around the room, lighting every candle.

'Alex and I have been acquainted since childhood. Farrell knows I am a friend.'

But how good a friend?

Jack dared not ask the question, afraid he might not like the answer. He stripped off his coat and turned his attention back to the unconscious man lying on the bed. Eloise came up to stand beside him, her hands clasped as if in prayer.

'Can you bind him up?'

'You need not look so anxious, madam. I dealt with much worse than this in the army. These are two clean cuts: there is no reason that they should not heal perfectly well. Help me get him out of his clothes.'

Sensing her hesitation, he glanced down at her, his brows raised. She swallowed and nodded.

'Of course.'

Silently they set to work. Eloise was already unbuttoning the coat and waistcoat so Jack pulled off Alex's boots and began to unfasten his pantaloons. By the time Farrell returned with a jug of hot water and an armful of clean linen, the bed had been stripped back to its bottom sheet and Mortimer was lying naked in the centre.

Farrell took one horrified look at the bloodied body of his master and turned an anguished glance towards Eloise.

'Madam, you should not—'

'Enough, Farrell!' she interrupted him swiftly and bent a frowning look upon the valet. 'We can involve no one else in this,' she said crisply. 'Major, what do you want me to do next?'

'Keep the pad pressed to that hole in his shoulder,' he told her. 'I'll deal with the cut on his leg first.'

He was pleased at the way she responded. No tears or vapours and with her hands shaking only a little she folded a pad of clean pad and held it against the wound. 'Very good,' he murmured, giving her the glimmer of a smile. 'We'll make a soldier of you yet, madam.'

They worked quietly together, Farrell tearing the linen into bandages while Jack cleaned and bound up the cut on Alex's thigh.

'Should we not call a doctor?' suggested Farrell. 'Perhaps we should bleed him.'

'After all the blood he has already lost?' Jack shook his head. 'No. The slash on his thigh looks bad but it is not that deep. I am hopeful that with rest the leg will be as good as new, except for a scar.'

'And the shoulder?' asked Eloise. 'It is not bleeding so very much now.'

She was still pressing one white hand to the wound; the other was tenderly brushing Alex's fair hair from his brow. A memory slammed into Jack. He recalled how she had brushed his hair from his eyes when they had been alone together in the shepherd's hut. Just before he had overpowered her, grabbing those slim white wrists and turning her until she was trapped beneath him. How those blue eyes had glared up at him, her breast heaving with indignation, her soft mouth so close to his, just asking to be kissed. His body stirred at the very thought of it. He dragged his eyes and his mind away from her and back to Alex Mortimer.

'He may find it painful to use his arm for a few days, but that should soon pass.'

Some of the anxiety left her face.

'Perhaps a little laudanum would help,' she suggested.

'Yes, if there is some in the house. He will be in pain when he wakes up.'

She nodded.

'The housekeeper will have some. Farrell must fetch it. Of the three of us, it will cause less comment if he is seen abroad at this time of night.'

'I'll go at once, my lady.'

'But you will tell no one that Lady Allyngham is here,' ordered Jack. 'You had best tell the housekeeper that Mr Mortimer was attacked in the woods. By poachers.'

The valet slipped out of the room and a silence descended. Jack tied the final knot around Alex's thigh.

She said quietly, 'Thank you, Major Clifton.'

'For what?'

'For coming to our aid. For being here.'

Jack nodded. He poured water on to a fresh cloth and began to wipe the blood from Alex's shoulder.

'I assume it is Deforge who is threatening you?'

'Yes. He sent me a note to meet him tonight. Alex came with me, for protection.' She looked up. 'But what were you doing there?'

'I followed Deforge.' He observed her look of surprise and shrugged. 'I have my own reasons for hating the man. And I saw the way he looked at you tonight. I thought he might be dangerous, so I had my man watch him. When he told me Sir Ronald had slipped out of the house I went after him. I saw you go into the temple and guessed he had sent for you, but it was not until I realised Mortimer was hiding in the woods that I was sure. What did he want this time?'

She hesitated, as if debating with herself how much to tell him.

'More money. Alex was angry and thought he could stop him.' She gave a little sob. 'It almost cost him his life. If you had not been there…'

'I should have run Deforge through with his own sword-stick!' muttered Jack savagely.

'Then all would have been lost. He—he says he has left the journal with his lawyer, with instructions to publish if anything happens to him.'

'Very clever.' Jack gave a little huff of frustration. 'And you plan to settle with him?'

'The alternative is to have the Allyngham name disgraced. Our private affairs would be discussed in every coffee house, reported in the newspapers for everyone to read, even lampooned like the Prince Regent! No, I will not risk that.'

'So you will allow a man like Deforge to impose upon you.'

'While he has the journal, yes. I see from your frown that you do not approve, Major.'

'No. It galls me to see you under any obligation to that man.'

She took the bloodstained cloth from his hand and handed him a clean one.

'You said you hate Sir Ronald. Will you tell me why?'

Jack's jaw set hard: she dared to ask, yet she refused to tell him her own secrets! He said lightly, 'Would you have me bare my soul to you, lady?'

His barb went wide. She merely met his mocking glance with a gentle smile.

'They say confession is good for the soul, Major. I feel there is some great bitterness in you when you think of Deforge, as if he has done you a great wrong. It cannot be good for you to keep such a thing to yourself.'

Jack did not reply immediately. At last he shrugged.

'Perhaps you are right,' he said at last. 'I will share it, since Deforge is our common enemy.' He placed a clean wad of cloth against the wound in Alex's shoulder and concentrated on strapping it into place with the bandages. 'It goes back a long time—five years or more—and concerns Lady Deforge.'

'His wife? She died three years ago, did she not?'

'Deforge killed her.'

Eloise gasped.

'Do you have evidence for that?'

'I do not, but knowing the man, and the lady, I believe it to be true. Oh, I know he was not at Redlands at the time of her death, but if he did not actually commit the deed I believe he drove her to it. Clara and I were childhood friends—more than friends, I thought. I believed she loved me as I loved her. True, she was a little wilful, but who could wonder at it if her parents spoiled her, for she was such a beautiful, delightful girl. Her father was against our marrying. I thought at the time it was because we were so young. She was her father's only child and I was a lowly captain, but later...' He paused, conscious that in his anger he was pulling the binding far too tight about Alex's shoulder.

Eloise reached across him and gently took the bandage from his hand.

'Here, let me.'

He watched her for a moment, part of his mind noting how deftly she readjusted the dressing. He walked to the fireplace and stared down at the hearth.

'Five years ago Clara's father died and I came home thinking that there would be no impediment now to our marriage, but when I arrived in London I found she was already betrothed. To Sir Ronald Deforge.' The story had been locked inside him for years, but now he had started he knew he must finish it. He said, 'I think, I believe, that when I first joined the army she intended to wait for me. We had agreed that there was no possibility of our marriage until I had achieved some promotion and could afford to keep a wife. She was far too good, too innocent to deliberately mislead me. When her father died she became the target of any number of men looking for a wife, and I suppose I was just too far away.' He shrugged. 'By the time I returned to London Clara had been swept off her feet by Sir Ronald. He was a wealthy, fashionable man of the town; by comparison I must have seemed a very callow youth of four-and-twenty, and how could I compete with a baronetcy? When I met her in London she seemed very happy with her choice.' His face darkened. 'I knew nothing of Deforge, save that he was a gambler, and that is a common enough trait. So I wished her well and went back to the Peninsula, where I tried to forget her.' He exhaled slowly. 'Wine, women and war—I survived them all. I fared better than my poor Clara. Two years later she was dead, drowned in the lake at Redlands, her family home. There was talk that she was not happy, that Deforge had married her only for her fortune. I do not know, but I can well believe it. After that one meeting in London I never heard from her again.'

'It is common knowledge that Sir Ronald's wife died soon after giving birth to a stillborn son,' said Eloise slowly. 'If the poor woman was unhappy, that would be cause enough, I think.'

'Of course, but I cannot believe he ever really cared for her. What I do know is that when Deforge married Clara he had already run through his own fortune and within two years most of Clara's money was gone. Since her death he has been selling off his properties and is almost at a stand. I have no doubt he is now looking for another rich wife.'

Eloise thought of her meetings with Sir Ronald Deforge and a cold chill ran through her. He was a cruel man: he would certainly publish the journal if she refused to marry him, but if she gave herself into his power, what then? Would he make her life so miserable that she would be willing to end it? She looked down at her shaking hands.

'Perhaps you could finish binding up Alex's shoulder,' she said, moving aside.

Jack returned to the bedside and she watched his strong, capable fingers take up the bandage. She screwed up her courage. It would be better to tell Jack Clifton the whole truth, to let him deal with Deforge. Even as she searched for the words to begin, the valet returned and the opportunity was lost.

Jack tied the final knot in the bandage around Alex's shoulder and straightened, easing his tense shoulders. 'There,' he said. 'I have finished.'

He wiped his hands on a cloth and dropped it on to the pile of bloodied rags on the floor.

'You may leave him to me now, Major.' Farrell tenderly pulled the covers over his master. 'I will clear up here and watch him until morning. I was obliged to explain to the housekeeper why I needed to disturb her, so I did as you suggested and told her my master had been attacked by poachers. I took the liberty of saying that it was you who found Mr Mortimer in the gardens and brought him upstairs, Major. No one need know of Lady Allyngham's part in any of this.'

'Thank you, Farrell.' Jack looked at Eloise, who was hovering beside the bed.

'I think it is time you returned to your own room, madam. Come, I will escort you.'

She hesitated, smoothing the sheet and straightening the covers until Farrell said quietly, 'You should leave now, my lady. Our situation will be much worse if you are discovered here.'

'Yes, yes, of course.'

With a final look at Alex she turned and accompanied Jack out of the room. The lamps burning in the corridors made it unnecessary to carry a bedroom candle but their low light threw black, wavering shadows against the walls. He sensed rather than saw her step falter and put his hand under her arm.

'No need to be afraid, ma'am, you are safe enough here.'

'I am not afraid. It is just—after all the excitement, I feel a little…'

She collapsed against him. Jack caught her up as she fainted. For a moment he stopped, staring down at the lifeless figure in his arms. Her head was thrown back, the dark lashes fanned out across her pale cheeks, the fine line of her jaw accentuated by the flickering light. What the devil was he to do now? They were in the part of the house known as the bachelor wing. The main reception rooms lay between here and the other guest rooms. To carry her all the way to her bedchamber would be to court disaster, for there were at least two flights of uncarpeted stairs to negotiate as well as a number of long passages. It would only take one light sleeper to open a door and look out…

With sudden decision he turned and carried her to his own bedchamber at the end of the corridor. It was similar to Mortimer's room, a square, panelled chamber with a fireplace in one wall, a window in another and a large canopied bed taking up most of the floor. He laid Eloise gently on the covers and turned to throw a couple of logs on the smouldering fire. He lit a candle from the glowing embers and placed it beside the bed.

She was lying as he had left her, pale and still against the dark coverlet, her hair in wild disorder and gleaming in the soft light. She was still wearing the blue gown she had put on for dinner but the embroidered skirts were in disarray and displaying her shapely legs in their fine silk stockings. As he reached out to straighten the skirts he noted that her shoes were stained and wet. His mouth twisted as he looked at the elegant satin slippers. They were designed for dancing 'til dawn on polished floors, not walking at night through wet grass. He began to untie the ribbons, his fingers shaking a little when they brushed her slender ankles. As he eased the wet satin from her feet Eloise stirred.

'What are you doing?'

'Your shoes are wet through so I have removed them.'

'Where am I?'

She put up one hand and he caught it in his own.

'You are in my room—do not be alarmed. You fainted, and I did not want to risk being seen with you in my arms.'

She sat up, but made no attempt to release his hand. If anything, her grip tightened.

'I am sorry; I do not know why I should suddenly have become so weak.'

He smiled at that.

'A reaction to the excitement of the night.'

'Where is your valet?'

'Gone to bed. When I went out I told him not to wait up for me.' Jack leaned a little closer. 'You are very pale. Shall I fetch you a glass of wine? I have a decanter here.'

'Yes, thank you.'

As Jack turned away Eloise glanced around the room. Everywhere there was evidence of the major's presence, illuminated in the golden glow of the firelight. His shaving kit spread out on the wash stand, silver-backed hair brushes lying on the dressing table. Even here on the bed beside her was the garishly coloured silk banyan he would wear over his nightshirt. Her fingers reached out and touched it. The silk was cool and smooth beneath her fingers. She imagined Jack wearing the banyan, the thin silk fitting snug across his broad shoulders—directly against his skin perhaps, since she knew some men did not wear nightshirts. Eloise snatched her hand back, quickly pulling her mind away from the sensations such thoughts aroused in her. Nervously she slid off the bed and stepped across to sit in an armchair drawn up beside the fire. She perched nervously on the edge of the chair. She should not be here. Everything in this room was alien to her. Masculine. She and her husband had always had their separate apartments, and she had never entered Tony's bedchamber when he was there. She swallowed hard. Jack Clifton was not Tony: he was very much more dangerous.

She should leave, now. Slip out of the door while Jack was pouring the wine, but her wayward body would not move. She realised with a shock that she felt secure in this man's room, where the air was redolent with wine and wood smoke, with spices, soap and leather. And, knowing that Sir Ronald Deforge was still a guest in the house, she did not want to be alone.

Jack carried two glasses of wine across the room and offered one to her. He was not surprised to see that she had moved from the bed to a chair by the fire. She was sitting bolt upright, rigid with tension. Pity stirred within him when he saw the anxious look on her face. She took the glass and held it in both hands, staring down at the dark liquid.

Jack hooked his toe around the leg of a footstool and dragged it across so that he could sit at her feet.

'Drink it,' he urged her. 'It is not drugged. I have no evil designs upon you.'

She looked at him, a faint smile breaking the rigidity of her countenance.

'I would not think that of you. I left my cloak in Alex's room.'

Jack indicated his shirt sleeves, billowing out from the tight-fitting waistcoat.

'My frockcoat is there, too. We must trust Farrell to return them to us in the morning.'

'So there is nothing to worry about.'

He met her eyes, hoping his smile would reassure her.

'No, madam, there is nothing to worry about.'

As she sipped at the wine Jack sensed the tension draining out of her. After a little while she leaned back in the chair and they sat in a comfortable silence. Jack stared into the fire, his elbows resting on his knees as he cradled the glass between his hands. He was very aware of the woman sitting in the chair. If he leaned slightly towards her, his arm would be touching her thigh. By turning just a little more he could rest his head in her lap. How pleasant that would be! How pleasant to be able to sit like this every evening. He glanced down at her dainty ankles and little feet. Her stockings were stained with mud and grass, reminding him of what had occurred that night. He would make no progress with her while she was in danger. If only he could extricate her from this mess, then perhaps she might consider his suit.

His suit?

Jack caught himself up. What was he thinking of? Not marriage, surely. It had always been his intention to settle down one day and this had included some vague plan to find himself a wife, but he had envisaged proposing to someone like his childhood sweetheart, Clara, an innocent maid of good family, not a widow whose past was so dubious that it was ripe for extortion. He glanced again at the woman before him. All at once her past seemed unimportant: he was certain in his own mind that whatever she had done it could not be so very bad. If she had had a string of lovers—well, who was he to criticise that?

Eloise stirred in her chair. She finished her wine and put down her glass upon the hearth.

'Thank you. I should go now.'

'Stay a little longer.'

'I—um—my feet are wet. I should dry them.'

Her blue eyes flickered over his face. There was nothing of the coquette in the look she gave him, only uncertainty, and a shy wistfulness. Suddenly his heart was hammering against his ribs. *Why not?* whispered the voice in his head. *If the lady is willing.*

'You can do that here,' he murmured. 'If you will allow me.'

Eloise gripped the arms of the chair as he put out one hand and gently pushed her skirts up to expose her knee. One word, one tiny gesture would stop him, she knew that, but she said nothing. She remained motionless as he untied her garter. An aching excitement pooled low in her body, her skin tingling in anticipation of his touch. She watched him roll the silk stocking down her calf and gently pull it away from her toes.

'There, that's better. Now, shall I remove the other one?'

No! She knew she should be running from this room, screaming. He was undressing her, carrying out a task that no one other than a husband should be permitted to perform. It was wrong. Immoral. Indecent. She should stop him. She looked at him, opening her mouth to object, but Jack was smiling at her and she felt the last remnants of her resistance melting away. Her mouth closed again and she was aware that she was nodding.

'Yes, please.'

The lightness of his touch was an almost unbearable

pleasure and when his hand cupped her heel as he removed the second stocking she gave a little moan.

Jack glanced up.

'Is anything wrong?'

He was still holding her foot, his thumb idly stroking her ankle and inducing a wonderfully soothing lassitude throughout her body. It was an effort to speak.

'I did not realise how chilled I had become.'

She bit her lip to prevent herself protesting as he released her foot and turned away.

He picked up the poker and began to stir up the fire.

'Stay here, then, until you are warm again.'

Relief suffused her, and a warm rush of gratitude for this man. She smiled and stretched, luxuriating in the warmth of the fire and the calm, soothing atmosphere of the room.

'I should like to stay here for ever,' she murmured. 'To sit by this fire, warm and comfortable and not worry about anything—it is my idea of paradise! But it cannot be. I must get back to my room before anyone begins to wake.'

'It is still dark,' said Jack. 'The servants will not be abroad for another hour or so yet.' He reached for her hands and pulled her to her feet. 'Stay here and let me show you my idea of paradise.'

Eloise gazed up into his face, mesmerised by the glow of the firelight reflected in his dark eyes. She trembled as his hands ran lightly over her arms and on to her shoulders. Her lips parted in a tiny gasp of expectation when he bent his head towards her. Her last, conscious thought was that he was going to kiss her—that she *wanted* him to kiss her, but the sensation of his mouth sliding across hers drove everything from her mind, save a desire to kiss him back. She threw her arms around his neck, leaning against his hard body while his tongue explored her mouth and played havoc with her senses. She felt as if she was floating and realised that indeed her feet were no longer on the floor, for Jack's arms were crushing her against him, lifting her as easily as a rag doll.

Desire consumed her. She returned Jack's kisses with a passion that was both exciting and confusing. She followed his lead, and if her kisses were inexpert he did not seem to mind, but held her even more closely. There was a crash as he kicked the footstool aside and carried her to the bed where he placed her down, all the time covering her face and neck with warm, heady kisses. When he raised his head she reached out and pulled him back towards her, intoxicated by his presence. He lay down with her, measuring his length against her, and she gasped as his hand came up to cup her breast. His thumb slipped beneath the lacy edge of her bodice and stroked gently over her nipple. She pushed against his touch, her skin tightening as the excitement built within her. She fumbled with the buttons of his waistcoat, eager for him to remove it yet sighing with frustration when Jack broke away from her. He gave a soft laugh.

'Patience, my lady. There is time to undress: I'll not tumble you like some cheap straw damsel.'

He shrugged himself out of his waistcoat and as he pulled his shirt over his head Eloise sat up and slipped her arms around his waist. She laid her face against the flat plain of his stomach, caressing him with her cheek. He groaned and fell back on the bed, drawing her to him again and as his mouth captured hers he tugged on the drawstring fastenings of her bodice. Between frantic kisses they discarded their clothes until they were lying naked together on the bed, their bodies illuminated only by the residual light of the dying fire and a single, flickering candle.

Jack pushed himself up on one elbow and stared down

at her. Eloise did not make any effort to cover herself. She basked in the admiration of his glance, revelling in the novel sensation of truly enjoying a man's attentions.

'You are beautiful,' he murmured, resting one hand on her naked thigh.

She smiled up at him, putting her hand to his cheek and gently drawing his face down to hers. His kiss was slow and thorough and she never wanted it to stop. The hand on her thigh slid up and inwards. Her body responded instinctively, pushing against his fingers while a heady excitement grew inside her, spreading through her body. She arched her back, gasping, only vaguely aware of Jack's body shifting on top of her. She dug her fingers into his back and cried out as they were united. There was an exhilarating, joyful satisfaction in knowing they were as physically close as any man and woman could be but even that was not the end. Their bodies were moving together, the blood singing in her veins as the dizzying excitement rose higher and higher until there was no more conscious thought. She cried out and clung on tightly as she felt herself tumbling and crashing into oblivion.

Jack lay with Eloise in his arms. He was breathing heavily, dazed and exhausted by the physical and emotional ferocity of their union. It had never happened before, even after battle when he had taken comfort in the arms of a woman; he had never experienced such an all-consuming passion. His arms tightened possessively. Whatever secrets the lady's past might hold he did not care. She stirred in his arms.

'Awake, sweetheart?' He nibbled gently at her ear. 'Did you enjoy that?'

'I—yes.' Her voice was hardly above a whisper. 'I never knew.'

The wonder in her voice made him smile.

'You have been alone for a long time. Perhaps you have forgotten.'

'No, not forgotten. I…that was the first time.'

He nuzzled her neck.

'Then I am very honoured, although I am sorry for it if all your other lovers failed to give you such pleasure.'

'No, you misunderstand,' she murmured. 'I am…*was* a maid. Until tonight.'

Jack grew still.

'A maid? But Allyngham…'

'Our union was never consummated.'

In one swift movement he rolled over and sat up on the side of the bed.

'A maid!' He was still intoxicated with her, his mind in turmoil. Nothing made sense. 'But you were married to Tony Allyngham for seven years! And in London, all those men—'

'Nothing more than flirtation.'

'Then by God, madam, you played your part well!' he retorted, more sharply than he intended.

She said in a small voice, 'I am sorry if I have deceived you.'

'Deceived me! Aye, you deceived me!' He put his hands to his head. It had always been a point of honour with him to avoid innocent maids. She had been so willing, so eager for his kisses, how could it be that he did not know? Confusion swirled within him. 'By heaven, madam, I do not know what to say. Why in hell's name should you wish to act in such a manner if you were not…?'

She gave a little sob and scrambled away from him, dropping off the bed on the far side.

'Now you think me the very worst type of flirt,' she muttered. He watched her scrabbling around for her clothes. His brain was still reeling, trying to make sense of everything. He had been so bewitched that he had allowed his desire for her to overwhelm him. He shook his head, trying to clear his thoughts.

'A *flirt*, yes, but— Oh my God, I would never have taken you to bed if I had known you were a virgin!' He dropped his head in his hands again. 'I thought you a woman of experience, one who played by society's rules. A discreet little affair while it amused us, then we could both walk away...'

'Well, you need not be afraid. You can still walk away.'

He looked up. 'That is not what I meant.'

He watched, bemused, as she made an attempt to find a way into her gown, but the flimsy material seemed to defeat her. Impatiently she threw it aside and pulled his banyan from the bed. The silk wrap was much too big and it pooled around her feet. She looked absurdly young and vulnerable.

'I know exactly what you meant, Major Clifton.' She threw the words at him as she tied the belt around her with angry, jerking movements. 'It was never my intention to entrap you. I am only sorry that I confided the truth to you, although no doubt you would have realised it soon enough. The evidence on the sheets will be all too plain in the daylight!' She ran to the door.

'No—Eloise—wait!'

But she was gone.

Chapter Eleven

Eloise sped through the dim corridors and down the stairs,
scarcely aware of the cold boards beneath her bare feet. She
dared not cry and held back her tears until she was safely
inside her own room with the door locked, then she threw
herself on to the bed and gave way to harsh, gasping sobs
that racked her body.

She had been a fool to give herself to Jack Clifton. It was
mere weakness to blame the excitement of the night and her
anxiety over Alex for her inability to keep the man at arm's
length. He had despised her when he had thought her wanton,
and he thought even less of her now he knew it was all a
charade. It was very lowering to know that he had thought
her easy prey, someone to tumble into bed for a few nights'
amusement, but his reaction when she had told him she was
a virgin was even more upsetting. He was outraged, as if she
had deceived him on purpose. She beat her fists against the
covers. Did he think she wanted to trick him into marriage?
Hah! She would show him! He was nothing but a rake, a low
rascal, and she would have nothing more to do with him.

At length her sobs abated and she lay exhausted on the

covers, only the occasional hiccup interrupting her misery. She had felt so comfortable in his arms, so *right*. She had spent years listening to her married friends, smiling and nodding as if she quite understood when they complained of how tiresome it was to have to pleasure one's husband, or giggled over the attributes of their latest lover, but until today she had never known just how exciting and enjoyable it was to be swept up by a man, to be kissed and caressed and…and *loved* until one's whole being was convulsed with pleasure. More tears squeezed themselves between her closed eyelids. If only it had been someone other than Major Clifton!

Eloise pulled the banyan around her. The silk was cool against her skin, and in its folds she could smell the distinctive fragrance that was Jack Clifton. It was like being in his arms again. With a petulant cry she threw off the wrap and slid naked between the cold sheets of her bed. She had told Alice not to wait up for her, and the hot brick her maid had placed in the bottom of the bed was now a cool, hard lump and no comfort at all. Eloise reached out for the banyan and pulled it into the bed with her. Tomorrow she would be cold and distant when dealing with Major Clifton, but for the few hours that were left of the night she hugged the silk to her, curling her body around it. As sleep closed in and her acute unhappiness mellowed into a dull and aching despair, she found herself thinking that there was one tiny crumb of comfort to be found in all this: even if she was forced to marry Sir Ronald Deforge to secure the return of the journal, at least she would not be giving him her virginity.

A soft scuffling at the door roused Eloise. She lay, tense and alert beneath the covers, listening. Her straining ears detected the slight sound of footsteps padding away along the corridor. It was still dark, but the shutters of her window had not been closed and the faint glimmer of moonlight penetrated the room, leaving only the far corners in deep shadow. For the first time she noticed the pale shape of her nightgown spread out across the bottom of the bed and she quickly pulled it on, shivering a little as the cold cotton slid over her skin. Then she reached for her tinderbox. Once her bedside candle was alight she slipped out of bed and went to the door. It opened almost silently and she peeped out into the empty corridor. Looking down, she saw a grey bundle lying at her feet. She scooped it up, carrying it into the room. It was her cloak, still muddy and a little damp from her nocturnal ramblings. Wrapped inside it she found the rest of her clothes—shoes, stockings, her chemise and stays, the thin muslin gown with its muddy hem and traces of Alex's blood on the front. It was all there, except the embroidered ribbon garters. She chewed her lip. It was possible that Major Clifton had overlooked them, but she doubted it. She thought of his handkerchief, lying hidden at the bottom of her drawer. Perhaps it was a fair exchange.

The talk the next day was all about the poachers who had so savagely attacked Mr Mortimer. Alice informed her mistress of the news when she brought in her hot chocolate that morning.

'I have no idea what you and Mr Alex got up to last night and I don't want to know,' the maid told her mendaciously, 'but when Mr Farrell announced this morning that poor Mr Alex was at death's door it was as much as I could do to keep my lips sealed—and if I hadn't peeped in and seen you sleeping so peacefully before I went down to the kitchen I think I should have run straight back upstairs to make sure you was in your bed! And now I finds *this*.' The maid picked up the crumpled gown and held it out. 'Don't you try to tell me that's mud on your skirts, Miss Elle, because I know very well it's bloodstains.'

'Well, it is not all blood,' put in Eloise, sipping at her chocolate. 'There are grass stains as well, where I fell on my knees beside Mr Mortimer.'

Alice gave a gusty sigh and shook her head.

'Oh, my dear lady, I knew I should have waited up for you last night—'

'And you know I ordered you to go to bed,' retorted Eloise. 'You would have been very much in the way. Now do stop scolding me, Alice, and tell me instead how Mr Mortimer goes on. Has Farrell sent for the doctor?'

'No, ma'am: it seems Major Clifton bound up his wounds.' The maid shot a fierce, searching look at her mistress. 'Just what happened last night, Miss Elle? You told me you and Mr Mortimer was going out to put an end to those horrible letters that have been upsetting you.'

'And so we were, Alice.' Eloise hesitated, regarding her maid over the rim of her cup. Alice had been with her since she was a child, and it was impossible to snub her. Eloise never doubted her loyalty, but she dare not take her fully into her confidence. 'Unfortunately the man attacked Mr Alex. He drew a sword upon him, although Alex was unarmed.'

'Oh, mercy me, the villain!'

'Quite. Thankfully Major Clifton was in the gardens and helped me to carry Mr Alex back into the house.'

'Then we should inform the magistrate, my lady, and set up a hue and cry for the culprit!'

'That would cause far too much of a scandal, Alice, you must see that.'

The maid sniffed.

'There would certainly be a scandal if anyone was to know that you had been running around the country at night with

Mr Alex!' She looked again at the gown, then picked up her muddy slippers. 'And what am I suppose to do with these? Ruined, just like your gown and your stockings! And all left on the floor for me to fall over! You should not have had to undress yourself, madam: if I had been here when you came in last night I could have taken these away and cleaned them, but now the dirt is so dried on there will be no getting it out.'

'No, I think you should dispose of the gown and the slippers,' said Eloise. 'But do it discreetly, Alice.'

The maid snorted. 'Do you think I would take these things down to the servants' hall and announce to all and sundry that my mistress was gallivanting the night away?'

Despite her heavy heart, Eloise smiled. 'No, of course not. I am very sorry to be so troublesome, truly I am. There is something else.' She pulled the silk wrap from under the bed-clothes and held it out, saying airily, 'This needs to be returned to Major Clifton.' She observed Alice's shocked countenance and looked away, her cheeks growing hot. 'I was very chilled when we came back last night…'

Alice reached out and took the banyan, holding it at arm's length as if it was some contaminated rag instead of a very costly and fashionable item of a gentleman's wardrobe.

'Well, I never did!' exclaimed the maid. 'So you put this on over your gown? Ooh, Miss Elle, if anyone had seen you!'

'Well, they did not see me,' replied Eloise, her cheeks very hot. 'So see that it is returned to Major Clifton, if you please, and leave me to drink my chocolate in peace!'

Later, when she helped her mistress to dress, Alice was still muttering about the heathenish ways of the Quality. Eloise made no attempt to stop her, knowing her handmaid would talk herself back into a good mood all the sooner if she was allowed to have her say.

Thus Eloise was prepared for the talk and consternation of the party when she joined everyone in the breakfast room later that morning and she was able to assume a suitable expression of shock when Mr Renwick's sister greeted her with the news of the attack.

'Poachers,' exclaimed Mrs Briggate, 'and in the park, too! I do hope, brother, that you will take precautions to secure the house.'

'I have already done so, sister.'

Mr Renwick's response was calm and reassuring.

'How is Mr Mortimer?' asked Eloise as she took her seat at the table.

'Very poorly, but Major Clifton says his life is not in danger,' replied Mrs Renwick. 'It was Major Clifton who found Mr Mortimer and he has been looking after him.'

'He is with him now,' added her husband, 'I have told him he has only to say the word and a man shall ride for the doctor immediately, but he does not seem to think it necessary at present.'

Sir Ronald had sauntered into the room and he said softly, 'The question is, what took Mortimer into the grounds at night in the first place?'

Eloise wrapped her hands around her coffee cup and tried to ignore his sly look.

'Perhaps he likes those horrid little cigarillos that are so popular with the gentlemen today,' said Mrs Renwick.

'That would certainly explain what Clifton was doing in the gardens,' put in Edward Graham. 'Doubtless he picked up the habit while he was in the army.'

'Don't know what these young fellows should want with those things,' barked Mr Briggate. 'What's wrong with snuff, I should like to know? Good enough for m'father.'

Eloise glanced at the brown stains around his nostrils and suppressed a shudder.

'Or a pipe,' put in Mrs Renwick. 'I remember my father enjoyed a pipe of tobacco of an evening. I always thought it smelled quite delicious.'

'Yes, yes, this is all very well, but we are straying from the point,' put in Mrs Briggate with a nervous glance around the table. 'What is to be done about the poachers?'

'We will do what we have always done, sister.' Mr Renwick smiled at her. 'I shall put extra men into the grounds today, and tonight we will let the dogs loose, so I would warn all of you to remain indoors after dark.'

'We are shooting today, are we not, Renwick?' asked Edward Graham. 'Perhaps we can bag a few of the rascals for ourselves.'

There was general laughter at this, and the gentlemen soon went off to prepare for their day's sport. Mrs Renwick carried the ladies off to the morning room and Eloise slipped away. She was anxious to see Alex and since the back stairs were deserted she quickly ran up to the bachelor wing and scratched upon the door.

'My lady! You cannot come in here!'

Eloise pushed past Farrell, ignoring his half-hearted attempts to deny her.

'It is my fault your master is injured and I must know how he is,' she said, walking into the room.

Alex was propped up in his bed, looking very pale. He raised his brows when he saw her.

'Go away, Elle. You should not be here. What if the servants see you?'

'They will not, for I am very careful. Besides, it does not matter if they do,' she said bitterly. 'It will merely add to my reputation. I had to find out how you go on.'

'I feel devilish,' he muttered. 'I have a neat hole in my shoulder which is a little sore but the cut on my leg will keep in bed for a week at least. I suppose I should be thankful it is no worse.' He frowned suddenly. 'Farrell tells me you and Clifton put me to bed.'

She flushed.

'Yes.'

'Damnation, Eloise, there was no need for that!'

'Yes, there was. It needed two of us to undress you and Farrell had to fetch the bandages.'

'You should have made some excuse and left the room.'

She had been thinking much the same thing, but at the time she had wanted to stay, and Jack's calm assumption that she would not be shocked by the sight of a man's body had allowed her to override her scruples. She realised now that it had only added to his conviction that she was a woman of the world.

She said quietly, 'I wanted to help.'

'But, good heavens, Elle, what will Clifton think?'

'I neither know nor care what the major thinks,' she retorted. 'He is an odious man.'

She looked away from Alex's searching gaze.

'Quarrelled again, have you?'

'Of course not. But I beg you will not confide in him. Do not tell him anything more about us. I do not trust him.'

'Well, I think you should. Jack is sound enough, my dear.'

Eloise pressed her lips together and hoped she was not scowling. So it was Jack now, was it? Alex put a hand to his shoulder.

'He made a capital job of binding me up, and he was here first thing this morning, checking the bandages. You've no need to worry about Clifton.'

'Did I hear my name?'

Eloise whipped round as Major Clifton came into the room. Her face flamed but he gave her no more than a nod as he walked towards the bed.

As if we were no more than acquaintances, she thought. *As if he had forgotten what happened last night.*

She bit her lip, knowing that she was being uncharitable. Perhaps he was trying to spare her blushes.

'Aye, we were talking of you.' Alex held out his hand to him, grinning. 'I was telling my lady what a good sawbones you would make.'

'One picks up a little knowledge in the army.' Jack gave Eloise a half-smile but she turned away, determined not to respond. 'Lady Allyngham nursed you, too, you know.'

'And I am very grateful to you both. But, Elle, now you can see that I am getting better I do wish you would go away: we are not related, my dear, and there will be the devil to pay if you are found here.'

'You should have thought that way last night before you went off together to meet Deforge,' growled Jack.

'That was different.' Alex shifted uncomfortably. 'No one was meant to know about that.' He glanced at Eloise. 'What are they saying downstairs?'

'That it was poachers. I saw Sir Ronald this morning.' She shuddered. 'I could hardly bear to sit still at the breakfast table, for he was smiling in the slyest manner.'

'The devil he was! When I am back on my feet I shall take a pistol to the villain!'

'When you are back on your feet you may of course do what you wish,' replied Jack. 'But for now you must rest. I've sent your man down to fetch you some breakfast.'

Even as he spoke, Jack was very aware of the lady standing silently beside the bed. She looked so pale and forlorn that guilt wrenched at his insides. If only he could go back and unsay his hasty words of last night. He was furious with himself for his outburst. From the little he had overheard when he walked into the room he was sure she had not told Mortimer what had occurred, so he would follow her lead and say nothing, at least when they were in company.

He needed to talk to her, to explain his behaviour, but that was not possible here, with Alex Mortimer looking on. He was not at all sure that it was possible under any conditions. How could he make her understand just how he had felt, after the most glorious, the most fulfilling lovemaking he had ever known, to discover that she was still a maid? He had been shocked, mortified to think he had not known. True, she had responded to him, matched his passion with her own but that was no excuse. He was not inexperienced and he was horrified to think he had been so insensitive to her. She had thought his annoyance was directed towards her and by the time he had collected his dazed wits she had gone, fled back to her room. Unable to rest he had collected her cloak, wrapped up her discarded clothes and deposited them at her door. He hoped she would know from that gesture that he intended to be discreet, that he meant her no harm. Until he could find a way to talk to her privately, it was all he could do.

Mortimer was pulling angrily at the bedcovers.

'Breakfast! I had rather you sent Farrell with a challenge to Deforge!' He glowered. 'He has gone too far this time. I won't have it, Elle. I say let him publish and be damned to him, we'll fight!'

Jack looked up quickly. 'Why, what is Sir Ronald demanding?'

As Alex opened his mouth to speak, Eloise put up her hand, saying icily, 'Major Clifton is no longer party to our plans, Alex.'

'Gammon! If Jack had not rescued us last night we would have been in the devil of a fix!' Alex turned his angry eyes towards him. 'Deforge wants Eloise for his wife.'

'The devil he does!' Jack could not prevent the exclamation, nor the sudden, intense surge of possessiveness. No wonder she had looked so frightened when he had told her of his suspicions about Deforge. He wanted to gather her up in his arms but he knew that if he made any move towards her she would run away from him. Despite the fear he could see in her eyes, she bravely put up her chin.

'That is nonsense, of course. I told him so last night.'

'He must think his hold upon you very secure to suggest such a thing,' Jack said slowly.

The lady was silent, but something in her countenance caused Alex to sit up.

'Thunder and turf, you are not to think of giving in to that villain, Eloise!'

Jack saw a shadow cross her face but it was gone in an instant. Smiling, she reached out to push Alex gently back against his pillows.

'No, of course not. Now lie still or you will set your shoulder bleeding.'

'You are not to do anything until I am on my feet again.' Alex grabbed her wrist. 'Promise me, Elle! Clifton—you must look after her, make sure Deforge has no opportunity to bully her.'

'By all means.'

She flushed.

'That will not be necessary. I am going back to London in the morning. I shall tell Mrs Renwick that I have business to attend to.'

'I would rather you remained here, under my eye,' declared Alex.

She smiled at that.

'A poor chaperon you would be, confined here in your room!'

Alex sighed. 'I am sorry, love: I had thought for once I should be able to help *you* out of a scrape, but it seems I have only succeeded in causing you more problems.'

She squeezed his hand and smiled fondly at him.

'You must not worry over me, Alex. We will deal with everything once you are well again.'

'But you are determined to leave?'

'Yes. There is plenty to occupy me in London. You know, I still have hopes that I might persuade Lord Berrow to sell me his land.'

Jack watched them, beating down the little demon of jealousy that gnawed at his insides. They were not lovers—he knew that now—but they were very close and they shared secrets that he was not privy to. His frown deepened as he realised how much he wanted Eloise to trust him as she trusted Mortimer. She kissed Alex's cheek and moved towards the door.

'Wait,' said Jack. 'Let me go first, to make sure there is no one to see you.'

Silently he checked that the passage was empty and preceded her down the stairs. When they reached the great hall the faint sound of voices could be heard coming from the drawing room. Jack stopped.

'Will you join them?'

Eloise shook her head.

'I would rather not. I would like to be alone. I think I shall go to my bedchamber.'

Even as she uttered the words the door of the drawing room opened and Lady Parham's shrill voice could be heard. It could only be a matter of moments before they were spotted and Jack knew that the lady would insist upon carrying Eloise away with her. The hunted look in his companion's blue eyes decided him. They were standing by the entrance to the long gallery. It was the work of an instant to whisk Eloise inside and shut the door.

He said, by way of explanation, 'I thought perhaps you might prefer to avoid them.'

On the other side of the door he could hear Lady Parham talking with her hostess, their voices echoing through the marbled hall. Eloise moved away from him.

'Thank you. I can find my way from here.' She nodded dismissively and when he made no move she added sharply. 'Please, you may leave me now.'

Jack smiled, his eyes flicking towards the door.

'Would you throw me out? Lady Parham would be sure to pounce upon me and drag me in to tell them all how Mortimer goes on.'

A reluctant smile lurked in her eyes.

'Surely you are not afraid of a group of ladies, Major.'

'Terrified,' he replied cheerfully. 'I shall have to remain in here until I know it is safe to venture out.' He moved further into the room. 'Renwick has some fine paintings here; will you not take a few moments to look at them?'

She had been walking away from him but now she stopped, uncertain, and he added quickly, 'If you are leaving in the morning you may not have another opportunity of seeing them in daylight.'

It was clear from her expression that she was torn between a desire to look at the pictures and a disinclination to be alone with him. At least she had not refused to stay. He pointed to the nearest painting and said in a matter-of-fact voice, 'This Cuyp landscape is highly prized and this next is thought to be a Rembrandt, although there is some doubt about that: what do you think?'

She moved a little closer.

'I cannot tell,' she said slowly. 'It is certainly very good, if it is a copy.'

'But what of the colours, and the brushstrokes, are they not a little fine for Rembrandt?'

'Not necessarily. I think his style changed when he grew older. And the subject matter, a biblical scene: this is typical of his later work.'

He regarded her with admiration.

'And you say you are no connoisseur? I believe you misled us, my lady.'

'My husband was very interested in the old masters. I picked up a little from following him around Florence and Rome.'

'You would enjoy the Louvre, I think. Now Paris is free once more you might like to see it.'

'Perhaps. One day.'

He smiled to himself, thinking how much he would like to escort her there. His previous visit had been in the company of his fellow officers: how much more enjoyable to be with someone who really appreciated art.

'And who is this?' Her soft, musical voice recalled him with a jolt. He cleared his throat.

'This next is a portrait of one of Renwick's ancestors—can you see the family resemblance?'

Jack moved slowly along the gallery, drawing her attention to various pictures, asking her opinion, searching his brain to drag up long-forgotten snippets of information about the artists. His patience was rewarded: gradually she relaxed and gave her attention to the paintings. He stood beside her, close but never touching, enjoying her company and amused by her

forthright opinions. By the time they were halfway down the
long gallery she was chattering away quite naturally. She even
turned to him at one point, laughing at something he said.
Jack found himself wishing the gallery were twice as long.
He drew her attention to a small pen-and-ink drawing.

'There is an interesting picture here of the house painted
about sixty years ago, before it was remodelled into its present
state.'

She stepped forwards for a closer look.

'The formal gardens are much smaller, and there looks to
be a village where the park is now.'

'Yes, it was demolished by Renwick's grandfather, to
improve the view.'

'Oh dear, and the villagers?'

'You need not worry; he built houses for all his tenants on
the far side of the Home Wood. They were delighted to have
new, weatherproof houses. I hope my own people will feel
the same.'

She turned to look at him, her blue eyes wide with
surprise.

'Are you evicting your tenants?'

He laughed at that.

'No, no, but I plan to build better houses for them as and
when the funds will allow.'

'This is at Henchard, your estate in Staffordshire?'

He smiled, inordinately pleased that she had remembered.

'Yes. I have a very good agent, who has been looking after
matters while I have been away, but there is much to do and
I plan to spend more time there in the future.'

'And will you be content with such a quiet life, sir?'

'Quiet? It will be hard work, improving my land and the lot
of my tenants. The house needs to be enlarged, new kitchens

built—do you think I cannot be happy unless I have a sword in my hand?'

'No, of course not. I suppose I had not considered. I know so little about you, Major Clifton.'

'There is a great deal we do not know about each other, my lady.'

A shy smile lit her eyes and Jack's spirits soared. This was progress indeed: perhaps now he could talk to her about last night. As if reading his thoughts her cheeks flushed and she turned quickly back towards the paintings.

'This is by Ricciardelli.' She leaned forwards to read the label on the frame.

'Yes.' Jack nodded. 'It is a particularly fine view of Naples—do you agree? I remember Tony telling me you visited Naples on your honeymoon.'

Jack clamped his mouth shut, cursing himself. Eloise's face flamed. She turned to go and he reached out for her.

'I beg your pardon. I did not mean to remind you of your marriage, if it was not happy.'

He was holding her arm and she stood perfectly still, keeping her face averted.

'Tony and I *were* happy.' Her voice was so quiet he could hardly hear her. 'Despite what you now know of me, we were very fond of one another. Excuse me, I must go.'

He released her and she hurried towards the door. He followed, saying, 'And you are determined to leave for London in the morning?'

'I am.'

'Then first let me talk to you—let me apologise—for last night.'

'There is nothing more to say.'

She reached for the door handle but he stepped past her, putting his hand against the door to prevent her from escaping.

'Oh, but there is! At least let me tell you that I know now how much I had misjudged you—you were not what I thought.'

She turned to look at him, fixing him with eyes as dark and troubled as a stormy evening sky.

'You thought me wanton, which is the impression I have been at some pains to give. I cannot blame you for that.' She looked away. 'We enjoyed a night together and that is all there is to it. Now I would be obliged if you would forget all about me.' Her chin lifted: he thought he detected the faintest wobble in her voice. 'I am sure I am not the first woman to have enjoyed your attentions for a single night. There will be no regrets, no recriminations and if we are obliged to meet in company, I hope we can do so like civilised beings. As far as I am concerned the matter is over.'

Jack stared at her. His instinct was to drag her into his arms, to melt her icy resolve with a savage kiss, but he was haunted by the memory of her distress that morning. Despite her brave words she had been a virgin when he had taken her to his bed and he was ashamed that he had not realised it. That she had not told him, that their lovemaking had been as passionate and intense as any he had ever experienced, was no excuse for his lack of control. More than that, he was confused by his feelings for her. She did not trust him, she certainly did not confide in him—it seemed now that she did not even *want* him, so why could he not just do as she asked and leave her to her fate?

'My lady. Eloise—'

She closed her eyes and lifted her hand as if to defend herself.

'Please, let me go!'

Her impassioned whisper cut him like a knife. She did not

want him near her. He removed his hand from the door and stood back.

'As you wish, madam.'

Chapter Twelve

'My lady, are you going downstairs for dinner?'

Alice's voice roused Eloise from her sleep. She blinked and gazed around the room. As her mind cleared she remembered with a sinking heart the events that had resulted in her spending the entire afternoon curled up on her bed.

Alice was bustling around the room, pulling clothes from the linen press and chattering all the while.

'I made sure everyone thought you had the migraine, my lady: even fetched up a tisane for you, which I drank myself since you was asleep. Didn't want anyone connecting your malaise with Mr Mortimer's antics last night. Mrs Renwick sends her compliments and says that if you wish she will arrange for you to have dinner in your room, so I said I would come and find out how you are.'

Eloise sat up and rubbed her eyes.

'No, I must put in an appearance, I think.'

Alice gave an approving nod.

'I have brought you up some hot water. Shall I lay out your new gown for you?'

She allowed Alice to dress her in the white silk with its

exquisite silver embroidery. She pulled out the diamonds Tony had given her for a wedding present and as her maid fastened the necklace she gazed at her reflection in the mirror, feeling very much as if she was putting on her armour to go into battle.

When Eloise walked into the drawing room some time later she had the impression that there was a sudden lull in the conversation, that all eyes were turned upon her. She kept her smile in place and walked towards her hostess: not even by the flicker of an eyelid would she betray her inner trepidation.

'My dear Lady Allyngham, I am so glad you could join us: migraine can be most debilitating.' Mrs Renwick leaned forwards and peered into her face. 'But, my dear, you are still a little pale, are sure you are quite well?'

'Yes, ma'am, thank you. You must not worry about me, especially when we have a much more serious invalid in the house. Is there any news of Mr Mortimer?'

'I think Major Clifton can answer that for you,' said Mrs Renwick, beckoning to Jack. 'He has been most solicitous of poor Mr Mortimer and can tell us if there is any change, can you not, Major?'

Eloise berated herself for her stupidity. She should have realised that any enquiries about Alex would be directed to Major Clifton. Unable to escape, she fixed her eyes upon the floor as Jack approached. He did not look at her, but addressed himself to his hostess.

'I called in upon Mortimer on my way downstairs, ma'am, and I am pleased to tell you that he is looking much better.'

'So we have no need to summon Dr Bellamy?' asked Mr Renwick, coming up.

'Not in the least. In fact I expect to see him out of bed in a few days, once his leg has begun to heal.'

'That is excellent news,' declared Edward Graham. 'Poor Mortimer, he will be sorry when he hears what a good day's shooting he missed today. And you too, Clifton. Pity you didn't come out with us, but I take it you'll be able to join us tomorrow?'

'Yes, if the weather holds.'

The conversation turned to sport and Mrs Renwick went off to greet Meg Cromer, who had just come in. Eloise moved towards the fire to warm her hands. She did not know whether to be most relieved or disappointed by the cool reception she had received from Jack, yet what did she expect, after the way she had repulsed him that morning? Her mind strayed back to their walk through the long gallery. For a short time she had been able to forget her troubles and lose herself in discussing art and the paintings on the walls. It was as if they had been old friends, until his chance remark had reminded her that she was not free to indulge in such luxury. She and Jack Clifton could never be friends. After last night he knew too much about her—for him to learn more might endanger everything she had worked so hard to conceal.

She allowed her eyes to stray towards the little group of gentlemen: Jack Clifton's powerful figure immediately claimed her attention. His broad shoulders filled the black evening coat without the need for padding and his long legs encased in biscuit-coloured pantaloons gave him the height to stand out amongst his companions. Some called him saturnine, with his raven-black hair and hard, unsmiling features, but she had seen the kindness in his eyes, experienced the warmth of his smile and found more jovial countenances insipid by comparison.

I love him.

The revelation shocked her. She turned away quickly, afraid that someone might look into her face and discover her secret.

It could never be, of course. Witness his reaction when she had revealed that she was a maid—surely he would never have reacted in such a way if he cared for her at all. If he loved her.

Aye, there was the rub: she was being foolishly romantic. Jack Clifton was a kind man, an honourable man, but he did not love her. He had told her himself that he had loved Clara Deforge and she had been a sweet, innocent young maid, a paragon of virtue compared with the disgraceful Lady Allyngham, who flirted and teased and kept all manner of secrets! Jack could never love such a woman. He wanted to help her because she was Tony's widow. Lying on her bed that afternoon, she had relived the moment when she had told him she wanted nothing more to do with him, only in her silly, foolish, fairy-tale imagination he did not let her walk away from him. An unhappy lump settled in her throat. If only Jack had held her then, told her he would not let her go, that she was his and he would keep her no matter what happened. But he had said nothing. He had stood back and let her walk out, probably relieved to be free of her toils.

'A penny for your thoughts, Lady Allyngham.'

Sir Ronald Deforge's soft words brought an abrupt end to her reverie. This man had the power to ruin her, he had tried to kill her best friend, but she dare not denounce him. Instead she assumed the brittle, society manner that served her so well.

'They are not worth even a groat, Sir Ronald.'

He leaned closer and it was all she could do not to back away.

'I thought you might be thinking over my…proposal.'

'That requires a great deal of consideration, sir. It is not something to be undertaken lightly.'

'Very true, but I am not a patient man, and I want your

answer.' He took out his snuffbox and flicked it open. 'Our hostess tells me you intend to leave us.'

'Yes. I am going back to town.'

'This is very sudden, is it not?'

She was silent while he took a delicate pinch of snuff.

'I made my decision last night,' she said at last. 'I informed Mrs Renwick earlier today that I have business in London requiring my attention.'

His puffy, pock-marked face pushed even closer, so that she could feel his breath on her skin.

'I hope you do not plan to run away from me, madam.'

She raised her head, her lip curling disdainfully.

'Of course not. But I need time to think.'

'So you are leaving your lapdog Mortimer behind you? Do you think that is wise? Will he be quite safe, do you think?'

Her head came up at that. She fixed him with a steady gaze.

'Let us understand one thing, Sir Ronald. I shall not make any decision until Alex Mortimer is quite well again. It is in *your* interests to make sure he comes to no more harm.'

His look of surprise gave her some small satisfaction

'Perhaps you think Major Clifton will protect you,' he muttered. 'Let me warn you, madam, that I shall not be caught unawares again. Any attempt by the major to interfere in this affair will have disastrous results, for you both.' He added silkily, 'I shall not hesitate to kill him, my lady, do not be in any doubt about that.'

'Oh, I believe you capable of any base act,' she retorted haughtily. She turned on her heel and walked away, head held high, yet a deadly depression was already seeping into her bones: if she was to protect everything she held most dear, she could see no alternative. She would have to marry Sir Ronald Deforge.

* * *

London was cold. Eloise ordered fires to be lit in every room of her house in Dover Street but the chill never seemed to leave her. She told herself she was anxious for news of Alex, but even when his letters arrived, and she knew he was recovering well, still something was missing. She found herself re-reading the letters, searching for any mention of Jack Clifton, but Alex told her very little, save that Jack intended to accompany him back to town, as soon as he was well enough to travel, and with that crumb she had to be satisfied.

Everyone welcomed Lady Allyngham back to town and she threw herself into the round of breakfasts, parties, routs and balls that filled the days and nights of any society lady, but although she was relieved to be away from Sir Ronald's presence she could not relax. At one particularly tiresome party she began to think of going to Allyngham until Alex returned. She was idly making plans for this when Lord Berrow sought her out and invited her to tell him more about the foundling hospital she intended to build. He hinted that he might be persuaded to sell her the land she needed at Ainsley Wood, and it occurred to her that she should make sure that her plans for the hospital were well under way, and a trust set up for its support as soon as possible: she was all too aware that if she was forced to marry Sir Ronald she would lose all control of the Allyngham fortune.

Alex came in to London sooner than she expected. Eloise returned from the Green Park one afternoon to find a hastily scrawled note awaiting her.

'When did this arrive, Noyes?'

'It was delivered shortly after you left the house, my lady.'

She looked up, smiling.

'Mr Mortimer is back in town. Since I am dressed for walking I shall go and see him immediately.'

'I will summon your maid, madam.'

'No, I will not wait for that.'

'But, my lady!'

She waved an impatient hand at him.

'It is only a few doors away and not yet dark. Open the door, Noyes. I shall not be long.'

Ignoring the butler's tut of disapproval she hurried along the street, holding her skirts up to avoid the dirty pavement.

If Alex's butler was shocked to find an unescorted lady at his master's door he was too well trained to reveal it and merely ushered her to the drawing room. Alex was stretched out on a day-bed, one arm in a sling and a brightly coloured rug thrown over his legs. Eloise ran forwards and bent to hug him.

'Oh, my dear, I am so pleased that you are back! I am sorry I did not come earlier, but I was out walking with Lord Berrow when your note arrived. How was your journey, was it terribly painful for you?'

'Not as bad as I feared. Jack brought me in his new carriage, which is very well sprung. I scarcely noticed the bumpy road.'

'Oh, I beg your pardon. I did not realise you had company.'

She straightened and turned to see Major Clifton standing by the window. As he walked forwards she observed the warm look in his eyes and heat seared her cheeks. He was not deceived by the cool, polite smile she was giving him, and she scolded herself for allowing that first, initial burst of irrational pleasure to show. Jack bowed to her.

'You will want to talk alone,' he said. 'I shall leave you—'

'The devil you will!' retorted Alex. 'You promised to keep me company at dinner, Clifton, and I will hold you to that.'

'Then I should go,' said Eloise quickly. 'I wanted only to assure myself that you had survived your journey.'

Alex reached out and gripped her hand.

'No, there is no need for you to rush off, Elle. We three know each other well enough to take a glass of wine together, do we not? My dear, ring the bell for me. Then you must sit down. A gentleman should not lounge around in a lady's presence, but you know very well that I cannot get up.'

'Allow me,' said Jack, pulling up a chair for her.

She did not look at him but sank into it with a murmur of thanks.

'Have you seen Deforge?' Alex's question brought her eyes to his face and he said impatiently, 'For heaven's sake, Elle, there's no need to look daggers at me. It is not as though Clifton does not know what is going on.'

'But Lady Allyngham would prefer not to discuss the matter while I am here...'

She put up her hand.

'No,' she said carefully. 'I have no objection to you being here, Major. After all, you saved Alex's life.'

Alex nodded. 'I am glad you are being sensible at last, my dear.'

'Sir Ronald left Renwick Hall two days before us,' explained Jack. 'He said he was calling upon friends, but I thought he might try to steal a march by coming straight to town.'

'I have not seen him,' said Eloise. 'I have no doubt he will seek me out when he is ready.'

'Then we must decide what is to be done,' declared Alex.

'You will do nothing, my dear,' she said quickly. 'At least, not until you are well again.'

'Then perhaps Jack—'

'No!' She sat up very straight. 'Major Clifton need not involve himself further in our affairs.'

'But I should like to help,' said Jack mildly.

She glanced across at him. Her heart lurched at the sight of his smiling face and she squeezed her hands together in her lap, reminding herself of her resolution.

'That is very kind of you, Major, but there really is nothing to be done at the present time.'

She was relieved that the entry of a footman carrying the wine caused a diversion.

'Yes, yes, that will do,' said Alex, impatiently waving away the servant. 'Clifton, will you pour? I am weak as a cat.'

'Hardly surprising after a long journey,' said Jack. 'You will feel better when you have had a good night's sleep.'

He held out a glass of wine to Eloise, saying with a faint smile, 'I insisted he send for his doctor to call upon him in the morning.'

'I am glad of it, thank you.'

She was very aware of her fingers brushing Jack's as she took the wine. She remembered the feel of them on her skin and experienced a little *frisson* of pleasure at the memory. Giving herself a mental shake, Eloise put both hands around the wine glass. Heavens, she must curb such thoughts!

Jack had turned away to carry a glass of wine to Alex and she was able to watch the two men as they conversed. She remembered the icy dread she had felt when Alex had been wounded. It was nothing to the fear that now enveloped her when she thought of anything happening to Jack Clifton. She regarded his broad back. He was so strong, so assured, but even he was not proof against an assassin's knife or bullet. Deforge had promised to kill him, and she had no doubt that he would carry out that threat, if he thought Jack was involved. She squared her shoulders: she would talk to Alex tomorrow and make him promise not to divulge anything more to Jack Clifton. She finished her wine.

'I must go. I am promised to attend Parham House this evening.'

'But I thought you did not like Lady Parham above half.'

Eloise gave a little shrug. 'I do not, but I have hopes that I might be able to settle the question of Ainsley Wood this evening, so you see I must attend. I shall call upon you again tomorrow, Alex.'

Jack put down his glass.

'It is growing dark. I will escort you to your door, my lady.'

'Aye, please do, Jack,' said Alex, before Eloise could refuse. 'I'd rather not have her walking alone. It is only a step and you can be back in ten minutes.' He scowled. 'Do not argue with me, madam. Bad enough that you should risk your reputation by coming here!'

Jack grinned.

'I think we should humour him, my lady: opposition could render him feverish.' He held out his arm. 'Shall we go?'

Silently, Eloise allowed him to escort her out on to the street. The chill autumn night was already setting in and she was glad to push her hands deep into the large muff she was carrying.

'You said you were walking with Lord Berrow this afternoon,' said Jack, matching his step to hers. 'Was Lady Berrow with you, too?'

'No, she was not.'

'But she knows of your outing?'

Eloise shrugged. 'I presume so, Major. Why do you ask?'

'I think you should have a care, that is all.'

'Lord Berrow's estates border my own. We are neighbours. It is only natural that we should discuss matters together.'

'The gentleman may not see it in quite that way.'

She stiffened.

'Do not measure all men by your own standards, sir!'

'I do not,' he retorted. 'That is why I urge caution.'

She stopped and turned to face him.

'Major Clifton, allow me to know my own business,' she said angrily. 'I am perfectly capable of looking after myself.'

'I very much doubt that.'

She drew herself up.

'In case you have forgotten, sir, my husband was a military man and often absent. I am quite capable of running my own affairs and have been doing so for years!'

'No, I have not forgotten your husband, madam, which is why I am trying to protect you!'

She gave him an icy look and turned to walk on. He fell into step beside her, saying, 'While Mortimer is tied to his bed I would urge you to be more careful. You cannot deny that you are inexperienced in the ways of men.'

They had reached her house and she ran quickly up the steps. As the door opened to admit her she turned towards him and said in a low, shaking voice,

'During the past few weeks I have learned as much about men as I ever want to know!'

Chapter Thirteen

A quiet dinner alone did much to restore Eloise's good humour and by the time she set out for Parham House she was feeling quite optimistic. Alex was safe and recovering well, and although she was angry with Jack Clifton, she had to admit that it was very pleasant to have someone so concerned for her welfare that they were prepared to argue with her. Tony had been a kind and considerate husband, and Alex was a good friend, but neither had ever shown themselves quite so fiercely protective as Jack Clifton. She could almost believe he cared for her—but that was because he did not know the truth: he was far too honest to approve of the web of deceit she had woven with Tony and Alex. She leaned her head against the luxurious padding of her carriage and allowed herself to dream of what her future could be, if she could only destroy the journal and free herself from Deforge's clutches. Perhaps, once the secrets of her past were safely hidden she could start again; make a new life for herself that was not built on lies and deceit. And perhaps then Jack might be able to love her. It would not be easy, and escaping from Sir Ronald's clutches would be both difficult and dangerous, especially with Alex injured and unable to help, but she decided it was a future worth fighting for.

Parham House was hot, noisy and crowded. Eloise summoned up her society smile and wondered just how soon she would be able to get away. She took a glass of wine and scanned the room for Lord Berrow. During their walk that afternoon he had asked her most specific questions about her plans for the foundling hospital, and she had been encouraged to suggest he reconsider selling her the land at Ainsley Wood. When they parted he had hinted most strongly that if she attended the rout this evening he would give her his decision, so she had changed her walking dress for an evening gown of rose-coloured silk, secured the Allyngham diamonds about her neck and sallied forth to brave Lady Parham's barbed wit.

Despite her bold words to Jack Clifton, Eloise did not enjoy going about alone in town. She was used to turning off the gentlemen's flirtatious banter with a laugh and a witty rejoinder, but without Alex at her side she found their attentions a little more pressing, and it was necessary to give an occasional set down in order to keep the gentlemen at a distance. She could not be said to be enjoying herself at Parham House. The time dragged while she waited for Lord Berrow to arrive. She took a second glass of wine, then a glass of champagne, anything to occupy her. At last she was relieved to see the Earl approaching her, and she held out her hand to him, smiling.

'My lord, I am very pleased you are here! Such a squeeze. All the world and his wife must be present.'

Lord Berrow raised her fingers to his lips.

'My dear Lady Allyngham. You are radiant, as ever!'

'Thank you.' She looked past him. 'Is Lady Berrow with you?'

He chuckled.

'My wife is indisposed this evening, but even if she were not, we would not want her here upon this occasion, now would we?'

She realised he was still holding her fingers and gently but firmly pulled them away.

'No, I suppose not, if we are discussing business.'

'Business! Ha ha, well, if that is what you wish to call it.'

Her eyes slid away from him and as a distraction she beckoned to a passing waiter.

'Shall we take a glass of wine, sir?'

The room was very hot and the wine did little to cool her. Eloise wished she had sent the waiter to fetch her some lemonade instead. Lord Berrow seemed content to talk of trivial matters but she was impatient to get away.

'My lord, you said you would give me your decision on Ainsley Wood. Will you allow me to buy the land from you?'

'My dear ma'am, I shall be delighted to sell you anything your heart desires!'

'That is very gracious of you, sir, but it is only a small portion of land that is required.'

'Then it is yours.'

'I am so pleased. I shall instruct my lawyers to—'

Lord Berrow put up a hand.

'Yes, yes, of course, but there are a few little details I should like to talk over.' He held out his arm. 'Allow me to escort you out of this crush.'

She placed her fingers on his sleeve and was happy for him to precede her, his substantial bulk carving a path for her through the crowd. The double doors of the main reception rooms had been thrown open and Lord Berrow led her into the salon beyond. This room was just as crowded, but her partner carried on to a small corridor at one end.

'You appear to know the house very well, my lord.'

Eloise gave a nervous little laugh as he ushered her into a small, book-lined study and closed the door upon the noisy throng. A single branched candlestick and the glow from the fire provided the only lighting in the room, adding to her unease.

He tapped his nose, beaming at her.

'The advantage of spending years in town, one learns where one may be, ah, private in even the busiest houses.'

'But is this necessary, Lord Berrow? Would it not be better to discuss these things at your house, or even with my lawyer in the City?'

'Oh I don't see the need to involve the lawyers for this,' he said, drawing her down on to a sofa placed before a crackling fire. 'At least, not yet.'

He sat down beside her. She edged away a little, suddenly suspicious.

'My lord, I thought you had agreed to sell me Ainsley Wood.'

'I have indeed.' He moved closer 'But there are a few little details we must discuss.'

'Must we?'

'But of course. You know that I was not at all in favour of having a foundling hospital located so near to me.'

'So near? My dear sir, your house is quite five miles away from Ainsley Wood, and I have already said I would offer you a very good price to buy the land from you.'

'I am sure you would, my dear, and I am very happy to sell you the wood, but I think we need to discuss terms.'

'T-terms?'

'Oh, yes.' He was smiling at her, so close that she could see the tiny, broken veins in his cheeks. 'We are neighbours, after all, and it would be very pleasant to know that whenever I stayed in the area I should be welcome at Allyngham.'

'You and Lady Berrow may call at any time, my lord. Of course I did not receive visitors when I was in mourning, but—'

'You misunderstand me,' he murmured, his voice thickening. 'I shall call upon you *alone*, to enjoy those charms that you display so lavishly. Now let us seal our little bargain with a kiss, shall we...'

His arm slid around her waist and he pulled her to him. She turned her head and felt his hot breath on her ear. She pushed ineffectually at his chest.

'My lord, let me go! This is not what I intended!'

He chuckled, his mouth pressed against her skin. She felt his teeth nibbling at her neck. Her flesh began to crawl.

'How dare you. Leave me alone!'

'No need to be coy, my love, I have said you may have Ainsley Wood, and I will not object to you building your hospital, but you must give me something in return...'

He was forcing her back upon the sofa, his knee pushing between her legs and one hand firmly fixed upon her breast. She began to panic as she felt his weight pressing her down, pinning her beneath him. His hot, rasping breath was warm on her face. She closed her eyes and tried to scream, but she could not get her breath and given the noise in the main salons she doubted if anyone would hear her.

Then, miraculously, she was free. The suffocating weight was lifted from her body and she opened her eyes in time to see Jack Clifton delivering a crashing blow to Lord Berrow's whiskery jaw. Gasping for breath, Eloise sat up and straightened her gown.

Lord Berrow spluttered and struggled to his feet.

'Damn you, sir, how dare you assault me!'

Jack stood over him, scowling blackly. 'From what I could see, *you* were assaulting the lady.'

'Not I,' blustered Lord Berrow, moving out of range of Jack's clenched fist. 'Lady Allyngham and I have an arrangement!'

'That is not how I perceived it.'

'Then ask her! She will tell you she came here willingly.'

Jack looked at Eloise. 'What do you say, madam?'

She crossed her arms over her breast, her whole body shaking.

'Please, make him go,' she croaked.

'Well, sir. You heard the lady.' Jack took a step forwards. 'You had best be off with you.'

Lord Berrow straightened his coat and cast an angry glance towards Eloise. She shuddered and looked away.

'Very well, madam,' he said coldly. 'It would appear I misunderstood you. I beg your pardon.'

With a stiff bow he turned and stalked to the door. There was a sudden burst of sound as he left the room, then the door closed again and relative silence settled over them. Eloise glanced up. Jack was still scowling, his black brows drawn together. She said in a small voice, 'I suppose you will say now that you told me so.'

The heavy frown vanished.

'I shall say nothing so ill mannered.' He walked to a side table and filled a glass from one of the decanters. 'Here,' he said, sitting down beside her. 'Drink this.'

She eyed the golden liquid doubtfully.

'What is it?'

'Brandy.'

He put the glass into her hand. Cautiously she took a sip.

She grimaced as the pungent aroma stung her senses. She held the glass away but Jack pushed it back.

'Drink it. It will put heart into you.'

Obediently she lifted the glass to her lips again. The brandy burned as she swallowed it but gradually its warmth seemed to spread through her body. The horror of the past few minutes faded and she no longer felt faint.

'It would seem I am in your debt again.' Her eyes flickered over his face. 'Did…did you hear me cry out?'

'No, I came looking for you. Over dinner I questioned Alex about your interest in Lord Berrow. He told me that you had been trying to persuade Berrow to sell you some land.'

'Yes. I came here tonight because I thought…I thought he was going to agree to the sale.' She put her hands to her cheeks. 'But he wanted…'

'Hardly surprising.' Jack's hard tone heightened her remorse and she hung her head as he continued. 'When a beautiful woman seeks out a man to flatter and cajole him, is it any wonder if he thinks he can ask for certain favours? You have gone out of your way to give the impression that you are a woman of the world. No wonder Berrow thought you were his for the asking.'

'Well, I am not. I am not his or any man's!' She swallowed and said dejectedly, 'I do not suppose he will sell me that land now.'

'Was it so very important to you?'

Jack put his arm around her shoulders. She quickly damped the flicker of pleasure she felt at his touch. It was a gesture of comfort, nothing more.

'Yes. Did Alex tell you of my plans for a hospital?'

'A very little.'

'I want to build a foundling hospital, in memory of my husband.' His shoulder looked so inviting that she leaned against him. 'Tony knew there could be no children from our marriage. And I would have liked children, very much.'

'You are young, madam. There is still time.'

His words cut at her heart. She knew now that there was

only one man she wanted to be the father of her children.
He was sitting beside her now, his arm about her shoulders,
having rescued her from another foolish scrape.

'Tony and I had talked about setting up a charitable foun-
dation,' she said. 'When he died last year I thought it would
be a suitable tribute to him. As an orphan myself I know
what it is like to be alone. I was fortunate that Lord and Lady
Allyngham took me in and raised me in comfort and luxury
but I know that most do not have that advantage, and it is
even worse for those poor babes born out of wedlock, or those
whose mothers are too poor, or too ill to look after them. The
children are left in church doorways, or worse, left to perish
at the roadside. We have a good doctor in Allyngham who is
very keen to help the poor. He sees the injustice of leaving
these children to suffer. We have already financed a small
school in the town but I want to do more. I have discussed
with him my idea of a foundling hospital and there is some
support from the church: we have set up a trust and agreed
on a site to build the hospital, a piece of land from my estate,
but it is a long circuitous route from the town, unless we can
drive a road through Ainsley Wood.' She handed him the
empty glass and gave a large sigh. 'Well, there is no help for
it now. We will have to improve the existing lane.'

'No need to worry about that now.' He gently drew her
head down on to his shoulder.

'No. I have been such a fool.'

'A regular little ninnyhammer,' he agreed, resting his cheek
against her hair.

'I suppose I should go home, but I do not want to walk out,
through all those people. I do not want everyone staring at
me.'

'We do not need to leave just yet.' Jack leaned back against
the sofa, pulling her with him.

'You will stay here?'

'As long as you need me.'

She sighed, murmuring, 'You are a very good friend to me, Major Clifton.'

Eloise closed her eyes. She was so very comfortable. The dim light, which had unsettled her when she had entered the study with Lord Berrow, now gave the room a cosy air. She felt safe, lying with Jack's arm about her and her cheek resting on his chest. The folds of his freshly laundered neckcloth tickled her nose. A strange inertia had invaded her mind and her body. Perhaps it had not been wise to take quite so much wine.

'I should not be here with you,' she murmured, snuggling even closer.

'You should not be here with anyone.'

She shook her head slightly.

'No, but definitely not with you. You are dangerous.'

'Not to you, my dear.'

She smiled as his fingers gently brushed a stray curl from her cheek.

'Oh, but you are.'

'I only want to protect you.'

The words rumbled against her cheek.

'How delightful that sounds.'

'It *is* delightful. Let me protect you from Deforge.'

'How could you do that?'

'I could force a quarrel on him. He is reluctant to meet me, but—'

She sat up, anxiety cutting through her drowsiness.

'No! No, if you do that his lawyer will publish the journal!' She clutched his coat. 'Promise me,' she said urgently. 'Promise me you will not challenge him.'

'How else would you have me deal with him?'

Her head was swimming, but it was imperative that she make him understand.

'I have no idea. I only know that if anything should befall him he has given instructions for the journal to be made public. If that happens—! No, please, Jack; tell me you will not call him out.'

'Very well, if that is your wish.'

She shook her head, wincing a little as something like a brick banged against the inside of her skull.

'No, you must swear it.'

'Very well,' he said solemnly, 'I swear I will not call him out.'

She looked into his eyes, frowning a little because it was so difficult to focus. At last, satisfied, she nodded and subsided against his shoulder once more. Everything seemed such an effort. She closed her eyes as Jack enfolded her in his arms again.

'But I still want to help you fight Deforge.' he murmured the words into her hair.

Secure within the comfort of Jack's arms, Sir Ronald seemed to pose no more threat to her than a troublesome fly. Her hand fluttered as if to swat him away.

'I can deal with him,' she said.

'He is a dangerous man, my dear.'

'To you, perhaps.' Deforge would not hurt her, at least not until he had made her his wife. That thought made her shiver, but she was resolved to wed him, if it was the only way to retrieve the journal. Once the damning evidence was destroyed then she would do what was necessary to escape a husband she hated. But Deforge had threatened to kill Jack. She could prevent that. She could protect him, just as she had always protected Alex and Tony—and now she knew that Jack was as dear to her as either of them. Her hand crept up to rest against his chest. 'Alex wants me to let you help us, but I cannot allow that.'

'Why not?'

She shifted impatiently. She was so tired. Why did he keep asking her questions?

'Because Deforge might kill you. Besides, you might discover the truth.'

'The truth? And what would that be?'

She shook her head.

'Oh, no, I won't be tricked into telling you.'

Even in her sleepy, comfortable state she knew she dare not tell him: he was far too good, too honourable. He would despise her for ever if he knew how deceitful she had been. And he would turn against Alex. She sighed.

'Poor Alex.'

'Why poor Alex?' asked Jack.

Had she spoken aloud? She pressed her lips together. She had drunk too much wine this evening and she must guard her tongue. She must not allow Jack to know any more of her secrets. And she must not allow him to fight Sir Ronald. She gave a little sob and Jack's arms tightened around her.

'Eloise? What is it?

She was drifting into oblivion, but even so she knew it was up to her to keep them all safe. As Sir Ronald's wife she could do that.

'Why poor Alex?' Jack asked again.

She said sleepily, 'I will marry him, and never see you again.'

'Curse it, no!' Jack exclaimed, sitting up.

Eloise remained slumped against him, fast asleep. Damnation, perhaps he should not have given her brandy, but she had been such a pitiful sight, pale and shaking so much he feared she might faint. Growling in frustration, he settled back against the sofa and gathered her against him. So she was going to wed Mortimer. Jack cursed under his breath. They weren't lovers; he knew that only too well. So why had they been at pains to make the world believe otherwise? And why marry now?

It had something to do with that damned journal. What secrets did it hold, if not a catalogue of the lady's scandalous affairs? His mind began to race with outlandish conjecture. Treason, spying, perhaps murder? He could not believe it, but even if it was true, did she think that by marrying Mortimer that would be the end of the matter? Deforge would publish anyway. If the contents were as scandalous as he had been led to believe then what life could she have? Marriage to Mortimer would not save her. They would have to go abroad, to live with the other exiles in Calais or Paris or Rome.

And he would never see her again.

His arms tightened around the slight figure sleeping against his chest. He would not let it happen. Jack put his head back and stared at the ceiling.

'By heaven, what a coil.' He looked down at Eloise, her golden curls resting against his dark coat. She was an enigma. She had been at pains to hide her virginity from the world. She was happy for the world to think her fast and immoral, so what on earth was it that she dare not tell him? She had said it was not her secret, that others were involved. Suddenly he recalled Alex's words: *she was loyal to a fault...spent most of her time rescuing Tony and me from our more outlandish scrapes.* Perhaps she was innocent after all. Perhaps she was merely trying to protect others. It would certainly fit in with what he knew of the lady.

Jack sighed again. Conjecture was useless. There was only one certainty in his mind. She was his, however scandalous her past, and he did not want to see her married to Alex Mortimer.

Chapter Fourteen

Eloise was sitting at the breakfast table, her head on her hands when Noyes announced Major Clifton. Before she could tell him to deny her there was a heavy footstep in the passage and Jack entered the room. His knowing grin annoyed her.

'I did not know if you would be out of bed yet,' he said as the butler closed the door upon them. He eyed the untouched food upon the table and his smile grew.

'I have the most pounding headache,' she told him crossly.

'I am sorry for it.' He took a seat beside her. 'I find that a good meal helps.'

'I could not eat a thing!'

He buttered a piece of toast and handed it to her.

'Oh, I think you can. Try this.'

After a few pieces of toast and two glasses of water Eloise had to admit that she was feeling a little better. She knew she should not be entertaining a gentleman alone at breakfast, but several questions had been nagging at her since she had woken up that morning, and she needed Jack to answer them.

'How did I get home last night?'

Jack poured himself a cup of coffee.

'I brought you home in your carriage.'

'Thank you. I cannot remember leaving Parham House.'

'No, you were asleep at the time. I carried you out.' He grinned at her horrified stare. 'I waited until most of the guests had left, then put it about that you had been taken ill. However, I have no doubt that the Wanton Widow's latest escapade will be the talk of the town this morning.'

She dropped her head back into her hands.

'Until now my...*escapades* have been nothing more than conjecture.'

'And they are still. Your going off with Lord Berrow appears to have attracted little or no comment and by the time we left it was very late. No one can be sure how long we were alone together.'

'We should not have been alone at all!'

'I did not take advantage of your powerless state. Many men would have done so.'

'I know,' she muttered. 'I know and I am grateful to you.' She added in a low voice, 'I do not deserve your kindness.'

He put down his coffee cup.

'Elle—'

She recoiled at the use of her pet name: it was too intimate, too painful.

'No, please,' she beseeched him, 'do not say anything. I am in no fit state to talk to you this morning.'

He took her hand.

'Very well, but we must talk at some point. There must be no more misunderstanding between us.'

His clasp on her fingers was a bittersweet comfort. Once there were no misunderstandings he would not want to be near her.

'Yes, very well,' she said, fighting back tears. 'But not today.'

She looked up as the door opened and Noyes entered.

'This has arrived for you, my lady.'

The butler brought a letter to her on a small silver tray while a footman followed him into the room, carrying a large package. Her smile faded as she recognised the black scrawl upon the note.

'Thank you, Noyes. That will be all. Please, put the box down over there.'

'What is it?' asked Jack, when they were alone again.

Silently she handed him the note.

'Sir Ronald is back,' she said, her voice not quite steady. Steeling herself, she crossed over to the side table and began to open the parcel.

Jack scanned the letter. 'He will be at the Lanchester Rooms tomorrow night and expects you to be there.' She heard the note of disapproval in Jack's tone. 'They hold public balls there. Masquerades.'

'I know it.' She untied the string and lifted the lid of the box. Inside she found an elegantly printed card lying on top of a cloud of tissue. 'He has sent me a ticket. And I presume this is the costume he wants me to wear.'

Jack came over to her and while he perused the card she lifted a heavy silk gown from the box and held it up. The full skirts fell in folds of deep green and orange to the floor.

'It is in the old style,' she said, observing the laced bodice and straight, elbow-length sleeves.

'Even older,' muttered Jack. 'This goes back to the time of the Stuarts. Look at the motif embroidered here.' He lifted out a cream petticoat. 'Oranges. You are to go as Nell Gwyn.'

She stared at him, then turned back to look again at the gown with its wickedly low-cut neckline.

'He wants me to go out in public dressed as a…as a…'

'An orange seller,' supplied Jack. His lips twitched. 'One cannot deny that Sir Ronald has a sense of humour.'

'He is a villain!'

She dropped the gown back into its box as if it was contaminated.

'Then do not go.'

She put out her hands.

'What choice do I have? You have read his letter: if I am not there he says the journal will be public by morning.'

He caught her hand.

'Elle, let him publish! I will take you out of town, tonight if you wish. I can protect you.'

She looked up at him. Her heart contracted at the concern she saw in his face. She reached up and touched his cheek.

'Then you, too, would be tainted by association,' she said softly. 'Besides, there is Alex. He is not fit enough for another long journey.'

He dropped her hand.

'And of course you cannot leave him.'

His cold tone cut at her. She said quietly, 'No. I will not leave him.'

'Yet you will not tell me what it is you have done that is so very terrible.'

She shook her head, not looking up. She heard him sigh.

'Very well, but you cannot go to the Lanchester Rooms unattended. I shall go with you.'

That brought her head up.

'No. It is too dangerous. I will not allow it.'

'Madam, you cannot stop me attending a public ball!'

Eloise looked up into his face, noting the stubborn set to his jaw. With a tired shrug she turned away and rested her hands on the table, bowing her head. Her brain felt so dull that she could not form an argument, especially when in her heart she knew she wanted him with her. She felt Jack's fingers on the back of her neck, rubbing gently, easing her tension.

'You need not be afraid. I will be in disguise. Deforge will not know I am present, but I will be close by if you need me.'

'Well, I must say, my lady, you looks a picture and no mistake.'

Alice stepped back to admire her handwork, a satisfied smile on her face. Standing before the long mirror, Eloise had to admit that the costume supplied by Sir Ronald appeared most authentic. From the brocade shoes with their leather-covered heels to the fontange headdress perched atop her golden curls she looked every inch a king's mistress. A whore. Eloise shivered. A green-and-gold mask had been supplied to hide her identity, but she allowed Alice to apply a coating of powder and rouge to her face to complete the disguise and the result was reassuring: Eloise did not expect to see any of her acquaintances at a public ball, but she would defy even as close a friend as Alex Mortimer to recognise her now.

'Your carriage is at the door, madam.' Alice interrupted her reverie by placing her cloak around her shoulders. 'I shall wait up for you, my lady, and won't rest easy until you are safely returned.'

With a nod and a brief, strained smile, Eloise hurried down the stairs and was soon on her way to Lanchester House.

She had never attended a public ball before and as she walked into the large echoing entrance hall her first instinct was to turn and run back to the safety of her carriage. Not that she could find fault with the bewigged and powdered footmen on duty at the door. Their livery was as fine as any she had seen, but the shrieks and unbridled laughter coming from the masked and disguised guests was very far from the genteel murmur of a *ton* party. Uncultured, nasal voices clashed with the over-refined accents of females whom she suspected to be the wives of wealthy tradesmen, dressed as fine as duchesses and gazing about them in surprise and disapproval at the free and easy manners of some of the revellers.

Eloise wanted to clutch her cloak about her but an insistent footman blocked her way and it was quite clear that she would have to give it up. As she moved to the stairs she put her hand up to her mask to check that the strings were secure, then, squaring her shoulders, she moved up the sweeping staircase towards the huge ballroom, where the strains of a boulanger could just be heard above the noise of the crowd.

In the ballroom she looked about her, dismay in her heart when she observed so many strangers, all attired in gaudy costume. She wondered if Jack was present. Perhaps he was one of the figures disguised head to foot beneath an enveloping domino. A waiter approached and offered her a glass of wine. She waved him away: she needed to keep a clear head tonight. She moved to the side of the room and turned to watch the dancing. It was not yet midnight but already the crowd was very wild. A Harlequin skipped passed and grabbed at her, trying to pull her on to the dance floor. Eloise dragged her hand free and stepped back even further, until she was standing at the edge of a small, shadowed alcove.

'Not inclined to dance tonight?'

Jack's low murmur drew a gasp from her and he added quickly, 'Do not turn. Keep your eyes on the dancers.'

She began to fan herself, holding the sticks high to cover her mouth as she replied,

'How long have you been here?'

'Not long. I saw you come in.'

'I am glad you are here. I did not expect it to be quite so…
raucous.'

'Do not be afraid. I will let no one accost you.'

'Let me see you.' She wanted desperately to look at him.
'How shall I find you?'

She heard him chuckle.

'There are many black dominos here tonight. Best to let
me find *you*.'

'Oh, but—' A laughing couple cannoned into her and she
was knocked back against the wall. They ran on, heedless,
and by the time she had recovered and turned to peer into the
alcove, it was empty.

Eloise wandered around the room. Her low-cut gown was
attracting attention and she studiously ignored the many invitations from gentlemen to dance or to join them for supper.
It was a comfort to know that Jack was nearby, although she
could not see him. Her eyes sought out anyone wearing a black
domino. There were several, but most were far too short to be
Jack. She was so engrossed in her thoughts that she did not
notice the gentleman in an old-fashioned coat and large black
periwig until he spoke to her.

'So you came, Lady Allyngham.'

She stiffened immediately, but knew an irrational desire
to laugh when she looked at the speaker.

'I had no choice.' Her lip curled. 'You see yourself as the
merry monarch, Sir Ronald?'

He bowed.

'It seemed appropriate, since you are Nell Gwyn. Allow
me to say how well you look in that costume, my dear.'

She waved her hand impatiently.

'Say what you have to say and let me leave this place.'

'I want your answer. Will you be my wife?'

'I have not yet decided.'

He placed a hand under her elbow and guided her, none too gently, to the far end of the room, where a series of pillars supported a minstrels' gallery. The area beneath the gallery was not lit, and the heavy columns cast deep shadows across the space. At first Eloise thought the area was deserted, but as her eyes grew accustomed to the gloom she could see that there were couples in each of the shadowy corners, their bodies writhing against the walls. She averted her eyes.

Sir Ronald turned to face her.

'My patience is running low, madam. I have given you time enough to make a decision. You know the consequences of refusing me. Are you prepared to suffer that? Your name disgraced, Mortimer branded a criminal.'

She snapped open her fan and began to wave it angrily.

'I am well aware of the risks, but what you ask...'

His lips parted in an evil grin. She took a step back and found a cold, unyielding pillar behind her.

'Would you rather I traded the journal page by page?' he said, leaning so close that she could feel his breath on her face. She averted her gaze and he continued softly, 'I could do that, you know.' He trailed one finger across the low scoop of her bodice. 'I would give you a sheet from the journal for each night you spend in my bed. As long as you pleased me, of course.' His lips brushed her neck and she froze, gritting her teeth to suppress the shudder of revulsion. He laughed softly. 'You do not like that plan, so I will be generous and honour my original offer: marry me and you shall have the journal immediately.' He grasped her jaw, forcing her to look at him. 'And do not think that you can ask Major Clifton to help you.' He took her arm and turned her towards the room again. 'Oh, yes, I know he is here, thinking he can protect you. Look—' his voice grated in her ear '—that is your precious major over there, is it not? In the black domino. But you see the two rustics on his right, and the piratical figure behind him? They are all my men. I realised at Renwick Hall that Clifton was likely to be a threat so I had him followed. I only have to give the word and they will cut him down like a dog.' Eloise gasped, her hand flying to her mouth. Deforge hissed, 'You have alarmed him. You had best signal to him not to approach. And quickly!'

The tall figure in the black domino had taken a few steps towards her. Behind him a huge bearded man in a pirate's costume was reaching for the gleaming, evil-looking blade in his belt. Frightened, she shook her head. Jack stopped and with a struggle she summoned up a reassuring smile.

Behind her, Sir Ronald murmured, 'Well done. You have averted a tragedy.'

'You would commit murder to achieve your ends?'

'Not I, my lady. It would have been a drunken brawl. No one could connect it to me.'

'You are an out-and-out villain!'

'No, I am merely protecting my interests. You have only to agree to marry me and Clifton will be safe.'

She shook her head and looked at him, bewildered.

'What happiness can there be with a wife that hates you?'

His thick lips parted into a leer and his grip tightened on her arm, the fingers digging into the flesh.

'Schooling you will be part of the enjoyment. And you must not forget that you bring with you the Allyngham fortune. So, madam. Your answer, now, if you please.' She swallowed nervously. A net was closing around her, cutting off every means of escape. At last she said in a low voice, 'You leave me no choice.'

'Then you will marry me. Say it.'

'Yes.' Eloise lifted her head. 'I will marry you.'

His triumphant look made her shudder. She watched him raise his hand, an innocuous gesture but immediately the shepherds and the pirate hovering behind the black domino melted away into the crowd.

'I shall send a notice to the newspapers in the morning, announcing that the wedding will take place on Friday next.' He held out his arm to her. 'My lady?'

She stepped away from him.

'If that is all you have to say to me I shall leave now.' She fixed her eyes upon his face. 'But be warned, sir. If anything happens to Major Clifton I promise you I shall cry off, do what you will with the journal!'

His hateful smile appeared.

'My dear, I think you care for the major even more than your good name. But have you told him what is in that journal? No, I thought not.' He leaned closer. 'Do you suppose the honourable Major Clifton will want any connection with the Allyngham family once he knows the truth?'

'That is none of your concern. I merely want your word that you will not harm him.'

'As long as you stick to our bargain the major is safe, but his continued well-being depends upon you.' He ran a finger down her arm. 'Be a good wife to me and there is no reason why Major Clifton should not enjoy a long and peaceful existence.' He gripped her arm and added, 'If you prove troublesome, however, I will make sure that your precious major meets a very slow and painful death. There are ways, you see; methods that would have even Jack Clifton begging for it to end. Do you understand me, my lady?'

Eloise shook off his hand. She said in a low voice, 'I understand you.'

'Then everyone is happy.' The smug note in his voice angered her but she said nothing and he continued. 'I must hold a party, to celebrate our betrothal. It is short notice, but I believe the *ton* will come, if only out of curiosity. What think you?'

She shrugged.

'Do as you please.'

'Oh, I will. It shall be next Tuesday, at my house in Wardle Street, and I expect you to be at my side. I shall be the envy of the *ton*, shall I not? The man who won the Glorious Allyngham.'

Eloise turned away. She felt slightly sick. Sir Ronald made no attempt to detain her and she hurried out of the ballroom. She was aware of the black domino shadowing her but she ignored him. She did not want to talk to anyone, least of all Jack. She retrieved her cloak and waited impatiently for her carriage to arrive at the door. The black domino had disappeared and her drooping spirits sank even lower. Did he think that now she was leaving she no longer needed his protection? Perhaps he considered his duty done, and had returned to the ballroom to while away the rest of the night with some pretty woman who made no demands upon him.

'Your carriage, m'lady.'

The servant's sonorous tones recalled her wandering thoughts and she went out into the busy street. Her own footman held open the carriage door and she climbed in, closing her eyes with relief as she fell back against the thickly padded seat.

'Thank heaven you are out of there.'

Eloise screamed and opened her eyes. Jack Clifton was sitting in the far corner of the carriage, his black domino merging with the shadows to make him all but invisible.

'I beg your pardon. I did not mean to startle you.'

'How did you get in here?' she demanded.

'I jumped in,' he said. 'From the street side. I want to know what Deforge said to you.'

'Sir Ronald knew you were present,' she replied cautiously. 'His people have been following you.'

'I thought as much.'

'You *knew*?'

She saw a brief flash of white as he grinned.

'That big oaf dressed as Blackbeard has been tailing me for days. His bulk makes him far too easy to spot.'

'But tonight there were others, I saw them.'

'The rustics? I saw them too—I had to throw them off my track before I climbed into your carriage.' He untied the strings of his domino and shrugged it off. 'They need not worry you, my dear.'

'But they might have killed you!'

'Not they! Trust me, they were never a threat to me. Only once have I been taken unawares, and that was by a beautiful woman on Hampstead Heath.'

There was a laugh in his voice but it awoke no response in her. He was far too reckless. If he would not protect himself then she must do so, even if it meant she would never see him again.

'But enough of that,' he said. 'Tell me about Deforge. I didn't like the way he kept leering at you.'

'He is growing impatient,' she responded quietly.

'And?'

Eloise hesitated. Sir Ronald's threats echoed uncomfortably in her head. At last she said, 'He wants my decision soon.'

'Hmm. Word is that he is rolled up and his creditors are pressing for payment. I thought he might have demanded you marry him at once.'

She forced herself to keep her eyes upon Jack. It was very

dark in the carriage, but she would take no chances that he would catch her out in the lie.

'No. Not yet.'

'Not ever!' he growled. 'We will find some way out of this coil that does not involve you giving yourself to that fiend, or marrying Mortimer.'

She blinked.

'M-marrying Alex? How could you ever think I would do that?'

'You said so, at Parham House.'

Eloise was silent. She had only the haziest recollection of what had happened after Jack had rescued her from Lord Berrow. She was afraid she had given herself away and admitted her true feelings: now it appeared that Jack had misunderstood her. He continued harshly, 'If you must marry anyone for expediency, then you will marry me!'

'M-marry you?' she gasped, surprised. 'What, what reason can you have for w-wanting to marry me?'

'Reason!' He gave a crack of laughter. 'If you want reasons—' He raised his hand and counted them off on his fingers. 'Well, for one thing it would foil Deforge, and for another Tony was a good comrade: I owe him my life.'

'That is very chivalrous, sir, but—'

He crossed the carriage to sit beside her. 'Not chivalrous at all, my dear. I have my own plans for you.'

She did not pretend to misunderstand. She swallowed, trying to clear the sudden constriction in her throat. His arm was around her and she allowed herself to lean against him.

'I thought you disapproved of me,' she murmured

He took her hand in his.

'I disapprove of the fact that you will not trust me with your secrets.'

'They are not my secrets to share.'

'Then I will not force them from you, but you must know that I am yours to command, now and always.' He put a hand under her chin and tilted her face up. 'I want you for my wife, Elle. My land isn't in such good heart as Mortimer's but with careful management and a little investment I know we can turn it around.'

We? The word made her heart give a little lurch. If only that were possible.

'I could want nothing better,' she whispered, sighing.

Jack kissed her and she clung to him, returning his kiss with such a passion that when he broke away they were both breathing heavily.

'I have only the one estate, now, plus a few acres at Brighton where I plan to build houses. Little enough to bring you, I know—'

'Do you think I care how wealthy you are?' Her fingers crept up to touch his cheek. 'Let us not talk of it now.'

He reached up and trapped her hand with his own.

'No,' he said thickly, 'Let's not talk.'

He slid his mouth over hers again and instantly she responded, her lips parting as his kiss deepened and she felt herself surrendering. She drove her hands through his thick hair, strong as silk between her gloved fingers. He unfastened her cloak and pushed it away, running his hands over her shoulders, his thumbs caressing her collar bones. Her skin was on fire beneath his touch. Her body remembered the delights of his lovemaking and she was overcome with an urgent need to repeat the experience. He planted a trail of feather-light kisses over her neck and she said, her voice not quite steady, 'When we reach Dover Street, will…will you come in and take a glass of Madeira with me, Major Clifton?'

He lifted his head to look at her. Even in the darkness she

could see the gleam of desire in his eyes. He replied solemnly, 'I would be delighted, my lady.'

She stifled the voice in her head that urged caution. Tomorrow the announcement would be in all the newspapers, everyone would know that she was going to marry Deforge, but tonight—she closed her eyes. Tonight she would enjoy one last night with Jack before he was lost to her for ever.

Chapter Fifteen

Sitting in the darkened carriage with Eloise in his arms, a quiet, joyous elation swept over Jack. She was his, every instinct told him so. Whatever hold Deforge might have on her they would fight it together. When the carriage pulled up in Dover Street he jumped down and handed her out of the carriage. It was as much as he could do not to sweep her up as if she was a new bride and carry her into the house, but instead he must walk quietly beside her, exchanging idle chit-chat while they handed their cloaks to the butler and she requested refreshments to be fetched. Jack prowled around the drawing room while they waited for the butler to return, knowing that if he came within arms' reach of Eloise he would have to kiss her. He was almost painfully aroused, his body ached to hold her but he must go slowly, he must remember that she had little experience of love, despite her reputation. He watched her as she stood before the fire, pulling off her gloves. There was a solemn, almost melancholy cast to her countenance.

'If you want me to leave—'

She glanced up and gave him a fleeting smile.

'No, truly, I want you here.' She turned away as Noyes came in and placed a heavy silver tray upon a table.

'Thank you, you may go now. And, Noyes...'

'Yes, m'lady?'

'You may go to bed. Major Clifton will see himself out.'

'But the bolts, my lady—'

She waved him away impatiently.

'I am quite capable of dealing with those. Now go to bed, if you please. And on your way tell Alice I shall not need her again tonight.'

There was no mistaking the butler's look of mingled shock and surprise. Eloise caught Jack's eye and blushed. She poured two glasses of wine and carried them across the room. Jack watched her, noting the way the wide skirts of her costume swayed with the movement of her hips as she walked. A smile tugged at his mouth.

'That gown suits you, but I do not like your hair to be so artificially contained.'

She stopped before him, a full wine glass in each hand but he made no move to take one from her. Instead he reached out and pulled off the headdress and tossed it aside.

'What are you doing?'

'Making you a little more like a king's mistress.'

Deftly he removed the pins and the gold curls cascaded over his hands. He spread his fingers and eased them into her hair, coaxing it to fall like a golden curtain around her shoulders. He nodded approvingly.

'Much better,' he said.

A shy smile lit her eyes.

'I do not believe Nell Gwyn ever appeared with her hair thus.'

'Not in public, perhaps, but in private. For her lover.'

She blushed profusely. Jack took the glasses from her and put them down on a side table. Time for wine later.

She kept her eyes on his face as he began to unlace the bodice of her gown. Her breasts rose and fell, temptingly close to his fingers but he resisted the urge to run his hands over their soft swell. She stood statue-like while he undressed her. The heavy skirts sank to the floor with a whisper and he continued, slowly discarding her clothes until she stood before him wearing only her chemise and a pair of creamy embroidered stockings.

'Now it is your turn,' he told her, smiling.

Shyly she reached out and began to unbutton his waistcoat. Despite the layers of material between them, her touch sent little darts of heat through his body. He experienced a jolt of excitement when she began to unfasten his breeches and, unable to restrain himself, he pulled her to him, his mouth seeking her lips. They finished undressing by the light of the guttering candles and then he drew her down on to the daybed.

Jack gently pushed her back against the padded silk. She did not resist. She was so trusting he tried to put aside his own urgent desires and concentrate on pleasing her. His kiss was long and languorous and he felt her relaxing, responding to him. When at last he raised his head, his heart sang out at the message he read in her eyes. They were dark and luminous and as he sat up she reached for him, pulling him back down against her. She gave him back kiss for kiss, tangling her tongue with his. Then he released her mouth and began to explore her body with his hands while he trailed kisses over her breasts and down across her stomach. Her body arched beneath him, pliant and yielding, inviting his touch.

Eloise closed her eyes, giving herself up to the sweet pleasure of his caresses. The past and the future were as nothing, she was aware only of the present: the crackling fire, the cool smooth daybed beneath her, Jack's hard body above and the faint, masculine scent of his skin. There was such an excitement building within her, such a cresting wave of joy waiting to burst that she could not keep still. Her body moved of its own accord and her skin was sensitive to the lightest touch. Jack's long fingers explored her, making her gasp with delight. At one point her body seized, and for one heady, heart-stopping moment she could not move, could not breath.

Jack stilled. He raised his head.

'Love?'

'No,' she whispered urgently, 'Go on, go on!'

She began to move against him, an instinctive, primal rhythm that she didn't understand. She wrapped her arms about him, pulling him on top of her, gasping as they were united, their bodies moving as one, faster, harder, the excitement building until they cried out together as the wave finally burst and Eloise clung to Jack as they collapsed back on to the daybed, gasping and exhausted.

Lying snug in the circle of Jack's arms, with his breath ruffling her hair, Eloise was aware of a sudden *tristesse*. The certainty she had felt earlier was gone, replaced by the thought that she should have sent him away. It would have been better not to know the wonder of being loved by Jack Clifton. She stirred. His hold tightened and he placed a soft, sleepy kiss on her cheek. She closed her eyes and pressed herself against him. No, she could not regret it. The memory of this night would be with her, a constant comfort in the bleak future that stretched ahead of her.

A cold, grey dawn was filling the London streets when Jack finally stepped out into Dover Street. His coat and waistcoat hung open and his neckcloth was missing but he didn't care. He felt alive and ready to take on the world. A sudden gust of wind reminded him that winter was on its way and he threw the black domino around his shoulders. Heaven knew what his friends would think if they saw him now. He grinned to himself. They would most likely think he had just left his mistress, and they would be right. Only she was more than his mistress. She was the woman he was going to marry.

When he reached King Street Jack ran up the stairs to his rooms, ignoring his man's remonstrations as he opened the door to him.

'Be done with your scolding, Robert,' he said, throwing himself on to his bed. 'I am going to sleep now, and I'd be obliged if you didn't wake me until at least noon!'

It was in fact some time past midday when Jack eventually awoke, and some hours more before he was bathed and dressed and Robert considered him fit to be seen. Having missed his breakfast, he was extremely hungry and decided to go off to White's to find something to eat.

As he turned into St James Street Jack spotted Sir Ronald Deforge descending the steps of the club. Jack frowned, the memory of the man's dealings with Eloise darkening his mood. He wanted to force a quarrel upon him and put a bullet through his black heart, but the villain had her journal and until Jack knew just what it contained he must go carefully. And he had given her his word he would not force a quarrel. He was thankful that Deforge did not see him, and had strolled away up the road towards Piccadilly before Jack reached the entrance to White's. There would be time enough to deal with Deforge later.

Jack found several acquaintances in the card room; they greeted him cheerfully and invited them to join him.

'Thank you, but no,' he said. 'I need to eat first.' He nodded towards a thin young man sitting by the window, his face as white as his neckcloth. 'What is wrong with Tiverton? He looks as if he is about to cast up his accounts.'

'Dished,' declared Edward Graham, shaking his head. 'He's just lost ten thousand to Deforge.'

'You have to admit the man's luck is in,' wheezed a portly gentleman in a grey bag-wig. 'Last night poor Glaister lost everything he had to him.'

'Well they say luck goes in threes, let's hope he's had his share.' Mr Graham slapped him on the back. 'But it's put paid to your hopes, eh, Clifton?'

Jack smiled.

'What's that, Ned? I don't understand you.'

'The Glorious Allyngham.' Mr Graham pointed to the newssheet lying upon the table. 'Seems Deforge has beaten you to it, old man.'

Bewildered, Jack picked up the newspaper, which was opened to display a large announcement. He stared at it, the letters dancing before his eyes.

'Aye,' said Mr Graham, resuming his seat at the card table. 'So Deforge is to marry Lady Allyngham next week. Damme if I'd have put money against his winning that trick! Waiter, bring me another pack of cards, will you?'

Slowly Jack folded the paper. Then, his appetite forgotten, he turned and walked out of the club.

'Major Clifton, my lady.'

Noyes barely had time to finish his announcement before Jack burst into the morning room. Eloise put down her embroidery and folded her hands in her lap. She had been expecting him, but she was not prepared for the violence she saw in his eyes. Her mouth went dry and she had to moisten her lips before she could speak.

'Won't you sit down, Major?'

He ignored her, and waited impatiently for the butler to close the door upon them before he spoke.

'What the hell is all this about?'

'All what?' She feigned surprise.

'This.' He threw the newspaper into her lap. 'The announcement of your marriage to Deforge. Will you tell me when that was agreed?'

She swallowed nervously and looked away from his furious glare.

'Yesterday. At Lanchester House.'

'And why did you not tell me?'

'Because I knew you would be angry.'

'Hell and confound it, woman, of course I am angry! Even more so because of what happened here last night.'

She rose from her chair.

'Pray lower your voice, sir. Would you have the whole world know our business?'

He laughed harshly.

'Your blatant actions last night can have left your people in no doubt of *our business.*'

She flushed and looked down at her hands. He came towards her and grasped her shoulders. She tensed herself for his tirade, but it did not come.

'Why did you do it, Elle?' His quiet tone flayed her even more than his anger. 'I thought that we understood each other. I thought you loved me.'

Too much to marry you!

The words pounded, unspoken, in her head. She shrugged off his hands and turned away.

'I…forgot myself.'

He pulled her round to face him.

'You must not do this! Send another notice, refute this and announce that you are going to marry *me*.'

Even as she raised her eyes to look at him in her mind she could see Deforge's men closing in, daggers drawn.

'I cannot. I gave him my word. Besides, there is the journal.'

'Ah, yes, that blasted book.' He let her go and took a hasty turn about the room. 'What is it, Elle, what have you done that is so bad you cannot tell me?'

She turned to stare out of the window. It was a bleak day, matching her mood. She said quietly, 'There are others involved: I cannot break faith with them, even for you.'

'So you would give yourself to this, this monster to protect other people. Hand over your fortune to a man who spends most of his day at the card table! Damnation, woman, he has already lost his own fortune and that of his first wife—he may even have driven her to her death! I will not allow it.'

She turned quickly.

'You cannot stop me.'

'I could put a bullet in him!'

'No!' she cried, alarmed. 'You gave me your word!'

'Hah! What do I care for that now?'

Even through her unhappiness she smiled at that.

'But you do,' she said. 'You are a man of honour.'

And I love you for it.

'But I will fight for what is mine.'

She said impatiently, 'Is that how you think of me, a chattel to be fought over and possessed?'

In two strides he was across the room and dragging her into his arms.

'You know it isn't. I think of you as my wife!'

She dug her nails into the palms of her hands to stop herself responding to him.

'No.' She forced out the words. 'I am tired of fighting the inevitable. I am going to marry Sir Ronald. It is agreed and I will not go back on it.'

'Not even for me?'

'Not even for you.'

His arms dropped away from her and the leaden band about her heart squeezed even tighter.

'I see.' He turned away and walked to the fireplace. For a few moments he stared moodily down into the flames. 'Does Mortimer know?'

'Yes. I told him this morning.'

'And he does not object?'

She hesitated, remembering the strong words that had passed between her and Alex. At last she said, 'Of course he objects, but he is still too unwell to do anything to stop me.' She raised her head and directed a look at him. Her heart was breaking but she met his eyes steadily, determined not to show him how much this was costing her. 'I have made my decision, Major Clifton. I…enjoyed our brief liaison, but it is over. Now we must say goodbye.'

She held out her hand. Jack stared at it, scowling blackly, then, without a word, he turned on his heel and left.

Chapter Sixteen

It was only to be expected that Sir Ronald Deforge's party would be the crush of the Season. He brought in his cousin, a colourless little widow of impeccable birth, to act as hostess, and even the creditors who had been baying at his door for the past few weeks had suddenly disappeared, reassured by the news that he was about to become master of the Allyngham fortune.

Any hopes Eloise had that her forthcoming marriage would pass off with little comment were dashed as the carriages turned off Oxford Street and queued up outside Sir Ronald's tall town house, waiting to disgorge their fashionable occupants. The interminable evening began with dinner. Eloise had tried to refuse but Sir Ronald insisted, pointing out that his cousin's presence would prevent any hint of impropriety.

'Although with your reputation I am surprised to find you worrying about *that*,' he said, with a grin that made Eloise long to slap his face.

'Until we are married,' she said frostily, 'we will observe every propriety.'

'Of course, my dear. I can contain my impatience a few more days.'

The dinner was long and cold, despite the dining room being on the ground floor and not far from the kitchen. Sir Ronald's cook was obviously unused to entertaining. The wine, however, was excellent, but she refused to take more than one glass. She was the only guest at dinner and her attempts to make conversation with her hostess could not be deemed a success. The widow was patently in awe of her blustering cousin and made no answer without first looking to Sir Ronald for approval.

'Once we are married I shall expect you to take over the running of my household,' said Sir Ronald, refilling his glass. 'I have no doubt that you are a very capable housekeeper.'

'I could certainly do better than this,' she retorted, pushing a piece of tough and stringy beef to the side of her plate.

'Well, we will not require two cooks when we are in town so I shall turn mine off,' he said. 'But what about the house— shall we live here, or would you rather I moved into Dover Street? You see, I am minded to be magnanimous about these things.'

The thought of Sir Ronald living in Dover Street appalled her. It had been her husband's home, not to mention the memories it held of the night spent in Jack's arms. She could not bear to think of it being desecrated by the boorish animal now sitting at the head of the table.

The meal dragged on, the covers were removed and she was wondering how soon it would be before her hostess gave the signal to retire when Deforge said suddenly, 'Time is getting on. Our guests will be arriving soon and I have something for you. Come along to my study. Oh, don't mind Agnes,' he added, as Eloise's eyes flickered towards her hostess. 'She should be off now to make sure everything is in readiness for our guests. Should you not, Cousin?'

'Oh. Oh, yes, Ronald, immediately.' The thread-like voice could hardly be heard above the scraping back of her chair, and the little woman scuttled away. Sir Ronald picked up a branched candlestick and walked to a door at the far end of the dining room. Eloise hung back.

'How do I know this is not a trick?'

'What need have I of tricks? In three days' time you will be mine, you have given me your word. Now, if you please, madam.'

He led her up the stairs and past the main salon to a room at the back of the house. At the door he stopped.

'No one enters here without permission,' he said, fishing in his pocket for a key. 'Not even my valet.'

The room was very dark, and Sir Ronald held the candles aloft as he entered. The light flickered over a large wing chair and across a number of tall bookcases. Eloise glanced about her nervously: a tall chest of drawers stood against one wall with a wooden-framed mirror and a number of small objects on the top. In the dim light she thought perhaps they might be snuff-boxes and scent bottles. She edged back towards the open door.

'This is your dressing room.'

'It is used for that purpose, yes, since it adjoins my bed-chamber. Perhaps you would like to see where we will spend our wedding night?'

She fought down her panic.

'With the first of the guests about to arrive I think we should return to the salon with all speed,' she retorted.

Sir Ronald shrugged and moved towards the large mahogany desk by the window.

'I realised I have not given you a ring to seal our betrothal,' he said. He put down the candlestick and unlocked the centre drawer. Eloise watched as he pulled out a small leather box. 'I have no family heirlooms to give you, so I have bought you this.' He laughed. 'Let there be no secrets between us now, my dear. To tell you the truth I have it on credit, the jeweller knowing that I shall pay him just as soon as your fortune passes into my hands!'

He opened the box and held it out to her.

'There, I knew you would like it. Never met a woman who could resist a trinket.'

Eloise's gasp was genuine, but it was not the large diamond ring winking in the candlelight that had caused her exclamation. She had watched Sir Ronald pushing aside the contents of the drawer to get to the ring box, and nestling amongst the clutter she had seen a small, leather-bound book bearing the Allyngham crest.

Quickly she raised her eyes and gave Sir Ronald what she hoped was a warm smile.

'It is quite…breathtaking,' she said, moving around the desk. 'May I wear it now?'

'Of course.' Delighted, he pulled the ring from the box and slipped it on to her finger.

'There, now you have something to show the tabbies tonight.'

He shut and locked the drawer again, slipping the key into his pocket. She heard the thud of the knocker, and the sound of feet running down the stairs. Sir Ronald looked up.

'Now, shall we go and greet our guests?'

Eloise stood between Sir Ronald and his cousin as a steady stream of people made their way up the stairs towards her. Her smile was pinned in place and she greeted them all mechanically. If she had not been so busy with her own thoughts she might have felt a little self-conscious of their stares. Everyone was curious to know what lay behind the sudden betrothal, but her mind was elsewhere, thinking about what she had seen in the study. By walking around the desk she had managed to take a quick look through the unshuttered window. A pale moon illuminated the night, showing her that the room looked out on to a narrow yard bounded by a high brick wall. Half the space was taken by a small outbuilding that butted against the wall of the house, its roof only a few feet below the window ledge. And the journal was in the desk drawer. For the first time in days she began to feel a glimmer of hope.

'I am disappointed,' said Sir Ronald as he escorted Eloise through the crowded rooms. 'I know your friend Mortimer is indisposed, but I had hoped that Major Clifton would be here.'

'I do not see why he should be,' she replied shortly. 'He is no friend to you.'

'But I made sure to send him an invitation, because I know he is a special friend of *yours*,' he purred.

'You are mistaken.'

He turned to look down at her, an evil smile curling his lips.

'What is this, a lovers' quarrel, perhaps?' When she did not reply he laughed softly and patted her hand. 'What a pity. I had hoped he would be here tonight: I wanted him to know just what he had lost. But never mind, my love, I may even allow you to take him as a lover again, if he will have you once I have done with you.'

Disgusted, Eloise pulled her arm free and went her own way. The rooms were so crowded she thought it might be possible to spend the rest of the evening without talking to Sir Ronald. His comments about Jack Clifton had touched a raw nerve. She had heard nothing from him since he had walked out of Dover Street. A casual enquiry of Alex had elicited the information that Jack was preparing to leave town. Alex had questioned her closely, had asked if she and Jack had quarrelled and she had been at pains to laugh it off, but secretly she was forced to conclude that she had succeeded in driving Jack away.

Nothing of her melancholy thoughts showed in her face as she circled the room, talking and laughing with everyone. By the end of the evening her cheeks ached with the effort of smiling. She was so tired she could hardly stand and there was no attempt at deception when she told Sir Ronald that she was too exhausted to remain another moment, once the last of the guests had quit the house.

'If that is the case,' he said, 'then surely it would be easier to walk to my bedchamber than to take your carriage to Dover Street.'

She had no energy to prevaricate. He merely laughed at her look of revulsion.

'Very well, my sweet. Go home and rest.' He placed her cloak about her shoulders. 'I am engaged to dine at the Forbes' tomorrow night: Mrs Forbes did send me a little note to say that, having seen the announcement of our engagement, I might bring you with me, but it is a long drive to Edgeware and I want you to be looking your best for Keworth's party on Thursday.'

'Thursday! But we are to be married on Friday. I need to prepare.'

'No. You will accompany me to Keworth House. His lordship's parties are always well attended. I want everyone to see you at my side.'

She grimaced.

'A card party! I have no interest in gambling.'

'But I have, and I want you beside me. You need not play.' He ran a finger down her arm. 'You may stand by my chair and bring me good fortune!' He laughed as she shrugged him off. 'I want everyone to see that I am lucky in cards *and* in love!'

With barely a nod she left him, and made her way downstairs to the tiled hall, where a vacuous-looking footman was waiting by the door.

'Your carriage is sent for, m'lady, but it ain't here yet,' he mumbled as she approached.

Eloise gave him a tired smile and moved towards a large button-backed arm chair. 'Then I shall sit here and wait. Unless, of course, this is your seat?'

The lackey jumped and looked a little flustered. She suspected he was unused to being addressed in anything but the curtest of terms.

'No, m'm, that seat's only used by Stevens, the master's valet, when he waits up for Master to come in o' nights.'

'Well, it is very comfortable. I have no doubt Mr Stevens has a little sleep while he is waiting for his master, what do you think?' She twinkled up at him and the lackey flushed, shifting uncomfortably from one foot to the other. Then he nodded.

'Aye, m'm, I think he does. Ah, and here's your carriage now, m'lady.'

Eloise hurried out, relieved to be leaving the gloomy and oppressive house at last. But the depression that had enveloped her for much of the evening had lifted. She had a plan.

Alex Mortimer was stretched out on the daybed in his morning room, struggling to eat his breakfast one-handed when Eloise was shown in.

'Thunder and turf, Elle, you cannot come in here!'

'Fustian,' she replied calmly, pulling off her gloves. 'Farrell told me you were going to get up today.'

'Yes, but I am not yet dressed. It is most improper for you to walk in here as if we were related. I won't have it!' He gave her a quick, searching look from under his brows. 'Unless you have come to tell me you're not going to marry Deforge after all.'

'No, I am not going to tell you that, although I hope now it might not be necessary.' She could not quite keep the excitement out of her voice. 'The journal is at his house, Alex! I saw it in his desk when I was there last night. I suppose he had his lawyer deliver it, ready for the wedding on Friday.'

'Very likely.'

'Or perhaps it has been there all the time,' she mused, 'and he only told me otherwise to make sure no harm came to him. It is in his study, which is at the back of the house, on the first floor.'

'And what has that to say to anything?'

'Well, it should not be too difficult to break into that room and take the journal.'

Alex's knife clattered on to his plate.

'*Are you out of your mind?* You know the penalty for stealing!'

'The journal is not Sir Ronald's property, and once it is destroyed—'

'Eloise, you know if I was fit I would do this for you, but it is as much as I can do to climb the stairs at the moment.'

She looked at him, her bottom lip caught between her teeth.

'I thought, perhaps, you might speak to Major Clifton for me…'

'Well, you thought wrong,' he retorted brutally. 'Jack has left town.'

'L-left?' A chill rippled through her, starting in her core and spreading rapidly throughout her body. 'He's gone?'

'Yes. When he came to see me yesterday he said he was off to Staffordshire.' Alex scowled at her. 'I take it you quarrelled with him.'

'Not, not quarrelled, exactly.' She looked down at the gloves held tightly between her fingers. 'He was very angry about my marrying Sir Ronald and I told him it was none of his business.'

'What? After all he's done for us?'

'No, what he has done for *you*,' she flung at him, angry colour burning her cheeks. She was filled with a disappointment as bitter as gall. 'As far as I am concerned, Jack Clifton has been nothing but a nuisance!'

'Oh, nuisance, is it? Well you had best look at what he's left you, over there.' He waved towards the side table. 'I was going to bring it to you later today but since you are here you may as well read it now.'

Eloise picked up the letter and broke open the seal. The thought flashed through her mind that Jack had written to her, but the hand was unfamiliar, and as that first flare of hope died away she had to concentrate to make sense of the words. Alex pushed aside his breakfast tray and waited for her to finish reading. At last she looked up.

'I don't understand,' she said slowly. 'This is from Lord Berrow, agreeing to the sale of Ainsley Wood.'

Alex nodded.

'Aye. Jack brought it round to me last night.'

'But...but why did he not bring it to me?'

'He said he didn't want to see you again, and from what you have just told me I can't say I blame him! He persuaded Berrow to sell you the land so you can build the road to your foundling hospital. Jack suggested you should get the papers signed today. Once you marry Deforge you will lose control of Allyngham and your fortune.'

Hot tears pricked at her eyelids.

'Oh. That was so very good of him.' She hunted for her handkerchief.

'You were a damned fool to turn Clifton away, Elle.'

'What else could I do? Deforge threatened to kill him if he interfered.'

'I would back Jack Clifton against a dozen men like Deforge.'

She shook her head.

'I could not take that risk. Until last night I thought that any attempt to thwart Sir Ronald would result in the journal being published, and if M-Major Clifton was involved then he would be implicated in our disgrace.'

'So you sent him away.'

'Yes.' Eloise wiped her eyes. 'It is done, and that's an end to it.' She looked again at the paper. 'But I do not understand: after my last…meeting with Lord Berrow I was sure he would not sell. What made him change his mind?'

Alex grinned.

'Jack saw him coming out of the house at the end of the street. Kitty Williams's house.'

She stared at him.

'But Mrs Williams is a…'

'Exactly. Jack made a few enquiries, found that for a price the fair Kitty was more than willing to divulge all the sordid details of Lord Berrow's visits to her establishment. Then he went to see the old hypocrite and told him that if he didn't want the whole world to know about his dealings with that Cyprian and her sisters, he should sell you Ainsley Wood.'

'And Lord Berrow agreed?'

'Aye, immediately, Jack said. It seems he was eager to

protect his reputation. He was especially anxious that his friend Wilberforce should not find out about it, nor his wife.'

'Then, then we can go ahead with the foundling hospital.' She folded the paper and put it in her reticule. 'That is wonderful news. I must write to the major and thank him—'

'No.' Alex interrupted her. 'Jack said to tell you he wants no thanks from you. He is doing this for Tony, because he wants a lasting memorial for a fallen comrade. I think you have hurt him very badly, my dear.'

'I know.' She put her hands to her cheeks. 'I know, and I am sorry for it. But it is not as if he l-loved me.'

'No?'

She heard the disbelief in Alex's tone and she shook her head.

'No. He told me himself that he was in love with Sir Ronald's first wife. That is why he is so keen to challenge Deforge.'

'That may of course be an added reason—'

'It is the *main* reason,' she interrupted him. 'My reputation is sadly tarnished, Alex.'

'But Clifton knows now it was all a lie—!'

'But the world believes it, Alex! How could a man as good, as honourable as Jack Clifton live with that, when he has carried the memory of a sweet, innocent woman in his heart for so many years?'

Alex did not answer and a long silence fell over the room. She struggled to smother her unhappiness. She had succeeded only too well: Jack Clifton had left town and he wanted nothing more to do with her. He was safe from Deforge and his henchmen. That was what she had planned, so she had no reason to feel aggrieved, and certainly no reason to be surprised. He was gone. Even now she could feel the loneliness settling over her like a heavy cloak. Eloise squared her shoulders: there would be time for tears later. Now she had to decide just how to proceed.

She looked at Alex. He still had one arm in a sling and by his own admission he was unable to walk more than a few steps. He could not help her. There was only one solution. Having made up her mind, she looked up, saying brightly, 'I had best take this paper to my lawyer and have him deal with it immediately.'

'And what of the other business—the journal?'

'You must not worry about that, Alex.'

'I always worry when I see that look on your face.'

She gazed at him, her eyes very wide.

'What look?'

'That innocent, butter-would-not-melt look. I insist that you tell me what you are planning, madam. No, don't walk out on me—Elle—*Eloise*!'

But she was already at the door and as she closed it behind her she heard his angry exclamation and the clatter as his breakfast tray slid to the floor.

Chapter Seventeen

Jack was putting the finishing touches to his neckcloth when he heard voices on the stairs outside his rooms. He nodded to Robert.

'Go out and send them away. Tell them I've already left town!'

He shrugged himself into his waistcoat, scowling as he heard the low rumble of voices growing louder. Damn Robert, could he not even obey a simple order?

'Sir, 'tis Mister Mortimer, and he says he knows you are here and he must speak with you.'

Jack's frown turned to a look of exasperation as he watched Alex limping into the room.

'What the devil are you doing here?' he demanded. 'You are as pale as your shirt!'

He quickly lifted the half-filled portmanteau from the chair. 'You had best sit down.'

Alex was leaning heavily on his stick and with a grimace he lowered himself on to the chair.

'Yes, well, I wasn't planning on coming this far today!'

'You walked here? Damned fool.'

'No, of course I didn't walk! I took a cab, but just those stairs to get up here have taken their toll.'

Jack waved his hand impatiently.

'And what has brought you here? I don't suppose you came to see me off.'

'It's Elle,' said Alex without preamble. '*I* can't help her, so I need you to do so.'

Jack looked towards Robert, dismissing him with the slightest movement of his head. 'Does Lady Allyngham know you are here?'

Alex shook his head.

'She came to see me this morning, and I did as you asked. I told her you had already gone.'

'Thank you. Now I suggest you go home and let me get on with my packing.'

'But this is important, Jack!'

'Not to me! I am done with her. She does not want my help; she has made that very plain on more than one occasion.'

'This is not about what Elle *wants*. I am afraid she is going to do something foolhardy.'

Jack gave a bitter laugh.

'There would be nothing new in that! No, she has chosen her path. God knows I tried to befriend her. I even thought— but she is done with me. She is going to marry Deforge. I won't try to stop her.'

'But the fellow's a rogue!'

Jack shrugged. 'I have told her what I think of the man,' he said coldly. 'If she chooses to ignore it then I can do nothing to help her. I only hope she fares better than his first wife.'

Alex waved his good hand.

'I am not talking about her marriage,' he said impatiently. 'I think she has conceived some madcap scheme to recover the journal!'

Jack looked at the pale face staring up at him and bit back a stinging retort.

'Alex, tell me why I should put myself out any more for this woman? She is not at all grateful for anything I have done so far and at our last meeting she made it very clear that she wanted nothing more to do with me.'

'I thought you loved her.'

Jack looked away. He picked up his brushes from the dressing table and threw them into the portmanteau.

He said coldly, 'It is impossible for me to love someone who is not honest with me.' He turned, subjecting Alex to a fierce glare. 'From the very beginning she has refused to share her secrets with me. I wanted to help her—hell and damnation, I wanted to *marry* her, regardless of the crimes she may have committed in the past, but I am convinced now that there is no future for us. She is determined not to confide in me. She does not trust me.' He snapped shut the portmanteau. 'All she will say is that the secrets are not hers to share.'

'She is correct,' said Alex slowly. 'But they *are* mine. And I will share them with you.'

There is an hour when the fashionable London streets to the west of the City are silent and deserted, between the night-soil cart rumbling through to collect the pails and the moment when the cook's boy emerges, yawning, and waits to follow his master to the market.

Eloise stood in the shadows, looking across the street at Sir Ronald's imposing town house. The windows were dark and the only light from the house was the dim glow of a lamp shining through the fanlight. With her heart thudding heavily against her ribs, she slipped across the road and into the deep shadows of a side alley. She ran freely and realised with some little shock that it was more than ten years since she had last worn breeches. She had bought them that afternoon at one of the less fashionable bazaars off Bond Street. Her maid had been surprised at her purchases but she had explained that she was buying a set of clothes as a present for a young relative. Even as she counted along the windows to find the right house, part of her mind was thinking of what she might do with the clothes when this night's work was over. *If* she was successful.

The third set of windows from the alley belonged to Sir Ronald's house. Everything was in darkness. She had been watching the house for some time, and thought that by now everyone would be asleep, even Sir Ronald's valet, who would be dozing in his chair by the front door. She only hoped that his master would not come back early: it was well known that Josiah Forbes preferred dancing and theatricals to cards, but he and his wife were exceedingly rich and influential, so those receiving an invitation to one of their select little parties deemed it expedient to make the long drive out to Edgeware. For once she was thankful that her reputation as the Wanton Widow had so far spared her that treat.

She crept along the dark, narrow alley, trying not to think of the dirt and debris beneath her shoes. The brick wall was a good six feet high, but she had climbed higher. Not for a long time, of course: not since she was a girl, making up wild adventures at Allyngham with Tony and Alex. How long ago that seemed now!

'Can I help you over the wall, my lady?'

Eloise smothered a scream as she spun around to peer at the black shape towering over her. It was far too dark to see, but there was no mistaking the deep, mellow voice, and even as her heart settled back into a steady beat she felt her fear subsiding.

'Jack! What are you doing here?' she hissed.

'I have come to help you.'

Her spirits lifted. She said gruffly, 'I thought you had left town.'

'No. Alex was worried about you and since he is not fit enough to help you, it seems I must.'

The elation she had felt a moment ago was somewhat dimmed. Could it be that Jack was doing this for Alex's sake? From his angry tone it seemed likely. She reached out in the darkness and gripped at his coat with her fingers.

'You must go away, Jack, now,' she urged him. 'It is far too dangerous for you. If *I* am caught, then Sir Ronald may be angry, but he will still want to marry me to gain control of my fortune. I may even be able to placate him, if I am alone...'

He silenced her by pressing his fingers to her lips.

'Let us be quite clear about one thing, madam, you are *not* marrying Deforge, whether we succeed tonight or we fail. Now no more talking or the sun will be rising before we get out of here!'

His tone brooked no argument. Eloise allowed herself to be lifted up on to the wall and she nimbly swung her legs over and dropped to the ground on the other side. Jack followed a moment later. Fitful moonlight illuminated the yard in shades of blue and black, and she concentrated on finding the best route up to the study window. She scrambled on to a water barrel and from there climbed on to the roof of the outhouse. Her soft shoes made no noise on the tiles: she gave a fleeting smile, remembering Alice's comments that a pair of solid leather boots would be more fitting for a schoolboy than dancing slippers. That, of course, was before she had shocked her maid into silence by explaining the real reason for her purchases.

The moon slipped behind a thick cloud, plunging her into momentary darkness and she stopped, unable to see her way.

She felt Jack's hand on her shoulder, steadying her. As the darkness eased she moved forwards until she was standing directly beneath the study window. When she had been inside the room with Sir Ronald she had noted that the window had a new sash frame, secured only by a brass fastener. She took out her penknife and reached up, planning to slide it between the two frames and push back the fastener. Behind her she heard a faint snort and Jack leaned close to breathe his words into her ear.

'You need to grow another six inches to reach the catch, my dear. Allow me.'

In an instant the deed was done and Jack was carefully pushing open the window. Another moment and they were both standing in Sir Ronald's study. The moon shone directly in through the window, bathing the room in a silvery light and making it unnecessary for Eloise to use the tinderbox and candle she had thoughtfully tucked into her pocket. She moved swiftly to the desk, penknife in hand, but once again Jack forestalled her.

'Did your education include picking locks?' he whispered.

'Of course not.'

'Then let me do this. If we are careful no one will know we have been here.'

From his pocket he drew a thin length of wire. It was bent at one end and he carefully inserted it into the drawer lock. He gently moved the wire until she heard a faint but distinct click and Jack pulled open the drawer.

'Where did you learn that?' she breathed, wide-eyed.

He turned his head to grin at her.

'Some of the men in my regiment came from the stews and rookeries of London. They would have been very much at home here.' He reached into the drawer and lifted out a

small, leather-bound volume. 'Is this what you have been looking for?'

With shaking hands Eloise took the book and ran her
thumbs over the embossed cover. An ornate letter *A* was
enclosed in a circle of acanthus leaves: the Allyngham family
crest. Quickly she pushed the journal inside her jacket.

'Thank you,' she whispered, fastening the buttons of her
coat. 'Let us go now.'

She watched Jack slide the drawer back into place and lock
it again. He straightened, looking around him as he put the
metal rod back into his pocket. Eloise touched him arm.

'We must go,' she hissed.

Jack raised his hand. He was looking towards the wing
chair, where a shaft of moonlight fell upon a bundle of straps
lying over one arm. He walked over and picked them up.
Eloise thought at first it might be a belt, or a dog's leash, but
when Jack held it up she saw the straps were connected into
an intricate webbing.

'What is it? It looks very much like a pony's head-collar,
only it is far too small.'

'This is no head-collar,' murmured Jack, carefully draping
the harness back over the arm of the chair. 'It is something
much more interesting than that.'

There was a thud from somewhere below and she froze,
her heart beating so hard she thought it might break through
her ribs.

'The front door,' hissed Jack. 'It must be Deforge returned.
Quickly!'

He pushed Eloise towards the window. She slithered out on
to the roof and descended hastily to the yard with Jack close
behind her. He threw her up over the wall and she huddled
in the shadows until he joined her. As soon as he reached the

ground he took her hand and they set off at a run out of the alley.

Jack did not stop until they had crossed Oxford Street and were out of sight and sound of the highway, where carts and wagons were beginning to make their way into the town. At last he slowed his pace and Eloise was able to catch her breath. She pulled her hand from his grip and leaned for a moment against the wall. She felt very light-headed. When she had set out that night she had been nervous, but determined upon her course of action: as soon as Jack had appeared her fear had diminished—in a strange sort of way she was even enjoying their adventure.

Jack was watching her, his hands on his hips and his feet slightly apart. She was pleased to note that he, too, was breathing heavily. In the dim light she realised that he had come dressed for the night's work: he had replaced his modish jacket and light pantaloons with a tight-fitting black coat, black breeches and stockings, and instead of his snowy white neckcloth he wore a dark woollen muffler wrapped around his neck. She glanced down at her own apparel and a quiet laugh shook her.

'We look like a couple of housebreakers!'

'We *are* a couple of housebreakers.'

'Are we safe now, do you think?' she asked him.

He took her arm again.

'As safe as one can be on the streets of London at this time of night,' he retorted, making her walk on. 'Of all the ill-judged starts! Don't you know how dangerous it is to come out alone at night?'

She put up her chin.

'How do you know I didn't take a cab to Wardle Street?'

'Because I followed you.'

She pulled her hand free and stared up at him. The flaring

street lamp cast deep shadows across his face. Eloise could not
see his eyes but she could almost feel the anger burning there.

'Alex told me you had left town.'

He let out a long breath, as if controlling his temper.

'That was my intention. I was finishing my packing when
Mortimer came to tell me he was anxious about you.'

'But he knew nothing of my plans!'

'He knows *you*. Once he learned you were not accompanying Deforge to Edgeware this evening he guessed you were
up to something. I merely had to watch your house until you
made your move. I was not fooled when a slip of a lad emerged
from the servants' door in the middle of the night.'

He began to walk on again, and she fell into step beside
him.

'Then I am very grateful to you.' She tucked her hand into
the crook of his arm. 'I am *very* glad you came, Major.'

He put his hand up and briefly clutched the fingers resting on
his sleeve and her spirits rose a little. Perhaps he was not quite
so angry with her. She glanced around, suddenly anxious.

'Sir Ronald's men, the ones who were following you—'

'No need to worry about them any longer. They are even
now on their way to the coast where they will be pressed into
service on one of his Majesty's frigates.' His wicked grin
flashed. 'Deforge is not the only one who has fellows willing
to carry out his more—er—dubious orders.'

'Oh.' She digested this in silence for a few moments.

'I shall write to Sir Ronald immediately,' she said, 'to ter-
minate our engagement.'

'No, do not write to him just yet. I was careful to close the
window when we left so I hope our visit to Sir Ronald's house
will not be noticed, and if that is the case I do not believe he
will discover the loss of the journal immediately. I understand

he is attending the Keworths' party tomorrow, that is, tonight. Do you go with him?'

'Yes, I am engaged to join him there, but now—'

'I want you to go, Eloise. Act as if nothing has changed. I have a plan to rid the town of Sir Ronald Deforge for good, but it will work best if he does not suspect anything.'

When they turned into Dover Street, Eloise noticed that the lights were still burning in Kitty Williams's house.

'I have not thanked you for securing Ainsley Wood for me,' she said. 'For making Lord Berrow agree to sell it.'

'I want no thanks for that.'

'You have been very good to me. It is more than I deserve, after I was so impolite in sending you away.'

'Hush, now. We will talk later.' They were opposite her house and Jack stopped. 'When you get inside, make sure you burn that damned book.'

'I will.'

He led her across the road and followed her down the area steps to the basement door. The scrape of the bolt told Eloise that her maid had been looking out for her. She looked back at Jack.

'Will you not come in?'

'No, dawn is breaking and I must get back. I would have no one guess just what we have been doing this night.'

She was disappointed, and her hand fluttered as if to detain him. He caught it and held it for a moment.

'You have the journal now. Destroy it before it can cause any more harm.' He raised her fingers to his lips. 'And no sooner have we secured the good name of Allyngham than I shall be asking you to change it!'

Eloise sat before the kitchen fire, tearing sheets from the leather-bound book on her lap and feeding them into the flames.

'Never seen anything like it, in all my born days,' muttered Alice, bustling around behind her. 'Running about the town dressed as a boy and breaking into houses! Why, miss, I've never heard of such a thing. Even Master Tony's most outlandish tricks never included thievery!'

'Enough, Alice,' said Eloise, frowning. 'I told you I was merely recovering my property, it was not stealing.'

'And heaven knows what would have become of you if Major Clifton hadn't been there to protect you. Still, all's well that ends well, as they say, and now that you have burned that book you have no need to marry nasty Sir Ronald Deforge. I must say I was never in favour of that, even when you explained to me why it must be so. And unless my ears was deceiving me, it's Mrs Clifton you'll be before the year's out. You couldn't wish for more, could you, my lady?'

Eloise did not reply. She pushed the last of the pages into the fire and sat back. The euphoria of the last few hours had melted away, replaced by a heavy depression.

There was no mistaking Jack's last words; he meant to marry her, but even if his plan worked and Deforge was no longer a threat, she must still tell him the truth about her marriage. He had not asked to read the journal: he was willing to forget her past but she could not. He had said he wanted no secrets. Well, there would be none.

An inner demon whispered that it was not necessary: Jack need never know. She clasped her hands together so tightly the knuckles showed white in the firelight. No. He had to know. If he loved her then perhaps it would not matter, but she was not sure how deeply he cared for her. He desired her, she knew that, but love—she dared not believe it. She was an obligation, the widow of a comrade, left to his care. And perhaps part of her attraction was the fact that in marrying her, Jack could thwart Sir Ronald. But could Jack really love her for herself? She found it hard to accept. She was so different from his first love, the incomparable Clara. She trusted him not to expose her, but once he had taken his revenge upon Sir Ronald, once he no longer needed her help, she must tell him the truth about herself, and give him the chance to walk away.

So you would throw away your chance of happiness. The demon in her head would not be silenced. *Do you think he can love you, once you have shattered his opinion of Tony and destroyed his friendship with Alex? You have only to keep quiet and you can all be happy.*

'No. I will not lie to him.'

'I beg your pardon, my lady?'

Eloise started, blushing as she realised she had spoken aloud.

'Nothing, Alice.' She pushed herself out of the chair. Suddenly she felt desperately tired. 'It is time for bed, I think.'

Chapter Eighteen

A sleepless night did nothing to relieve Eloise's depression, but neither did it shake her resolve to tell Jack everything. And once the truth was out, she doubted very much if he would want her for his wife.

She dressed quickly and dashed off a note to Alex, telling him that the diary had been destroyed and asking him to call. She sent her groom to deliver the message and remained at the window, watching, until his return.

'Well,' she demanded, 'did he send me an answer?'

Perkins tugged his forelock.

'Mr Alex says to give you his regards, m'lady, but I'm to tell you that he is gone out with Major Clifton and he will see you at Keworth House tonight.' The groom nodded, smiling. 'I must say it is good to see Master Alex looking so well, ma'am. Left off his sling, he has, but he is still using a cane.' He winked at her. 'He'll do his best to put that aside before he has to walk you to the altar and give you away, I'll be bound!'

'That is enough of your insolence, Perkins, you may go now!'

Eloise hunched her shoulder and turned away from the groom's knowing grin. That was the problem with having retainers one had known since childhood, they were more like family than servants. Her irritation died away: at least she would still have Perkins and Alice to keep her company in her lonely future. She put a hand up to her cheek, her dilemma growing greater the more she considered it. By confessing everything to Jack she could lose Alex's friendship, too, once he realised she had divulged the truth.

These depressing thoughts combined with her fears that Deforge might discover the theft and call upon her. She tried to stay calm, telling herself that there was no longer any danger, but she knew that Deforge was capable of revenging himself upon those who moved against him. Jack might have removed some of Sir Ronald's henchmen, but there would be others. Her anxiety made the day one of the longest Eloise had ever spent and it was with some relief when the time came to change her dress and order her carriage to take her to the Keworths' card party.

'Shall I be coming with you, m'lady?' asked Perkins, when she descended the stairs, the candles glinting from the diamond cluster at her neck and the tiny diamond drops hanging from her ears.

Eloise looked at the groom as he stood before her, twisting his cap in his hands. She had received no word from Jack or Alex all day, and at that moment Perkins seemed to be her only friend in the world.

'Yes, if you please,' she nodded. 'Jump up on the back and stay with the carriage.'

Keworth House was ablaze with light when the Allyngham town coach rumbled up to the door. Reluctantly she prepared to alight. She had no idea what Jack was planning. He had

asked her to trust him and she would do so, but once this
was over she knew he would ask her to marry him, and she
would have to tell him the truth. In her imagination she saw
the blaze of desire die from his eyes, to be replaced by a look
of revulsion. It could not be avoided. Better now than in the
future.

A light drizzle was falling. She put up her hood and grasped
her cloak about her, glad that the chill night air gave her some
excuse for her trembling. However, once she was inside the
house there was no escape: she was obliged to straighten her
shoulders and make her way to the main salon, no sign of her
inner anxiety showing in her face.

The news of her betrothal was still the talk of the town
and there were more congratulations to be endured as she
made her way up the grand staircase. She was relieved to
move into the candle-lit salon where dozens of little tables had
been set up and nothing more than a gentle murmur disturbed
the players who were intently studying their cards. Lord and
Lady Keworth were renowned for their card parties. In the
past Eloise had always declined their invitations because she
found nothing to amuse her in games of chance, but looking
around the room she realised how few of her acquaintance
shared her view, for the cream of society was seated around
the room.

'We are delighted to have you join us tonight, Lady Allyngham,' her hostess beamed. 'We are very fortunate to have so
many friends here tonight.' Lady Keworth bent an arch smile
towards Lord Berrow, who was passing at that moment. 'You,
too, are a veritable stranger to our little parties, my lord.'

Unable to ignore his hostess, the Earl stopped and gave a
little bow.

'It is unfortunate that I am so often otherwise engaged...'

Lady Keworth laughed and tapped his arm.

'Well, I am very glad that you are not engaged elsewhere this evening, sir, especially when we have such delightful company.' She glanced towards Eloise, gave her an encouraging smile then turned away to greet another guest.

Lord Berrow looked around him, clearly uncomfortable to be left in Lady Allyngham's company. She held out her hand to him.

'My lord, I am glad we have met: I wanted to thank you personally for allowing me to buy Ainsley Wood. It was very generous of you.'

His lordship flushed.

'Oh, yes, well,' he muttered, 'it is in a good cause, after all.'

'Indeed it is, sir,' she replied warmly. 'When the trustees are drawing up their records I shall make sure your generosity is recognised.'

With an inward smile she watched him puff out his chest.

'Oh, no need for that, dear lady,' he said, looking considerably more cheerful. 'We must all do a little something for those less fortunate, eh?'

He gave a fat chuckle and looked as if he would say more but Sir Ronald's voice cut across the room.

'Ah, and here is my lovely bride. Come along over here, my dear, and join us.'

Play was suspended as everyone's eyes were fixed upon Eloise. Not by a flicker did she betray her nerves. She nodded to Lord Berrow and moved across to Sir Ronald. He was sitting at a table with several other gentlemen, including his host and Mr Edward Graham. Lord Keworth rose and began to offer Eloise his chair but Sir Ronald waved at him.

'Sit ye down, sir. Lady Allyngham ain't one for cards, are

you, my dear?' He reached out and caught her wrist, pulling her closer. 'She will stand beside me, my lucky charm.'

'Damme, sir, I think you may need it,' laughed Mr Graham, giving Eloise a good-natured bow. 'There are a number of gamesters here tonight, ma'am, some of 'em quite reckless. The game is bassett, you know: I fear the play will be very deep.'

She glanced around at them all and managed a smile.

'Then pray be seated, gentlemen and go on with your game. Sir Ronald is quite correct, I am more than happy to observe the play, if you will let me.'

'Bless you, my lady, of course you may watch,' declared Lord Keworth, picking up his cards. 'Though tedious work you may find it. Once Deforge has his mind on the cards, nothing will sway him!'

Lord Keworth was right; Eloise found it very dull standing at Sir Ronald's shoulder while he played. Cards were taken and discarded, wagers were made and she found herself surprised at the high stakes. Glancing around the room, she realised that although the players at every table were doing their best to win, none had the intensity of those pitting their skill against Sir Ronald.

A light-hearted game of quadrille was just breaking up and she used the diversion to move away. As she did so Lady Parham beckoned to her.

'My dear Lady Allyngham, I was so sorry to miss Sir Ronald's little soirée.' She glanced at the diamond winking on Eloise's finger. 'It was such a surprise to hear that you are to be married, and to Sir Ronald, too.' She hesitated before giving another of her thin smiles. 'I had not thought him one of your *particular* favourites.'

Silently Eloise inclined her head and moved to pass on but Lady Parham stepped in front of her.

'I had thought Mr Mortimer had the advantage, especially since you have known him for so long. He is your neighbour at Allyngham, is he not? It must have been *such* a comfort to have him so close while your husband was away.'

The implication was plain. Eloise realised she had played her part as the wanton widow far too well. She replied evenly, 'Mr Mortimer has always been a very good friend, Lady Parham.'

'And what does he think of your betrothal to Sir Ronald?' The sly look that accompanied these words angered Eloise, but at that moment there was a distraction at the door. She looked up.

'You had best ask him that yourself, ma'am,' she said, smiling in relief and surprise as she watched Alex limp into the room with Jack close behind him. Until that moment it seemed to Eloise that she had hardly been breathing. Now her heart swelled with pride and pleasure as the two gentlemen greeted their hostess. Alex was looking a little pale and leaning heavily upon a cane. Jack, standing tall and dark beside him, looked at the peak of fitness. Surely there was nothing to fear while she had two such champions.

'Lady Allyngham, I fear you have forgotten your role this evening.'

Sir Ronald's voice boomed out once again. Her eyes narrowed angrily. She wanted to tear the ring off her finger and throw it in his grinning face. She looked across the room at Jack, who gave the tiniest shake of his head. Putting up her chin, Eloise fixed her smile and walked back to Sir Ronald.

'Stand close, my dear, you are here to bring me luck.'

He reached out and put one arm possessively about her hips. She forced herself to stand passively until Sir Ronald released her and returned his full attention to the cards. Jack was watching them, but his countenance was inscrutable. She

must play her part until he gave her a sign. She watched the
game progress, alarmed at the large amounts the gentlemen
were prepared to wager on a single card. As banker, Sir Ronald
had the advantage, controlling the cards and dealing them with
practised ease. Across the room Jack and Alex were talking to
Mr Renwick. They were moving closer, but so slowly that the
tension made her want to scream. No one at the table had eyes
for anything other than the play. Mr Graham had thrown in
his hand and now sat with his head bowed, rubbing his eyes.
Another gentleman pulled off a ruby ring and placed it on his
card, only to see it join the growing pile of notes and coins in
front of Sir Ronald.

'Hell's teeth, Deforge, you win again!' With a laugh Lord
Keworth stared at the cards Sir Ronald turned up on the table.
'What luck!'

'And skill, Keworth,' murmured Sir Ronald, smiling.
'Although having my future bride at my side is undoubtedly
an advantage.' He glanced up at that moment and saw Jack
standing nearby. His smile grew more unpleasant. 'It is a case
of winner takes all, I think. What say you, Major Clifton?'

'Oh, undoubtedly,' replied Jack, 'Only tonight I do not
think the winner will be you.'

His words were quiet but uttered with such cool conviction
that a sudden hush fell over the table. The players were very
still, while other guests drew closer, drawn by the sudden
tension in the air. Sir Ronald raised his quizzing glass and
stared at Jack, his smile turning into a sneer.

'Oh, I think you are wrong there, Clifton. You only have to
look at the fortune on the table to see how successful I have
been. And tomorrow, you may come to the church to watch
me claim this beautiful woman as my bride.'

Jack's slow smile was even more menacing than Sir
Ronald's.

'I think not.'

Eloise eased away. All eyes were upon Jack and Sir Ronald: there was violence in the air, she could almost taste it. She wondered what had become of Alex. She could not see him, but there were so many people standing around the table now that her view of the room was quite limited. Lord Keworth gave an uncertain laugh.

'Gentlemen,' he said, 'There are tables and cards enough for everyone. Perhaps, Major Clifton, you and Deforge would like to settle your differences with a game of picquet.'

'My dear Keworth, we have no differences to settle,' said Sir Ronald, rising to his feet, his cold eyes fixed upon Jack. 'The major does not like to lose.' His lip curled in an ugly smile. 'Losing to me seems to be your lot in life, does it not, Major? First your childhood sweetheart and now Lady Allyngham. But you must resign yourself to it. You have no choice because, you see, I hold the winning hand.'

'Aye,' said Jack steadily, 'you hold all the aces.'

Deforge gave a soft laugh.

'I am glad you realise that, Clifton. Now if you do not mind—'

'Not only aces,' stated Jack, raising his voice a little, 'but kings and queens, too.'

There was a movement in the crowd. Alex stepped up behind Sir Ronald and pulled his coat off his shoulders.

'What the—!' Deforge gave a snarl of rage, but the coat was already halfway down his arms and he could only struggle against Alex's hold.

Lord Keworth sprang to his feet. 'Good God, Mortimer, what do you mean by this?'

'I think it is quite clear,' said Jack.

Alex yanked the coat even further, revealing a web of leather straps around Deforge's left forearm. Sir Ronald stood before them, his fists clenched as he glared at the horrified faces around him. Jack stepped around the table and pulled a card from beneath one of the straps.

'I was right, you see. A king.' He withdrew a second. 'And a queen. You have already played the knave, have you not, Deforge?'

With a roar Sir Ronald turned on Jack but immediately Alex grabbed him and held him fast. A low murmur broke out and rippled around the room.

'By God,' muttered Mr Graham, 'the man's nothing but a cheat!'

Lord Keworth stared across the table, shaking his head in disgust.

'And to think I called you friend,' he muttered. 'I think you can release him now, Mortimer. I will have the servants escort Sir Ronald from my house.'

Alex stepped away and Deforge angrily shrugged himself back into his coat, his heavy pock-marked face almost purple with rage and humiliation. He looked at Eloise.

'Come, madam. We are leaving.'

'I will not.'

His eyes narrowed and he said menacingly, 'You are promised to marry me, my lady. You know the consequences of denying me.'

Slowly she withdrew the diamond ring from her hand and placed it on the table.

'You coerced me, but that is all at an end now.'

Jack stepped up beside her.

'There will be a notice in tomorrow's newspapers, announcing that the engagement has been terminated,' he said. 'In the circumstances I do not think anyone will be surprised. Lady Allyngham will not dishonour her late husband's memory by marrying a cheat.' He fixed Sir Ronald with a steady look. 'You have no hold over the lady now, Deforge.'

Sir Ronald stared at him.

'What have you done?' he ground out, his chin jutting pugnaciously.

Jack merely smiled. Two burly footmen appeared behind Sir Ronald and Lord Keworth said coldly, 'I would be obliged if you would leave my house immediately, Deforge. You will not touch the money lying on the table,' he added, as Sir Ronald glanced towards it. 'I do not need to tell you that you are no longer welcome here.'

An expectant silence hung over the room. Eloise found herself stiff with tension as Sir Ronald cast a venomous glare in her direction. She returned his look with a haughty stare until at last he looked away. One of the footmen put a hand upon his shoulder and with a snarl Sir Ronald shook him off. He straightened his coat and headed for the door. As he passed Eloise he stopped and turned towards her, his eyes menacing. Immediately Jack stepped in, as if to shield her.

'Just go, Deforge. If you have not left town by the morning it will give me very great pleasure to call you out!'

Eloise caught her breath. The two men glared at one another for a long, angry moment before Sir Ronald turned and flung himself out of the room. Jack turned back to her, the angry light in his eyes replaced by something much softer. He said quietly, 'It is over, my lady. Now you may be easy...'

She struggled to concentrate. His voice seemed to be coming from a great distance. Blackness was closing around her. The last thing she saw was Jack's face smiling at her before the darkness overwhelmed her and she fainted.

Jack did not hesitate. As Eloise began to fall he swept her up into his arms.

'Ah, poor thing,' exclaimed Lady Keworth. 'Bring her this

way, Major, into my sitting room.' She led Jack out of the salon and across the landing to a small, cosily furnished parlour. 'I will have the fire banked up…'

'No, thank you,' said Jack, gently laying his precious burden on a chintz-covered daybed and sitting down on the edge. 'I think it was the heat in the salon that caused Lady Allyngham to faint. It is quite warm enough in here.'

Alex appeared in the doorway.

'Is she all right?'

Lady Keworth hovered over the daybed.

'Lady Allyngham will be very well, I am sure. Perhaps you would like to leave her with me…'

'No!' Jack softened his first, instinctive response by directing a charming smile at his hostess. 'I feel responsible for Lady Allyngham, I shall look after her.' He pulled off her gloves and began to chafe her hands. 'But perhaps a glass of water?'

'Yes, yes, of course.'

Alex stood aside to allow Lady Keworth to hurry away.

'I did not see,' he said, stepping into the room. 'Did Deforge attack her?'

'No, she has fainted, nothing more,' said Jack, not looking up. 'Is he gone now?'

'Aye. Keworth's men showed him to the door. He was looking as black as thunder, as well he might. No one will receive him after this night's work.' He glanced down. 'She's stirring.'

Jack felt the little hands tremble and his own grip tightened.

'Be easy,' he murmured. 'You are safe now.'

She looked up at him, her eyes as dark as sapphires. Her fingers clung to his and only the knowledge that Alex was in the room prevented him from pulling her into his arms.

'Aye,' said Alex, coming to stand beside him. 'It is over, Elle. Deforge is finished.'

Lady Keworth bustled back into the room with a glass of water.

'Well, my dear, I am so glad to see you have come round,' she said. 'Such a fright you gave us, but I am sure you will be better now.'

Eloise struggled to sit up. Jack went to rise but her slender fingers clung to his hand so he remained perched on the edge of the daybed.

Lady Keworth held out the glass. 'There, my dear. Are you sure there is nothing else I can do for you; shall I summon a doctor?'

Eloise's fingers were shaking when she took the glass and Jack immediately reached out to help her, putting his hand over hers to steady it. She cast a swift, grateful look in his direction before turning to address Lady Keworth.

'Thank you, ma'am. I am sure I shall be very well, if I may only rest here quietly for a little while.'

The lady hovered uncertainly.

'I shall look after Lady Allyngham, ma'am,' said Jack again. 'I am sure you want to return to your guests, they will be growing anxious.'

'Well…' Lady Keworth hesitated and Alex stepped up.

'Indeed, ma'am, we should go: so much excitement—we would not wish it to spoil your card party. You may be easy, madam; before he died at Waterloo, the late Lord Allyngham consigned his wife to Major Clifton's care.' He held out his arm to her. 'Let us leave them now, I am sure they have much to discuss!' He looked back over his shoulder as he escorted the lady from the room, giving Jack a grin and the suggestion of a wink.

Chapter Nineteen

'I thank Providence for Alex Mortimer,' said Jack, unable to suppress a smile. 'I thought our hostess would never go away. He has closed the door upon us, too. I fear your reputation will be ruined after this, madam, unless you agree to marry me.' He turned to Eloise, but his smile quickly disappeared when he saw her pale cheeks and the stricken look in her eyes. He said quickly, 'Dearest heart, what is it?'

She shook her head.

'Please, do not call me that!'

He took the glass from her shaking hands and placed it on a small side table.

'Now, Elle,' he said, taking her in his arms. 'What is all this?'

She put her hands against his chest to hold him off.

'I c-cannot marry you!'

'No?' He let her go and she turned away, hunting for her handkerchief. Silently he handed her his own.

'No. At least,' she muttered, dabbing at her eyes, 'not until you know the truth about me.'

He smiled.

'I know everything I need to know about you.'

She choked back a sob. How was she ever to explain it to him? He put his hands on her shoulders and she jumped, moving to the far end of the sofa.

'Please,' she said quickly, 'do not touch me, not until I have t-told you.'

'There is no need—'

'But there is!' she cried. 'I w-would have no secrets from you, Jack, not any more. But once you know everything I am very much afraid you will want nothing more to do with me.' She turned back towards him, her hands clasped so tightly the knuckles gleamed white. 'I must tell you. I could not bear for you to find out in the future and…and hate me.'

'I could never hate you.' He reached out and took her hands. He said quietly, 'Elle, if this is about Allyngham and Alex, I know. Alex told me everything.'

'He did? But…when?'

'The night we broke into Deforge's house. I was determined to leave town. I told Alex that if you would not trust me then I wanted nothing further to do with you. So he told me what you would not—what you felt you could nott—out of loyalty to your husband and your friend. After all it was their secret, was it not?'

She gazed at him wide-eyed.

'You are not…outraged?'

He smiled at her.

'Despite your reputation, my lady, you really have led quite a sheltered life. No. I was not scandalised to learn that Alex and your husband were lovers.'

'But…in the eyes of the law it is a criminal offence—men can be hanged for it.' She squeezed his fingers, not sure that he understood her. 'Lives have been ruined, reputations lost— Tony and Alex were so careful to protect their secret. Tony knew his name would be disgraced for ever if the truth came out—no respectable person could ever acknowledge him.'

'Then perhaps I am not quite so respectable as you think me,' replied Jack, smiling slightly. 'Alex's disclosure did not shock me. I was more shocked to learn that you had married Allyngham to protect them both. Mortimer said that you are very loyal and he is right, is he not? A little too loyal, perhaps. You were prepared, nay, willing, to be thought fast—a wanton widow indeed!—rather than have anyone suspect the truth.'

She bowed her head.

'I am glad Alex told you,' she said quietly. 'I did not want to betray him, or Tony. But neither could I let you marry me without you knowing the truth.'

'Thank you,' he said, giving her a smile that tugged at her heart. 'Once I knew you were a maid I suspected the affairs in the journal might be Allyngham's rather than yours, but I was at a loss to know why you would not trust me with the secret, until Mortimer explained it all.'

'I am so very sorry.'

'Elle, you have done nothing wrong,' he said quietly. 'You were merely protecting those you loved.' Jack squeezed her hands. 'What a burden for you to carry! I admire your loyalty towards Tony and Alex, my dear.'

She bit her lip.

'I seem to have spent my life looking after them,' she murmured.

'And now I am going to look after *you*,' he told her, smiling. 'Tony said that you deserved better, I didn't understand him at the time, but now, I hope I can be a worthy husband for you. I shall obtain a special licence: we can be married and away from London within a se'ennight, what do you say to that?'

'It—it sounds delightful, if you are sure you still want to marry me.'

'It would be an honour to marry Tony Allyngham's widow,' he told her solemnly.

She closed her eyes, suddenly exhausted by the events of the evening. Jack leaned forwards and kissed her cheek.

'Poor love, you look very tired. I should take you home.'

She nodded.

'Yes, if you please.'

'Wait here, then. I must find Alex and tell him we are leaving. And I must speak with our hosts.' He gave her a rueful smile. 'It may take some time: you will not mind being left alone here?'

'No, I shall be well enough, but please, be as quick as you can!'

Alone in Lady Keworth's elegant sitting room, Eloise reclined upon the daybed, her arms folded over her stomach. She was aware of a little seed of happiness inside her, but she was afraid to allow it to grow too much. She was very weary, but she did not want to sleep, only to lie still and go over in her mind all that Jack had said to her. He knew the truth and he still wanted to marry her. She went back over his words again. He cared for her, he desired her, she knew that, but at no time had he told her loved her. She hugged herself a little tighter. Perhaps, given time, he might grow to love her for her own sake, and not just as his comrade's widow.

A light scratching on the door made her sit up.

'Come in.'

A liveried footmen stepped into the room. He carried her blue silk cloak over his arm.

'If it please your ladyship, Major Clifton is waiting for you with the carriage.'

She rose and followed him out of the door, throwing her wrap over her shoulders.

'This way, madam.' He pointed to the backstairs. 'The major thought you might like to leave by the side door, rather than go out through the main salon.'

'Of course.' She followed the servant down the stairs, smiling to herself. How thoughtful of Jack to know she would not wish to speak to anyone.

The side door stood open and she could see her carriage drawn up on the street, the flickering streetlamps illuminating the Allyngham crest on the door. A fine drizzle was falling and Eloise threw her hood up over her hair. The footman went out before her, opened the door and handed her into the waiting carriage. Almost before she had climbed in the door was closed behind her and the carriage pulled away with a jerk, toppling her on to the seat.

'Goodness, Herries is eager to get home tonight!' she laughed, addressing the figure lounging in the far corner of the carriage.

Her laughter died and a cold, sick dread came over her as Sir Ronald Deforge leaned forwards.

'I, too, am very eager, my lady, but we are not going to Dover Street.'

Eloise shrank back into the corner of the carriage.

'How did you get here? Where are my people?'

'Trussed up in an alleyway, along with one of Keworth's lackeys. We needed his livery.'

'So the footman was one of your hirelings.' Her lip curled. 'I did not think you would stoop so low.'

'I have not resorted to housebreaking,' he retorted. 'Do not look so innocent, my lady: I gather from Clifton's words that you have somehow managed to retrieve Allyngham's journal.'

'Yes,' she said defiantly. 'It is destroyed. You have no further hold over me.'

He laughed gently and a shiver of fear ran down her spine.

'Since you are here now, I think I have quite a substantial hold over you, madam.'

Eloise bit her lip, her eyes sliding towards the carriage door. Sir Ronald said coldly, 'If you are thinking of leaping out, my dear, let me assure you that it will not help you: you might easily break a limb in the process and in any event my men would catch you and bring you back immediately.'

'Where are you taking me?'

'To Redlands, a little property of mine near Thatcham. It belonged to my late wife—all that remains of her not inconsiderable fortune. Being a gambler is an expensive business, my dear: I need the Allyngham fortune to replenish my own.'

'So you have abducted me,' she said, her voice heavy with anger. 'When it is discovered that my servants have been attacked and I am missing, everyone will guess you are the culprit.'

'But that may not be for some time, madam, and how are they to know where we have gone? We shall be at Redlands in a few hours: the rector there owes his living to me: I have the special licence in my pocket.' She saw his evil grin appear. 'We shall have our wedding today, as planned.'

'I will never marry you!'

'Oh I think you will, madam,' he said softly. 'And you will learn to please me, if you do not want me to hand you over to my stable hands for their plaything.'

'You will not get away with this,' she retorted. 'When they come after me—'

'They!' He gave a cold, cruel laugh. 'Who do you think will put themselves out to chase after you, madam? Mortimer is not fit to ride, and as for the rest, do you think they care what happens to a woman with a reputation such as yours? That leaves only Major Clifton, and what can one man do against myself and the three fellows travelling on the top? You have overplayed your hand, my lady: the *ton* will say that the Wanton Widow has received no more than she deserves!'

Eloise glared across the carriage at Sir Ronald, who lounged carelessly in his corner. Perhaps he was right and the *ton* would leave her to her fate. She had no doubt that Jack would try to find her, but even if he had Alex to help him how long might that take?

Sir Ronald rubbed his chin thoughtfully. 'And yet Major Clifton is such a resourceful fellow, he will go to great lengths to do me a disservice,' he purred. 'I think I shall hire a room at Maidenhead and take you there, just to make sure of you.'

She curled her lip.

'Do you think that will save you from him? It will only make him more determined to kill you!'

'I am well aware that Clifton wants to put paid to my existence. He wants revenge upon me for marrying his childhood friend, the love of his life. You are little more than a pawn in this game, my dear. Did you think you could ever replace Clara in his heart? She was a veritable angel, my dear, as pure as you are wanton. Taking you from me might redress the balance a little, but where would be the satisfaction for him if I had already bedded you? He will not want you then, madam, knowing that I have already sampled your delights. How could he ever lie with you after that, knowing that I had enjoyed you?' He laughed. 'But this is mere conjecture. No one knows our direction and it is most unlikely that they will find us before I have wed you. And once we are married I shall make sure you have no opportunity to escape me.'

'And will you kill me, like you killed your first wife?'

'Is that what Clifton has told you?' Sir Ronald gave a bitter laugh. 'Aye, he would like to believe that. Much more comfortable for him to think I was villain enough to beguile Clara into marrying me and then find a way to dispose of her once I had run through her fortune!'

'Is that not the truth?' she challenged him.

'Far from it. Clara was a sweet, innocent beauty. We were madly, hopelessly in love within weeks of being introduced. Such passion could not last, of course, and I confess that her devotion outlasted mine. She liked to live at Redlands, I preferred town. Once she knew she was with child she settled down, although she seemed to think I should come and live with her. I kept putting it off, making excuses why I could not join her, until it was too late.' He paused and turned his head to gaze out of the window. 'I was in London when she drowned herself, driven mad with grief at the loss of her baby. Our son.'

'I am so very sorry,' murmured Eloise.

He turned back to her, saying harshly, 'You need not be. Clara has been dead for three years and unlike your precious major I gave up mourning her long ago. Truth to tell, I cannot say that her death was anything but a relief. I had grown very weary of her maudlin airs and clinging ways. You, my dear, have so much more spirit.' He stretched out his foot and rubbed it against her leg. She quickly drew back, pulling her skirts about her. Sir Ronald merely laughed again. 'By Gad, madam, it will be amusing to bend you to my will.'

Eloise returned no answer but huddled in the corner, staring resolutely out of the window, watching the dark landscape flying by. Jack would come after her, she was sure of it, but she was less sure of his reasons for doing so. Sir Ronald's words had lodged themselves in her brain. Her reputation, even her actions in giving herself to Jack, proved her to be far beneath the paragon that was his first love. She knew he wanted to marry her because she was Allyngham's widow, but what if he also he wanted to thwart Sir Ronald? Would he still want her once Deforge had taken her to his bed? Even if by some chance Jack decided upon the right road, there was little chance he would catch them before they reached Maidenhead.

Chapter Twenty

They rattled on and Eloise kept her gaze firmly fixed upon the window. She forced herself to consider her position. It did not look promising. Sir Ronald might dress as a fop but he was too strong for her to overpower him, and she did not even have a hatpin with which to defend herself. Once he had her alone in a room she feared all would be lost. The idea of his hands on her body made her shudder with revulsion. She shifted closer to the window and peered down. She had never considered the distance from a carriage to the ground before, but now she was determined that if they slowed at all she would attempt to run away. Sir Ronald took out his watch and held it, turning it towards what little light there was coming into the carriage.

'We shall soon be at Maidenhead, my dear. You had best prepare yourself.' He leaned across to run his finger along her cheek. 'What, still not speaking to me?' She flinched away and he sat back, chuckling. 'You will soon learn to enjoy my caresses, Eloise.'

Her stretched nerves noticed immediately when the pace slackened. They were entering a village: the dark outlines of buildings could be seen on either side of the road, although not a light was visible from any window. She tensed, surreptitiously noting the position of the door handle. The carriage slowed still further and began to turn off the road towards the lighted yard of a large inn. Sir Ronald was peering out of the window beside him.

'What the devil, this isn't the Bear—'

Eloise seized her chance. She sprang up, released the door catch and leaped from the carriage as it turned off the road. She landed heavily and rolled over, hoping she was clear of the wheels. Her voluminous cloak billowed out and settled around her even as she scrambled to her feet. She could hear Sir Ronald's outraged roar and knew she had only seconds to escape. As she raised her head she saw there was a line of horses stretched across the road, blocking the way. That was why the carriage had turned off the highway.

It took her a moment to recognise Lord Keworth and Mr Renwick amongst the horsemen. A glance back showed her that more men were surrounding the carriage, their pistols directed at the coachman and the two accomplices who were clinging to the back straps of the coach-body. Sir Ronald had jumped down and was coming towards her. Eloise quickly moved towards the horsemen.

'Thank God we have found you, Lady Allyngham!' Lord Keworth dismounted and held out one hand to her, the other levelling a pistol at Sir Ronald. 'That is far enough, Deforge. Stand, or I shall shoot!'

'Elle!' Jack was running towards her. 'Elle, dearest! Are you all right?'

His voice was shaking, and suddenly she felt close to tears. With a sob she threw herself on his chest.

'Yes, yes,' she said, 'I am well enough now.'

'Why did you jump from the carriage?' He held her away from him, staring into her face. 'If he touched you—!'

Eloise shook her head.

'No, but he p-planned to hire a room and—' She broke off, shuddering, and Jack pulled her back into his arms.

'Then thank God we were in time.'

She leaned against him, secure within his embrace while all around them was confusion.

The riders were dismounting and moving forwards to stand around them, effectively cutting off Sir Ronald's escape. She could hear a familiar voice barking orders to the men on the coach.

'Climb down now, me boys, and steady does it: there's more than one finger here itching to pull the trigger!'

She raised her head.

'Perkins?'

'Yes,' said Jack. 'It is thanks to your groom that we were able to find you so soon. He was returning from a local gin shop when he saw your carriage pulling away from the side door at Keworth House. If the speed of its departure hadn't made him suspicious then the fact that a Keworth footman scrambled up on the back told him something was wrong. He immediately raised the alarm and had the presence of mind to follow the carriage until he ascertained that it was leaving London by the Great West Road. We followed, and thankfully, even at this hour of the night there were enough people abroad to notice your flight.'

'And you all came to find me,' she said, looking around at the familiar faces. 'I am very grateful.'

'Not at all, dear lady.' Lord Berrow pushed forwards and gave a little bow. 'When Major Clifton set up the hue and cry we were all most happy to oblige!'

'Very touching,' sneered Deforge, glaring at them all. 'Especially when you know you would all like to have the wench for yourself!'

'Enough!' barked Lord Keworth. 'You will keep a civil tongue in your head when addressing the lady.'

'Lady? I know better,' cried Sir Ronald. 'She has taken you all in with her smiles and fine airs, but she is nothing but an imposter! She was never a virtuous wife to Allyngham— their marriage was a sham, a cover to mask her husband's unnatural practices with Alex Mortimer! No *lady* would have agreed to such a pretence. Who knows what went on in their bedchamber between the three of them? And she knew, she *knew* when she married him that Allyngham was a—'

He got no further. Jack stepped forwards and smashed his fist against Sir Ronald's jaw. Deforge's head snapped back and he crashed to the ground.

'Well done, Clifton, just what was needed,' declared Lord Berrow, coming forwards. 'I have no doubt Mortimer would have done the same, had he been well enough to ride with us.'

'Aye,' declared Lord Keworth. 'A dastardly act, to accuse Mortimer, a man who you know is already wounded and in no condition to demand satisfaction.'

'Not only Mortimer, but Allyngham, my friend and neighbour,' roared Lord Berrow, turning to glare at Sir Ronald who was slowly picking himself up. 'Why, you filthy scoundrel, how dare you attempt to blacken the name of a hero of Waterloo? One, moreover, who is no longer alive to defend himself! Tie him up, gentlemen.'

'It is true!' cried Deforge, struggling as Renwick and Graham secured his hands with a length of whipcord. 'And I had the proof, before they stole it from me! Ask them,' he spat. 'Ask Clifton to deny that he broke into my house!'

Putting her hand up to prevent Jack from uttering an angry retort, Eloise took a step away from him and looked at the men gathered around her. She said clearly, 'But of course, knowing that he had the means to blacken my husband's good name, I went to Wardle Street to retrieve it. I climbed in through his window at dead of night, stole the proof and burned it!'

An instant's shocked silence was followed by hearty laughter. Jack took her hand.

'As if any woman would have the nerve to do such a thing,' he murmured, grinning at her.

'Curse you,' snarled Sir Ronald, 'I shall swear to it, on oath!'

'Do you think, sir, after your behaviour tonight, anyone will take your allegations seriously?' retorted Mr Renwick.

'Aye,' nodded Lord Berrow. 'You had best beware, Deforge: false accusations of this kind are punished very severely. Come, gentlemen, let us take this villain and his cronies back to town. We shall haul them before the magistrate in the morning.'

'You may use my horse,' offered Jack. 'I shall drive Lady Allyngham home in her carriage.'

'I'm coming with you, m'lady,' put in Perkins, walking up at that moment with the major's man, who added,

'And if you'll allow me, madam, I can handle a coach and four: it'd be an honour to drive you.'

'Thank you,' she murmured.

'Aye, thank you, Bob,' said Jack, putting his arm about Eloise. 'Now, if that is settled, tell that rascally landlord to bring us some fresh horses and we'll be away.'

The first grey streaks of dawn were edging into the sky as they rumbled back towards London. Eloise sat beside Jack in the dark carriage, her head on his shoulder and her hand snugly held in his comforting grasp.

'I was so frightened,' she murmured. 'I never doubted you

would come for me, but I did not know how soon, or if you
would be alone.'

Jack put his arm about her.

'After he had ruined the card party so spectacularly this
evening, the gentlemen were only too pleased to have an
excuse to come after Deforge,' he said, resting his cheek
against her hair. 'And your groom's quick thinking put us
on the right track immediately. I have quite forgiven him for
hitting me over the head on Hampstead Heath.'

'And me?' she asked shyly. 'Have you forgiven me for being
so foolish?'

'Of course. The person I do find it difficult to forgive is
Allyngham for marrying you. And for committing a record
of his indiscretions to paper. Damnably irresponsible for such
a clever man.'

Eloise was silent, leaning against Jack and listening to the
thud of his heart.

'I think he began his journal because he was away from
home and missing Alex,' she said at last. 'He continued to
write it when he was at Allyngham for those few short months
before Waterloo. I did not know what was in it and when it
went missing I was not unduly concerned: I thought perhaps
Tony had destroyed it himself. From what Sir Ronald told me
I believe now it was stolen by a servant I had turned off for
dishonesty. I knew the man had taken a few pieces of clothing when he left—a few shirts and a pair of boots.' She gave
a little sigh. 'Things of such little value I did not pursue it. I
thought the poor man would have a hard enough time of it,
being turned off without a reference. He was illiterate, so he
had no idea what was in the journal.'

'And you think he passed it on to Deforge?'

'Yes.' She shuddered. 'It was not until Deforge left me one
of the pages in the gardens at Clevedon House that I realised

just how, how *explicit* Tony's journal was, and how dangerous that could be. Not to me.' She sat up and looked at him, her eyes begging him to understand. 'Not to me, but to Tony's name, and of course to Alex, if it became public knowledge that they were...*lovers*.'

He put up a hand to stroke her cheek.

'So you had to protect them, just as you had always done.'

'Yes.' She nodded. 'We grew up together, you see. Tony and Alex were two years older and I thought they were wonderful, everything older brothers should be. They were never cruel, or spiteful, as boys often can be to a younger child, and we were always friends. We were allowed to run wild at Allyngham. Tony was the leader; he liked excitement and danger. Somehow I seemed to be the one who found ways to extricate us when Tony's madcap schemes went awry. Even when the boys went off to school I was still the one they called upon in a fix. I remember I sold my pearls once, when Tony became embroiled with a moneylender and was too afraid to tell anyone in the college, and he certainly would not tell his father. But he paid me back as soon as he was able,' she added quickly. 'Tony was always very generous. And very kind.'

'Kind!' Jack muttered an oath under his breath. 'I do not call it *kind* of him to wed you, to rob you of the opportunity to marry the man of your choice, to have children—'

She sat up and put a finger to his lips.

'He *was* my choice. I loved him as a brother. And Alex, too. I wanted them to be happy. It was always plain to me that theirs was a very deep and abiding love. Alex still feels the loss, more keenly than I.'

'Allyngham should not have married you!'

She shrugged.

'I had to marry someone. I was the poor relation, brought

up with the family but expected at some time to repay their kindness by making a good marriage of my own. Lord and Lady Allyngham did not attempt to force me into a marriage, but it was apparent—never said but always implied—that I *must* marry.' She paused, looking back into the past. 'Tony was army mad, so Lord Allyngham bought him a commission. Then his elder brother died and Tony was the heir. Suddenly his family were pushing him to marry—whenever he was home on leave they would invite a series of young ladies to meet him. Of course he did not want to wed any of them. He was far too kind to allow any woman to marry him unless she knew the situation and he could not risk *telling* anyone, so when he suggested that we should wed, it seemed the perfect solution, for all of us. Lord and Lady Allyngham never liked the match, but when they saw that Tony was adamant they relented.'

'And how old were you then?'

'I was seventeen.'

'And he explained everything to you? You knew you were entering a sham marriage?'

'I knew Tony could never love a woman as he loved Alex.' She raised her chin and looked directly into his eyes. 'That was all I needed to know. Sir Ronald thought Tony had…had corrupted me, but that is not so. Tony and Alex were always very discreet when I was present. I think I had a much happier marriage than many women. Tony always looked after me, always treated me with the utmost kindness. To the outside world he was the perfect husband.'

'Except in one regard.'

A slight flush tinged her cheeks.

'I never noticed the lack,' she said softly, 'until I met you.'

A low growl escaped Jack and he swept her into a crushing

embrace. She clung to him, pressing her body against his as she gave him back kiss for kiss. Tiredness forgotten, Eloise found her body responding to his caresses. When at last he raised his head she lay in his arms, her head thrown back against his shoulder as she gazed up into his face. Suddenly she could not bear the thought of being apart from him for even a moment. She reached up and touched his cheek.

'How, how soon can we be married by special licence?' she whispered.

'Ah. I have been thinking about that.'

'Oh. I—um—I thought you wanted to be married with all speed.'

'Yes, I know that is what I said, but after all that has happened I am afraid I have changed my mind.'

Eloise struggled to sit up. It was impossible to read his expression in the darkness, but his words sent her heart plummeting. Swallowing, she began nervously to smooth her gown over her knees.

'I, I quite understand,' she said, trying not to cry. 'I am aware that you consider yourself under an, an *obligation* to Tony, but after all you have done for me, I think you have more than fulfilled that duty.'

'Why, I think so, too.'

Her heart sank. Eloise gazed out of the window where the dawn was washing the landscape in shades of dirty grey. So he had reconsidered, he had realised how damaging it would be to marry her. He would have to love her very much indeed to risk everything for her. And he did not love her, he loved Clara Deforge. With great resolution she turned to face him.

'Jack, there is something else I must tell you.'

He was leaning back in the corner of the carriage, half-asleep, but now he opened his eyes and regarded her.

'More secrets?'

'Not exactly.' She did not smile. 'When I was in the carriage with Sir Ronald, he—he mentioned his first wife.' Jack did not move but she knew she had his attention. She continued, 'He, um, he told me that he and Clara had fallen hopelessly in love when they first met and, and although their passion had cooled a little by the time she drowned herself, I do not think he wished her any harm.'

She waited, holding her breath, for his reply.

'And you believe him?'

'Yes.' She nodded. 'He had no reason to lie to me.' She took his hand. 'I wanted you to know that, Jack. I know it will hurt to think that she was not faithful to you, but she and Sir Ronald really did love one another.'

'Thank you for telling me.'

He closed his eyes again. Anxiously she studied his face. There was no guessing his thoughts. After a few moments Jack opened his eyes and looked at her.

'I beg your pardon,' she whispered. 'I thought it might help...'

He smiled.

'It does. I am glad, truly, that she was not unhappy.'

She blinked rapidly. 'I am sorry that she did not always love you...'

'I am not. Not now. I did love her, but that is in the past, and knowing that she made her choice for love, not greed, or ambition—I will let her rest now.' He reached out to stroke her cheek. 'Did you think I still loved her? I don't, you know. She will not come between us.'

She nodded, the knot of misery still tight in her chest. She had been foolish to think a respectable man would want her for a wife, but even as her hopes crumbled she realised that she did not want Jack to suggest she become his mistress: she had thought him different from those other men. She had thought him truly honourable. A lump filled her throat. It was her own fault; she had always been too fanciful. She knew very well that even honourable men had mistresses. Eloise had never considered herself in the role of a mistress, and she would not, even for Jack. Especially for Jack. She blinked, hard. Alex wanted to go home to mourn his lost love. She would return to Allyngham and do the same. As Jack went to pull her into his arms she held him off.

'Please,' she said, her voice not quite steady. 'I know you think me fast, I know I have given you every reason to do so, but please, no more! I quite understand why you no longer wish to marry me, but—'

She heard Jack chuckle.

'No, you don't understand, Elle. Come here.' He pulled her back into his arms. 'I never said I didn't want to marry you, but I will not wed you by special licence, my foolish love, because I intend to marry you with as much pomp and ceremony as we can muster, and that will take a little time to arrange. The only decisions you have to make, my sweet, are what you will wear, and whether you wish to be married from Allyngham, or from Henchard.'

She stared at him.

'Truly?' She put one hand up to his face, her fingers rubbing against the faint dark stubble on his cheek. 'You would really do that for me?' she said wonderingly. 'But, but *why*?'

He gazed down at her. Even in the grey dawn light she could see the warm glow in his eyes.

'Do you really have to ask?'

'Y-yes,' she whispered, hardly daring to hope. 'Yes, I do.'

'Because, my sweet innocent, I want the whole world to know how much I love you.'

'Oh,' she said, tears welling in her eyes, 'you r-really love me?'

'To distraction,' he muttered, hugging her even tighter. 'I cannot imagine life without you!' He kissed her savagely. 'I want you for a wife, Elle. A lover, a friend—a partner to stand beside me against the world!' He kissed her again. 'And we will be married in a positive *fog* of respectability.'

With a little sob she threw her arms about his neck.

'Oh, Jack, it is what I hoped, what I dreamed of, but never dared believe…'

'Well, you may believe it now,' he murmured, gently nibbling her ear. 'And as long as you love me, there is nothing to stand in our way.'

'I do,' she told him, hugging him tightly. 'I love you more than I ever thought it possible!'

He gathered her to him and kissed her, gently at first, but as the kiss deepened his arms tightened protectively around her. She leaned into him, revelling in the way his body hardened against hers. He swung her round and pulled her across his lap, covering her face and neck with kisses while she clung to him, exulting in the hot, passionate embrace. When at last he released her they were both panting. She lay in his arms, her head resting on his chest and the steady thud of his heart beating against her cheek.

'Happy now?' he murmured, dropping a kiss on her hair.

'Mmm. Jack?'

'Yes?' He began to nibble her ear.

'Your plans for a respectable marriage,' she murmured, closing her eyes as his lips trailed gently across her neck, painting a line of warm kisses on her skin. 'The banns, a new gown—this will take at least a month. Does that mean I must hire a chaperon, and only see you in company until our wedding day?'

His mouth was moving across the soft swell of her breast, but at her words he raised his head and looked at her. There was sufficient light in the carriage for her to see the gleam in his dark eyes and what she read there sent a delicious tingle running down to her very toes.

'Well,' he said, giving her a wicked smile, 'I don't think we need to be *quite* that respectable!'

* * * * *

THE CAPTAIN AND THE WALLFLOWER

LYN STONE

*This book is for my wonderful and courageous
friend, Garland Whiddon Rowland.
This is for all those discussions about what
love is when we were teens still anticipating it.
Oh, and for being my maid of honor once
I found it! So happy that you found it, too!*

A painter of historical events, **Lyn Stone**
decided to write about them. A canvas, however
detailed, limits characters to only one moment
in time. 'If a picture's worth a thousand words,
the other ninety thousand have to show up
somewhere!' An avid reader, she admits, 'At
thirteen, I fell in love with Emily Brontë's
Heathcliff and became Catherine. Next year I
fell for Rhett and became Scarlett. Then I fell
for the hero I'd known most of my life and
finally became myself.'

Prologue

Caine Morleigh studiously avoided touching the cloth bandages covering his eyes as he waited for the physician to arrive. For five long weeks, his injuries had remained under wraps, the bandages changed by feel in pitch-dark to avoid further damage from the light. And to avoid revelation, he admitted to himself. Today, he would know whether his sight had been destroyed.

There would be so much for him to learn if that proved so. Already, he had begun counting steps from one place to another so that he could eventually get about the house unaided. He fed himself in private still, but was becoming good at it.

Control would not be beyond him. In time,

he would be able to manage the impediment, if forced to it. Damn, but he hated being dependent. Impatience warred with apprehension as the wait dragged on in the drawing room of his uncle, Earl of Hadley.

He heard his aunt Hadley gasp again as Trent, his best friend and companion, regaled her with prettied-up details of their final day on the field of battle. Caine paid little heed to the words. He'd heard it all before in considerably more graphic terms. Hell, he had lived it. Trent talked entirely too much, but his effort here was admirable, Caine admitted. It was Trent's way of lessening the tension and distracting everyone from the purpose of the gathering.

"We were wounded on the charge along with most of our brigade, most never to rise again! Caine fell beside me, unable to see, and I, my leg badly twisted, could not hope to walk. But did we lie there and die? No, ma'am! I served as his eyes whilst he got us to my horse. His horse had collapsed, you see, so we mounted double and rejoined the charge, galloping full speed. There was no going back...."

Someone cleared their throat and Trent, thank God, left off his narrative at the interruption. "Dr. Ackers and Miss Belinda Thoren-Snipes," Jenkins, the butler, announced.

"Show them in! Show them in!" his aunt exclaimed. Caine heard the rustle of taffeta skirts as Aunt Hadley approached and laid a hand on his shoulder. "I thought he would never come."

"How convenient they've arrived together," his uncle said. "I sent a note round for your Belinda to join us, too. I knew you would want her here."

Caine sighed, wishing he had not. He wanted to discover for himself whether he could see before he encountered his fiancée. If he was to be blind for life, she should not be held to the betrothal. For that reason, he had not initiated any contact at all since his return to London.

He had no trouble recalling how she had looked the last time he had seen her. He hoped against hope he would see her again. She was a blonde, rose-cheeked beauty, his Belinda. Her image had sustained him for nearly two years as he had faced the ugliness of war.

He heard approaching footsteps, the physician's heavier masculine tread interspersed with the soft click of Belinda's dainty shoes on the marble floor of the corridor. Did he actually smell the scent of her lilac perfume as she entered, or was that merely a fond brush of memory and expectation? Caine was convinced he loved her and had from their first meeting.

Despite that, he realized he knew very little about his future wife. He had courted her, of course, but not for long and always under the strictest of supervision. Their desultory conversation then, and later her infrequent letters filled with frivolous details of life at home, had not told him much.

In fact, he did not know a great deal about women in general, other than in the biblical sense. That paid-for expertise was helpful only in the bedchamber, but valuable nonetheless. Perhaps that was all that any man could hope to understand fully or, in fact, would need to know.

He employed respect with all females, regardless of rank, as well as chivalry and what charm he had acquired. Common courtesy demanded that much of a man, and rightly so.

He forced a smile to greet Belinda even as he wished for her own sake, as well as for his, that she were elsewhere this morning. Her scent of lilacs, the essence he had recalled with fervent longing in the midst of war, now nearly overpowered the senses he had left.

"Captain Morleigh!" she said with obviously forced brightness.

"How are you, my dear?" he asked, sick with apprehension, holding his smile in place by sheer force of will.

"Fine, thank you," she replied, the brightness slipping, replaced by a tremor.

He noted that she did not return the question. Her fear of the answer must be nearly as great as his own, at being faced with the very real prospect of having a blind husband to look after. He would release her from their betrothal if it came to that, but she did not yet know it.

Caine identified the sound of the medical bag being opened.

"Could we get on with it?" he asked, impatience winning out. He wanted this over with, whatever the outcome.

"Certainly, my boy," the doctor answered, his tone entirely too sympathetic and tinged with worry. "Let's turn you away from the lamps to the soft light from the window."

Caine moved as directed and heard the others in the room, Trent, Aunt Hadley and Belinda, shifting positions, as well.

"Belinda, you must stand just there so that you will be the very first thing he sees!" his aunt said.

Belinda muttered her thanks as the doctor slid a scissor blade beneath the bandage at Caine's right temple and began to cut. He carefully peeled the cloth away and dabbed something wet over both eyelids, soaking them thoroughly. "There," he said finally. "Now open your eyes slowly."

Caine concentrated as he did so and sensed the doctor move to one side and expose him to the window.

He blinked, saw blessed light…and heard the screams.

Chapter One

London
Cavanaugh House
August 25, 1815

"Spot the homeliest of the lot, Trent, and speak to her sponsor on my behalf." Caine Morleigh smiled at his friend as he handed his cane and top hat to the attendant. "She should look utterly frightful, perhaps be a bit dull of wit and wanting in every respect, or she won't do."

Trent sighed, rolling his eyes as he tugged at his gloves. "You don't have to do this. You're making far too much of that girl's reaction." He scoffed. "Porridge for brains, that one."

"That's as may be, but I have a more significant reason for this than the way *I* look." The receiving line had dispersed, and apparently they weren't to be announced, since they had come so late. He led the way, following the music down the wide corridor. He glanced inside a smaller room, which had been set up for card playing and refreshments, then turned and entered the ballroom.

He kept his voice low as he leaned sideways to continue his conversation with Trent. "I need someone who will require little attention, a woman satisfied to simply change her marital status and then leave me alone. I shall have more than enough to do as it is."

Trent huffed. "A woman who needs little attention? Is there such a creature? In my experience—"

"I know all about your *experience*. Now, stop blathering on and help me look."

The gathering at Lord Cavanaugh's was far from a crush, since it was past the regular London season and many had retired to the country. Decorations had been held to a minimum and this appeared to be a rather modest affair. Still the columned entry, the great expanse of highly polished floor and elegantly curved staircase needed little embellishment to shout wealth.

The musicians sounded rather good, though they were few in number compared to events he had attended in years past. He watched the dancers move through their measured steps without much gaity or conversation.

"Not much of a rout, is it," Trent commented

with a sigh of resignation. "I've seen more excitement at funerals."

"Suits my need perfectly," Caine responded. Most of the single women present would be the leftovers and their sponsors, hoping for a late-made match. Perhaps with a bit of luck, he could make one of the hopefuls content, if not happy.

Trent snorted. "Damned harebrained idea. You're obsessed with controlling every aspect of your life. Always have been. And it's not possible, y'know."

"I can but try."

"You're treating this like a military campaign, and you know how I hate taking orders!"

"Think of the compensation. You may go for the best-looking one for yourself. It's a small thing I'm asking of you," Caine said, applying his most reasonable tone. "*Asking,* not ordering. And as a friend, Trent."

"Fine! It's your own throat you're cutting. Your uncle was wrong when he put the condition on you to marry. I wouldn't do it if I were you. You'll have his title no matter what you do or don't."

Caine shrugged. "Yes, but it's the fortune that will go to Cousin Neville, plus the estates, since none is entailed. Think of all the people now employed by the earl who would suffer if Neville lost everything over a stupid game of cards or on a damned horse race. He could, and probably would, piss away everything the family has worked for these last two centuries."

"You don't know that he will. You haven't seen him since you were children."

"Oh, I've heard enough of his maddening exploits from my uncle. Knowing such things, I cannot imagine why he would even consider leaving *anything* to Neville, but Hadley seems amused by it all and oddly unconcerned. Therefore, I must prevent it however I can. So I will marry, as he stipulates. I don't have any strong objections. He is my uncle, after all, and I do care about his feelings. I should settle his mind before he gives up the ghost."

"But why must you have a woman who's desperate to marry?" Trent clicked his tongue, exasperated. "Not every female in London runs screaming from the room when she sees you."

"One certainly did."

"Well, *only* that one, and as I've said before, she's not all there." He tapped his temple with two fingers and shook his head. "Silly witch."

"Well, she's not *here,* either, which is why I came." Caine heaved out a breath of frustration and began strolling the perimeter of the room, Trent at his side.

"Watch how each miss gives me a look of repulsion as we pass, terrified I will take an interest." He shook his head. "Times such as this, blindness would be a blessing."

"Well, I'm damned glad you're *not* blind and you ought to be, too! Perhaps their regard is merely a reaction to your grim expression. Try smiling now and again. They could do far worse than you, and you know it. So you have a few scars. A wife would get used to that after the first shock of seeing them."

"I hope you're right." Caine stopped beside a towering plant and picked absently at one of the leaves. "But I think it best to choose a woman not prone to play the social butterfly. The most beautiful exist for it. I despise these sorts of occasions and would like to be done with them."

He hadn't used to hate social events, not when he'd been a young lieutenant, flirting, dancing, assessing the newest crop of preening lovelies, giving Trent solid competition. That's how he had found a little beauty of excellent birth, whom he had thought would be the perfect mate for a rising army officer. A young fool's mistake, that. Now he knew better.

He had been only third in line for the earldom then, with a military career underway. However, with the deaths of his father and a brother during the years Caine had served in the army, he was now set to inherit from the eldest of that generation, his uncle. He had not been born to the title, nor had he been trained for it. The responsibilities were enormous, greater than he had ever imagined. There was so much to learn. So much to sort out.

The old earl, who admittedly was not long for the world, demanded that his heir be settled and ready to assume his duties. That involved Caine's getting a wife immediately, so here he was, shopping. He surveyed the goods, evaluating faces, postures, attitudes.

This time he knew he must rely on different currency for the negotiations. The women he had been well acquainted with in his life thus far had proved rather shallow, valuing a handsome face, charm and practised manners well above anything else in a man. They left it to their practical families to ascertain whether their choice possessed the necessary means to support them.

Now he must find a suitable woman desperate enough to overlook his altered appearance and lack of social inclinations to settle for his prospective wealth and title. More important, as he had impressed on Trent, he needed one who would not impact on the time he would require to fulfill his duties as earl. The task of handling the earl's business matters already proved daunting. He must live up to it.

Trent's words troubled him. Did such a woman as he required actually exist? He continued scanning the ballroom, dwelling on the corners where the wallflowers perched, trying to conceal their hopes and dreams behind fans and half smiles. None of their smiles were directed at him.

Suddenly, his good eye landed on one in pale yellow, a painfully thin figure with lank brown hair, a colorless complexion and enormous, doe-like eyes. Caine immediately sensed in her a mixture of hopelessness and resignation, yet she somehow maintained an air of calm dignity he admired. "A definite possibility there," he muttered, more to himself than to Trent.

The girl was not precisely ugly, but it was certain no one would describe her as pretty. He felt a tug of…what? Sympathy? No, more like empathy. She did not wish to be here, either, most likely for similar reasons. Yet they must be here, probably striving toward the same goal—a suitable match.

These mating rituals were such a trial for any not blessed with the allure necessary to attract the opposite sex. At least he would have wealth and the title to recommend him. She had only her dignity apparently. If she were an heiress, she would certainly be better dressed, coiffed and bejeweled. Her pale neck and earlobes were completely bare.

If he could look past her surface, perhaps she would be willing to look past his. But he must put it to her in a way she would find palatable. He couldn't very well say "You look like a quiet, unprepossessing chit I could count on to not complicate my life any further than it is already."

Could he summon enough charm, persuasion and outrageous bribery to convince this one to have him? Yes, he decided, approaching her might be worth the risk of rejection.

"Yes, I think so," he said to himself. "That one, Trent," he said, nodding toward the candidate. "The one in the lemon-colored frock. She'll do."

"What? She's a bean stalk, Morleigh, and the beans don't appear to have developed yet."

"I'm not out for beans," Caine said tersely, his gaze still resting on the waiflike girl.

"Well, she looks like death on a plate. I doubt she'll live through the month, much less the rigors of a wedding." He nudged Caine with his elbow. "Besides, you said you'd let me choose."

"Don't be tedious. I believe she's the one, so go. Do what we came to do," Caine said simply, straightening his sleeves.

He hoped to have the selection completed with this one foray into society, because it was damned uncomfortable submitting himself to all these stares. He knew he wasn't that monstrous looking and that they were mostly curious, but it bothered him.

His left eye bore only a few scars, but those surely made everyone imagine the very worst of the one he kept covered. The right, he always avoided looking at in the mirror and concealed it behind a rather large eye patch whenever he was in company.

That was probably a useless vanity due to the well-broadcast observation of Miss Thoren-Snipes, his former fiancée. She had declared to one and all that he was a horrible sight that turned her off sick, a fright she would never forget, one that caused her nightmares.

To her credit, his aunt's reaction that day had verified that Belinda did not exaggerate by much. He made women faint, cast up their accounts and scream in their sleep. Avoiding that hardly qualified as vanity on his part. No, more like a gentleman's consideration, he thought.

Trent did not understand, and why should he? He had the wherewithal to pick and choose and take his own sweet time about it. No woman would refuse Gavin Trent, handsome as he was, a hero of the wars and witty as hell. Caine owed him his life, admired him enormously and wished him well. Envy had no place in a friendship as enduring as theirs. But Trent's eternal optimism and infernal teasing tried his patience to extremes.

The girl in yellow was now getting an earful from one of the other unfortunates, an overweight dumpling who seemed entirely too vivacious to qualify as second choice if he needed one. Her glance left no doubt about whom she had chosen to revile.

Caine wondered if perhaps he was overly sensitive and tried not to be, but he was unused to it yet. He had attended none of these functions since his return to London. He was grateful that he was still able to see and wished he could simply bypass mirrors forever and ignore how he looked. If not for this acquiring of a wife, he could be content with himself as he was.

The object of his future suit looked up and her very direct gaze again met his across the room. He should march right over and ask her to dance. Three times running. That would seal the deal. But not yet.

Caine snagged a glass of champagne off the silver tray of a passing waiter circulating among the guests. He raised it slightly, toasting the girl, and forced a smile as he spoke to his friend. "Go, Trent. Find out who she is. I'll wait here."

"You're certain you want to go through with this?"

"Yes, quite." He sipped the sparkling wine and concealed a wince. He preferred a stouter drink with some substance to it.

A quarter hour later, Trent rejoined Caine. "She's Wardfelton's niece, Lady Grace Renfair," he declared. "His lordship laughed in my face when I spoke with him. Told me she has no dowry. She's penniless. *Worthless* was the word he used to describe her, an ailing, aging millstone around his neck and none too bright."

"Aging? How old is she?"

"Twenty-four or thereabout. I inquired of a few others, as well as her uncle. Lady Nebbins, that old talebearer, told me the chit was orphaned at sixteen, engaged to Barkley's second son, a lieutenant in the navy, who died aboard *The Langston* six years ago. She lived as companion to the lad's widowed mother until that lady remarried. Lady Grace has been with Wardfelton for these past two years."

"Ah, good. Of suitable birth then. And something in common already, noble uncles with a foot on our necks. Perhaps she's ready for a change."

Trent hummed his agreement. "I don't doubt that. Rumor about town had it she was perhaps dead. People had begun wondering aloud whether she was deceased and how she came to be so. It's thought Wardfelton has trotted her out tonight to dispense with the gossip. I must say, she might yet make it a fact. To call her frail would be kind."

Caine smiled. "No matter. I can go forward with it then."

"Ah, well, there's a fly in the ointment," Trent informed him. He rocked to and fro as he spoke. "Wardfelton didn't take me, or my request on your behalf, seriously at all. He thinks

we are making fun of his simpleminded niece
and seemed to find it highly amusing that we
should do so."

"Simpleminded?" Caine didn't believe it for
a second.

Trent shrugged. "He doesn't think much of
her, obviously. Probably exaggerated. I would
remind you, you did ask for dull of wit."

"He didn't refuse outright to let me address
her, did he?"

"No, he doesn't really expect you to," Trent
admitted. "I spoke with Lord Jarvis, too. He says
she is the daughter of the previous earl. Wardfelton's actually the third brother to hold the title.
The second, Lady Grace's father, was a physician until he inherited. Only held it for a couple
of years before he died of the cholera during the
outbreak here, along with his wife. The girl was
left home in the country and escaped their fate.
And as I said, Barkley's mother took her in."

Caine nodded. "Ah, an earl's daughter. Uncle
should consider the match entirely acceptable. If
she is willing and I could obtain a special license
from the archbishop, we could marry this week."

"You know what they say about marrying in
haste."

"Never put off until tomorrow what you can
do today," Caine retorted. He shoved his glass
at Trent. "Hold this for me. Better yet, get me

another with something more bracing than bubbles. Courting's thirsty work."

He left Trent standing there staring at the delicate crystal stem and went to ply his suit.

Chapter Two

❦❧

Grace Renfair shifted her gaze elsewhere, determined not to look back at the man standing across the ballroom. His intense regard unnerved her. Why did he single her out so pointedly? Probably wondering who was so witless as to sponsor a creature such as herself.

She felt exposed, woefully underdressed and incomparable in the worst sort of way. No matter. She lifted her chin and paid only scant attention to the vile chatter of the girl beside her.

"I could never abide a man so tall and large as Captain Morleigh, even if he were handsome!" exclaimed Miss Caulfield. Grace did not reply, even to nod or shrug.

He was large, yes, but not frighteningly so. Grace thought he cut quite a figure when compared to the fashionably slender or the aging portly gents milling around him at the moment.

"He would frighten the life out of anyone! Belinda is well out of that match! She says he has turned unbearably cold and cruel since the war. Why, he probably slew dozens of people before he was nearly killed himself!"

Wasn't he *expected* to do that when he was a soldier? Grace ignored Miss Caulfield's comment. Would the girl ever change topics? No, she prattled on. "Look at his shoulders! All that swordplay, I should think. No padding there, I'd wager!"

Not a bet Grace would take. She had also noted that his features were well defined and rather stark above that square jaw and stubborn chin. The eye patch added a dash of interest, as perhaps it was meant to do, though if he had been wounded in battle, it probably was not simply for show.

The black evening attire topped by a snowy neckcloth looked impeccable, though his straight-shouldered military bearing was such that he might as well have worn regimentals. His height was remarkable, too, putting him at least half a head above the men around him.

"Yes, his looks are compelling," Grace said, before remembering she should not speak at all.

So why should she mind if he caught her looking at him, since everyone else seemed to be? Perhaps she should thank him for drawing inquisitive stares away from her.

When she finally gave in to curiosity and shot another glance in his direction, she saw this Captain Morleigh heedlessly interrupting the progress of the quadrille by walking directly through it. Now, there was a man who did precisely as he pleased. She would give anything to be that bold.

She had been once, but had changed so much she hardly knew herself any longer. The face in her mirror seemed a stranger, as did her almost-lifeless form swathed in the dated ball gown her uncle had provided. There had been no maid to dress her, to help with her woefully straight hair or even produce pins for it.

Her uncle had brought her here to show her off, so he said. She believed that to be true in the very worst sense and wondered if perhaps he thought he must. He had kept her a virtual prisoner for well over a year. Did anyone question where she was keeping these days and what had happened to her? Or did anyone remember her at all?

She had never made her debut, having been betrothed so early on. Then her mourning had been extended much longer than usual. She had lost both parents and soon after, her husband-to-be. The comfort of his mother, Lady Barkley, had been such a balm, she had been loath to give up the sweet lady's company. Not one to intrude on her dear friend's newlywed state, Grace had insisted on removing herself to the care of her only relative. Such a mistake that had been, and so irrevocable.

She and Wardfelton had gotten on quite well in the beginning. She even played hostess for several entertainments he had held at the country house. Then, literally overnight, things had changed. He suddenly turned into nothing short of a jailer, insisting she remain in her rooms except for a supervised walk about the enclosed gardens when weather permitted. Her meals were sent up. Her correspondence disallowed.

It seemed he thoroughly enjoyed humiliating and even frightening her in every way he could devise. She shuddered just thinking of the tales he had told of young English women disappearing, sold into white slavery, never to be seen or heard of again. Though not an outright threat, there had been warning in his eyes. Why, she could not fathom, but he obviously meant to keep her terrified and biddable for some reason or other.

Perhaps he feared being called to account for squandering her inheritance, if indeed she had ever possessed any such thing. She could not look into it herself and whom did he think would do so on her behalf? No one cared.

Well, her looks were gone now and she much

doubted any foreign sultan with proper eyesight would want to buy such as her. What more could Uncle do to her other than offer her up to ridicule as he was doing tonight?

Murder was still an option, even though he would be the most obvious suspect. She had pointed that out to him when he deliberately had left out that book of poisons for her to see. He had laughed at that, but she had sensed his unease. More likely, he intended to drive her to suicide so he would look blameless.

If only she knew someone here, she would plead for escape. But would anyone believe her? Would anyone care?

"He's coming this way!" Miss Caulfield announced. "Should we venture to speak to him?"

Grace knew she was being watched, for Wardfelton had told her she would be. He also warned rather adamantly that she was to hold no personal conversations with anyone present. She was only to been seen, not heard. Grace held her head high despite all that. He would not steal what little dignity she had left.

Nor would this man approaching with a patently fake smile upon his face. He stopped directly in front of her.

"My lady, please allow me to presume and introduce myself."

"You would be Captain Morleigh," she replied, to save him the trouble. She held out her hand and watched with interest as he lifted it almost to his lips. Damn Wardfelton. Let him do his worst. Damn them all. She was sick of living in fear.

"Lady Grace," he said, holding her gaze, as well as her hand. "I see that our reputations have preceded us. Such a pleasure to meet you. Would you do me the honor of the next dance?"

Grace cocked her head to one side as she continued to peer up at him. He bore a few scars from the war, pinkish and still healing, random marks upon his forehead and around his uncovered eye. They did proclaim the validity of the eye patch he wore that lent him his roguish air.

Misses Caulfield and Thoren-Snipes were so wrong. The man was not hideous at all. More's the pity. She had never trusted handsome men, especially *arrogant* handsome men who presumed too much, as he did now. She forced a half smile. "Not for all the gold in England would I dance with you, sir."

His eye twinkled and he smiled more sincerely, a crooked expression that warmed something inside her. "I'm not offering *all* the gold," he said, "but a significant portion could be yours if you're amenable."

"A proposition, sir?" She raised an eyebrow with the question. "Am I to run weeping at the insult or deal you a resounding slap? How do the bets go that I will respond?"

"No bets and no proposition. I have a very decent proposal in mind."

"I am already the object of ridicule," she told him frankly, withdrawing her hand from his, flipping open her fan and giving him the signal to leave her alone. "Go, find another to tease who will at least earn you points for originality."

He inclined his head. "Certainly no ridicule intended, my lady. I merely ask to be considered. I have some trouble in that quarter as you have no doubt heard." He cast a pointed look at her overfed companion, who promptly blushed and hurried away.

Morleigh returned his attentions to Grace. "Will you not grant me a small favor, at least, and take a turn about the floor?"

Perhaps this was an arranged jibe, compliments of her uncle. "Do you know Wardfelton?"

"I have not met him yet, but I shall seek him out immediately if you will give me leave to ask him for you."

"For my *person?* Not only a dance? How droll."

"For your hand in marriage," he said without equivocation.

A short laugh escaped in spite of her dismay. The man was either woefully desperate, quite mad or downright cruel. "I should give you that leave, my lord, and hold you by law to your word. It would serve you right for carrying this jest too far."

Amazingly, he stretched his hand closer, his expression totally devoid of sarcasm, his deep voice rife with sincerity. "Please do. I would be forever grateful. Perhaps we could dance and discuss it further?"

His madness must be contagious. Whatever he had in mind could hardly lower her any more in public estimation than did the way she looked tonight. And why should she care if it did? None of her former friends were in attendance, not that she had ever had many who would be here in town.

She had hoped at first to appeal to someone she knew to give her some respite from her uncle, but he had warned her no one would. In fact, she had nothing provable to complain about except his clearly implied hatred and her suspicion that, for some cause unknown, he wished her to wither and die. She could not run away again, for even if he were disposed to let her, where would she go and what would she do?

Revealing her fears to anyone and asking their interference might imply hysterics on her part. Wardfelton had accused her of that himself, cleverly attributing it to her martyring grief and self-induced illness. No doubt he had already broadcast that diagnosis to anyone willing to listen. Secluding her in a madhouse was a distinct possibility, and perhaps tonight was meant to set the stage for that.

Damn the man and his threats! This was no way to live, and she was sick of it. Why had she stood it for so long?

Let him do his worst. She probably would die soon one way or another. Sad, but that fact seemed oddly freeing at the moment. It wasn't as if she stood any chance of ever making another match or doing any of the things a young woman of means might undertake. She had no means. No prospects at all. Why not do as she pleased tonight and damn the consequences?

Without thinking any more about it, Grace placed her gloved hand in the captain's again. He swept her onto the dance floor and into a scandalously close waltz.

She was not so familiar with the steps, but he held her firmly and guided her as if they had practiced daily for weeks. Grace found it exhilarating, being held so near and whirled about so expertly.

After one turn around the floor, she looked up at him. "Why do you do this, really? You have already made us a spectacle, so honesty will lose you nothing."

His expression smoothed out. "Honestly? I need a wife. And I am guessing that you need a husband. That *is* why we are here, is it not?"

"You *do* know Wardfelton. He has put you up to this."

"We have never met, I vow it on my life. I will admit I sent Lord Trent as my emissary to ask Wardfelton's leave to court you."

"Oh, he would never agree to that," she stated, quite sure of it. Who knew what her uncle would do to her simply for having this dance and conversation?

"Well, he did not refuse, either. Probably too deep in his cups. I can only hope he's drunk enough to let me have you. Assuming you are willing, of course. Are you?"

She laughed a little. "What idiot steered you in this direction, I wonder? I've not a farthing to recommend me. I would come with nothing. Surely he made that clear enough."

"I come with everything you will need. Make your demands and I shall meet them."

Grace shook her head and kept a smile on her face, unwilling to let him see how painful it was to be toyed with in such a way. Yet she decided the best way to deflect this sort of jest was to laugh along with the jester. "Ah, well, if you put it that way… A thousand quid per annum, two maids and a shiny new phaeton. Oh, and diamonds, of course. A lady must have diamonds."

He gave a satisfied nod. "Done and done, my lady. Only, you shall have two thousand, all the servants you like, plus a matched team to pull the phaeton."

"Why, thank you!" she exclaimed with her widest smile. "But what of the gems, my lord? Does that break the deal?"

"No. Do you prefer blue or yellow stones?" He whirled her again, causing her stomach to flutter wildly.

"White diamonds," she declared, leaning back and challenging him with her eyes. "You know, this is most entertaining. For you, that is to say. As for me, I should like to kick you in the shins and spit in your face. Manners prevent, however, so if you would kindly lead me back to my place by the wall and collect whatever sum you have riding on this farce, I would be most appreciative."

He stopped dead still in the middle of the floor and stared down at her. The music faltered and the noise died down. With no apparent care for who was watching and listening, he took both her hands in his and brought them to his lips. "Lady Grace, you've quite stolen my heart and I cannot live without you. Would you do me the great honor of becoming my wife?" His voice was even deeper than before. And rather loud in the gathering hush.

A collective gasp shook the cavernous room. Someone dropped a violin and the strings pinged, the only other sound to be heard.

"Say you will have me, or my heart will break." A stage whisper if she had ever heard one. It fairly echoed round the room.

Grace barely resisted the urge to throw back her head and laugh out loud. She had not laughed that way in so long, perhaps she had forgotten how, but the urge was there.

She glanced over the group surrounding them and saw Wardfelton had entered the ballroom and was standing there with his mouth agape. She realized at that moment she would do virtually anything to discommode him further. And anything to get away from him permanently, even if it landed her in a worse fix. Well, here was her chance.

She recalled the old expression, *better the devil you know...* Balderdash, that wasn't so in her case. The devil she didn't know could hardly be any worse than Wardfelton. She had nearly forgotten what it was like to live without constant terror. And for some unfathomable reason, she had no fear of Captain Morleigh. None at all.

Grace looked back into the eye of the presumptuous man who held her hands. Here was no devil, only a slightly disfigured fellow who doubted his appeal to women so devoutly he would settle for the one he thought most desperate. Well, he had found her right enough.

The description of him that Miss Thoren-Snipes had passed around had been widely dispersed, according to Grace's companion earlier this evening. Perhaps Morleigh suffered more than anyone knew, especially if he was now reduced to pleading with the least-agreeable woman in the room to marry him.

He began to look hopeful then, taking her hesitation for wavering, she supposed. It certainly was that. She felt him draw her closer as he leaned down to speak privately. "All that I promised you, plus independence," he whispered, then added, "no conditions attached."

"None?" Yes, he *was* mad.

"Well, faithfulness, of course," he said against her ear. "We will vow that much when we wed. But otherwise, you shall do as you please, go where you will, act as you choose."

"Your word of honor?" she whispered back, actually considering it seriously. She might be trading one threat for another. Morleigh could beat her, lock her away or possibly get rid of her permanently as she was sure her uncle planned to do. Even as she thought that, it seemed more likely this man would simply leave her to her own devices if she displeased him. Or even if she didn't. It certainly was a gamble, but she really had nothing to lose.

"Then yes," she replied in a whisper.

"Louder," he suggested. "That will make it official and irrevocable."

"I will!" she declared, flashing her uncle a

steely glare. "I would be honored to marry you, Captain Morleigh. My heart is lost and I simply cannot wait to be your wife." Who cared if that sounded like a line from some mawkish play. So had his loud proposal.

Morleigh kissed her hands, each in turn and signaled to the orchestra. "Gentlemen, if you please, a celebratory waltz!"

Stunned, shaken, still feeling the urge to laugh wildly, Grace followed his lead until the music stopped.

Lord, she felt dizzy, overcome with heat from the exertion. The moment he released her to applaud the music, she swooned. Her last thought was that she had finally starved herself into wild delusions. This night could not be real.

Chapter Three

"Fetch a doctor!" shouted Caine. He felt her wrist for a pulse and found one. It seemed steady enough and only a trifle weak.

No one came forward to help. Highly unlikely that a mere physician would be present at the assembly, so he scooped her up in his arms and strode out, barking an order to have his carriage brought round on the instant.

"Where do you think you're going with her?" Wardfelton demanded loudly. He followed them out the front entrance and scampered around to hamper Caine's progress.

"She needs a doctor. I know one. Stand aside. She's mine now."

"She is *not* yours!" The man's outrage seemed real enough. "I forbid this!" he shouted. "Put her *down,* I say!"

"Come with us if you're worried about her. Otherwise, stand clear!"

Half the attendees had followed them out to the steps and stood transfixed. Better than a horse race or a boxing match, Caine figured. More food for gossip at any rate. He needed the audience, so he didn't mind.

"Someone call the watch! This is abduction!" Wardfelton cried, wheeling right and left, searching for someone to interfere.

Caine faced him down, the lady's inert form between them. "Lord Trent is my witness. He spoke for me and you did not deny my asking for her hand. I have done, and with intentions most honorable. She is of age to accept without your consent. Lady Grace will be properly chaperoned by my aunt, the countess of Hadley, until she recovers and then we shall be married."

"This is absurd!" Wardfelton announced, still looking around for support amongst his peers.

"Is it? What is your objection, sir?" Caine noticed the carriage making way along the thoroughfare to where they stood at the edge of the steps. "I marry her not for money or property, for you and she both swear she has none. I admire her enormously and find her delightful."

He appealed to the crowd, whose female members had just uttered a sigh and were looking rather dreamy eyed. "Beauty is as beauty does, you know. And she does beautifully so far as I am concerned."

Another collective sigh and numerous eager nods of approval. As he meant them to, the women present were eating this up with a spoon.

His carriage now awaited with the door open. Caine turned sideways and stepped into it with his featherlight fiancée still in his arms, her head resting on his chest.

She had revived on the steps. He had felt the tension in her thin body the moment he had faced down Wardfelton, but she continued to feign unconsciousness. He didn't blame her in the least, and it did suit his purpose of keeping crowd sympathy.

"Don't come round yet," he warned her in a whisper as he waited for the footman to close the door. "Your lady friends are sighing at the romance of it all. Add that to their relief that I'm no longer in the market for a bride and we two could become legend."

"Thank you for a moment I shall never forget," she whispered back. "Even should you dump me in the nearest ditch, I would still feel beholden. The look on his face was priceless. I peeked."

He grunted in response as he shifted her more comfortably on his lap. "You are guaranteed more than a moment. Can you survive all this or do you plan to faint on me regularly?"

She shook her head. "No, it was merely the exercise. I've not danced in ages. Or eaten of late. Is there food where we're going?"

Caine relaxed. "I believe we can find something."

The carriage was well away from the crowd now. Grace sat up, moved off his lap and onto the opposite seat. She leaned forward and clasped her hands on her knees. "So we are going to your home now?"

"My uncle's house here in Mayfair, where you'll be properly chaperoned, as I promised."

She nodded. "All right. This is no jest, is it? You truly were not in collusion with him."

"With Wardfelton? You heard our exchange."

With a heartfelt sigh, she leaned back against the seat and closed her eyes. "Thank God."

"I'll send someone round for your things tomorrow," he said. He reached up and started to shift the patch from his eye, then stopped himself.

"Oh, go ahead. The binding must be dreadfully uncomfortable," she said with a flap of one hand. "My father was a doctor and I assisted with patients. I shan't be shocked by an empty socket."

Still he didn't remove the patch. He merely studied her in the carriage light. "You seem a different sort from the lot I've known."

"Truer than you could ever guess," she admitted, then stifled a yawn with her hand.

"Are you ill, Grace?" he asked, then seemed to realize his impertinence. "Sorry. May I call you Grace in private?"

"Address me as you like. I suppose you have a given name?"

"Caine," he replied, looking a trifle uncomfortable.

He had a strong face and very fine skin where it wasn't scarred. His hair was rather too long, but a lovely shade of brown and with a slight wave to it.

She imagined he had been far too handsome for his own good before his injury. In fact, he was even now, though he would never believe it should anyone say as much. "How were you wounded?" she asked.

For a full moment, he remained silent and she thought he would refuse to answer. Then he did. "Artillery fire." He gestured to his face. "A shell exploded nearby and I was struck by fragments. Killed my horse."

"But you survived," she said, fascinated and wishing he would tell more. "That's the important thing."

"So I thought at the time. Wouldn't you like to lie down? I'll make a pillow of my coat." He began to take it off.

"No, don't bother. Is it very far?"

He glanced out the window. "Almost there. How do you feel?"

"Exhausted, if you must know," Grace admitted. "But I shan't need a doctor. A good night's rest should put me right. And food, as I said before. I'm famished."

"Good God! Has he been starving you?" Caine demanded.

She laughed, giddy and a bit light-headed. "No. I've done it to myself."

His worried expression said what tact prevented. He thought *she* was the mad one. And given her present situation, perhaps he was right.

Caine would not second-guess his choice. That was not his way. He made decisions and lived with them. If one proved wrong, he worked it to his advantage as best he could. Never vacillate, never look back on what might have been. And now he had chosen a wife. Granted, this decision had been made more impulsively than most any other in his life, but he would stand by it.

He would stand by *her*. For some uncanny reason, he felt an odd kinship with the little Lady Grace and had from the moment he had first seen her across the ballroom. Odd.

Trent had followed them home and stood in the foyer behind him as he introduced Grace to his uncle's housekeeper, Mrs. Oliver. The older women curtsied even as she frowned at the new-comer. Caine could sense her disapproval, or perhaps it was only concern. The earl might mirror that when he met Grace, since she did not possess the appearance of a healthy breeder. No matter.

"Mrs. Oliver, could you arrange something to feed us?"

"The three of you, milord?"

"Yes, but nothing fancy. A simple tray in the breakfast room will do nicely. And a pot of strong tea for the lady."

"Only brandy for me," Trent supplied. He turned to Grace with a succinct bow. "I am Gavin Trent, friend of this nodcock you're now attached to."

"And his second this evening, so he tells me. Thank you for your assistance with the arrangements," she said with a curtsy.

"My pleasure."

"This way," Caine said, ushering Grace down the corridor.

"A lovely residence," Grace observed, sounding a bit breathless. "Your uncle is...?"

"Earl of Hadley."

She turned to him. "And you are his—?"

"His heir. Yes, you will one day be a countess. I understand your father was an earl, so perhaps you won't mind the station." Caine hoped she wouldn't faint again and took her arm in case she did.

"My goodness!" she exclaimed, her hand clutching her bodice. "Why *me?*"

Caine might not know much of women's minds, but he certainly knew better than to be completely honest in this instance. "You looked positively regal standing there. I was quite smitten."

She laughed out loud, a full-throated, joyful sound he hadn't expected. It was contagious and he laughed with her. Trent shot him a frown and, obviously not amused, went straight for the brandy decanter when the butler appeared with it.

They sat at one end of the breakfast-room table, Grace on his right, Trent to the left. "So, here we are," Trent said on a sigh as he poured a draft into three snifters. "What now?"

"Would you see about getting the license?"

"If you like." Trent gulped a swallow and winced at the burn. "But first I'll need information you haven't given me yet. Where will you marry?"

"Do you have a preference?" he asked Grace.

She gave a shrug and a small shake of her head. "Anywhere."

"The chapel at Wildenhurst," Caine stated. "It's close enough that Uncle can attend comfortably, but not here in town where we might be plagued by hordes of the curious. Have you friends you wish to witness or attend?" he asked her.

Again, that small, disbelieving shake of her head. She knocked back the entire contents of her glass and coughed.

"Easy there. Are you quite all right?"

She nodded uncertainly as if the full impact of the evening's events had suddenly hit her.

"No more plans tonight. You need to eat and then sleep. Tomorrow is soon enough for arrangements," Caine declared. He looked meaningfully at Trent.

Trent set down his glass and stood. "I'll just be off then." He held out a hand to Caine. "Congratulations on your betrothal." He bowed to Grace. "My lady, I wish you every happiness. And with that, a good night to you both."

Grace exhaled audibly. "Thank you."

Caine grinned at Trent's wry expression. "See you in the morning."

When they were alone, Caine sought to soothe Grace's concerns, since she surely must have a few. "Everything will be done for you and you needn't worry about anything."

A kitchen maid arrived with a tray laden with cold meats, bread, sliced oranges and a pot of tea.

"You may leave it," Caine told her. "I will

serve the lady." He proceeded to slather butter on a slice of bread for her.

She hurriedly rolled two slabs of ham and attacked the food without pause. Or anything resembling manners. Caine stopped what he was doing and watched with fascination as she ate. Eyes closed, she moaned softly and chewed rapidly.

After a few moments, she stopped and covered her mouth with her serviette.

"Too much, too fast?" he asked. "Perhaps you should rest a bit first."

"She should and that's a fact," Mrs. Oliver declared. Caine turned to see her standing in the doorway Trent had just vacated. The heavyset retainer marched forward and virtually lifted her charge out of the chair. "You come right along, miss."

He stood quickly to bid Grace good-night, noting that she plucked up the slice of bread he had buttered before being hauled away.

Caine sat down again when they were gone, eye fixed on the remnants of the cold supper without actually seeing it. Why would Grace admittedly starve herself, then gobble down food with such abandon? Had she lied about Wardfelton's treatment? Had the man withheld sustenance? And if so, whyever would he do such a thing?

This would bear some investigation, but there

was no rush. His little Grace would be perfectly safe now and hereafter. He would see to that.

For the first time since the morning of the battle that nearly blinded him, Caine felt a wave of calmness and well-being. He dearly hoped it would last.

The next morning, Caine awakened late, but fully alert and eager, for once, to face the day. He ascribed that to having a meaningful and interesting project other than the tedious business of straightening out his uncle's affairs.

Grace must take second place, of course, immediately after their marriage. Once he had grown accustomed to the new duties he would assume and felt confident he could handle them, he would investigate Grace's situation or have someone do it.

No sooner was he dressed and on his way downstairs than Trent arrived with news. Caine motioned him toward the library.

Trent began speaking before he even took a chair. "The archbishop will provide the special license to wed any place you wish," he announced immediately. "However, Jarvis says that you will still have several weeks' wait."

"I thought we could wed at any time thereafter." Caine made himself comfortable behind the earl's desk and began rearranging the papers he had been working on the day before.

"Well, these days, a special license has become a status affair and everyone wants one. So why not have banns called at the Wildenhurst chapel and do things in the regular way?"

Caine steepled his fingers beneath his chin and thought about it. "I had hoped to have it done sooner, but I suppose there's no great reason for haste."

Trent nodded his agreement. "He also said it might be wise for either you or the lady to repair to the country for the duration in order to establish residence. Though, that could likely be waived, since it was your home before the war."

Caine considered that for a moment. "Very well." Truth was, he didn't mind leaving London, but he would need to convince his uncle to accompany them. "Would you see to retrieving Lady Grace's belongings from Wardfelton's house for me?"

Trent sighed and threw up his hands. "I went by to accomplish that after I asked about the license. Her uncle refuses to part with a thread of hers, or to countenance what he's calling her abduction. He swears he plans to bring charges against you, but I doubt it will come to anything. Too many witnesses heard her accept your offer."

"I suppose the town's abuzz with last night's antics," Caine said.

"If that was your intention, it was wildly successful. Still, public approval of your little romance doesn't help clothe the lady, does it?"

"No matter. I'll send for a dressmaker. Grace will need a trousseau. But absolutely nothing in *yellow*," he added with a shake of his head. "Atrocious."

Trent was staring at the doorway and wincing. Caine turned to see Grace standing there, wearing the awful garment he had just referred to. "Sorry you heard that, but you must admit…"

She nodded thoughtfully, staring at the floor. "I am well aware of how I look. No need to mince words on my account."

Caine wished he could call her beautiful, but he did not want to begin their relationship with lies. She was not beautiful. The poor little dear looked pitiful this morning, even worse than last evening. Her light brown hair hung from a middle parting in stick-straight strands, the ends uneven about her shoulders. Pale as death, her features seemed far too small for the large blue eyes. Remarkable eyes. His heart went out to her in that moment.

"It's the color yellow that I object to, Grace. And only that," he said with conviction.

Trent cleared his throat, breaking the spell. "Yes, well, if you two will excuse me, I have errands of my own."

Caine thanked him absently as he left.

"Mr. Trent is a good friend to do so much for

you," Grace said as she ventured farther into the library.

"It's *Lord* Trent, Viscount Trent. His father's Marquis of Alden. And yes, indeed he is my best friend." Trent had been that since they were boys. "We schooled together and served under the same command in the army. I would scarcely know what to do without him," Caine admitted.

She traced her fingers along a row of books before facing him with a sigh. "Would you grant me permission to go to the country alone while the banns are being called?" she asked.

"Not to Wardfelton's estate. Unless you've changed your mind about the marriage."

"Heavens no on both accounts," she answered with a little huff of laughter. "I will go anywhere you say *except* there, but I would like some time to myself before the wedding if you wouldn't mind."

"If you would be willing to take a companion and the dressmaker I mentioned, you could go on to Wildenhurst. It's one of Hadley's minor properties, but well appointed. And I could remain here. I understand that my company is probably—"

"Oh, no!" She frowned and shook her head vehemently. "No, I swear, it isn't anything to do with you at all!" For a moment, she looked at him with a plea evident in her expression. "You promised me freedom. I would like a taste of it."

Yes, he had promised. He nodded.

"There you are!" Mrs. Oliver came marching in, hands on her hips. "You come with me now, miss. You've not had your chocolate and toast yet and aren't even dressed proper for the morning, showing shoulders and such. Excuse us, sir, and go on with your business. I shall see to the little miss."

In spite of himself, Caine liked the old lady, overbearing attitude and all. Everyone in the household, regardless of rank, obeyed her. Even Jenkins, the earl's snobbish butler, didn't dare oppose her. How she had gained so much power, he couldn't guess, but she was one to reckon with. Still, he felt an urge to defend Grace. "Little Miss has a name, Mrs. Oliver."

"Well, she's Little Miss to me until she's a married lady. Got to look after young misses, we all do, till they grow up and marry."

Caine could see Grace hiding a smile behind her fingertips. So she understood and didn't mind the heavy-handed martinet. Perhaps she would enjoy being fussed over and looked after. "Go with Mrs. Oliver then and have a good day. My aunt and uncle will want to meet you, but I think we should wait until tomorrow for that."

"She'll be ready," Mrs. Oliver assured him. "Now, come along, luvvy, so I can put you to rights. A good feed and a hot bath should do the trick."

"Could I have eggs?" he heard Grace ask her as they left.

"And black pudding. Good for strength and such," Mrs. Oliver declared.

Caine smiled at Grace's groan. A fair beginning. They had two dislikes in common. Black pudding and Wardfelton. He toyed with his pen as his gaze lingered on the doorway. He wondered idly whether they shared any likes. And then, why such a question should occur to him at all.

Chapter Four

Caine promptly went to work, but found he could not concentrate. Impatiently, he pushed aside the account books for his uncle's largest estate. The figures were not in good order, but today there were more pressing matters.

There were inquiries to answer, orders for supplies and letters of instruction to be prepared for signature. He arranged the paper, dipped a pen in the inkwell and began to write.

In all his life, he had never thought to do anything but soldier. He liked the structure of army life in general, but had hated the chaos of battle and the incompetence of leadership. If not for his wounding and the earl's illness, he would have continued trying to rise in rank until he could displace some of that inefficiency. But now here he was, facing the ever-increasing responsibilities of an earldom. So many people were dependent upon his ability to manage well. And soon, so would a wife.

Thankfully, Grace shouldn't pose a problem or even much of an added responsibility. She would remain practically invisible, by her own choice, he expected.

She was easily led and apparently preferred solitude. An excellent match indeed with which to satisfy his uncle's demand and Caine's own need for time and space to acclimate to the nobility. Yes, he had his personal affairs arranged precisely as they should be. Well, almost. There were matters there that needed his attention before he could relax.

That afternoon, he put aside the earl's business for his own. A meeting with Grace's uncle was necessary and might as well be accomplished as soon as possible to get the unpleasant errand out of the way. He changed his coat, ran a comb through his hair, adjusted his eye patch and set off on foot for Wardfelton's town house.

The man was not at home, but the maid who answered the door did advise Caine where the earl might be found at that hour.

Caine had avoided the clubs since returning from the war. Before that, he and Trent had frequented White's on occasion. His leanings were

Whig, as were his uncle's. Apparently, Wardfelton preferred Brooke's, overwhelmingly Tory.

Things had worked out well, after all, he thought as he strode down St. James road. A public place would be better than a private meeting.

Caine used his uncle's cachet and feigned interest in joining in order to gain entrance. He strolled room to room. Attendance proved low in midafternoon, most of the cardplayers and drinkers still at home, readying for the next night's revels, he supposed. He found Wardfelton upstairs, sitting alone in one of the assembly rooms and reading a newspaper.

Grace's uncle certainly looked the part of an earl, though he, like Caine, had not been born to it. He was a third son. The elder brother had died accidentally, thrusting the title on Grace's father. Then the country doctor, cum lord, had perished of cholera two years later, leaving Wardfelton to inherit.

Caine assessed the man who had not yet noticed him. The suit appeared to be Saville Row, tailored to perfection, the linen snow-white. His black hair, stiffly pomaded, showed no gray. The waxed mustache curled upward in direct opposition to his thin, pale lips. His hands were smooth, long-fingered and as delicate as a woman's. Nothing else about him looked effete, considering that he was nearly the size of Caine.

Wardfelton looked up suddenly, glared at Caine and folded the paper into a neat rectangle. He did not speak and he did not stand. The gaze of steel held fast as his lips tightened to a straight line.

Caine pasted on a smile in an offer of civility. This was Grace's uncle, her only family. And though she obviously had no love for the man, nor he for her, it would serve no purpose to irritate him further.

"Good afternoon, milord," Caine said as he approached the table and executed a congenial nod in lieu of the bow convention demanded.

"You have no business in this club. Or with me," Wardfelton said, his tone flat. He slapped the paper on the leather tabletop.

"Surely I do, sir. We should discuss the contract. The marriage is in three weeks."

"There is nothing to discuss," Wardfelton snapped, looking past Caine, a deliberate cut. "I made it clear that my niece is destitute, without property or funds."

"I thought you might want *her* interest served, since I am *not* destitute. We should decide her portion, agree to provisions should I drop dead before I inherit."

Wardfelton sighed, rolling his eyes. "Very well. Sit down, Morleigh. I see I shall have to speak with you about her, but it's nothing that you'll enjoy hearing."

"Nothing that will dissuade me, either." Caine pulled out a chair and sat, certain that the man had suddenly decided to stifle his anger over Caine's appropriation of his niece and be reasonable. "Understand that we must amend today's contract after I inherit, for there will be more to settle on her then."

"I doubt either will be needed once I've had my say. What has Grace told you?"

"Very little," Caine said truthfully, unwilling to share how much he had divined from the bits she had revealed. "But I have heard that her parents died, as did her betrothed. She served as her fiancé's mother's companion, then came to live with you almost two years ago. Have you something to add?"

Wardfelton nodded and sighed again. He pressed his fingers to his brow. "I'm afraid I do. I had hoped not to have to reveal this. The grief affected her mind, Morleigh. I regret to tell you that Grace is quite mad. She conceals it at times, but she is rarely stable for long."

Caine froze, locked in denial. Of course it could not be true. Still, a shadow of doubt began to flirt, tempting certainty to desert him. Grace's response to him had been unexpected, definitely out of the ordinary for a young unmarried woman. There was that sudden faint. And she had expressed unusual candor on such short acquaintance with him. Then there was the fact that she had admittedly starved herself, no reason given.

She certainly seemed lucid enough, however, and he had witnessed no hysterics or incomprehensible tirades. How did this supposed madness present itself?

"I cannot blame you for what happened," Wardfelton declared. "Grace can be quite persuasive when she chooses and I do not doubt she fabricated some tale of woe to stir your sympathy. Some imagined plight to do with me. You see, I've had to keep her confined for her own safety, no choice about the matter. I thought it better than sending her to strangers in some institution."

Caine listened well enough, but observed even more carefully. His army command and dealing with all sorts of men had taught him that. Tongues could easily lie, but the body often spoke the truth. Wardfelton's eyes met his only briefly now and again, as if gauging whether Caine trusted what he was saying. The man often shook his head as if he couldn't believe himself.

"Yet you took her to a public ball where you knew she might embarrass you before the ton?" Caine asked.

"And so she did," Wardfelton said with a huff. "But I had to do it. Rumors were gathering. Some thought I had done away with her. As if I would harm my own flesh and blood! They have no idea how difficult it has been to care for her at home rather than relegate that duty."

"That must have been a difficult decision. Did you even consider it, putting her somewhere?" Caine asked, projecting sympathy he did not feel. Wardfelton struck the wrong notes in this song of woe. It simply did not ring true.

The earl pressed his fingers to his forehead, hand concealing his eyes, and groaned softly. "I am ashamed to admit that I did inquire. Not Bedlam, of course, but a licensed house in Houghbarton that provides such care. You see, Grace has wandered away twice and had to be brought home, kicking and screaming."

"But you decided against sending her? Why?"

"Even though our own king is so afflicted, poor devil, I dreaded the scandal to my own house," Wardfelton confided, his voice deep and sorrowful. "Madness in the family, you see... You understand my conundrum, surely."

"Indeed. An unfortunate situation for anyone to imagine," Caine remarked with a nod. He drummed his fingers on the tabletop, letting the silence gather, wondering what the man would say next to fill the void.

Once again and once too often for his act, Wardfelton heaved a sigh of regret. "So you must bring her back to me, Morleigh, or let me fetch her. No one has to know why the betrothal was dissolved. We can put it about that Grace herself had second thoughts."

Aha. The crux of the matter. Caine stood, now impatient to be away. "No, sir, that won't do. I said I would marry her. Once my word is given, I hold to it. Grace and I will wed, come what may."

The earl stumbled to his feet, almost upsetting his chair. "No! I insist… Wait. I implore you, Morleigh. Think, man. You'll be disgraced!"

"Better I than you, eh? You should be relieved. If Grace's madness is ever discovered, everyone will believe I am the cause. They shall have Miss Thoren-Snipes to verify once again that Morleigh's become a monster." Caine smiled. "I gave *her* nightmares!"

He looked directly into Wardfelton's eyes and read fear. Caine wondered at that. "Good day to you, sir. You may have your solicitor call on me regarding a contract and your niece's future."

Caine left him standing there, obviously dismayed.

On reaching the street outside, worry began to gnaw at Caine like a ravenous rat. Could there be a grain of truth in what her uncle said? Had Wardfelton's fear been for Grace, or for the earl himself, should his treatment of her be revealed?

The path to truth lay with Grace and her behavior. Caine hurried back to Hadley House to observe that, praying all the while that Wardfelton was simply a mean-spirited man trying to gloss over his abuse of a helpless relative.

Good lord, he should have listened to Trent. What had he gotten himself into with this hasty arrangement? But, as he had stated to Wardfelton, his word was his bond. His decision had been made. Grace was his now, for better or worse, whether that wedding vow had been repeated or not.

Caine felt apprehensive about talking to Grace, though he certainly needed to after his meeting with Wardfelton. The man must be lying, but his words had required careful reflection, in case Caine's reasoning about this was faulty.

He spent hours after returning home reviewing the visit with Grace's uncle. His preoccupation was so intense, he barely tasted the meal Mrs. Oliver brought him on his tray. He ate absently as he considered every word, every move, every sigh Wardfelton produced.

Caine denied himself that last element of consideration, the woman herself, until he had examined the rest in detail. That accomplished, he would now have to judge her for himself in light of her uncle's declaration. He was resolved that, mad or sane, he would never return her to Wardfelton, but Caine felt he should know her state of mind one way or the other.

Grace had been left to her own devices all day. How must she feel in strange surroundings among people she hardly knew? He wanted to give her no reason to reconsider their betrothal, least of all because of his neglect of her when she was most vulnerable.

The visit with Grace could prove awkward. Now that the matter of their marriage was settled, what would they discuss? Most of their conversation thus far consisted of fielding insults, arguing away her mistrust and convincing her that he meant business.

His trepidation annoyed him. She was only a little bird of a girl after all, hardly anything to dread. If grief had stolen her reason, then he would restore it if he could, keep her comfortably if he could not. He would see that she was as happy as he could make her and as free as possible. She would know that she was cared for.

Caine postponed calling for her. The evening would be soon enough, he figured. He resumed working, poring over numbers in the earl's accounts.

Late that afternoon, the butler interrupted the never-ending effort. "A Mr. Tinroy to see you, sir. He insists it is urgent."

"Show him in," Caine said, shuffling the paperwork into a neat stack and setting it aside, welcoming the intrusion, whatever it was. The visitor's name was unfamiliar. Perhaps it was Wardfelton's man.

"Thank you for seeing me, sir," the spindly little fellow said after Jenkins had introduced him. Hat in hand, he stood before the huge oak desk like an errant schoolboy called up for an offense.

"What is this urgent business, Mr. Tinroy?" Caine demanded, the former commander in him responding naturally to the man's subservient attitude.

"It concerns your betrothal," the man said with a timid smile. "I should say, the original one made with Miss Thoren-Snipes."

"Ah, a thing of the past then. What of it?" Caine replied, clasping his hands atop the desk and leaning forward.

"The thing is, she never officially ended it, sir. Her brother has retained me to speak on her behalf and tell you that, as a gentleman, you are obliged to carry through. He mentioned a breach-of-promise-suit if you prove unwilling."

"So she would sue?" Caine almost groaned at the irony. "How can one be a *gentleman,* Mr. Tinroy, when he has been quite publicly declared a beast? Please inform your client that unless she wishes a countersuit for defamation of character, the matter is best considered closed."

"Oh, sir, she meant no harm by her words. You know how young ladies natter on to one another when they are upset. But *never* did she cry off the engagement!"

No, she had *screamed* it off as far as Caine was concerned. He sighed, unclasped his hands and stood. "No contract was ever signed, because her brother originally opposed it. Of course, I was not heir to the title at that time. Perhaps that has inspired his sudden inclination to find me an acceptable match?"

Tinroy rolled his hat brim and tried a smile. "Oh, no, sir, not at all! It's merely that the young lady has realized her foolishness and had a change of heart!"

"So have *I*," Caine declared, rounding the desk and towering over the little toad. "Good day to you, Mr. Tinroy."

He watched the solicitor back out at a near run. Caine felt like dusting his hands and hoped he never heard the name Thoren-Snipes again in his lifetime. Greedy buggers, the lot of them.

After a day fraught with confrontation, he knew he had one more to face before he could rest. Grace. Only, this meeting, of course, was to be more in the nature of an evaluation to see whether Wardfelton's accusation held any semblance of truth.

He flagged a maid in the hallway and sent her up with a summons for Grace. They might as well meet here in the library. If she were a reader, they could discuss books. There, that was settled. He waited.

Grace appeared within five minutes, almost breathless as she entered the room. Had she taken the stairs at a run? Her hair was pulled back into a rather untidy bun at the nape of her neck and several strands had come undone. She raked them back with an impatient hand. "You wished to see me?" she asked with a nervous laugh.

"Yes, of course. Good evening, Grace," he replied as he stood and surveyed the change in her. It was not so remarkable. She wore a plain gray long-sleeved dress, not a good color for her, but better than the yellow. It was a bit short and so large it hung rather loosely at the waist. He figured she must have borrowed it from one of the maids. In fact, she looked like a young maid on her first day of work, sans apron and reporting late.

He could not help comparing her looks to the stunning, yet shallow, beauty of Belinda. Somehow, even in her plainness and disarray, Grace did not seem wanting. Surface attraction held little appeal for him, especially now. Grace's smile was sincere and she seemed honestly happy to see him. Lord, maybe that alone made her unhinged.

He smiled. "How was your day, my dear?"

She cocked her head and studied him for a

minute, then seemed to form a conclusion. "Interesting, indeed. How was yours, Captain?"

Caine sensed she was really interested instead of just being polite. "Honestly? I have had better." He indicated she should take one of the large wingback chairs beside the fire. He sat across from her in the other as he elaborated. "Business matters consumed me, being new to the chore of managing properties. I must have been born to soldier. That was never so difficult for me."

"Ah, but you love a challenge," she guessed with a sly grin that lighted her slender features.

"That's true enough," he agreed, noting that she had a foxlike manner, watchful, knowing, quick to respond. "Do you?"

She inclined her head and nodded once. "I suppose I do, come to think of it. We certainly took on this one without much hesitation, so it seems we have something in common from the start."

"Apparently."

The silence drew out between them. Caine wondered if there were any more to say. He had to think of something. "You seem quite… rested." Truth was always appropriate. Her eyes were brighter, such a true, clear blue. Like a cloudless sky at its best. "I take it that you slept well?"

She sat back in the chair, perfectly relaxed,

though her feet, clad in her soft yellow dancing slippers, didn't quite touch the floor. She swung them idly as he watched. "Oh, yes, and I haven't slept much of late, so that was a great relief. And the food here is remarkable!"

Ah, there was that prodigious interest in food again. "I shall commend the cook," he promised. "Have you already eaten this evening?"

"An hour ago. You were busy and Mrs. Oliver said I shouldn't wait for you. I understand your aunt takes a tray in the earl's chambers early in the evening to keep him company."

"Yes. We seldom dine together at table these days." Caine felt guilty that she'd had to eat alone. He should have joined her. But she must grow used to his being absent, since he would have little time to entertain her in future.

He grew impatient to end the exchange that was beginning to seem forced. And yet, he needed to evaluate her condition. Nor did he want her to feel dismissed. Or lonely. She had probably had far too much time alone in Wardfelton's care.

"I look forward to traveling to the country," she declared with another bright smile. "It has been a while since I have been anywhere at all if one doesn't count the trip from the manor to the house here in Town." She leaned forward, her expression animated. "Do tell me about your estate, the one where we are to go."

"Wildenhurst is not mine yet, though it is where I was born." Immensely relieved to have a topic he could expand upon, Caine let himself meander back to childhood. "It's the lesser of two properties owned by Hadley, the grander one being Hadley Grange, his seat near the Eastern Coast."

"A grand mansion, or perhaps a castle?" Grace asked.

He answered absently, "A country house, quite impressive and easily thrice the size of Wildenhurst."

"But what is Wildenhurst like? Has it a great history?"

"Well, I suppose it has that. The property was purchased by my great grandfather who had the house built directly over the site of an old monastery destroyed by King Henry. The stones lining the underground floor are still there. The rest is relatively new."

"You have a dungeon!" she exclaimed. "I love old things and places!"

Caine hated to dash her streak of romanticism. "Not a dungeon at all. It consisted of monk's cells originally, and with the new structure over it, it became a rabbit warren of storage rooms and a marvelous place for a boy and his imagination."

"Even better!" She listened avidly and Caine saw yearning for a real home in her faraway look. The place where she had played, laughed and loved now belonged to someone else. Perhaps one day she could think of Wildenhurst as hers.

He continued, "I think of it as home. My father managed it for the earl until his death. As I said, it's where I first saw light of day, where I lived until I went away to school and then where I took holidays. There are the greenest of hills to ride, a river at the back, trees in abundance and wildlife to watch. Gardens with flowers of every sort you can imagine."

"I *adore* flowers," she said, clasping her hands beneath her chin. "And herbs are a must. Is there an herb garden? Say there is or I shall make one for you."

Caine searched his memory. "I believe so. Yes, I'm sure of it." He went on. "The house itself is rather modest, comfortable and not too elegant, but with plenty of rooms. When I retreat to a place of peace in my mind, that is where I go."

"Oh, I know I shall love it!" she exclaimed. "Your description makes it sound heavenly. Why would anyone ever leave it to come to Town?"

He laughed, quite liking her exuberance and her optimism. Caine could use a dose of both, and hers were infectious. "Well, there is the season, of course. And meetings in the House of Lords, though I've yet to experience that and hope I shan't in the near future. Uncle could not attend this year, but remains in town now to be near his physician."

"I see. Well, I do hope you may spend some days in the country to restore your sense of peace after your time at war. It would probably do you a world of good," she said with a succinct nod.

He thought so, too, but did not see it as possible the way things were now. However, he agreed with her anyway. "I expect it would. You know you may take complete charge there if you like. My aunt has declared she will do no more with it. I think she always felt somewhat isolated in the country. For all intents and purposes, other than formally deeding it over, my uncle has consigned the place to me."

"On condition that you marry," she guessed with a wry purse of lips.

Caine nodded again. "With that stipulation, yes." He looked at her. "Grace, I sincerely hope you will be content. And I thank you for accepting my offer. This cannot be easy for you and I do appreciate that."

She laughed, a merry sound and not at all bitter. "I did admit I welcome a challenge. Here's proof of it. I hope you will be happy, too. There. We have set our goals—contentment and happiness, each for the other. So be it. Now, if you would excuse me, I believe I shall visit the kitchens, nick some milk and biscuits and retire. I understand tomorrow is to be a busy day."

Caine stood when she did and reached for her hands. "Good night, Grace. Sleep well."

"Thank you. I'm very grateful," she said with all seriousness. "I never thought to have such good fortune again in my life." She gave his hands a fond squeeze and let go.

Caine watched her leave, wondering how he could have dreaded her company. No one could be less intimidating than Grace. Or less mad. Wardfelton was a bounder and ought to be hanged.

Chapter Five

Mrs. Oliver had managed to find her another more appropriate gown to wear, though gray seemed to be the signature color for the help hereabouts. For a price, one of Lady Hadley's maids had parted with her Sunday best, a plain gray broadcloth with long fitted sleeves, a simple black pelisse and a close-fitting bonnet to match.

Grace met Morleigh at the earl's chamber door, where she had been escorted by Mrs. Oliver. He knocked gently as he spoke to Grace. "Don't be afraid," he said, smiling. "I think he's too weak to bite."

She mustered a smile of her own as he ushered her into the room. "Uncle Hadley, Aunt Hadley," he said in a formal tone, "May I present Lady Grace Renfair, my fiancée. Grace, Lord and Lady Hadley."

"Come closer, gel," the earl demanded just as Grace was in the midst of a deep curtsy. He beckoned clumsily, so she approached his bed-side.

His lordship was a white-haired, florid-cheeked old fellow who had trouble breathing. He had a heart problem resulting in dropsy, Grace determined from the swelling in his arms and hands. That looked different from ordinary corpulence. His condition could probably be im-proved by a small concoction of foxglove. She had seen a number of gents in his fix when she had assisted her father in his practice.

It would be rude to suggest a dose of any-thing, however, since he had a physician in at-tendance who would surely take offense. The physician was frowning at her from his posi-tion in the corner of the room. Perhaps he wasn't reading her mind, but only judging her state of health at the moment.

Caine must have noticed the interaction. "Par-don me. Lady Grace, Dr. Ackers, his lordship's physician."

The man bowed. "My lady."

Grace nodded. "A pleasure to meet you, sir. My father shared your profession when we lived in Norfolk."

"Renfair? Oh, my, yes!" The man's eyebrows rose and his face livened with recognition. "I believe I knew him. *James* Renfair? He studied in Edinburgh?"

"Yes, he did!" Grace said, pleased to meet someone who had known her father.

The earl noisily cleared his throat, obviously to direct her attention back to himself. Grace immediately attended to her audience with the family, smiling her apology for the interruption to his lordship.

She did, however, decide on the instant that she would correspond with Dr. Ackers with regard to his knowing her father. And perhaps when they were better acquainted, see whether he would be willing to entertain Dr. Withering of Birmingham's research papers on treatments of the heart. Her father had found them invaluable.

Her mother had objected to Grace helping her father at first, but Grace had explained how foolish it would be to forego the opportunity to learn as much as she could about healing and tending the sick if she was to run her own household one day. She wondered if she would have the opportunity to treat anyone where she was going or if they would simply think of her as a useless lady.

"How is it you met the boy?" the earl demanded, huffing as he peered up at her from beneath hooded and wrinkled lids.

"At Lord Cavanaugh's ball, sir. He charmed

me instantly." Grace glanced nervously at the countess, who stood on the opposite side of the earl's bed, studying her carefully.

The countess looked pleasant enough, not much younger than her husband, at least a stone too heavy but blooming with health. Her hair and eyes were both as dark as a Spaniard's, though her complexion was very fair. Her mouth formed a little bow faintly lined with wrinkles. She wore a flattering green silk taffeta trimmed in black that was the height of fashion. Quite a beauty in her youth, Grace imagined.

"You are Wardfelton's child?" she asked Grace.

"His niece, ma'am, though my father held that title before he passed on."

The earl transferred his attention to his wife, reached for her hand and spoke in a near whisper, "Caine told us of her lineage, remember, my dear?"

"Yes, of course. Where are you staying?" the countess asked.

Grace glanced at Morleigh, wondering what to say. Did the countess not know what had transpired at the Cavanaugh's and that he had invited her here? Grace thought the events of that evening must be all over London by today.

"She is here with us of late, Aunt," he said. "However today, she's going on to Wildenhurst, where we will have the wedding in three weeks."

"The season must be over," the countess said, her free hand fiddling with her ear bob as she stared across the room at nothing.

"Almost over, Aunt. Soon we'll all be breathing the country air," Morleigh said, sliding an arm around Grace as if to protect her. "We should leave now."

"I haven't dismissed you, boy!" the earl exclaimed, shaking a finger in their direction. "What provisions did you make her? What of her dowry and such? Agreeable terms?"

"We are satisfied with the arrangements, Uncle. I'm handling the business matters until your health is restored, so you needn't worry. Everything's well in hand."

"The estates?" the earl asked.

"Thriving, sir. Bills paid, rents collected. Everything is as it should be."

The earl closed his eyes. "Or will be when you're wed. She'll do, then. Got to have a wife to be settled. A helpmate. Eh, m'dear?"

The countess nodded. Her smile was for the earl. They were still holding hands. Grace felt tears threaten at the sweetness of it all. She thought of all the years these two had been together and the bond they obviously had formed.

Morleigh quietly guided her out of the room and closed the door.

"He never dismissed you!" she whispered. "Will he be angry that we left?"

Morleigh patted her back where his hand rested. "No. He only likes to remind me now and then that he's still in command."

Grace liked the kind way Morleigh handled the delicate situation with his uncle. Here he was doing all the work of the earl and yet allowing the old gentleman to preserve his dignity.

The earl and countess had not seemed to notice that Morleigh's future bride looked like a mouse. At least they had not remarked on it. Grace was just happy not to have appeared before them as a molting duck in her old, jaundiced, limp, ruffled frock.

Grace was glad, too, that the audience with Caine's family had been a short one, so as not to tire his uncle.

She and Caine headed downstairs, since she was to leave immediately for the country. Caine had informed her it was a distance of only eighteen miles to Wildenhurst.

When they were halfway down the stairs, she saw that Lord Trent had arrived and stood speaking to the butler at the open door. He must be a constant fixture in Captain Morleigh's life. Mrs. Oliver had told her Trent was a born adventurer and a dear friend to Morleigh.

Trent was handsome, a real head-turner, though Grace had scarcely noticed that until now. He was nearly as large as Morleigh, though his features were slightly more refined. He was of fairer complexion and his chestnut-colored hair had a reddish glint. She quite liked his looks, but not the way he assessed her, as if he worried she might harbor some ill intention toward his friend.

She had been told he would bring Madame Latrice, the dressmaker, and a trunk full of fabric lengths for the trousseau.

"Your seamstress and Mrs. Oliver are probably waiting to board the coach," Caine commented to her as he saw Trent.

"Everything is happening so quickly," Grace said as they continued to descend.

He had hold of her elbow, a firm but gentle grip. "I know, but in a few hours you'll be settled and have plenty of time to rest and absorb it all." He patted her arm with his free hand. "I promise you'll have nothing to worry your little head about but the cut of your gowns and whether tea is on time."

Grace decided not to push him down the stairs. He was only a man and they were all taught that women needed coddling. She sighed. "I suppose it's not your fault, really."

"What isn't?" he asked, and she realized she had spoken her thought aloud. Oh, dear!

How could she be so ungrateful? Just because she was feeling renewed strength and boundless energy after deep sleep and a few decent meals was no reason to turn uppity. Captain Morleigh had her best interests at heart and he truly could not deny his ingrained, overprotective nature. She should be kissing his feet!

"Uh, it's no fault of yours that my shawl was left behind last evening. Is there a blanket in the coach?" And it was not even cool outside this time of year. How ridiculous did she sound?

"Not to worry. I have your shawl. Trent fetched it, so you'll be warm enough." He looked so proud, as if he had already procured for her all he promised her last evening.

She stopped, halting their progress for a moment. "About what you said as we danced…and all those things I asked you for?"

"You will have them, Grace. I always keep my promises."

"No! What I mean to say is that I was merely playing to what I believed was a jest." She lifted her hand in question. "Now, what would I do with a phaeton and team? And as for diamonds…" She scoffed.

He was smiling at her so fondly. "Then perhaps for the nonce, you'll accept a purse with pin money. It is a wife's due." He pulled a small velvet pouch from his pocket and placed it in her hand, folding his around hers.

"I'm not yet a wife," she reminded him, stunned that he had prepared this just for her. What a thoughtful man he was.

He laughed softly. "So practical. I'll deduct

this from your first quarterly allowance then if you'll take it now."

She shrugged. "Very well, if you insist. But I must ask what you want from me, aside from the faithfulness you require and an heir, of course."

"I never mentioned an heir," he said, sounding a bit surprised. And confused.

Grace rolled her eyes. "Well, that's a given, isn't it? If you're to be the earl, everyone *knows* you'll need at least one. Isn't that the whole purpose of marrying?"

His gaze dropped to the stairs as he seemed to consider it. Perhaps he dreaded the very thought of doing what it took to get the heir.

Then, without responding to her question, he took her arm again. "You should be on your way so as to arrive before dark. There'll be plenty of time to address details later."

Details? An heir was but a detail? "Yes, of course," she muttered, doubt setting in that she had made a wise choice after all. He had declared his need for a wife and was taking her without a penny to her name. Her looks certainly had not captured his heart.

So why had he married her if not to continue his line? A condition of the will, she supposed. Mrs. Oliver had hinted at something of the sort and he had all but confirmed it when they'd spoken of the ownership of Wildenhurst. But surely that was not reason enough to bind himself to a wife he had no intention of bedding.

She looked up at him, then allowed her searching gaze to travel the length of his body, wondering if perhaps he was incapable of relations due to some unseen injury. Was that why he had chosen her, a woman who would be too grateful to insist on her rights as a wife once the marriage was a done thing? No, she could not imagine him capable of such deceit. She would put that right out of her mind and forget it.

Madame Latrice and Mrs. Oliver had already seated themselves inside the coach when Caine handed her in.

"Goodbye for now, Grace," he said. "Take care you don't tax yourself these next few weeks and send word if you need anything."

Grace nodded and added a simpering smile for good measure. If he wanted a milk-and-water miss who didn't know bedding from biding, she supposed she could pretend. At least for a while.

What a pity that was all he desired, since she had spent the entirety of yesterday and last night looking forward to her marriage to him and imagining, even dreaming about, what it might entail.

Now that she had escaped Wardfelton's threat, she would be back to her old self in no time. However, Morleigh had arrived in her life as the answer to her fervent prayers and she would try to be precisely what he wanted whenever he was around.

She could not help but like his straightforwardness and felt quite attracted to him as a man, but he was obviously not interested in her as a woman, despite his playacting last evening. Perfectly understandable.

He had baldly stated that he needed a wife, but apparently wanted one in name only, probably one who would not bother him with her presence. Grace smiled inwardly, imagining herself as the invisible countess. What a role to play, but she certainly preferred it to playing Wardfelton's clueless prisoner.

The question she had to ask was whether she could keep up the act in future just to accommodate Morleigh. She was grateful to him, of course, but gratitude wasn't everything, was it?

She had always wanted to have a child, and if she were completely honest with herself, she wanted the man even more. However, she was not yet ready to explore too deeply the reasons for her odd reaction to him. Perhaps it was merely because he presented a challenge.

The coach rumbled over the cobblestone streets as Grace studied her companions. Mrs. Oliver appeared a comfortable grandmotherly type, short and rather rotund, dressed in her sturdy black wool. The ruffles of the mobcap beneath her plain bonnet framed graying hair, bright green eyes and sweetly rounded features. But though surely nearing fifty, the retainer possessed the strength of a man and the iron will of a mule. Nothing intimidated the woman. Grace quite admired her for it.

As for Madame Latrice, that one obviously felt her importance and dressed it splendidly. Grace judged her to be close to thirty, very self-sufficient and more than a trifle haughty. She wore a lovely traveling costume of forest green made of fine bombazine that rustled with every move she made. Her black bonnet sported dyed green ostrich feathers and a fringe of jet beads that dangled off the brim. Stylish to a fault. However, the prune-faced expression spoiled the effect.

Grace attempted conversation, but the woman seemed loathe to discuss anything, even her plans for Grace's new wardrobe. Mrs. Oliver merely raised one eyebrow and gave Grace a conspiratorial look.

The well-sprung coach afforded such comfort and traveled so slowly, Grace found herself nodding off now and again. It was twilight and they had come quite a ways when the coach rolled to a stop in the middle of the road. The horses neighed and she heard a man's shout. Then a shot rang out.

Madame screamed.

The coach door flew open and a man stood

there, holding a double-barreled flintlock pistol. "Get out, all of you!" he shouted. "Now, and look lively!"

Madame exited first, then Mrs. Oliver and Grace followed. She glanced around to see whether the man acted alone. No one else was in sight. She looked up and saw John Coachman slumped sideways on the box, reins still clutched in his fist.

"Which of you is Morleigh's woman?" the highwayman demanded.

"She is!" Madame cried, pointing a shaking, leather-gloved finger at Grace. "It's her! She's the one!"

The highwayman grinned at Madame, showing several missing teeth. He scanned Grace's length and shook his head slowly. "Don't think so. Easy t'see who's the fancy piece here. Beggin' yer pardon, ma'am," he said, sounding coy.

Then he shot Madame point-blank in the chest. She crumpled slowly to the ground as Grace and Mrs. Oliver watched, stunned. The gunman kept grinning as he reached into his pocket.

Grace knew at that moment he would not let them live. He was going to stand there, bold as you please, reload and shoot them both! She had to do something.

He wasn't terribly big, but she couldn't overcome him on her own and had no idea whether Mrs. Oliver would help her or faint dead away. But if he managed to reload, they had no chance at all!

Grace knew she must use the dirty trick Father had told her about, the last-ditch effort to save herself that he had declared every woman should know. Could she do it? What if she missed? There would be no second chance.

"Sir?" Grace said softly. "Look." She slowly began to raise the front of her skirt and petticoats to get them out of her way. She bared ankles, knees and even higher to entice him.

He looked, all right, and slowly began to walk toward her. She pasted on an inviting smile and waited for just the right moment. When he was near enough, she kicked for all she was worth, thanking God for the borrowed ankle boots she wore. He dropped the still-empty pistol, grabbed his essentials and buckled forward with a harsh cry of pain.

Mrs. Oliver snatched up the pistol and hit the back of his head with the butt of it. He fell like a tree, right at Grace's feet. Mrs. Oliver hit him again, several times, then stood away. "Think he's done for?" she gasped, breathless with exertion.

"Not yet. Give me the gun," Grace ordered. She knelt and fished in the man's pocket for the small powder flask and bag of caps and shot she figured he had been reaching for earlier. She hoped she recalled the correct method of loading. It had been years since she had done it and her hands were shaking now, but she finally managed.

"Take this and point it at him in case he wakes," she ordered the housekeeper. "If he moves, pull the trigger. And do *not* miss."

She hurried over to Madame to feel her neck for a pulse, but knew the woman was dead even before she touched her. Grace shook her head at Mrs. Oliver's silent question, then returned to check the highwayman again. His breathing had stopped and a puddle of blood surrounded his head. "He's dead," Grace said.

She lost no time climbing the wheel and mounting the driver's box to see about the coachman. "He's alive and coming to," she called down. Then of the driver, she asked, "How far are we from our destination?"

"Five miles or so," he rasped.

"You have a wound in your neck, John. Hold this end of your neckcloth over it tightly so it will stop bleeding. I don't believe it's serious, but I shall drive."

"You, my lady?"

"Of course. We can't have you bleeding to death."

"What of...them?" he asked, pointing down at the ground.

"I'll be back up in a moment, just lean back, sit still and keep pressing steadily on that cloth. You should be fine."

She scrambled down, catching and tearing her skirt in the process. "Mrs. Oliver, you and I will have to load the bodies into the coach. I'm afraid you must ride inside with them, but we only have a few miles to go."

"Can't we leave *him* here for the carrion eaters?"

Grace shook her head. "No, I think it best if we return him to London along with Madame Latrice. Perhaps he can be identified. Someone must have hired him to do this, Mrs. Oliver. Someone who knows Captain Morleigh."

"Aye, Lady Grace. Somebody paid him to kill *you!*"

Chapter Six

Grace still shook inside as a footman assisted her down off the coach box. The Italianate facade of Wildenhurst manor looked impressive, much like the home she had lived in before her parents' demise. The house didn't intimidate her and neither did the rolling meadows and beautifully landscaped grounds. What did strike fear in her heart was the sudden assumption of responsibility for all of it. Morleigh had said she might take charge, and Grace knew she must do so at the outset.

None here would outrank her. Therefore, all would look to her for a solution to this particular problem, as well as for the ordering of the estate in the earl's or Morleigh's absence.

She straightened her skirts, took a deep breath and firmed her resolve. Prepared or otherwise, she must assert herself. This was to be her home for the nonce, perhaps for good and all. "Might as well begin as I mean to go," she muttered under her breath. Then aloud, she asked the footman, "What is your name, young man?"

"Harry Trusdale, ma'am." He eyed her curiously, but did not presume to ask who she was.

"I am Grace Renfair, Captain Morleigh's intended. We were assaulted on the road and the coachman is wounded. Help him down and take him inside, then summon the earl's steward to me immediately."

Mrs. Oliver joined her, still eyeing the coach. "What shall we do about the uh—"

"Leave them as they are for the return trip." She turned to the two grooms who were holding the team. "You there, unhitch the horses here and have another pair brought 'round. We shall need a driver and another man to accompany him back to town. See to that, then await my written message, which you will deliver to Captain Morleigh at his lordship's house in Town."

She marched up to the front door that stood ajar. An elderly woman stood there, watching, mouth agape.

"Are you housekeeper here, madam?" Grace asked her.

"Mrs. Bowden. We were not notified anyone was to arrive today. I fear—"

"No need to fear, Mrs. Bowden." Grace

brushed past her. "We have a wounded man needing attention. Where shall we put him?" She peeked into the room to her right, a morning room with a divan, several chairs and a large round table in the center. "In here will do. Bring me strong spirits, whiskey if you have it, vinegar, needle and thread and any medicaments you have on hand. Heat water and have a bed prepared on this level. We shall have him moved once I've seen to him here."

Mrs. Oliver took her cue. "Look lively, Mrs. Bowden! Her ladyship won't abide delay. Summon some maids to fetch and carry." To Grace, she announced, "I'll see to the patient if you need to speak with Mr. Harrell. He'd be his lordship's factor."

"Thank you, Mrs. Oliver." She moved aside for the footmen to help the coachman into the room and onto the divan. "I'll have a closer look at John's injury first."

Mrs. Oliver closed her eyes for a moment and released a heavy sigh. "What a day this has been!" she murmured.

"It is not over yet," Grace reminded her in an aside meant only for Mrs. Oliver's ears. "Steady on until things are settled. We can fly to pieces later."

Mrs. Oliver grunted a wry laugh. "Just so. I shan't be calling you *Little Miss* any longer, my lady."

In the next hour, Grace tended the coachman's wound, apprised the steward of the incident on the road, penned a brief letter to Morleigh and ordered the coach containing the bodies back to London. She insisted that Mrs. Oliver retire to the upper servants' quarters and rest.

By that time, Mrs. Bowden had assembled the staff for introductions. Immediately after, Grace and Mr. Harrell interviewed several of the menservants and determined which ones were handy with weapons.

"Collect all weapons and the hunting guns, load them and arm yourselves," Grace ordered. "Post guards at all entrances to the house. No one is to enter unless you know them well and they have business here. If there is any question regarding that, hold them at gunpoint and report it to me. Is that understood?"

The men nodded, excited to have a break in their routine, she expected. Mr. Harrell assured her he would see to everything, and herded the men away.

"Now then," she said to Mrs. Bowden, "where am I to stay?"

"The rose room should do nicely, my lady. Jane here will show you up and draw a bath for you. Would you like to come down for supper or have a tray sent up?"

"A tray, please," Grace said on the instant. "And send it as soon as may be. Hearty fare and plenty of it, but it need not be grand. Whatever you have already prepared."

"But 'tis only beef and cabbage, my lady. I could—"

"I know, but tomorrow will be soon enough for Cook to show expertise. Tonight, I'd as soon not wait."

"Of course," Mrs. Bowden said, eyeing Grace askance. "Anything else you require, my lady?"

"Yes. Make certain that John is given restorative broth and red wine every two hours tonight. He lost a lot of blood. Also, please see to Mrs. Oliver's comfort. She's had rather a shock and an enormous demand on her courage. Were it not for her, we should both be dead."

Mrs. Bowden's mouth rounded and her eyes flew wide. "Mrs. Oliver saved your life!" she exclaimed in a whisper of awe.

Grace nodded somberly. "She dealt the highwayman a deathblow with his own pistol."

"I will see to her myself, Lady Grace! Poor woman must be fashed indeed! But you are an angel to think of the others so kindly when you had the fright of a lifetime yourself. Will you be all right in Jane's hands?" She darted a look at the plump young maid who stood waiting.

"Go along, Mrs. Bowden. Jane is highly capable, I'm certain."

Finally, Grace thought, she could afford to retire and collapse. The mantle of command slid off her shoulders in a heap. Had she filled her new role as a future countess? She hoped she had done her mother proud, as that woman had been saddled with a like situation years ago when Father had inherited. Grace recalled how graciously Mum had stepped from her life as a mere country doctor's wife into the exalted position.

Countess. Wife to an earl. Mistress of a large household. That would be her lot when Morleigh inherited. What a daunting thought. Even more daunting was the wifely part of it. Would she be a bride in truth to Caine Morleigh? She admitted she felt more anticipation than apprehension at that thought. She wondered just how he felt about it.

Her stomach growled loudly and she pressed a palm against it as she and Jane climbed the stairs. For now, she would concentrate on other pleasures. Like food.

"There's apple dumplings left, I expect," the shy little maid ventured. "Custard, for sure."

Grace laughed. The girl must read minds. "I think you and I shall get on like a runaway horse, Jane."

Caine cursed as he tossed Grace's letter on his desk. "Damn me, I promised to protect her!" He turned to the butler, who stood waiting in case

he wanted to send a reply. "Jenkins, send someone for Trent. Have them tell him it is urgent."

She had written that Caine must stay in London and not hie to Wildenhurst, as would probably be his first inclination. She guessed correctly
there. It was all he could manage not to mount
up and set off immediately and see for himself
that she was unhurt. However, the danger to her
originated here. She was also right about that.
Whoever had sent that cretin to kill Grace would
not yet know his minion had been unsuccessful,
so she would be safe for a while.

This needed to be kept quiet until he could
investigate. That might be difficult since the
deaths of the dressmaker and the highwayman
would have to be reported. Caine only hoped it
would not appear in the news sheets and alert
the mastermind that his plot to murder Grace
had failed.

Who in the world would want her dead and
why? Considering the highwayman's words, it
obviously had to do with Caine's marriage to
her. There was his cousin, Neville, who would
be heir to the earldom if Caine did not marry
and produce an heir. Getting rid of the prospective bride would prevent that. However, why not
go directly for Caine? Perhaps because he would
prove harder to kill?

Then there was Wardfelton. He had no love
for Grace and it had already been rumored that

he had done away with her before he quelled the gossip by bringing her out for all to see. Of course, one could not accuse the man, a peer of the realm, of attempted murder without solid proof. How was one to get evidence of that when the hireling was dead?

Trent arrived within the hour, appearing a bit disgruntled at having been awakened so early. He was shaking rain off his hat and handing it to the butler as Caine met him in the foyer. "Damn nasty out." Trent straightened his cuffs and blew out a sigh. "What's the crisis of the day then?"

Caine got right to business. "A highwayman attacked Grace's coach, killed the dressmaker and wounded the coachman before the women did him in. His body's in the carriage house along with that of our unfortunate modiste, whom he mistook for my fiancée."

Trent had frozen in place, his eyes wide. "What!"

Caine continued. "I need assistance in identifying the corpse and discovering who employed him to do murder. Have you time to help me?"

Trent snapped his mouth shut, thought for a moment, then nodded. "Of course I'll take the time. This is…abominable!"

"Come," Caine ordered. "We'll go and have a look at him. I thought perhaps you could draw a likeness of him and we could show it round in quarters he might have frequented. I shouldn't have called you out so early, but the sooner the better, before his features are too sunken."

"I'll need charcoal and paper," Trent said, hurrying along now that Caine had proposed the task.

An hour later, Caine looked from the drawing Trent had made to the actual face of the dead man. "Excellent. Even better than that one you did of Colonel Colbert for his wife. Amazing likeness, really. We'll put it under glass to protect it from smearing and then be off to make inquiries."

"What of the woman?" Trent asked. "Shouldn't you send her remains to her family and make some sort of explanation?"

"The undertaker's been notified and will come before noon to take both bodies. I've sent someone to search for her relatives and have prepared a letter for them when they're located."

"You've notified the authorities?" Trent asked, an eyebrow raised in doubt, obviously aware that no one was present and questioning the deaths yet.

Caine shook his head. "I will, but I'd like a head start on identifying the man before word gets out. I'd not like it known yet that the attempt was foiled."

"How was it, by the way? You said the *women* did him in?"

"Grace wrote that she and Mrs. Oliver overcame the man when he was reloading his pistol. I wish she had seen fit to give more details, but I guess it's sufficient for now to know they were successful and neither was harmed."

Trent grinned as they made their way back to the main house. "I'd love to have seen it. I expect Mrs. Oliver must have torn into him like a she-cat with kittens. Not hard to envision, is it!"

Caine could visualize it with no trouble at all. "I owe her more than I can repay. Perhaps a generous sum put by for her retirement would go a ways toward that."

"I dare say. Poor little mite you picked to marry probably just fainted again. Will you go and see about her?" Trent asked.

"I'm debating with myself on that. Even she realizes that the plot was hatched here in town and suggests I remain to investigate. Grace has a good head on her shoulders. She writes extremely well, concisely and to the point. Pragmatic girl, if I do say so."

Trent issued a wry laugh. "And in no way modest, is she? Taking credit for a part in downing a highwayman." He shook his head. "I can't see her doing much other than fluttering those thin little fingers and wilting to the ground."

Caine stopped and glared at Trent. "Leave off diminishing her! She's a brave girl, who's endured entirely too much."

Trent laughed again. "You've gone sweet

on her! God, Morleigh, you've been without a woman for so long any kind will serve!"

Caine grabbed Trent's lapel and jerked him to his toes. "I *chose* her, Trent. She's to be my wife. You keep your tongue behind your teeth or I'll have to knock them out!"

Hands up as if to ward off a blow, Trent backed away when Caine released his coat. "Settle down, man! You know I don't mean half I say and the rest is a joke. I *do* like her. She seems quite…well, polite." When Caine continued to glare a threat, Trent added, "Gentle. Well-spoken. Hell, Morleigh, I don't know her well enough to say more in her favor!"

"Don't speak of her at all then," Caine advised.

Trent straightened his lapel and wisely changed the subject. "Shall we go to Whitechapel first? We can show the sketch at the pubs. Perhaps he's a regular at one. Or the brothels. Haven't been to one of those since we came back to London, have you?"

Caine didn't trouble to answer that. He had thought about it, but somehow had not wanted a woman he had to pay for. There was too much pretense in the world as it was. And any woman who lay with him would have to pretend. Oh, they would do anything he wanted for pay, of course, but he was well aware that not one would look forward to it.

He wondered how he would deal with Grace in that respect. By only coming to her in the dark? Or granting her the right to refuse him? She probably wouldn't require either favor. His looks didn't seem to bother her all that much. She herself had brought up providing an heir. And she had said she was very grateful. He supposed he would have to resign himself to accepting her gratitude or else do without.

"Would you like me to go to Wildenhurst and see how she's getting on?" Trent asked, his tone conciliatory. "I promise I'll treat her with all kindness and care."

"No," Caine snapped. He didn't want his friend, or any other gentleman, foisting himself on Grace as a houseguest. "I'll go myself as soon as we have a name for the dead man."

Trent laughed and shrugged. "Sudden decision, eh? May I come, too?"

Caine shot him a nasty look. "Why do I put up with you?"

"Must be my good humor, since you have obviously lost yours. To think, you used to be such fun," Trent said with a weary sigh. He tugged on his gloves. "Shall we be off to the stews?"

Grace looked around the Wildenhurst library as she paused in rereading the letter she had just received from Dr. Ackers, the earl's physician. She had written to him the day after her arrival here. He said he had studied with her father more than twenty years before and was quite interested in his success with the heart patients Grace had told him about in her missive to him.

He replied that he would certainly obtain and explore Dr. Withering's papers on the subject and thanked her for the information. She was pleased that he would consider it and would write to tell him so. She had truly missed writing and receiving letters after Wardfelton had denied her the pleasure.

This room was the perfect place to do her correspondence, plan menus and simply sit and read. She had been struck immediately by the comforting familiarity. Her father's favorite retreat had possessed nearly this same ambiance and almost as many books. Few of these were medical texts, however, but many were interesting all the same.

In fact, Wildenhurst proved everything Morleigh had related and much more. Aside from the generous welcome from the staff, the house itself seemed to embrace her. Grace took an hour whenever she could find a free one, to explore the manor.

The four floors were simply laid out in rectangular shape. A modest vestibule lined with beautiful paintings led one to a highly polished, gently curving staircase. It also opened to the right into a lovely morning room and through that, the formal dining hall. Behind that lay the kitchen areas, containing the buttery, scullery, still room and the kitchen proper.

To the left, off the vestibule, Grace could enter the formal drawing room, an enormous space that had obviously been three rooms at one time, probably set up originally as a state apartment for important or even royal guests. Beyond that was a small conservatory that opened onto a flagstone terrace at the north end of the house.

Off the main corridor behind the stairway, she had found this wonderful oak-paneled library redolent of lemon-oil polish, sweet-scented pipe tobacco and the unique essence of old books. Floor-length windows swung open easily and led to the gardens out back.

She loved this room best of all. An interior door led to a small business room where the estate accounts were kept and managed. The rest of the ground floor consisted of living quarters for the upper servants in the household.

Up the stairs on the first and second floors were the family and guest bedrooms opening off the corridor that ran along the middle of the house lengthwise, as it did on all levels. The attic chambers for the maids occupied half the third level, while the other half contained a large area for proper storage.

Below it all lay the cellar she had yet to explore, but she had been told the menservants had quarters in the northern end, while the root cellar, wine cellar and various other utility areas held up the kitchens.

Grace was no student of architecture but she applauded the Wildenhurst designer for his attention to convenience. This was no rambling, added-onto conglomeration of wings wherein a stranger might lose her way! Efficiency had a home here and she hoped she had, as well.

The gardens were rather casually formed, rife with roses of all description, but the herb beds were in overgrown disarray. She planned to remedy that as soon as time permitted.

Yes, she thought with a sigh, Wildenhurst felt like home after only four days. She wondered if Caine would allow her to stay on here after they were married or whether he would send her to some other property to live.

She had begun to think of him as Caine in her own mind. It seemed so much more friendly than either Captain or Morleigh. More intimate, as if they already knew one another quite well, though they really did not. One day they would—and soon, she hoped—but until then it hurt no one to think of him that way.

He invaded her thoughts constantly. And her dreams. He would suddenly appear, that big strong body, the seriousness of his expression, his occasional flash of humor that seemed to surprise even himself, the way he strode across a room, owning the space.

She loved how he could change his demeanor from stern and commanding to wry and gentle in a heartbeat. Somewhere inside Caine, Grace suspected there was a well of good humor waiting to be fully tapped. Vestiges of it escaped now and again and she longed to have him reveal it completely, to hear him laugh with abandon and let go of his demons.

The thing that appealed to Grace most about Caine was that he appeared to care what happened to her. That made him the only one in the world who did and certainly dear to her because of it.

She loved his face, scars and all. He would never credit that, so she might as well not tell him. Grace was mightily afraid that, on all counts, she was hopelessly infatuated with the man.

Mrs. Oliver fussed over her constantly, yet treated her quite differently than she had before the incident on the road. Now she asked instead of telling. She deferred instead of demanding. Amazingly, the other servants followed her lead implicitly. Grace found herself completely in charge for the first time in her life and took full advantage.

"Mr. Harrell?" She looked up from the writing desk in the study as Hadley's factor appeared in the doorway. She feared he had been neglecting his estate duties of late to concentrate on her protection. Thus far there had been no threats apparent. "Is there a problem, sir?"

"There are two riders approaching along the main road, ma'am. I thought you should know." He pursed his lips and raised his bushy gray eyebrows as he awaited her response.

She tensed, heart in her throat. Surely it wasn't her uncle or men he was sending to collect her. He would not dare such a thing. Would he? "I doubt anyone bent upon mischief would ride in at midmorning."

Even as she said it, she could not erase from her mind the memory of the times, twice before, that she had been found by her uncle's minions and returned to him.

Chapter Seven

Mr. Harrell rushed to reassure Grace, "Oh no, ma'am, the visitors are not anyone you should fear. One of the riders appears to be the captain, judging by the mount he's on."

Grace jumped up from the desk and flew past him on the way out of the room. "Notify Cook. We'll need something special prepared to feed them," she ordered over her shoulder. "I will receive in the drawing room."

She hurried there to wait. After a few calming breaths, she pinched her cheeks for a bit of color and brushed back an errant strand of hair that had escaped the confines of her morning cap. Then, on second thought, removed the foolish cap and stuffed it under a cushion.

It was too late to change her gown, but there was little choice to be had in that direction anyway. Most of her new clothing, the morning gowns in particular, were still in pieces awaiting construction. The borrowed gray would have to suffice.

Grace had to laugh a little at herself. That she should want to look pleasing to the captain surprised her. He had chosen her when she was at her very worst and his expectations today would doubtless be quite low in any case.

She heard the commotion outside when he arrived and arranged herself on a divan to wait for him.

"Captain Morleigh and Lord Trent, ma'am," Judd, the butler, announced in a somber tone.

Grace rose and smiled as the two men entered. "Welcome!" she said, and held out her hands to Caine. He looked so fine, even in his travel dust. Rather rakish, in fact.

He raised her fingers to his lips. "I trust you've recovered from your misfortune on the road?" He seemed to take in every detail of her appearance as he asked.

"I have indeed." Grace withdrew her hand and offered it to Trent. He reacted less familiarly, merely bowing over it. "It was good of you both to come, but not at all necessary. Would you join me, or have you other business to conduct?"

Trent cleared his throat. "If you would excuse me, I will leave you two to speak privately."

Grace nodded. "Please consider yourself at home here, Lord Trent. We shan't be long."

"Why thank you, ma'am. I shall do that," Trent replied, and promptly left with Judd.

Caine smiled. "I see you've assumed command." He gestured for her to sit, then joined her on the divan. "Does Wildenhurst agree with you then?"

She brightened. "Oh, yes! I knew I would love it here and I do. Everyone has been very agreeable and we're getting on quite well. I can hardly wait to meet the neighboring families and perhaps entertain a bit. But I suppose that will have to wait awhile."

"Oh. You would enjoy company? Parties and the like?"

"Yes, of course!" She gestured around the drawing room. "This is a perfect size for dancing, isn't it? Please don't judge my social abilities by my dislike of the ball where we met," she said, laughing at his concern. "Even though I never had a London season, I attended all our local events and helped my parents host a few. All of that was curtailed by mourning, of course. Wardfelton's evenings were rather dark events with few ladies in attendance. I've quite missed the dancing and gaity."

"I see. Yes, I suppose you would," he said, apparently still troubled by something.

She leaned toward him, hands clasped in her

lap. "And how have *you* been? And Lord and Lady Hadley, how do they do?"

"Well enough, thank you," he said, a frown still marring his strong features. "I've come to let you know Trent and I have discovered the identity of the brigand who accosted you. His name does us little good, however, since we have not yet been able to connect him with anyone of means who might have hired him to do the deed." He sighed. "Do you think it was Wardfelton, Grace?"

She nodded. "He came immediately to mind."

"To me, as well," Caine admitted. "However, I am at a loss when figuring his motive. Any ideas?"

"None at all. When I first came to him, we got on rather well. After that first year, things changed abruptly. He acquired a sudden dislike of me, a hatred, really."

Morleigh shifted to face her fully. "Do you know *why?*"

Grace shook her head and shrugged. "No. He never declared it outright, but I began to feel very strongly that he wished I would cease to exist."

He placed a hand over the one she rested on the cushion beside her. "Was he very cruel to you, Grace?"

"Not to my person," she admitted. "All his threats were implied."

She noted a hardening of his expression as he spoke. "Well, you won't have to endure that again, I assure you."

Grace hesitated a moment before venturing a notion that had occurred to her well after the attack. "Perhaps my uncle is not the culprit. Is there anyone you know who might wish *you* to remain unmarried?"

"It is possible that my cousin, next in line for the title, might want to prevent it. He will be my heir if I don't marry and produce an heir. However that seems rather far-fetched, the more I consider it. Doesn't it seem more likely he would simply try to eliminate *me?*"

"Well, I wouldn't dismiss him out of hand. The assassin did ask for Morleigh's woman instead of using my name as my uncle might have done."

She hated to mention the other possibility. This one, he would not like. "What of your friend Trent? I felt from the outset that he does not approve of me in the least."

Instead of anger, he offered an indulgent smile. "You may strike Trent off your list of suspects, Grace. He has been my best friend since we were lads and has saved my life twice."

She pursed her lips, but could not hold back the words. "Perhaps he believed he was saving it yet again. Or at least protecting your future."

"No, Grace. It most definitely is not Trent.

He would not need to have you killed to prevent our marriage. All he would need do is seriously object and give me valid reasons for it. The worst he has done is to tease me, which he has always done about everything under the sun. Please trust me on this."

He patted her hand again. "Now, I want you to stop worrying. You will be perfectly safe here. I will go back to London, find whoever is responsible and take care of the matter."

Grace turned her hand palm up to grip his. The move seemed to surprise him.

"I do trust you," she said.

He looked taken aback, but finally spoke. "Thank you. I've given you precious little reason to do so as yet, but I appreciate that."

"Nonsense! You have given me every reason," she said, meaning every word.

Trent entered in something of a rush, stopping just inside the door. He looked from one to the other as he bit his bottom lip. Something had obviously upset or excited him.

Grace raised an eyebrow. "Is something amiss, Lord Trent?"

"Uh…no, not amiss exactly. I wonder if I might have a private word?"

"With me?" Grace asked, unable to resist testing his patience.

Trent shook his head and fastened a concerned gaze on Morleigh. Grace tugged her hand from Caine's clasp and rose. "It is a bit early in the day, but there's brandy in the cabinet there if you'd like a tot while you confide." She gave Trent a saucy grin as she swept out and left the men to their business.

Her hand still tingled with the warmth and comfort of the captain's touch. She cradled it beneath her breast, even as she warned herself not to read too much into his attentions.

She was of mixed feelings about his treatment of her today. While a part of her resented his superior "I shall handle everything for you" attitude, another part enjoyed his promise of security.

To be fair, the first impression he must have had of her was that of helpless female. She clearly saw now that she had let herself become a victim of her uncle's intimidation. It was as if Caine had awakened her somehow when she had been at her lowest point. And the unfortunate incident on the road had shaken her fully out of her former grief and apathy. No, she could not blame him for viewing her as weak and inept, but she could change his opinion and gain his respect in time.

He would never regret choosing her, she decided with a firm nod of her head. Never. She would see to that.

"You won't credit what Mrs. Oliver has told me!" Trent exclaimed as soon as they were alone.

Obviously agitated, he began pacing the plush turkey carpet and rubbing his forehead with his thumb and forefinger. "I still can't credit it."

Caine waited for him to relate whatever it was, his mind still on Grace's calm assertion of trust.

"It was *she!*" Trent said, stopping to offer a gesture of disbelief. "Grace herself disarmed that man! Can you believe it? Mrs. Oliver hit him, yes, but it was Grace who saved them both." He strode over and plopped down beside Caine. "She lifted her skirts, man. She enticed him on purpose. Then she kicked the stuffing out of his privates and brought him down!"

Caine stared wide-eyed at Trent. "What?"

Trent nodded, then shook his head. "Oliver finished him off with the pistol's butt. According to her account, Grace then helped her load the bodies, clambered atop the coach, saw to the coachman's wound, then drove them here herself!"

"Give over. The woman must be exaggerating."

"Not so! She swears it's all true." He shook a finger at Caine. "You have sorely underestimated this girl, Morleigh."

"*I? You* are the one who had her wilting in a faint." Belated fear rose in his chest at the mental image of Grace physically confronting a full-grown man. "Go. Find her and send her to me."

Trent threw up his hands as he stood. "Find her yourself, man. I'm still coming to terms with this." He resumed pacing and scratched his head. "I cannot believe I have so *misjudged* anyone, especially a woman. It's not like me at all."

Caine huffed. "This is not about you, Trent." He strode out to locate Grace, intent on giving her a real dressing-down for risking her life that way.

He ran into her in the vestibule, literally. She backed away laughing and rubbed her nose. It had collided with his chest.

"What were you thinking to do such a thing?" he demanded.

"Sorry, I didn't see you in time to stop."

"Not that, wigeon! The brigand. Oliver told Trent it was you!"

"Oh, that. Well, Mrs. Oliver actually did him in. I told you that."

Caine rolled his eyes. "Yes, but it was you who lifted your skirts. Do you have any idea what might have happened if—"

"Well, he was reloading and meant to kill us, so I redirected his thoughts to something less fatal."

Morleigh grasped her upper arms and shook her once. "Did you consider what might have happened if you hadn't had enough strength to—"

"Unman him?" She laughed nervously. "But I did."

"What if you had missed your mark, Grace? What if he had—"

She shook off his hands and raised her chin. "You're more worried about his defiling my person than shooting me dead as he did Madame?"

"Well, no, of course not, but—"

"Then stop treating me like an idiot! It was our only chance and I took it! If he had thrown me to the ground to have his way, I trust Mrs. Oliver still would have had sense enough to take advantage of his lust and bash in his head."

She exhaled a gust of anger while a moment of silence ensued. But apparently she wasn't finished asserting herself. "Do my actions offend your male sensibilities?"

He stood back, took a deep breath and inclined his head. "Somewhat, but I will rethink it. I beg your—"

"Indulgence? Forgiveness? And if you say *attention,* I shall hurt you!"

He smiled, all anger erased. "Come now, Grace, what you did merely shocked me, that's all. I'm relieved you were so quick-minded. And happy you weren't hurt or worse. In fact, I'm rather proud—"

"Very well then. So long as we have an understanding. You are wrongheaded, as most of your gender usually is, and I am—"

"Absolutely rude for completing almost every thought I put into words."

She looked to be hiding a smile herself. "If I promise to cease my rudeness, what shall you concede?" she demanded, arms crossed and foot tapping with pretended impatience.

"To hear you out before going on the attack," he promised.

"So be it."

She sparred really well, Caine thought, proud of her spirit.

"Are you hungry?" she asked. "I'm famished. I was coming to tell you the meal is ready."

"Thank God," Trent piped up. He had been listening, propped in the doorway. "I thought we were about to be put on the road back to town."

He strode forward and tucked one of Grace's hands through the crook of his arm. "Never contradict this woman, Morleigh. She scares me to death and I'm staying firmly on her good side."

"One wise man on the premises," Grace said with a wry laugh. "Come along, Captain," she said over her shoulder. "Food usually improves a man's temper."

"A woman's, as well, one would hope," he replied, taking her other hand. They walked three abreast to the dining room for the noon repast.

Caine was still too shocked to say much, but his mind whirled with varying emotions. He alternately felt a great need to spank or salute her.

One thing he was certain of, life with Grace would never be boring. However, he was not certain if that was a good thing or bad at this point.

"You could remain here for a while," Trent suggested to Caine after they had finished eating. "There's nothing you could do in London that I can't do for you. Would you leave a lady alone after such a scare?"

"I'm not frightened in the least, but I would welcome your company," Grace said with a smile. "Please stay if you like."

Caine knew he had no right to stay at Wildenhurst, that he should return to London forthwith and dedicate himself to discovering their enemy. However, Trent could continue the investigation and Caine supposed he really should remain for at least a few days. "Very well, if you're sure."

Trent was right that Grace should not be left alone. Heaven knew she had fended for herself for too long as it was.

They bade Trent farewell and stood together out front, watching him canter down the long drive. "I know I promised you solitude for three weeks. Are you certain you won't mind my intrusion?" he asked her.

She shook her head and answered firmly, "It is your home, after all, and this would give us the chance to become better acquainted."

Caine made his decision. "Then I shall stay,

of course." He knew he might regret the hasty choice if he thought about it for too long. But regret was not something he entertained often and he made up his mind he would not in this instance. Grace wanted him to remain, so he would.

They met at breakfast the next morning. Caine had no idea what to do with her now that he was to keep her company. As if she read his thoughts, she asked, "What shall we do today?"

He looked out the window at the rolling meadows beyond the lawn. "We could ride if you like. You do ride?"

Her little bounce of excitement answered before she did. "Oh, yes! And I've missed it so much," she said, eyes bright with anticipation. "I dared not do it without your leave. I thought it might not be safe."

"I'm glad you didn't go out without me." Caine admired her sense of caution and prudence, noting that this was the first he had seen of those qualities. "However, we should be fine if we stay on open ground and well away from the wood. There is no access to the back acres, except through the river."

She pulled away and lifted her skirts to take the steps. "I'll run up and change!"

"You're fine as you are. We'll not see a soul who would question your attire."

"I haven't a habit yet anyway, but I need my borrowed boots!" she said, holding up a slipper-clad foot.

Caine noted the smallness of it. How dainty she was all over and how thin. He could scarcely believe she'd had enough strength in that tiny foot to unman a killer. "Meet you at the stables then," he said as she hurried inside.

When she arrived, he had the horses saddled and ready, his own gelding and the gentlest mare for her. Grace still wore the serviceable gray gown, but had topped it with a bright scarlet spencer. "Most becoming," he commented, delighted to see her in bright color for a change. "Puts roses in your cheeks."

"Thank you, kind sir! My one completed garment from the materials you purchased. As for the pink face, I but needed the fresh air and sunshine your garden has supplied. It is such a gorgeous day, isn't it?" She handed him a small cloth bag with a strap. "Hang this over your shoulder, if you please."

He took it. "What's in it?"

She grinned, helped him adjust the strap. "Bread, cheese and wine. My contribution to the outing."

"Brilliant." He grasped her waist and lifted her onto the worn sidesaddle no one had used for years. "I'll order you a new saddle when I get back to Town," he said.

She laughed. "I'd rather have that than the curricle you offered. See how frugal I can be?"

He mounted his gelding. "Aha, then perhaps a young mare instead of the matched team?"

"Definitely preferable! However, I've grown quite fond of Betsy here. I have spoiled her with apples already, haven't I, old girl? Yes, I brought you one for later!" She patted the mare's neck and was rewarded with a loud neigh.

Caine laughed with her at Betsy's unexpected response and felt a release of tension he hadn't realized was there. They would get on well, he thought with relief. They both loved horses, riding and the country air. He might look forward to future visits. If he found he had the time to spare.

They set out across the meadow at a gallop. She sat a horse as though born to it and didn't appear to suffer at all from lack of practice. With the wind tearing at her hair and her face alight with joy, Grace looked incredibly young and almost beautiful.

Her small-breasted, thin-waisted, narrow-hipped figure appeared that of an adolescent only just crossing the threshold into womanhood. She wore no cosmetics to enhance her features and her silky hair flew freely, undone by the wind and set free of hairpins.

Caine wished for boyhood again and the chance to have known her in early youth before grief and war had turned their lives grim. Perhaps, just for today, he could dismiss all worry and pretend it was so.

"Race you to the water's edge!" he called out.

With a shout of laughter, she urged Betsy to full speed. Caine held back a bit in order to let her win.

He had not felt so happy in years. Surely the fabric of his life would hold together if he abandoned responsibility and stole a few days of pleasure for himself. He looked at Grace, a vision of total abandonment, and envied her precious ability to live in the moment. Perhaps she could show him how to do that, if only for today.

Chapter Eight

Caine dismounted at river's edge and went to assist Grace. He reached up and grasped her waist. She felt so slender and so soft. The fact that she wore no corset registered immediately. Both her hands rested on his shoulders as he lifted her. He couldn't seem to help holding her entirely too close, sliding her down his front until her feet rested on the grass.

He told himself it was just to see what she would do, how she would react to his nearness. She never once protested or braced herself away. Instead, her direct blue gaze never left his.

She didn't smile, but neither did she frown. Her lips were slightly open and her expression was…well, the best he could describe it was inquisitive.

Caine had to remind himself to release her,

and only then did she step back. And smile up at him, a knowing smile, as if she was fully aware that he suddenly saw her not as a girl, but a woman.

"I like this," she said in a breathless voice. Then she looked around and pointed. "There is the perfect place." Without a pause, she scampered over to sit on a large flat stone, removed her boots and stockings and dangled her feet in the water. "Come on," she urged, patting the space beside her. "It feels wonderful!"

She was right. Neither even mentioned the impropriety of exposing bare feet and ankles. Hers were narrow, dainty and rather pretty. She lifted them out of the water and wiggled her toes when she saw he had noticed. Caine laughed at her childlike impulse, doubting there was another in the world as unaffected and natural as Grace.

"Tell me about your parents," she said, idly watching as she swirled her feet in the lapping waves, accidentally brushing his foot now and then. Or perhaps she meant to, as a small gesture of comfort or something. "Did they die when you were very young?"

The topic was painful, but Grace certainly had a right to ask questions about his family. "Mother contracted scarlet fever when I was ten. It weakened her heart and she died soon after. My father, as well as my older brother, were still living when I bought my commission six years ago."

"What happened to them? Do you mind my asking?" Her gaze fastened on him then, rife with apology or concern. Caine realized it felt good to have someone really care how he felt.

"No, of course I don't mind. You have every right to ask." What woman wouldn't want to know? For all she knew now, they might have succumbed to some inherited malady that her children could fall victim to in future. "They were caught in a sudden storm as they were sailing off the coast, a pastime they shared often." He looked out over the river.

"But you have no love of that, do you?" she guessed.

He smiled. "No sea legs and no stomach for it. Getting from here to the Continent with my company proved a problem. Trent's ever-present flask was a godsend, I can tell you."

She laughed softly. "We all have our embarrassments. What of your friend Trent? What does he do now that he's no longer your lieutenant?"

Caine wondered whether her interest in Trent could be personal. His best friend was rather handsome and the thought stirred a small worry that Grace had noticed that. "Oh, well, Trent does a bit of everything and next to nothing since he sold his commission. His father, the marquis, kicked up quite a fuss when Trent followed my lead into the army. Trent's an only child."

"Ah, the heir," Grace said with a nod. "So one day both you and he will sit together in the Lords, all pompous and stodgy in your wigs and robes."

"Now, there's a picture." Though it would more than likely happen, it was hard to imagine. "The pair of us, as we were at our schools and on our belated grand tour with the army."

"Aha, Bonaparte's wars kept you from the usual acquiring of continental polish, so you two joined the fight to pay him back!"

"That, plus an equal part of rebellion against our fathers' expectations. Then there were the uniforms, of course." He turned and winked at Grace. "Drew the ladies like lodestones." Speaking of those times now, even considering how his engagement turned out, he decided the years hadn't been a total waste.

"Dashing comrades-at-arms," she said with a chuckle.

"We really were comrades, y'know. Still are that. He's been more of a brother to me than my own ever was." Caine looked up at the clouds, lost in the past. "In fact, I hardly knew Trevor at all. He was already away at school when I was born and on his visits home, he and my father were usually out sailing or busy in Town."

"Poor little left-behind," she said. "At least you had your boon companion. Denied that grand tour to sow your oats, you and he must have set London on its ear when you came of age." She cut him a sly glance and grinned. "Didn't you?"

"We certainly tried." Caine appreciated her way of lightening a conversation. "Sorry, but I refuse to bore you with details of my misspent youth."

"And I have no business asking," she said. "It's only that my past is so boring. I thought to live vicariously in hearing of yours."

"Boring?" he asked, curious to know what her life had been like. "You assisted your father, which must have proved exciting at times. And you met someone dashing to love very early on. Were you happy before your great losses and these past two years?"

She looked off into the distance. "Yes," she said simply with no further explanation of what might have made her so.

After a few moments lost in her thoughts, she looked at him and smiled. "I am happy at this moment and I believe one should relish that where one finds it, however small the measure." She nudged his elbow with hers. "Now you are meant to say how profound you find that observation and declare that you agree completely. Go on…"

"I do agree and it was profound." Caine noticed that she liked to touch and was in no way reticent about it. That nudge, for instance, an occasional hand on his sleeve or the soft bat of her palm on his hand, the touch of her foot. It seemed so natural, as if she were totally unaware she was doing it. He was unused to touches that were not deliberate and a means to an end.

"You're very unusual," he said. "And that is a compliment, by the way."

"What a kind way of putting it. I suppose I must thank you."

Only moments later, in the silence that ensued, did it occur to him that Grace might have thought he meant her appearance unusual. And he didn't know how to explain what he had said without making it sound worse.

"Ah, this is heaven," she crooned, leaning back, propped on her hands, her face lifted to the sun. She turned to him and opened one eye. "Tell me, do you fish?"

So she had forgiven him. "Not for a long time. Have you ever?"

"Of course! Many were the days I provided dinner." She sighed theatrically and faked a sad frown. "Life was hard for a poor doctor's family, you see. I was forced to fish for variety in the diet. Father was paid with chickens so many times, I thought I should grow up clucking!"

Caine threw back his head and laughed.

"Bring me fishing tomorrow!" she exclaimed, pressing her hand on his. "Please, please?"

"We have a holding pond behind the gardens, Grace. Full of fish, unless Harrell's a slackard."

"Not the same," she declared, giving his hand a slap and resuming her position of soaking up the sunshine. "Nothing tastes better than a trout that made you work for him. You'll see."

"So I shall. Maybe Harrell can scare up poles and hooks."

"In the back of the tack room," she said immediately. "Along with flies and a bucket for worms."

"Which you will dig yourself, no doubt," he said with a chuckle. "This I must see."

"Oh, you will see and assist me, too. I shan't be the only one with grubby fingernails and dirty knees. Your soft life is over, Morleigh."

So, of course, the next day found them at water's edge again. Her patience with fishing surprised him a little, as did her willingness to bait her own hook. There were moments when he suspected the activity brought back memories she had hidden away for a while. Perhaps she had sat on a bank before in this same way with another.

He wondered if she had been very much in love with young Barkley and if she missed and mourned him still. What would it be like to lose to death someone you greatly loved? He had suffered over the loss of Belinda, of course, but that was not the same thing at all. The woman he had loved was still very much alive and he'd had pride and anger to sustain him while recovering from losing her. The love he had felt for Belinda must not have been very deep and it had certainly been misplaced. His recovery felt quite complete now. He wondered if Grace's was.

Caine hesitated to broach the subject, but he so wanted to know. "Grace, are you still in love with young Barkley?"

She sighed and inclined her head. "Well, I loved him but I'm not certain I was ever *in love* with him, if you know what I mean. We were childhood friends. He was great fun, quite the clown as a boy." Her eyes took on a dreamy look. "Then when he came home from school at last and was commissioned, he looked very dashing." She laughed. "I was sixteen, mad for the uniform, fascinated that he actually had grown side whiskers."

Caine smiled. "In love with love, then?"

"Oh, most assuredly. I confess I was curious, too. He proposed because I let him kiss me, you see," she admitted with a grin.

"Were you…intimate?" Caine asked before he could catch back the question.

She gave an elegant little snort. "Not quite *that* curious!"

Caine had to laugh, both at her words and

with surprise that she had taken no offense at his asking.

She set down her fishing pole. "And what of you?" she demanded, tossing a stick into the water. "Did that Thoren-Snipes girl entrap you as shamelessly I did my beau?"

"No such excuse," he answered. "She seemed…well, more than she actually was and I asked for her hand with all the eagerness of green youth and wild expectations."

"You fell in love with her."

"With the girl I thought she was, yes. Her brother objected, so there was a challenge for me, as well. Belinda promised to wait for me until the war was over. And so she did. You have heard the rest, I'm certain."

"To parrot your question to me, do you love her still?" Grace asked him, head cocked to one side in that probing way she had that made one feel compelled to answer.

Caine pursed his lips for a moment as he put his cane pole down and tossed a rock in the water where her stick now floated. He looked directly into Grace's questioning eyes and answered truthfully, "No. Absolutely not."

She grinned. "Older and wiser now, are you? But you should know, sir, no one of our gender is precisely what she seems. Ever." Her face contorted and her fingers formed into claws as she pretended to threaten him. "So best beware!"

Caine huffed a laugh. "An admitted shrew, I believe I can handle. Taming her with food should work! Are you hungry?"

"Famished!" she exclaimed, scrambling to her feet and brushing off her skirts. "Let's eat."

She helped him spread the blanket and arrange their small feast. "This is a lovely way to spend a day, isn't it!"

"Even if the fish aren't biting," he replied.

For some reason, he became obsessed with giving Grace more than a few days of well-deserved happiness if he could. He knew that, in doing so, he would find more than a little joy himself. He already had.

And so it went. Three lovely days of nothing but sport and sweetness, laughter and lolling about. By some unspoken agreement, neither of them mentioned Wardfelton, the attack on the road or their future as man and wife.

There were so many times he felt fascinated by her mobile lips, the way they pursed in that little moue when she was puzzled, or how they could stretch into a wide gleeful smile in an instant, lighting her whole face from within.

He thought about kissing her more than once, but it was too soon. It might make her think he was one of those men who had nothing else on his mind when he was around a woman. She might also believe he did it only because she had admitted kissing Barkley and withdraw from him completely. So he refrained. It would only have been a test anyway, he told himself, and she deserved more than that when he did kiss her.

The day would come when he would, of course. He would be her husband. But for now, for these few days, he simply wanted to be Grace's friend. To know her as a person. She had warned him that no woman was precisely what she seemed to be. But Grace was so open and honest, how could she not be?

Caine would always think of the time as the halcyon days, surpassing any other he had ever known, even as a boy. Grace had restored something in his soul that he had lost and forgotten. He only hoped he could hold on to it.

Reality intruded on the morning of the fourth day when Trent returned and Grace prepared herself for Caine's departure to London.

After the three of them shared the midday meal, Caine asked Grace to accompany him through the garden to the stables so that they could speak privately.

Trent had said his farewell and gone on ahead to have the horses saddled for their ride.

"This has been a poor attempt at courting," Caine said.

"No, no, it was wonderful, if far too brief," she said.

"I wish I had a longer time to visit, but I did

promise you your time alone to adjust." He looked down at her, directly into her eyes, as if searching for something.

She was first to look away. "So you did." Now she wished she had never asked for that.

Their lovely time out of time was over and he seemed to regret that as much as she did. That was some consolation.

All the matters they had forgone discussing for the duration should be addressed at some point. Grace decided to begin with what was most important to her. "Tell me, will we bide here after the wedding or return to Town?" She reached out and plucked a dead head off a rose-bush, watching the last of the petals drift to the ground.

"You may do as you like, of course. I promised you could. But I must remain with my uncle as often as possible. He believes his time is near and he has affairs that should be put in order."

"Will he not come for the wedding then?"

Caine shook his head, though his answer was positive. "He plans to attend. Insists on it, in fact. We can make him comfortable in the carriage, bring his physician and take the journey slowly. Unless his condition worsens between now and then, he'll be all right, I think."

She smiled up at him. "You care for him a great deal, don't you." It was not a question.

"I love the old fellow, even when his demands

drive me mad," Caine admitted. "He and my aunt were always like parents to me, even when mine were alive."

"You're a good man, Caine," she said.

He cocked an eyebrow. "If not so good to look at."

"I would never say that, nor would anyone with two good eyes." Then she realized the *faux pas* and covered her mouth with her hand. "Oh, I'm so sorry. I wasn't thinking."

"Not to worry. I was just teasing you. And thank you for the compliment, however undeserved."

"But it's not undeserved! You have to stop seeing yourself as that stupid girl described you." She reached up and touched his eye patch. "Take it off."

He backed away, glaring at her, his lips drawn into a firm line.

She braced her fists on her hips. "If I'm to run from you, wouldn't you want me to do it now before you're shackled to me for life? How can you bear wedding a woman you cannot trust to stay? Take it off and test me."

"You're a demanding little tyrant, aren't you?"

She nodded. "At times, but this is all I've asked you for and really meant it. Do it, Caine. I dare you."

To her surprise, he reached up slowly and removed the eye patch. She gasped with surprise. "You have your *eye!*"

He glanced away, obviously embarrassed.

"It moves with the other! Can you see out of it, Caine?"

One shoulder lifted in a shrug and he nodded once.

She threw up her hands in dismay. "I'd just begun to think you a sensible man! Why on earth would you cover your eye and give up half your sight for vanity's sake? If you place so much value on appearance, why take an ugly wife? Will you put a patch over *me?*"

"You are *not* ugly!" he replied. "Are you attempting to destroy our bargain with a fight?"

"Do you want it destroyed?" she demanded. "Have you second thoughts?"

"None! If anything, I am more resolved!"

"Why?"

He turned away, then back to face her. "Because I *like* you, damn it!" he exclaimed. "I need to protect you and I *care*. Make of that what you will!"

"I shall make the most of it then," she snapped, and crossed her arms over her chest. "So, goodbye, Captain."

"Goodbye, Grace," he said.

She marched right up to him, snatched the eye patch out of his hand and stalked back to the house alone.

Inwardly, she was bursting with happiness. *He could see!* How bloody marvelous was that! And his scars didn't signify at all. They were not pretty, she admitted, but they were not what she would deem disfiguring, either.

And he *liked* her.

She glanced over her shoulder as she reached the door. He still stood there, such an imposing figure, one hand on his hip, watching her.

Grace couldn't resist. She shot him a defiant grin and raised a hand in farewell before ducking inside.

Did she imagine she heard his laughter?

Caine's step felt light as he walked on to the stables. Mr. Harrell awaited him there, along with Trent and the saddled mounts.

"I did not wish to speak of this in front of Lady Grace, Mr. Harrell. Now that I'm leaving, you should assemble every able-bodied man on the estate and have them armed. Not only the few I've seen patrolling, but *all* of them," Caine ordered.

"Oh, that was done at the outset, sir, even before you came," Harrell assured him. "Many are stationed well out of sight so you or anyone approaching wouldn't notice. All are mindful of any traffic upon the roads leading in and guards are posted at every entrance to the house itself, night and day."

"Yes, I saw those few every day." Caine was impressed. He had been so preoccupied with Grace's company and so sure he could protect her himself, he hadn't thought to question the number of guards.

"The earl will be happy to hear of your initiative, as am I. In fact, I plan to suggest that you be properly rewarded for the effort that goes beyond your official duties."

"Thank you, sir." Harrell's chest puffed out. "I reckoned the need immediate when Lady Grace arrived."

Caine smiled and nodded. "Carry on, Mr. Harrell, and send word if you need anything. You have enough weapons?"

"Loaded and well manned, sir. There's more powder and shot on order. If it turns out we don't need that now, there's always the fall hunt."

Fall hunt? They had not had one since his father and Trevor died. Was Grace already planning one or was this Harrell's idea? In either event, it was not a good idea, but he would take that up later.

Caine mounted up. "We shall return soon," he told Harrell. "Keep a sharp eye."

He and Trent rode out, pacing their horses for the long ride to London. Trent's thoughtful look prompted Caine to ask, "Do you still think I'm mad to marry her?"

"I think you're mad if you don't," Trent replied. "How was your visit with her?"

"Enlightening," Caine replied, thinking that was the understatement of the century. He had come to like Grace enormously and fully appreciate her originality. Unless he was badly mistaken, she liked him, as well.

Her independence certainly suited their situation. He knew she would be fine by herself when he was occupied with business. And on occasion, when he was not, she would welcome his company. A perfect arrangement for both.

If there was a detraction from that perfection, Caine admitted it was his burgeoning desire for Grace as a woman. She managed to stir his senses even though he could not precisely explain it. Her *joie de vivre,* perhaps. She did embrace life with an energy he envied. The more he was with her, the more he wanted a taste of that, a taste of *her.*

Trent nodded his approval. "Well, I must tell you, Mrs. Oliver informed me last time I was here that Grace ordered armed guards the moment they arrived. Harrell merely followed her directions. You shouldn't give him the credit."

Caine smiled to himself. He had figured as much.

Trent continued, "True, Grace is no beauty and she could cut you to ribbons with that saucy tongue of hers, but she's amazingly resourceful and…well, quite interesting," Trent observed.

"Mmm-hmm."

Trent gestured, palm up. "You must admit, the girl's no henwit. Took a cartload of courage to do what she did to that highwayman."

"Daring."

Trent continued, his mood thoughtful. "And she has this way about her, y'know? A way of moving with a purpose. Not jerking about or anything like that, but efficient, I guess you might say."

"I noticed."

"Can't see how one could help but do that. However, she eats an enormous amount of food, did you see that? Last time I was here and this time, too. She'll beggar you at the market." Trent released a harsh sigh. "She could run to fat. Three helpings of pudding." He shook his head. "I would never mention that to *her,* you understand. But I expect she'll realize it herself before it comes to that, smart as she is."

Caine inclined his head in agreement. "I dare-say."

Trent sounded half in love with Grace himself, obviously taken with her boldness and courage, if not her face and figure. He had obviously given it much thought in the past three days. As had Caine, in a much more personal way. Grace was perfectly charming and he was happy that Trent could see it, too.

Her appearance had changed, though Caine had trouble pinpointing precisely how. Her features were the same, so that wasn't it.

She still wore her hair, straight as a rapier, scraped back into a tight little chignon unless the wind destroyed its severity. He loved when it did that. With outdoor exposure, it did look lighter, streaked with sun and with more shine to it. Like silk. Several times he had touched it briefly just to feel its texture.

Perhaps the difference he saw was due to the hair and the color of her complexion. She looked healthier, pinker. She had clear, beautiful skin, flawless, in fact, though it had looked deathly pale before. Country air obviously agreed with her.

Her vivacity and outspoken manner, something he had admired from the very beginning, certainly overrode any plainness. In truth, she no longer looked plain to him at all. He had been perfectly honest with her as far as his own perception went. She was not ugly.

She had an increased air of confidence that he certainly approved. Her humor enchanted him more than he could say. The girl could make him laugh out loud. Who would have thought?

And didn't she seem quite within her element running the Wildenhurst household! He hoped she would accept that there would be little opportunity to entertain as a couple after they were married. He hated to deny her that, but needs must.

She loved his old home. He looked back at the house that would belong to him when he became earl and then to his son if he ever had one. The impending death of his uncle, the event necessary to inheriting, saddened him.

"You're frowning. Was your parting with her unfriendly?" Trent asked, showing sincere concern. "You didn't quarrel again, did you?"

"Didn't you notice? She stole my eye patch," Caine said, turning back to view the road ahead.

"By God, she's precocious! I've wanted to do that for weeks! If you ask me, I always thought the thing looked a bit theatrical." He leaned toward Caine and squinted at his scars. "Not as red as they were, are they? Did she remark?"

"Only to exclaim that I still had my eye. She expected an empty socket. I suppose my having the eye mitigated the scars."

"You won't wear the damn patch again, will you?"

Caine shook his head. "The only person whose opinion matters to me doesn't seem put off, except by my vanity. I trust you now believe I chose that person wisely?"

Trent met his gaze squarely. "I think you picked up what appeared to be a rather ordinary rock and discovered a solid gold nugget. But I don't see how you could have known her value at first glance. How did you?"

"It was her eyes," Caine replied readily, surprising himself with a truth he hadn't fully realized until now. "I looked into her eyes and they hid nothing."

Chapter Nine

The next week provided little in the way of solving the riddle of who had hired the assassin, despite the leads Trent had amassed. Those came to nothing. In fact, his and Trent's questioning in all quarters only served to reveal publicly the fact that the attempt on Grace's life had failed. Word was out in Town. Now Caine had to worry that another attempt might be made.

On the Friday, he walked down Fleet to Rundell and Bridge Jewelers at Ludmore Hill, intent on purchasing a wedding ring for Grace, as well as a bride gift.

"Something with diamonds. White stones. Nothing ostentatious," he specified when Mr. Rundell asked his preference. "The lady is quite dainty and her taste, modest."

Once he had decided on a simple gem-studded

band of gold, he asked to see something worthy of a morning gift, perhaps with blue stones. Rundell nodded with satisfaction. "I have just the thing, a versatile parure fit for a royal. Understated and elegant and absolutely exquisite."

Caine lifted and examined a delicate necklace of fine blue sapphires, the exact color of Grace's eyes. He touched the matching combs and imagined how they would look in her hair. "Excellent! These are perfect," he commented as he returned the set to Rundell to have it properly boxed and wrapped.

"Captain?" asked a soft voice just behind him. He felt a hand on his back, a light touch.

He turned abruptly. Belinda stood there, radiant in a bright paisley shawl and white day gown that exposed far too much of her generous bosom. The lovely mounds heaved as she took a deep breath and smiled, focusing on his chin.

So she still could not look at his face. Caine sketched a perfunctory bow. "Miss Thoren-Snipes."

She looked away and gestured nervously toward the front window. "I saw you enter and finally summoned courage to follow."

"I commend your bravery." He turned back to the counter to await his purchases, hoping she would go away.

"Aren't you happy to see me?" she asked in a near whisper.

"No happier than you were the last time you saw me," he said without turning.

"How dare you!" she exclaimed. Did he imagine she stamped her foot? "I've come in here to explain why I ran from you. I was in a state of shock when I saw your wounds. Any woman of delicate constitution would have run!"

He turned and cocked his head. "And any woman of breeding would not have broadcast her reaction and unfairly labeled me a cold, unfeeling monster to anyone who would listen, would she?" He again faced the counter. Surely she would leave now.

The white-haired Rundell winced and busily adjusted his cravat.

"So now you would give me the cut direct?" Belinda whined.

"I am a direct sort. You would be wise to mark it."

"Oh, don't be mean, Caine! I heard that you are to be married to someone else. Surely a wicked rumor," she simpered, "since you are still betrothed to *me*. A gentleman never goes back on his word. He *cannot*."

Caine took a deep breath, trying to control his temper. "When you declared to one and all how you were so fortunate to escape such a gruesome match, I took that as a very public cancellation."

"I never cried off it to *you!* I know you do this to shame me. And you pretended to choose another in my stead, declaring *love* for her, proposing at an assembly?"

"Yes, at Cavanaugh's. No pretense about it. I am engaged."

"You cannot be! She is plain as a peasant and worth less than nothing! *Everyone* told me so!" She issued a patently fake sob. "You've made me a laughingstock among my friends!"

"You will recover. I did."

She uttered a cry of disbelief. "You are horrible! I have never known you to be so cruel!"

What more could he say to be quit of her? "You have no patent on that quality. If you wish forgiveness for all you have said of me, then I give it. If you think this tantrum will rekindle what is now a defunct attachment, I must disappoint."

She uttered a pitifully loud moan and ran weeping noisily from the shop. He could swear he heard her mutter a curse just before the door slammed behind her.

Mr. Rundell winced again and cleared his throat. "Lucky escape, indeed, if I may say so, sir."

"You may, this once." Caine opened his money folder and peeled off the notes to pay for the jewels, adding a generous gratuity. "A bit extra for your future discretion," he explained. "I should not like this incident repeated. Anywhere."

"Of course not, sir." Rundell inclined his head. "Unless you require my repetition of it... for legal reasons, you may consider it completely forgotten."

Caine himself would not forget it. The exchange with Belinda only served to reinforce his opinion of her vain and childish nature. Either she could not bear to be replaced by another in Caine's affections even though she had been the one to reject him, or she had reconsidered the benefits of attaching herself to him now that he was slated to become titled.

Neither reason spoke well of her. He understood her shocked reaction at seeing his scars for the first time, but he could not forget how she had branded him a monstrous sight to all of society. Adding, ostensibly to excuse her own behavior, that he had gone cold and ruthless in the bargain. That had not been necessary or in any way kind. Marriage to her would have proved a disaster and he knew he was well out of it.

He met Trent at the club as arranged, but recounted none of the Belinda episode. No need to upset a friend, when it would serve no purpose.

"We shall have to step up efforts," Trent remarked as Caine joined him in the reading room. "I've checked the papers daily to see whether an account of the incident has been officially reported. See here. No details, but what it does say is factual."

Trent read aloud, his voice barely audible. "'An attack on the carriage bearing Lady Grace Renfair, betrothed of Captain Lord Morleigh, was thwarted last week on the road south of the city. Unfortunately, her modiste, Madame Avril Latrice, was killed. The perpetrator was dispatched, as well, and is no longer a threat to travelers. Additional guards have since been posted to police that road. One must wonder why there was then a scarcity of protection that allowed such a vicious attack.'"

"Word of mouth probably preceded this by at least a day or two," Caine remarked.

"Undoubtedly." Trent folded the paper and laid it aside. "How soon do you think there will be another attempt now that the one who was responsible has been alerted of the failure?"

"Who knows? I suppose that depends on who wanted it done and why, what sort of resources he has and so forth. At least Grace is well protected where she is. Let's go again this afternoon and see whether we can locate Wardfelton's solicitor at his home address. It seems a strange coincidence that he should be away for—"

"Excuse me, Caine Morleigh?" a deep voice demanded.

Caine stood and faced the questioner. "I am."

"By God, it *is* you!" The man slapped Caine on the shoulder and laughed. "Caine! It's Devil Neville, man! Don't you know me, coz?"

Caine stared at the stranger. And that he was. He bore no resemblance at all to the skinny lad Caine recalled from his youth. But the wavy black hair and dark-fringed eyes looked familiar. "Neville?"

"So you made it home from the wars! I heard, but I've been away from Town since you came back. Are you well? I was told you sustained a frightful wound." He peered sympathetically at Caine's scars.

"I do well enough," Caine declared. He turned to Trent. "I present Neville Morleigh, my cousin. Neville, my good friend, Lord Trent." He watched as they shook hands and exchanged greetings. Then he asked, "What are you doing in London?"

"Can't a fellow settle down? I live here now." His smile faded. "I was so sad to learn of the deaths of Trevor and your father. Such heavy loss at once, and you were away at the time."

"I was," Caine returned, nodding, "And thank you."

"So now you are heir to Hadley," Neville said with a sigh. "The responsibility must be trying. I know I shouldn't like it myself."

"Neither of us was born with the expectation," Caine admitted wryly, "but I believe I shall manage, as I'm certain you would do if the opportunity ever arose."

Neville regarded him with a canny expression. "You must not think I envy you, Caine. I do not. You're infinitely more suited to the job than I would ever hope to be."

"How comforting to hear it."

"But you don't believe me, I can see, and think I can guess why. I read of your fiancée's trial on the road from London last week. Everyone with the slightest reason to have sought her death must be suspect. Even myself."

Caine said nothing to that, knowing that his silence would provoke Neville to explain himself more fully.

"I need nothing that you will gain, cousin. My own business ventures have been successful and I promise you the title would only hamper me in pursuit of those."

"What sort of business ventures? Gambling?"

Neville grinned. "Ah, thinking of those card games we used to play, eh? You know I never won. That taught me never to rely on chance and especially not on my limited skills at gaming. I'm in shipping, properly insured and closely monitored. But I'm not so busy that I wouldn't be happy to add my efforts to yours in determining who instigated this menace against your lady."

"Why?"

His cousin's shoulders shrugged with impatient resignation. "Word has it you're looking for the culprit. And because she is your betrothed and will soon be one of our family, but I see you are still cautious. So be it." He reached into his pocket and handed Caine a card. "This is my direction here in Town. Do come by if I can be of any assistance."

Caine tucked the card away without looking at it. "If family is so important, why have you not visited since we were boys?"

"I have done. It is you who were away, first at university, then at war. As for me, I went abroad and sought my fortune. Business has brought me to London at least thrice each year and I always make time for Uncle and Aunt while I am here." He smiled again. "So you see, I've not been remiss, except to keep correspondence with you." He shrugged. "I fear I am not a great letter writer, but I have asked after your welfare whenever I had the opportunity. Have you done likewise?"

"I have," Caine said. "The reports were not favorable."

Neville looked confused. "No? Whom did you ask?"

"The earl, of course. He posed you as a ne'er-do-well, a gambler, drinker and waster of funds."

Caine saw the instant hurt in his cousin's expression and it looked genuine. Perhaps it was an act, but if it was, Neville had missed his calling and should be on stage.

"Well, then," Neville said in a quiet voice. "I

should go. Nice to have met you, Lord Trent.
Good to see you again, cousin." He turned
abruptly and left.

"What do you think of him?" Caine asked
Trent.

"That he was sorely troubled by the earl's assessment," Trent remarked. "What will you do?"

"Speak to my uncle, of course. I begin to suspect there might have been devious machina-
tions afoot on his part to get me wed."

"So you won't comply with his condition if
the earl has lied about Neville?"

Caine cast Trent a look of surprise. "Not
marry Grace? I pledged myself to her and it
cannot be undone unless she decides otherwise."

Trent pursed his lips. "Can't risk another
breach-of-promise suit, eh?"

Caine had told Trent of Thoren-Snipes's
threat of that, and would discuss it no further.
He dismissed the topic altogether. "This distraction has cost us time. Come, we must find that
solicitor and see how Wardfelton's affairs stand."

Grace stitched for a week until her fingers
were sore, wondering all the while where she
would ever wear so many gowns. Four new ones
for morning wear hung in her wardrobe, already
finished. Two ball dresses were complete and
her wedding gown lacked but the hemming
and attaching the lace. She, Mrs. Oliver, Mrs.

Bowden, Jane and two women from the village worked as constantly as they could.

"There!" she exclaimed to Mrs. Oliver as she held up the short jacket. "This riding habit has all the button holes bound. If you will trim it with the grosgrain edging, Jane can apply the buttons and it will be done!"

"You have the blouse yet to do," Mrs. Oliver reminded her.

Mr. Judd appeared at the doorway to the morning room. "A young lady to see you, madam. I put her in the drawing room."

"Thank you, Mr. Judd." She laid aside the garment in her hand, happy for any excuse to leave the sewing to the other women. "Who is our visitor?" she asked the butler.

"A Miss Thoren-Snipes, ma'am. Should I send for tea?"

"No. I believe this will prove a rather brief visit," Grace told him. She did not intend to offer that chit so much as a stale biscuit. However, Grace figured it might do well to hear whatever she had to say.

Grace patted her hair and smoothed down an errant strand that had escaped her chignon. She regretted not wearing one of her new frocks today, but she was saving them for Caine's arrival. The old gray one she had on would have to do.

"Miss Thoren-Snipes. To what do I owe the

honor of your unexpected visit?" Grace said by way of greeting as she entered the drawing room. She did not invite the woman to sit. "Have you ridden all the way from London?"

"No, I am visiting friends at Hollander House, but three miles distant. I felt I had to come and speak with you."

"Concerning…?"

"Morleigh, of course," the woman said, frowning at Grace. "Apparently, knowing him is *all* that we have in common. I did not think you'd be quite so…"

"Quite so what?" Grace asked, forcing a smile as she appraised the beauty of Caine's former fiancée. Diminutive and dainty, dressed in a lovely riding costume of deep rose, Belinda Thoren-Snipes epitomized the English ideal of womanhood. She had perfect features, an hourglass figure, pale blond curls, dimpled cheeks and a girlish air. Any man would fall at her feet and worship her. Caine had been no exception.

"Forgive me, but you hardly seem the sort Captain Morleigh would ever choose to marry." The girl's comment was so sweetly made.

"Not *your* sort, you mean?" Grace kept her smile in place. "Well, I must suppose he decided against repeating past mistakes."

The woman sniffed as she dismissed Grace's words with a flick of her hand. "I came to warn you, not to suffer insults."

Miss Thoren-Snipes had an interesting pout as she fiddled nervously with her gloves. Grace noted that her breathing was rather rapid. No doubt she would like to say what she'd come to say and be gone. Fine with Grace.

"Warn me of what?"

Belinda's rosebud mouth took on an ugly twist, her lips barely moving as she spoke. "Caine Morleigh is a dangerous man, Miss Renfair. Not a proper candidate for marriage to anyone."

Grace pursed her own lips and raised her eyebrows as she digested that. "I have heard your opinion of the good captain repeated in Town. However your current version sounds considerably worse. Before he was only so ghastly looking you could not abide his presence. And cold, I believe you said. Now he's become dangerous, as well? How so?"

"He…he… He attacked me! With vicious words and in a public place in front of people! He's a horrible man with no tender feelings. None!"

Indeed, the woman appeared upset. It was entirely possible that Caine had said something to her if approached, but Grace could not believe he had sought her out to do so.

"So you believe that, on your word alone, I should cancel my wedding?" Grace asked.

"Yes! You must! I had to come and tell you. To

warn you!" She crossed the room hurriedly and stood directly before Grace. Her tone was vehement. "The man has killed people, you know, and it has unhinged his mind. You should have heard the things he said to me! So cold and forbidding! He is a crazed ruffian tricked out like a gentleman, but do *not* let yourself be fooled. He will do you harm one day if you are unwise enough to marry him. Why, I do not doubt he was the one who hired someone to assault you on the road, probably to *kill* you because he suddenly realized his mistake in proposing. Speculation about that is all over Town, you know."

Grace had heard quite enough. "If this is the new tale you're spinning for society's consumption, you go too far. Continue spreading these lies and I will encourage him in every way possible to sue you for defamation of his character."

"He would not dare sue me!" she cried.

Grace inclined her head as if thinking about that. "Perhaps not. He might simply *kill* you and prove you right."

"Ooh, you are a shameless, fortune-seeking hussy! Even worse than he! I hope you are miserable together, do you hear? *Miserable!* I hope you *die!*"

She stomped out of the drawing room and down the vestibule, the heels of her riding boots clacking rapidly on the tiles.

Grace stood at the drawing-room entrance

and watched as Judd opened the front door for her exit.

She had an enemy in that one. Then a darker thought dawned. The jealous Belinda was dead set against the wedding and had gone to quite uncomfortable lengths to persuade Grace not to carry through. Could Caine's former fiancée have hired the highwayman? Those parting words made Grace wonder.

Chapter Ten

Over a week had passed and Caine still had found no answer. He had written and reassured Grace that Belinda was incapable of arranging a bowl of flowers by herself, let alone a murder. The very idea was laughable. Her visit to Grace was nothing more than a vitriolic attempt to ruin his life because he had scorned her at the jewelers.

The investigation was proving futile in most regards, but at least Neville was less of a suspect now. It seemed he really was financially secure, had recently married and either owned or managed a shipping company. The details of his business remained a puzzle.

Today, Caine and Trent called upon him again, hoping to get answers and put the pieces of that puzzle together.

Neville's address had been the initial surprise, a town house right in Mayfair, his wife's inheritance from Lord Ludmore. Caine vaguely remembered the old man. Apparently, Neville had appropriated the very rich widow.

Caine and Trent were guided to an exquisitely furnished drawing room and announced. Neville was already there, along with a stunning young woman.

"Greetings!" Neville said with a welcoming smile as he stood. "My dear, I should like to present my cousin, Captain Caine Morleigh and his friend, Lord Trent. Gentlemen, my wife, Miranda."

Caine and Trent bowed over her hand in turn. "It is so good to meet you both," she said. "Congratulations on your impending marriage, Captain. And, Lord Trent, we are happy that our cousin has your kind support in the enquiry of the unfortunate attack on his betrothed. Will you stay for a light supper with us?"

"No, thank you. Kind of you to offer, ma'am, but not tonight," Caine said. "We are expected elsewhere."

"Another time, perhaps."

Neville smiled his approval of his wife's niceties and raised a brow in some unspoken suggestion. She gave an almost imperceptible nod to it, then addressed Caine and Trent. "If you will excuse me, sirs, I shall absent myself and leave you to your visit. I do hope we will meet again soon in happier circumstances."

"I'm certain we will," Caine replied politely.

They watched her leave and close the door behind her, a graceful exit. "She is charming and very beautiful," Caine told Neville.

"Titled and wealthy, too," Neville agreed with a grin. "So you see I can have no designs on the earl's largesse." He sighed. "I am content beyond imagining." He gestured to a grouping of chairs. "Please, do sit down."

"Thank you," Caine said.

"About this wealth and contentment of yours. Uncle knows, does he?" Caine asked, allowing his suspicion to show.

Neville's smile faltered. "I thought he did. After you told me the things he said to you about me, I went to question him, but he would not receive me when I called. Perhaps he was thinking of my father and confused the two of us in his mind. I regret the misunderstanding. His opinion matters a great deal to me, Caine. So does yours."

"Duly noted," Caine replied. "You could easily right things if you would agree to spill a few secrets about your business activities and recent whereabouts."

"Perhaps, but unfortunately I am unable to lay everything bare. My business affairs are my own and must remain so. My whereabouts these past few weeks consisted of traveling with my wife. Our wedding trip, you see. However, I take no offense at your asking and my offer to aid you still holds. Anything I can do, you have but to ask."

"Thank you," Caine said. "I will let you know." He rose to leave. "Come along, Trent. We should see the solicitor if we can find him."

"Wardfelton's man?" Neville asked as he followed them out of the drawing room into the foyer. His question revealed that he had already done a bit of detective work without being asked.

"Yes. Do you know him?" Caine asked.

"I know *of* him. Elusive, is he? Look, I have this friend, an enquiry agent of sorts," Neville declared. "He has worked for me on several occasions in my business doings and has an amazing way of locating people and ferreting out private information."

Caine wondered if the fellow might ferret out some of Neville's for a proper price.

Neville continued. "You think Wardfelton's solicitor is the one? Why would he be after Grace?"

"We haven't been able to find the man to ask," Trent declared. "Caine has done everything we know to locate him."

"My Mr. Cockerel will find him," Neville said. "Meanwhile, shouldn't you be readying for your wedding? It is…what? Only a week away now."

"Not to worry. I'll be ready," Caine assured him.

"Aunt asked if Miranda and I would attend. Would you mind if we came?" Neville asked. "I would appreciate the opportunity to square things with Uncle and also, Miranda and I would love to be there to meet your bride and help celebrate your marriage."

"Yes, of course you may come," Caine said. He would not feel at all comfortable with having Neville anywhere near Wildenhurst and Grace if there was a chance he could be the one responsible for the recent attack. But Caine felt he could hardly retract his aunt's invitation on a slight suspicion. In fact, he did not really want to believe Neville was guilty. "Why not plan to travel with the family? Six days from today, at first light."

"Excellent idea. But six days, when the wedding is in seven, Caine? Your lady must be wondering if you even remember she's there waiting."

They were at the front door now and Caine was past ready to leave, still uneasy about discussing plans in front of Neville, not ready to trust him fully. But the man stood between him and the door, obviously reluctant to end the conversation. Caine had to wonder if his cousin was that delighted to reestablish the familial connection or if he was busy formulating plans for the next assault.

"I will go to the country earlier than the others," Caine said, unwilling to reveal his exact itinerary to one whom he didn't fully trust.

"And I'll be with you," Trent announced. "There might be arrangements that require assistance!" He obviously realized Caine's attempt at misdirection. "I could attend to errands, all things a groomsman should do, eh?"

"Such as?" Caine asked, forgetting Neville altogether when faced with the idea of Trent hanging about Grace when he obviously liked her so much. Trent had hardly passed a day since their last visit to Wildenhurst without mentioning how marvelous Grace was.

"Oh, I don't know. I'll think of something," Trent said, winking at Neville. "Our lad here is somewhat green-eyed with jealousy, y'see."

Neville smiled fondly at Caine. "This bride of yours must be quite a beauty."

Caine merely shrugged. What could he say without disparaging Grace's looks. And yet, he thought perhaps Neville should be set right about what to expect. He might, by surprised word or expression, offend Grace when he did meet her.

"Grace is lovely in her own quiet way," Caine said at last, adding, "Quite unique."

"She is that," Trent agreed with a nod. "Well, we should be off."

"I'll send word when I learn anything from Mr. Cockerel," Neville told Caine. He stepped aside and opened the door for them and offered a firm handshake to both. "Godspeed, cousin. And to you, Lord Trent."

When they were settled in the carriage, Caine asked Trent what he thought of their second meeting with Neville.

"He seems sincere as the day is long," Trent said, "But he still holds secrets that even my sources can't unearth."

"Yes, and I have to wonder why," Caine muttered.

"So, will you actually go to Wildenhurst earlier than planned?" Trent asked.

"I don't know yet." Now that the idea of it had arisen, Caine began to feel an eagerness to see Grace again, to reassure her, even to argue with her. That anticipation boded well, didn't it? He thought of the future with Grace and how knowing her had already kindled a certain excitement.

Whatever life had in store for him, he had the distinct feeling that it would never be dull and complacent with her for a wife.

Her apparent fragility had proved deceptive, and though he had not been particularly drawn to her physically at first glance, that had changed. What he felt was not a burning urge to possess her body, but to hold her, to comfort and protect. It was a subtle desire, an inner need, he decided, and something that would last much longer than the hot flame of passion.

Yes, he liked that idea. It made perfect sense and would make marriage a less consuming effort. More comfortable, certainly.

The carriage bumped along in the gathering darkness as Caine and Trent headed back to Hadley House. Fog had settled over the city and lent a decided chill to the air.

Trent seemed content with the silence between them. Caine wondered if perhaps he had reacted too strongly to Trent's admiration of Grace. He didn't want his best friend to think his loyalty was in question. He also didn't like being labeled jealous.

"Would you do one of your portraits for me when you have time?" he asked, certain that a compliment to Trent's talent would mend fences. "I'd like a picture of Grace."

Trent sniffed. "I can recommend a good miniaturist. Does watercolor on ivory."

Caine sighed. "I don't want that. One of yours would mean something. You know Grace."

"Well, if you really want me to," Trent said, sounding somewhat mollified. "Perhaps she'd like one of you, too."

"Settled then. Those would make an excellent wedding gift. You'll stay for supper, won't you?" Caine asked. "You might as well stay the night. That way we could be off to Wildenhurst at first light. I've decided to go."

"Of course, if you're certain you want me to come," Trent said.

Caine grinned. "A week in the country will save you a fortune in gaming losses. And you can do the pictures then. What else have you got going on?"

"The investigation," Trent reminded him.

"Neville will carry on. He said he would. We can continue it after the wedding, since I'll have to come back to London anyway. Grace will come with me, of course. If she wants to."

"What do you mean *if she wants to?*" Trent demanded. "Why wouldn't she?"

"I promised her she could do as she prefers. She's had no freedom in years, Trent. I decided it was a fair term to offer."

"Damned fool!" Trent muttered under his breath. But Caine heard. And agreed.

When they arrived at Hadley House, Trent exited the carriage first. Shattering glass and a loud report greeted Caine as he followed. Both men instinctively dropped to the street as a second shot rang out.

"There!" Trent cried, scrambling to his feet at the sound of boots pounding the cobbles. Caine spied a figure dashing down the street at top speed. He jumped up and broke into a run.

"Caine, wait!" Trent called from a few steps behind. "Caine, you've been hit, man. Stop!"

Trent's hand grasped his arm and pulled him to a halt. "You're bleeding!"

Caine felt no pain, only red-hot rage. He yanked out of Trent's grip. "He's getting away!"

"Leave it, Caine! Look to your shoulder!"

Two of the Hadley footmen had caught up to them now, puffing with exertion. They looked at Caine with concern, as did Trent.

Then Caine felt the burn and looked down at his lapel where a round hole marred the wool. "Damn," he cursed with a cough of disbelief.

"There's an exit wound. Went straight through. Let's get you to the house. You there, find his lordship's doctor," Trent ordered as he and the remaining footman tried to assist Caine.

"I can walk, damn you!" Caine insisted, and did so.

Only when the burst of outrage and excitement faded and he faced the stairs inside Hadley House did faintness threaten to overtake him. He staggered down the hall to the library and collapsed in a leather armchair. "Who was he? Did you see?"

"Another hireling, I'd guess. No, I didn't see his face."

"This changes things," Caine gasped. "It's not only Grace they're after."

"Brilliant observation," Trent muttered as he

began helping Caine remove his morning coat. "Bring linen, man. And hot water," he ordered in an aside to the hovering footman. "Move!"

Caine allowed Trent to tend him until the physician arrived. Then he was helped upstairs to his room, undressed by his uncle's valet and put to bed.

All the while, he ignored the increasing pain and focused on the possible reasons behind the shooting. His and Grace's attacks were connected, of course. Who would want one or *both* of them dead?

"Preventing the marriage has to be the goal," he said to Trent.

"Again, marks for the obvious," Trent replied. "Now, leave off speculating and take the laudanum, Caine."

There would be no trip to Wildenhurst for him come morning. That was Caine's most worrisome thought as he felt the pain-numbing drug take effect. "Go on without me. Please keep her safe," he ordered Trent. "And don't like her… quite so much."

"I shall camp outside her door," Trent promised.

"Yes…*outside*," Caine muttered, knowing he must trust.

The next morning when he awoke, Trent was still there by his bedside. Caine pushed up, wincing at the sharp, pulsing ache in his bandaged shoulder. "Why are you still here?" he demanded.

Trent stood and walked over to the bed. "I'll be leaving as soon as I know you're recovering. In the meantime, I've recruited three more able guards and they're on their way."

"Hurry after them!" Caine snapped. "How do you know they can be trusted?"

"Because we served with them, Caine. Smythe, Vickers and Tombs. Found them at the Whistlefish down on the docks last night after you slept. They're loyal men, damn good shots and need the work."

"Oh. Well, that's good then," Caine said, clenching his eyes shut, relieved that Trent had taken charge. "I still wish you'd go now."

"Soon enough, but Grace will want to know how you are when I get there and I thought I would wait and see. So how are you?"

"Well ventilated. Where is Ackers? Did he say how soon can I travel?" Caine barked.

"He agreed to five days if you rally and show no sign of infection. Can you use the arm? He was worried about damage to the nerves, but I told him you seemed to move it naturally enough immediately after the shooting."

Caine flexed his fist and gingerly moved his arm side to side. "Hurts like the devil."

"There was that good half hour of digging

out threads of fabric and another of stitching
you up, but he says you should mend quickly if
you could move it and if it doesn't fester. How
do you feel otherwise?"

"Groggy. It's that vile dose. I won't take any
more."

"Then lie back and go to sleep." Trent reached
for a tasseled cord and draped the tail of it over
the head of the bed. "Here's the bell pull if you
need anything. There's nothing you can do at
present but heal and rest."

Caine worried that someone would make another try at Grace, since they had failed to kill
him. Of course, he could still die, he knew very
well. Even in war, blood poisoning killed more
soldiers than did actual wounds. "Gavin…if I
don't survive for whatever reason, promise you
will look after Grace?"

Trent smiled down at him. "Ah. You only use
my Christian name when you're desperate for
me to act like one. So I will. I promise if you
die, old boy, I shall marry her myself."

Caine shot him a go-to-hell look, even as he
realized that was only Trent's way of ensuring
a speedy recovery.

Caine had to get to Wildenhurst soon, but he
didn't think he could make it today. Besides, he
did not want Grace to see him in his current condition. Despite Trent's teasing and his own un-

reasonable jealousy, Caine knew he could trust his best friend.

The day passed in a feverish haze of uneasy slumber and the interruption of it by periodic bloodletting and the application of stinking poultices. His shoulder ached abominably. He finally agreed to another very small dose of laudanum that would allow some relief.

A scratch on the door awakened him. Sun streamed through the east window. This must be his breakfast. He had little hunger for it.

A maid entered without waiting for his leave to do so. And she carried no tray. That was curious. Caine pushed himself to a sitting position with some effort.

The woman curtsied, head bowed so he could hardly see her face beneath the ruffle of her mobcap. "A posset, sir. From the doctor. Says you should drink it all to speed your wellness."

Caine noted her attire, dark brown fustian half covered by a dingy white apron, its bib clumsily pinned to her bodice. The lowliest kitchen maids in Hadley House dressed better. He eyed the porringer she held out. Pewter. Not the silver always used to serve one of the family or guests. Suspicion shook him to full awareness.

"You brewed this yourself?" he asked conversationally.

"As the doctor directed," she answered, sounding a bit breathless. Her posture, dress and attitude were all wrong for whom she professed to be.

"In the kitchens *here?*"

She nodded.

He doubted Cook would allow such a creature near her implements. He took the small bowl with two handles when she held it out. "Have I met you before?"

"No, sir. I don't work here. I've come from the doctor."

"Ah, I see. So Dr. *Quentin* sent you? You work for *him.*"

"Yes, sir. Could you drink it now so I can be returning?"

There was no Dr. *Quentin.* Caine reached for the bell pull that Trent had arranged so that he could call for assistance and gave it a sharp tug.

The maid edged toward the door.

"Stay here," Caine ordered.

She turned and ran. Right into Trent, who grasped her upper arms.

"Bring her back in," Caine said. "I think she was attempting to poison me."

Trent turned her around and forced her back to the bedside while she struggled, shook her head and loudly proclaimed innocence.

Caine held out the porringer. "Fine. Then *you* drink it."

She began to weep and thrash wildly against Trent's grip on her.

Caine sighed and lay back, exhausted. "Take her below and confine her. Have someone locate a rat catcher and test the mixture on vermin. If it is poisoned, send for the authorities." He looked meaningfully at Trent. "Question her before you turn her over and find out who sent her."

When they had gone below, Caine made a decision. He would go to Wildenhurst and he would go today. If the would-be killer were this determined, there would be another attempt on either his life or Grace's. They could better defend against that on one front as opposed to two.

He yanked on the cord again, and when a familiar maid came this time, he asked for Hadley's valet to help him dress and pack.

The pain was nothing compared to his worry about arriving too late to save Grace if someone had already gone after her. Her guards there might never suspect a woman like the one who had tried to finish him off.

Chapter Eleven

Grace sat curled on the chaise beside the window in her bedchamber and hurriedly stitched the final inches of hem on the rose silk pelisse. She snipped the last thread. There.

They were behind schedule on her wardrobe and she feared they might have to seek more assistance if they were to complete her new wardrobe before the ceremony.

She laid the pelisse aside and looked up as the maid entered. "Yes, what is it, Jane?"

"Mr. Neville Morleigh awaits your pleasure in the morning room, ma'am," the maid announced.

Caine's cousin, the one next in line for the title and Morleigh fortune! The man had no reason to be here now unless it was to get rid of her.

She could not risk a confrontation, so she made a quick decision. "Hurry, Jane, summon Mr. Harrell. Tell him to have several of the strongest men apprehend and lock Mr. Morleigh away until we can notify Captain Morleigh that he's here."

Jane's eyes rounded. "But, my lady, Mr. Neville is—"

"I know very well who he is, Jane! Do as I say and make haste!" She watched Jane bob a curtsy and rush to obey.

Grace went immediately to her writing desk and dashed off a quick missive to Caine, informing him of his cousin's presence.

Perhaps this would end all the worry. If the ne'er-do-well cousin were the culprit and had come here himself to kill her, Caine would know what to do with him. If he had come for another reason—though, she could not imagine what that would be—then there would be no harm done other than to the man's dignity.

Hurriedly, she took the back stairs and ran to the stables herself. "Josh?" she gasped, approaching one of the grooms.

"Aye, ma'am. You'd be wanting to ride out again? Not sure that's safe without—"

"No. I need a messenger to hie to London straightaway and give this letter to Captain Morleigh."

She waited until he summoned a man for the task and handed him the letter. "Go armed and with all speed and if the captain decides to come here, stay and accompany him. Keep a close watch out."

That accomplished, Grace returned to the house. Mr. Harrell met her as she entered. "Mr. Morleigh is secured, ma'am. We locked him in the root cellar and posted a guard. I think you're right he came to cause mischief. He was a wild one as a boy and still is. Took three of us to subdue him."

Grace nodded. "I couldn't think why else he would come. The captain did tell me he was suspect in arranging the attack, so I thought caution the most prudent course. I've sent a messenger to London. So you spoke with Mr. Morleigh as he was locked away?"

"He was right heated up, ma'am, fighting, threatening me and my men and blathering on about how he'd come to offer you protection. Said someone shot the captain last evening."

"Shot him?"

When Grace gasped in fear, he shook his head. "Had suchlike happened, ma'am, the captain or his lordship would have sent for you without delay, or at the very least let you know. This cousin likely made up the tale so we'd let him near you. We should wait for the captain's orders. No doubt, he'll come post haste and take care of matters."

"Thank you, Mr. Harrell. That will be all," Grace muttered, distracted by the possibility that this Neville person spoke the truth. But neither the earl nor Trent would have sent *him* to break such news to her. Caine had told her of his uncle's low opinion of Neville Morleigh.

In any event, she would soon know one way or the other after her message reached London. All she could do at present was wait. And sew. And hope the cousin lied and there would be a wedding after all.

As the day wore on, she grew more fearful that something had happened to Caine. She almost had Jane pack her valise so that she could head for Town, but convinced herself finally that she should not risk it. Perhaps the cousin intended to have her do precisely that in response to his tale of Caine's being wounded. He could have someone waiting to accost her on the road.

Just as she sat down to tea that afternoon, Mr. Harrell appeared. "Ma'am, his lordship's carriage is coming down the road at breakneck speed!"

"It's too soon for an answer from the captain! Our rider would have only just arrived there!"

She hurried past the steward to the front entrance to await the approaching conveyance. The weather was fair, a perfect day for riding. Caine would have come by horseback as he had before. The sense of foreboding that had increased since Neville Morleigh's arrival hit her full force. Something terrible had happened. She could feel it in her bones.

The carriage halted and Trent bolted out. Two footmen joined him at the carriage door and Grace saw them half lift Caine from the interior. She ran forward. "Is it true? Was he shot?"

Trent nodded, his gaze still on Caine as the men carried him. "He wouldn't stay abed as Ackers ordered. The ride was too much. Now he's fevered and weak."

"Bring him upstairs," she ordered, running ahead of them to prepare. "Mrs. Bowden, Mrs. Oliver! Come quickly! Bring the medicines!" she shouted from the vestibule. Now was no time for decorum. Her captain needed care.

Late into the night Grace tended Caine, bathing his face, arms and chest with cold cloths and dosing him with feverfew and willow-bark tea. He was out of his head with fever.

The men had undressed him and covered him decently before leaving him in her care. Grace had ordered them out, along with Mrs. Oliver, ignoring the woman's protests that an unmarried lady should not attend a grown man's sickbed.

Doing so was in no way proper and Grace knew it, but she was to be the man's wife, after all. She had more knowledge of tending the ill than all of them together. And she was, given Caine's present inability to give orders, the ranking member of the household.

She held his head as he drank the willow-bark tea Mrs. Oliver brought up. "We will need more," Grace told her. "Prepare yarrow, as well. The receipt is in the medicine book. I will ring for you when I need it."

When the woman left, Grace removed the sheet that covered Caine. She recalled everything her father had recommended for a fever resulting from a wound, and all that she had read about it in his books.

The fever was natural, occurring with almost every injury of any consequence, but she could not let it grow so hot as to do damage of its own. He would not die from this, she thought, unless left untended. She silently thanked her father for all those valuable lessons and the freedom he had given her curiosity.

She determined to remain detached from the feelings generated by her first sight of Caine's unclothed form. There were scars he had never mentioned that few people would ever see but her. Those were probably nothing compared to the ugly ones imposed on his soul by things he must have seen in the war.

Every comment since, every look askance at the evidence of his last battle must dredge up the pain of it all. This man had suffered too much. "Poor lamb," she whispered as she bathed his body to cool it.

He was a well-made man, strong and vital.

She knew he would recover. And he would be hers. Eventually she would lie with him, feel the strength and warmth of his embrace. The very thought created a fever inside her that nearly rivaled his. Could she make him want her as she wanted him?

She shook off the salacious thoughts and sighed at her foolishness. He would be mortified if he knew of it and so would she if he woke up and found her looking at him.

For hours, Grace tended him diligently, then finally he began to sweat. When he groaned and shivered with cold, she wrapped him again in the sheet, added blankets and sat beside him as he slept.

Trent knocked and entered the room around midnight. "Let me sit with him awhile, Grace. You look done in."

"No," she said absently. "I'm well enough."

"Harrell spoke to me about your *guest* and I released Neville from your makeshift jail."

"Was that wise?" Grace asked.

"It's all right. He's returning to London in something of a snit. Neville's no longer a suspect. He has been helping us and insisted on coming immediately when he heard that Caine had been wounded and was unable to protect you. Said it was his duty as family to stand in for his cousin."

"So you and Caine do not believe he could

be involved in the attempts?" Grace turned to see Trent shake his head. "Well, he will get no apology from me until I know for certain he's innocent!"

Trent stood at the foot of the bed, his gaze fastened on Caine. "Is he improving?"

"The fever has broken, but he's exhausted by it and his sleep is deep. I must keep him cool."

"Here, let me." He took the cloth from her, dipped and wrung it out, then placed it on Caine's brow. "I owe him my life, Grace. Trust me to tend him awhile." He shot her a crooked smile. "Sorry, I realize you never offered me the privilege of dropping the courtesy. Do you mind?"

She sighed, flapped a hand and sat down heavily in the armchair by the window. "You might as well. I suppose we are to be constantly in each other's company."

"You don't like me, do you, Grace?"

She leaned her head back and closed her eyes. She did not want to have a conversation at all and certainly not about this, but unless she left the room, it could hardly be avoided. "I like you very well, Lord Trent."

"Just Trent, please. And yes, I daresay we will see much of one another in future. I hope to be your friend, as well as Caine's."

"Then answer me this, *friend.* You have never

approved of my marriage to him," Grace said. "Why is that?"

Trent met her gaze steadfastly. "I objected to his choosing you on impulse, almost without thought, so I believed. But since? Well, I now believe you are perfect for him in every way."

Grace wasn't sure he was sincere, but at the moment, hardly cared one way or the other, she was so tired. "Fine then. See if you can get him to drink more of that tea, will you?"

"What's in it?" Trent asked as he raised Caine's head and lifted the cup to his lips.

"Yarrow," she explained, too fashed to feel much other than impatience. "It rids a body of impurities and helps to fight off a return of the fever."

He gave a little grunt of a laugh. "I read once that yarrow's a witch's brew, used as a love charm."

"Ask him how loving he feels when he wakes and is calling for the chamber pot ever quarter hour," she retorted. An indelicate statement, she knew, but did not care in the least. She was exhausted and in no mood to be teased. "I'll leave him to *you* then."

"As well you should."

They settled into an uncomfortable silence for some minutes. Then he turned to her, keeping his voice low as he spoke. "Grace, do you know Wardfelton's factor?"

She was not surprised he had changed the topic from bodily functions. Though she would have preferred not to talk at all, she answered. "His solicitor? Yes. Mr. Sorenson. I met him a number of times. He was often at the house the first year I came. Less later on, I think, but I hadn't the run of the place then, so I'm not certain. Why? Do you suspect him of conspiring with my uncle in some way?"

Trent busied himself with the cloth, wringing it out and laying it again on Caine's brow. "I wonder if this Sorenson might have embezzled your inheritance and feared he'd be found out when the marriage settlement was arranged. That's the only motive he would have for getting rid of either of you. Of course, that could be Wardfelton's reason, as well. Could be either of them or they could be in collusion."

Grace sat up straighter and tried to clear her head. "My uncle told me often that I had no funds left to me. He could be right. I doubt my father had much personal wealth when he died, since he was a country doctor and hadn't many well-to-do patients. Whatever he had after he inherited was probably allied with the title and property that went next to my uncle."

"We shall see," Trent told her. "Meanwhile, you needn't worry. This place is proof against any threat at the moment and we will see it stays so until you and Caine are married. Then he will have the authority to sort out anything that has to do with your inheritance."

Grace thought about that. "Morleigh will own me then," she muttered to herself. "But he has promised me a certain freedom."

Trent laughed softly. "Straining at the bit already? What sort of wife will you be, I wonder."

"Perhaps an absent or an invisible one, a name on the marriage lines to satisfy his lordship's decree. That is what Caine was after when he chose me, was it not?" That sounded bitter to her own ears, and was in fact how she felt.

"Ah, but if I know you, you will never settle for that," Trent said.

Grace frowned and crossed her arms over her chest and closed her eyes, dismissing the topic and Trent. No, she would not settle for it. She wanted the captain and she would have him.

"He doesn't want to see you," Trent said as he met Grace in the corridor outside the sickroom the next morning. He had finally convinced her to go to bed and rest and now she was returning after a few hours of sleep. Then he clarified, "Rather, he doesn't want *you* to see *him*."

"But that's absurd! I spent most of the night in there. I've already seen him." More of him than anyone realized, Grace thought with a huff. "How am I to tend him if he won't let me in?"

Trent pointed to the stairs. "He had me send

for the village doctor. That's probably him coming up now." His voice dropped to a whisper. "With his lancet and bowl, no doubt. Or leeches."

"No!" She knew the man. He had been summoned by Mr. Harrell after John Coachman was shot. He was an apothecary, as well as a surgeon, and seemed competent enough for one of that ilk, but he was no physician. She trusted Caine's treatment to no one but herself.

Grace tried to push past Trent, but he held her back. She had the irresistible urge to stamp on his foot. "I will not let Caine be bled!"

"Simmer down," he insisted. "I won't allow it, I promise. The wound needs to be looked at, Grace. So go, have your breakfast and leave him to the doctor and me. Caine's surly now that he's lucid and you don't want to go in there."

"But I have to—"

"Grace?" Trent patted her shoulders as his hands rested there. "Humor me, please. Caine's somewhat indisposed and a female attending him would not be the thing at all."

"Oh." She felt her face heat. It was one thing to bandy about indelicate matters at midnight in a sickroom when feeling too exhausted for propriety, quite another to speak openly of them in the bright light of day.

The village doctor reached the top of the stairs and gave them a nod as he approached.

"Well, then…" She backed out of Trent's grasp and straightened her skirts with a nervous gesture. "Call me if I am needed."

"On the instant, trust me."

She watched uneasily as he ushered the doctor into Caine's bedchamber and closed the door behind them. For a few moments, she stood there listening, heard the muffled sound of Caine's angry protests and smiled. He sounded strong enough to fend off lancets and leeches on his own.

Filled with a sense of satisfaction that she had done the best she could for him, Grace went downstairs to see how the household had been faring without her direction.

For two days, she kept busy with the duties she had assumed, she sewed on her trousseau, she collected herbs and flowers from the gardens. And periodically, she attempted to gain access to the patient.

Caine was having none of it. He obviously did not want her to see him as he was, just as Trent declared. She wondered if he realized that she had seen him in a much more vulnerable state and felt embarrassed to face her.

She admitted that if the situation were reversed, she would probably feel the same. Still, she could not resist pushing, always unsuccessfully, for a brief visit. She quite missed Caine and was somewhat miffed that he was not missing her.

On the afternoon of his third day at Wildenhurst, Grace was just coming down for tea when the butler met her at the foot of the stairs. "An unfamiliar coach and four approaches, my lady," Mr. Judd informed her. "Mr. Harrell and the lads are at the ready."

Grace nodded. "If the visitors offer no threat, show them to the drawing room. I will be there directly."

She hurried back upstairs and went straight to Caine's room to fetch Trent. When she knocked, he opened the door immediately and blocked her view of the interior.

His dishabille surprised her. Trent was usually dressed to the nines wherever she saw him. Today, he appeared exhausted and unkempt in rolled-up sleeves and his shirt gaping open at the neck. "Sorry, his nibs still won't see you, Grace. Perhaps later in the day."

"It's you I wanted. Someone's coming to visit, in a coach and four, no less. Will you greet them with me? I fear it might be my uncle."

Caine piped up, ostensibly from the bed. "Trent! Send one of the lads to help me dress."

"You stay exactly where you are!" Trent ordered over his shoulder. "Give me a moment," he said to Grace. "Do not go down without me."

She agreed. He had to don his neckcloth, coat and, she hoped, a loaded pistol.

Her stomach tightened with a knot of apprehension. It would be very like Wardfelton to barge in unannounced, demanding she return with him, especially if he thought Caine was still in London. Or if he knew Caine was wounded. That would mean that he…

A sudden commotion and voices in the vestibule downstairs demanded attention. Grace peeked over the railing.

"How is he, I say? Someone get that gel here with answers! Judd, step lively, man. Go find her!"

Trent ran down the corridor and took Grace's arm. "Come, that's his lordship's bellow. Hurry down before he bursts a vein. What the hell is the old rascal doing here, I wonder?"

"Apparently he's come to see after Caine! We should have sent word."

"God, yes. I forgot," Trent whispered. "He'll be furious we haven't." They reached the curve in the stairs and saw the earl glaring up at them. "Rest easy, milord. Your heir is alive and well."

"You there," he said with a curt nod to Grace. "Is my nephew abed then?"

She dropped a curtsy. "He is, sir, but recovering nicely. Your rooms are ready for you, as usual. You must be exhausted after such a long journey."

"Yes, yes. Damned annoying," he admitted gruffly, leaning heavily on his countess's arm. "Not at all the thing, is it, Bewley? Haring about like we used to."

"No, dear," Lady Hadley murmured. She smiled rather vacantly at Grace. "We came early for the wedding. There is still to be one?"

Grace wasn't altogether certain there would be, but she nodded. "I believe so, ma'am. Would you like to go up to your rooms now? I'll send someone to lay a fire."

"Nonsense!" barked the earl. "Not cold enough to waste wood."

"A fire would take the chill off, Haddie," the countess said. "A nice pot of tea, too. And biscuits."

Trent had gone forward to assist the earl. "Mr. Judd and I will help you up, sir."

"Hmmph. Damned nuisance this. Used to bound up steps like a leaping buck. I could still do it if I took the notion." He issued a rumbling cough and slung one arm around Trent's neck. Judd took the other, relieving the countess, and they lifted his legs to carry him.

Grace watched their awkward ascent, then looked to Lady Hadley. "Is the earl getting on better these days?"

"Yes, it seems so," the countess said with a heavy sigh. "Dr. Ackers is to follow later today."

"Good news. He can see to the captain's wound when he comes."

Lady Hadley didn't remark any further.

"Come, take my arm," Grace offered. "We'll go up together and I'll send Jane down for your tea while Mr. Judd lays a fire for you."

"You're a sweet girl, Belinda," the lady said.

Grace smiled. "It's Grace, ma'am. Remember? Belinda…declined."

"Oh, yes, of course. Declined." A soft chuckle. "The pretty one."

"Yes, ma'am." Grace sighed and held the countess's arm as they slowly climbed up the stairs. "She was the pretty one."

"Aunt Hadley!"

Grace looked up. Caine stood beside the newel post at the first-floor landing, frowning at his aunt. He was barefoot, wearing a belted banyan over a wrinkled linen shirt and dark trousers. His hair was sleep tousled and he badly needed a shave. She felt the maddest urge to hug him.

"It's all right, Caine," she said with a slight shake of her head. "We have everything in hand. You should go back to bed."

"Darling boy!" his aunt cooed, "You look a fright! We so hoped to find you well of your ague! Are you fevered?"

He sighed and accepted the woman's embrace when she gained the landing and reached out.

"No fever, Aunt Hadley. I'm feeling fine." He peered at Grace over the woman's shoulder and mouthed the words, "I'm so sorry."

"Her ladyship is probably tired." Grace smiled at him as she passed by them, unable to resist touching his sleeve. "See her to her chamber, then, if you're up to it. I'll find Jane to tend her."

She wondered if anyone had told the Hadleys the truth about Caine's having been shot. More likely, the countess only imagined he had the ague rather than believe anyone would fire a gun at her nephew.

Grace wished to heaven the wedding were over and everyone but Caine would leave for London. Perhaps she was more like the countess than she realized in trying to deny unpleasantness.

Chapter Twelve

The afternoon had taken its toll on Grace. The Hadleys' arrival had further stirred the household, already in a state of flurry and worry due to Caine's wounded presence. Then Dr. Ackers had come from London to tend the earl, eager to have a private conversation with Grace about her father's patients and Withering's research.

In addition to that, Mr. Harrell interrupted her day several times with concerns over providing two newly hired men with weapons and temporary lodging. Mrs. Bowden and Mr. Judd had almost come to blows over discipline of a footman and tweenie who had formed a liaison. And so it had gone, one thing after another.

Late that evening, after everyone was settled, Grace sat down with a cup of tea in the library. It had become her favorite place of refuge. Here, she could escape the bustle of the household. Everyone usually assumed she was reading or going over accounts and left her alone. Yet this evening, Trent did intrude.

"Caine asked me to come down and see how you are. He's very upset about his aunt."

Grace set down her cup, rubbing her brow to banish the ache that had formed there. "Why so?" She motioned idly to a chair, a reluctant invitation for him to sit.

Trent hesitated for a moment, then sat down. "You know, what she said to you. Sometimes she doesn't think."

"Oh, the mistake in identity?" She dismissed that with a sigh. "I took no offense at that. The poor lady was weary and confused."

He sat back in his chair, apparently content to stay for a while. "No, about her other comment."

"That Belinda is the pretty one? Well, Trent, you can't fault her for honesty. Belinda *is* pretty."

"I didn't realize you knew her," Trent said, suddenly alert and leaning forward.

"A recent acquaintance. She came here to warn me not to marry her captain." Grace tossed her head and pulled a face, aping Belinda's haughty attitude. "He is *so* dangerous! Beware the captain!"

"She warned you off?" Trent's brow lined with concern as he sat forward. "Why didn't you tell us she had been here? When was this?"

"Before Caine was shot. I wrote to him about it and he answered immediately that she was only posturing. That it wasn't significant and we should ignore it."

"I can't believe she dared."

"You don't think she's the one who—"

Trent raised his shoulders in a shrug. "She hasn't the brains, but that brother of hers... I should speak to Caine about that." He pushed out of the chair. "Excuse me."

Grace jumped up and grabbed his arm to stop him. "Please don't put that in his mind, Trent! He might want to do something about it and he's not well enough. Let it go for now, please."

He turned and took her hands in his. "You're right, of course." He searched her face for a long minute. "May I make an observation? You won't misconstrue it?"

"Of course I wouldn't," she said, looking down at his grip on her fingers and back to his serious expression. "What?"

"Prettiness goes no deeper than the surface, but beauty shines out of the soul. You glow with it, Grace. I just wanted you to know that."

Speechless with shock, she just stood there as he released her hands, turned abruptly and left the library.

Caine remained in his room that evening, as did Trent, Lord and Lady Hadley. Grace dined alone, as usual, and spent another restless night.

Trent joined her for breakfast the next morning. "You look refreshed," she commented, toying with her spoon instead of facing him directly. "Sleeping better now that our patient is improving?"

"He's sleeping through the night without laudanum. Grace, about what I said—"

"So when will he emerge from his cave again, do you think?" She interrupted him because she had determined to forget his remark to her last evening and never speak of it again. Either he had made it out of pity, or worse, was developing some sort of tendre for her, which definitely wouldn't do.

He nodded and smiled. She hoped he understood the matter was finished.

"Caine will see you this evening. He apologizes for appearing in such a state yesterday and says he will make himself presentable and come down for supper."

"It is about time!"

"The man is vain past forgiving," he said with a shake of his head. "Doesn't want anyone to view him in any light but the best."

"No," she argued. "Not *vain* precisely. He simply has a low opinion of the female gender and believes all of us are that much taken with how a man looks."

"And you disagree with that, of course."

Grace shrugged. "Some of us obviously *are* that way, given his past experience."

"Ah, but not Saint Grace of the beautiful soul! Do you forgive me for yesterday's flirt? I can't seem to help myself."

She laughed. He wouldn't let her forget it. "You are an intolerable tease, Trent. How is Caine really doing this morning?"

"Bearlike, if you must know, but I've seen him in worse temper. You'll have your work cut out for you in future, jollying him out of those moods of his…" He let the sentence drift as he shook his head and rolled his eyes heavenward.

"Yes, dear old Belinda also warned me he was dangerous. So you'd both have me cry off and leave the poor man at the altar?"

"Of course. Then I would have a clear shot at you myself."

"There you go again! Restrain yourself till you get back to Town, will you?" She got up and paced to the window, hiding her smile, determined to give as good as she got. "If you use up all your good lines on me, what shall you have to offer the London belles?"

"Practice, love, practice! I'm only half serious at the best of times. Caine's a lucky man, but I would never tamper with the best match ever made. You will be incredibly good for him, y'know." Trent rose as he spoke. "I'm going for a short ride and dispense with some pent-up energy if you will excuse me."

She grinned. "Too right I will. Go and devil a horse."

The butler appeared in the doorway before Trent reached it.

"A letter for you from Mr. Neville Morleigh, sir." He handed it to Trent on a silver salver.

Grace approached as Trent tore open the missive, both knowing it must concern the investigation.

Trent read it quickly, then refolded it. "Come. We'll brave the bear's den together. Caine should hear this now. Trust me, he's well enough."

"Knock first," she said, huffing from exertion as they topped the stairs. "He might not be dressed."

Trent chuckled and shot her a sly grin. "Never tell me you spent half a night with the man and didn't peek under the covers once. Have you no natural curiosity?"

She felt her face heat with color. "Have you no natural shame?"

"No, and that would make two of us," he admitted as he rapped on the door. He raised his voice. "Make yourself decent, Captain! Female in the barracks!"

She heard Caine curse.

Trent opened the door without waiting for

leave. Grace couldn't resist entering right behind him.

Caine stood before the washstand, straight razor suspended and his face half covered with lather. He was bare, save for the bandage on his shoulder and buckskin breeches with the front flap only half buttoned.

She stared, again fascinated with the way his chest hair narrowed down his midsection to the indentation of his navel. He looked quite different standing up and nearly naked. Madly muscled and rather delicious, in fact. She couldn't quite stifle a smile of pure appreciation.

"Damn you, Trent!" Caine exclaimed, tossing the razor in the bowl and reaching for the drying cloth. He wiped his face and ran a hand through his hair. "Good morning, Grace."

She reluctantly lowered her gaze to the floor. "Good morning, Caine. You're looking *well*." She feared she had sort of sighed that last word.

Trent snickered, then must have remembered why they were there. He held out the letter. "Message from your esteemed cousin. Seems Wardfelton's solicitor has vanished along with his account books. Neville's man traced him to the docks and found he took passage yesterday for the Continent on one of the trade vessels. Sounds as if we've discovered the culprit, eh?"

"Indeed. What about Wardfelton's involvement?" Caine asked even as he scanned the letter. "Ah, I see Neville has put a watch on him."

Trent nodded. "The solicitor was probably working alone. Wardfelton would be gone, as well, if it was he who played false with Grace's inheritance."

"I told you there might have been no inheritance," she reminded Trent.

"I think that's highly unlikely, but we shall find out," Caine said as he laid the letter on the washstand. "You realize Wardfelton could not simply disappear? He is an earl, after all, and I believe he would brave it out and challenge any accusation rather than abandon his title and everything that entails."

When he turned back to them, he looked Grace over as if he had never seen her before. For a long moment, he said nothing. Then he turned away again. "If you two would give me a few moments to finish here and dress, I'll meet you downstairs."

"In the morning room," Grace said. "Trent and I just ate. The food's still warm. No one else is up yet."

"Coffee will do," Caine muttered.

"I'll do my utmost to entertain her until you interfere," Trent said.

They left and Trent closed the door behind them.

"You are a horrible man," Grace said in a

gruff whisper. "Downright perverse to tease him that way."

"I know," he said with a sigh. When they were on the stairs, he stopped and touched her arm. "Grace, he's going to want to leave today, so be prepared for that. He might even want to delay the wedding."

"He said nothing about—"

"He will. I know that look. I've known him for so long I can usually tell what he's thinking." He took her arm and continued their descent. "Did you see the way he looked at you just now, once the surprise of our intrusion was over?"

Grace certainly did recall. "Yes, and did you think he seemed more disappointed than usual in the way I look?" Jane had put up her hair in what Grace believed was a flattering style. Her morning gown was new, a bright shade of blue just the color of her eyes. And with regular meals, she had lost the gauntness of face and body. "I thought I might appear a bit better than when he was here before, but perhaps not."

She hated to admit, even to herself, that the countess's comment on Belinda's prettiness and Trent's touting her *inner* beauty had anything to do with her effort to improve her outer looks. She had made a real effort.

Trent huffed a sigh. "Ah, Grace. Ill as he's been, and not having really looked at you for over two weeks, Caine wouldn't have noticed the difference until just now."

"It might be blue he dislikes!" She shook her head. "You know, how he hates yellow. Or perhaps it's my hair." These curls were not natural to her, a vanity perhaps not as flattering as she had thought. "I knew I should have worn a cap, lace or something to properly cover it."

Trent turned her to him and stared into her eyes. "It's neither. You look beautiful. You bloom with health and confidence now. The problem is that you're no longer the wretched little wraith left on the vine for him to pick and tuck away, Grace."

"Why should he mind that?"

"Wait and see for yourself. I will lay odds he puts off your marriage, probably to give you a way out of it. When the matter is settled, I expect you'll have money, enough to marry where you please. Caine will see to that, one way or another."

"What? You can't possibly know if there ever was any inheritance and I will certainly never accept charity! Anyway, why would I want out of the marriage? I'm well content, even eager to have it done. What do you think of that, Lord Trent?" she demanded.

"Eager, Grace?" he asked with a touch of sarcasm. "Well, what I think is that you will have to convince Caine you really mean it, my dear, and that will be no easy task."

Caine finished shaving and dressed for riding. He intended to leave for London as soon as possible. His shoulder was healing well enough, though it still pained him. That pain was nothing to that which he expected to feel when he set Grace free of their engagement. He had to do it, because it was only right.

He had worried about it almost constantly since those wonderful three days they spent together at the outset. Seeing her yesterday and especially this morning had convinced him that he was not right for her.

Grace was so full of life, so appealing and now, exceptionally lovely, as well.

She was not the woman he had thought her to be now that she was herself again. Fear of Wardfelton had almost ruined her health. The man had damaged her spirit, too, but that had healed very quickly, in the space of days. Now, weeks later, she was a beautiful young woman with everything to recommend her except a fortune. He would have to be shameless and with no honor at all to take advantage of a betrothal she'd agreed to only to save her own life.

It might have been a marriage of convenience he had planned for them, but it had been a marriage of survival for her. She had been desperate. How could he hold her to such a promise?

She would have a dowry, too, if he could recover it for her from that damned solicitor. If not, he would see her well fixed so she could make her own choice of husbands. He knew in his heart that her choice would not be a battle-worn cynic, who was more prone to argue than entice.

He had done little to encourage her to like him, much less want to be shackled to him forever. He had promised her freedom and she should have the ability to freely choose.

Grace had observed close-hand what she would be getting if she married him. She'd seen him at his very worst, bloodied and sweating, probably worse than that while he was out of his mind with fever. Damn, he hated thinking of it.

He made his way down the stairs to the morning room, dreading what must be done. Grace and Trent sat nursing their coffee as he entered. She quickly hopped up and poured him a cup.

Caine watched her, noting anew how lovely she was now, how the roses in her cheeks blushed the pearled sheen of her complexion and how even her lips seemed plumped to perfection. The striking blue of her eyes looked more intense with the color she was wearing. Her hair seemed even lighter than the last time, swept up into a crown of curls, interlaced with a blue ribbon.

"How beautiful you are." The words slipped out before he could catch them.

She lay a hand on his good shoulder, set down his cup and offered a merry grin. "Pure artifice, I assure you. My maid is a wonder with a curling iron and face paint."

He cleared his throat and shot Trent a look of dismissal. It did not take. Trent merely raised an eyebrow and stayed right where he was. On second thought, perhaps it was just as well the conversation did not go private.

"Now that the solicitor has left the country, there should be little danger of another attack. No point to it, really. So I believe I should go to London today and question Wardfelton about the matter. It's time we got to the bottom of this."

Grace's smile faltered. "The wedding is in three days. Why not wait until after?"

Caine sipped his coffee before answering. "As to that, it would be best, I think, if we postponed the ceremony until we've cleared everything completely. Then we shall see." Somehow, he couldn't utter the words that could end things between them. Not yet.

Trent raised both brows then as he turned to Grace and pulled a comical frown. Caine could have boxed his ears.

She took her chair, propped her elbows on the table, rested her chin on her hands and looked directly into Caine's eyes. "No," she said simply.

"I am going to London," he declared. "I have to go."

"Fine. Go," she said. "But be back in two days."

Caine turned to Trent. "Please leave us."

Trent pushed back his chair, raised his hands in surrender and walked out. He shot Grace a smile over his shoulder, but she paid no attention. Her eyes were on Caine.

When they were alone, Caine started to state his case, but she interrupted before he could. "No," she repeated. "We will not delay, nor will we cancel the wedding, Caine. Everything is planned. Jilting me will be worse than anything my uncle ever did to me, you see."

She abandoned her recalcitrant pose and got up, going to the window to look out so that her back was to him. Caine suspected she was hiding tears. He'd had no intention of hurting her. He rose and followed, cupping her shoulders with his hands and turning her around to face him. "Grace, things have changed…."

"I know, but my mind has not." She grasped his face with her hands, raised to her toes and pressed her lips to his. When he would have pulled back, she held him, increasing the intensity of the kiss.

He couldn't resist her moan of encouragement. Damn, she tasted so sweet, so determined, as her tongue touched his.

He abandoned himself to the kiss, embracing her fully and holding her body as close as he could. How soft and giving, insistent, enticing. He wanted, needed… Until her hand accidentally brushed his wound and he jerked in pain. She jumped back, alarmed.

They stared at each other in shocked silence. The kiss was more than either of them expected, he reasoned. Grace didn't appear to have been quite that thoroughly kissed before and Caine wondered if he had, either.

He knew he'd never felt quite that out of control during a mere kiss. Huh. There was nothing remotely *mere* about it. He was aroused, breathing rapidly. He saw that she was, too.

"One week," he said finally, and added, "Please."

She sighed and nodded, looking rather helpless.

He kissed her again, keeping this one quick and perfunctory with no body contact. He could not afford to linger or there would be no waiting, even for a week. Perhaps distance would help solidify his thoughts on the marriage. Right now they were rather liquid. And hot. "Keep well," he whispered as he released her lips.

He left before she could recover and speak. Heaven only knew what she would say or how he would respond.

Trent was waiting in the vestibule with his

coat and hat. "Let's go then," he said. "Unless you'd like me to stay."

Caine didn't even bother to reply to that idiotic suggestion.

Trent insisted they take the carriage and Caine didn't protest. He knew he was not up to an all-day ride, and it did look as though it might rain.

Once on the road, Trent began his inevitable questions. "So is the wedding still on? I warn you, if you cast her off, I plan to—"

"Stop there. I have no intention of casting Grace off. She insists we carry through and, as you well know, I am honor bound. Only *she* can end this farce and is apparently unwilling to do so." *Thank God.* He leaned back against the squabs and closed his eyes. "Though I cannot for the life of me, think why she wouldn't. I promised her protection and couldn't even protect myself."

"She loves you," Trent said with a grin.

"You're a bigger fool than I thought if that's what you think. She's only grateful and feels obliged."

"So you no longer want her?" Trent prodded.

"I want her, all right. What man wouldn't want her? It's just that she's not the same she was before."

"Ah, I see, not what you bargained for," Trent

said, nodding sagely. "Now she's become the very sort you wanted to avoid, another Belinda."

"She's not a whit like that little she-devil, and you know it. But now she'll require a great deal of attention. Managing. Entertaining," he added. "She admitted as much when I was here before. She loves parties, balls and such. How can I be dancing attendance on a woman and fulfilling all my duties at once? Damn it, I have to figure a way."

"Oh, I'll gladly dance with her," Trent offered. "And I daresay, there'll be a crowd of admirers willing to do the same."

"Just so," Caine agreed with a sad shake of his head. "How long do you suppose it would take her to realize her mistake in tying herself to me? How could I compete with men who haven't a care in the world past what color waistcoat to wear?"

"You have a rather low opinion of her, Caine. She's not so shallow as that. Grace cares about you a great deal. Looks like love to me, or at least, the promise of it."

"No, it's only gratitude. Not an auspicious emotion on which to base a marriage."

"Neither is convenience, your motive for choosing her in the first place," Trent reminded him. He had gone serious now, all teasing aside. "Were I you, I would look again and see if I could find better reason. You might possibly love her, too."

Caine was afraid to look any deeper. He already knew he wanted Grace. He might find that he did love her.

Losing Belinda had nearly destroyed him, but at least that had been swiftly over and put behind him. He shuddered to think what it would be like to be married to a woman, truly loving her, and suffering *constant* rejection once she realized her mistake.

Chapter Thirteen

No matter what she did, Grace kept thinking about that kiss. That and the heat of his body pressed to hers had awakened a hunger she had not known was sleeping within her. She thought she had experienced desire before, but that chaste touch of lips and slight tingle she felt with Barkley had been nothing, a mere hint of the raging storm that Caine Morleigh's kiss could unleash.

Now she wished to heaven she had never read all those medical texts in Father's library when she was a girl. How had she ever thought herself worldly beyond her years merely because she knew how a man and woman fit together? Words on a page told nothing of the feelings that must accompany all of that. And she had only a brief taste of those feelings. All too brief.

Grace tried to dismiss the thoughts until they would be appropriate. It was all she could do, so she had to stay busy every minute with other things.

She was sick to death of sewing. The house was in order, menus all planned and there was nothing to do now but wait for the wedding. She hated waiting. So what next to do to keep Caine off her mind?

Maybe this was an ideal time to see for herself how the earl was progressing. He kept to his chamber, taking his meals there and she had hardly seen him since his arrival. All she had was Dr. Ackers's word that he was taking the concoction she had suggested and was much better. She wanted to see for herself.

Yesterday, they had spoken at length about her father, who had attended university the same years as Ackers, though they had known one another only in passing.

He assured her he had begun treating the earl, using Withering's writings as a guide. They discussed trusting apothecaries who furnished the substance and Grace convinced him that she could provide better quality from the plants growing wild in the wood. They talked of preparation and dosage.

He reminded her of her father in attitude if not appearance. He had the same intelligent eyes, but Ackers was a slight man with effeminate features, thickly pomaded hair and an overlarge mustache. Grace quite liked the doctor.

"I should like to speak with Lord Hadley," she told him as they met by chance at midmorning in the downstairs corridor. "Is he awake this time of day?"

"Always, unless he's very ill. Lady Hadley rises late, so he will probably be alone. Shall I accompany you?"

"That's not necessary. I won't be long and I promise not to tire him."

He agreed, so Grace went upstairs to the earl's chambers, knocked softly and entered without waiting for a reply. "Milord, I've come to see how you're feeling today."

"Eh? Well, come in, come in, gel. What is it, then?" He pushed up against the pillows and frowned at her. "Bad news?"

"No, sir, not at all! I thought I would keep you company for a little while, if you don't mind."

He squinted at her. "Looking pert today. Nice frock, that."

Grace curtsied, holding out the skirts of her new rose morning gown. "Thank you, milord! I see where Morleigh gets his way with the ladies." She put on her best smile and approached his bedside.

The earl chuckled. "Cozening his old uncle won't get you any more blunt, gel. He'll be getting it all soon anyway."

"I hadn't a single thought in that direction," she assured him, eager to get to the point of her visit. "Could we speak about your condition, sir?"

He appeared amused. "Heart's giving out. Shouldn't take long. You can wait, can't you?"

"It's nothing to do with me, or with your nephew inheriting. Dr. Ackers says that he told you my father was a physician and treated quite a few gentlemen with heart afflictions."

The earl nodded. "Gave 'em that stuff Ackers gives me."

"Yes, sir, what do you think of it? Do you feel any stronger?"

"I do." He cocked his head. "But it won't last, y'see."

She reached for his hand. "May I study your pulse for a moment?" When he shrugged and indicated he would let her, she pressed her fingertips to his wrist. After feeling the uneven pattern, she risked a further presumption. "Could I listen to your heartbeat?" He nodded and Grace leaned forward, laying her ear against his chest.

"Still fluttery," she remarked as she straightened again. "But I suppose you know that even better than I. We could make it steadier and stronger, but, as I'm certain the doctor told you, increasing the dosage carries risk."

He laughed, a rusty grunt of sound that ended in a cough. "Ackers is an old woman, more scared than I ever was that I'll die. I am his only patient, y'see, so he's overcautious."

"Not without cause, sir. There's a chance that increasing what he's given you might make you sicker than you are." She let out a sigh. "Or worse."

"Too much could kill me," he said, nodding. "Why should you prolong my old life when I'm worth more to you and Caine dead than alive?"

"Caine loves you, sir, and your living longer will make him happy. If he is happy, then surely I shall be."

She saw a sheen of tears in the weak old eyes. "Loves me, does he? Ha. Well, then calm Ackers's fears if you can and let's see what happens."

Grace conversed with him a few minutes longer, turning the subject to country life and happier things. Then she bade him good morning and left, eager to find the doctor again, glad to have a purpose that would occupy her mind.

The next few days crawled by for Grace. The nights were worse.

The only unusual occurrence was the arrival of a letter addressed to her. Mr. Judd had brought it to her that morning, along with several invitations to various events nearby. She had thought little of it at first, except to wonder who might be writing to her now that Dr. Ackers was here.

Then she read it and wondered whether she should send for Caine immediately. But she was safe as could be here, wasn't she? Caine would be back soon anyway and there was nothing he could do about it even if he were here.

So upset she could not sleep, she had donned a robe in the middle of the night and come down to the library to fetch something boring to read.

Certainly not that letter, she thought with a grimace as she glared at it. The horrible thing had arrived in the post and still lay open on the desk. She was unable to touch it, even to throw it away. In spite of her resolve, it drew her to it yet again. Perhaps she had overlooked some clue as to who had posted it.

This time, she tried to suppress her outrage and examine it objectively, as one who was uninvolved in the message.

It was addressed without title, simply to Grace Renfair. There was no greeting inside, only the one paragraph and, of course, no signature.

Ask yourself why he would propose marriage to someone of your sort. It was because you looked fit to die and he hoped you would. He has to wed, yet wants no wife. Cry off and run if you wish to live. Beware his tricks. Beware his friends. Save yourself.

Her first thought was that Belinda Thoren-Snipes had sent it. But Grace had made it quite clear to the woman that her warning held no credence. Why would Belinda bother with a second of the same nature? Surely the woman's pride would hardly allow that.

Grace tapped a finger against her lips as she studied the hand. The graceful penmanship indicated someone with much practice at it, one who had perhaps studied calligraphy.

Wardfelton's handwriting was spidery and backslanted. She had seen it on his outgoing correspondence that first year when he had treated her with civility. Trent's writing was entirely different, too, for she had a sample of that. Caine's was a bold hand with few curves and no flourishes.

Judging by the comparison of this to the writing of her uncle, Trent and Caine, Grace felt fairly certain none of them had written it.

It made no sense that Caine would write anything so self-incriminating anyway. He certainly couldn't be guilty of attempting to have her murdered. Someone had tried to kill him, too. She had come to trust Trent as a true friend. Despite his constant flirting, she knew he wanted her to wed Caine.

Perhaps part of the message might be true, however. She had looked *fit to die,* as the letter said. Wait! Whoever wrote that must have been there at the ball to see her the night Caine proposed. How else would the writer know how she had looked? Trent and her uncle had attended, among countless others. Belinda had not, but she had friends who were there.

Grace was eager to have Caine return and see this. She quickly laid a book over it, determined to leave it covered there until he came.

Trent had posted a brief missive to her the day before, stating that Caine was feeling amazingly well and the matter of the solicitor was *progressing,* whatever that might mean. Had they caught the man or not? Would Caine return as planned or delay the wedding further?

Her greatest fear was that he would postpone it forever. She knew he did not trust that she would make a good wife. The only way she could disabuse him of that notion was to actually *become* his wife and show him.

It angered her that her confidence in that ability waned with every hour that passed. Suppose he was right, she thought whenever her defenses were low. What if the feelings she had for him were, as he must think, only surface emotions guided merely by the desire to thank him for choosing her? To reward him. And herself, too, she admitted. She really wanted him.

Only when she was with him did she know for certain that the instant infatuation she had experienced that first night they met had deepened into something more lasting and undeniable. At least on her part, she was sure it had.

Suppose he really felt nothing for her? She had felt his desire when they kissed and he'd held her against him, but he might feel that, have that response, for almost any woman who virtually threw herself at him. She had been too forward. Scandalously forward and she should be ashamed.

However, she was not sorry at all and would kiss him again, given half a chance. Given a ring and vows, she would do a great deal more than that.

She hoped that she had at least shown him that he was not horribly disfigured, as Belinda Thoren-Snipes had declared. That stupid little idiot needed her hair yanked out by the roots.

Grace unfisted her hands and folded them sedately against her waist, determined to regain her composure and settle her thoughts enough to go back to bed and to sleep.

The arrival of Trent and Neville Morleigh the next morning surprised and disheartened her. Caine was not with them.

"We have news for you!" Trent announced as he entered the morning room, where she received them.

Grace gestured for them to sit down. "Good news, I hope."

Trent nodded. "The solicitor has been found. He was responsible for everything and is no longer a threat."

"Where is Morleigh?" Grace asked, more interested now in the absence of her bridegroom than in the apprehension of their suspect.

"Coming along in the morning by carriage. We rode, you see, and he still wasn't up to jouncing along on a horse for hours," Neville explained. "We came on early, thinking you would be relieved to know the man who tried to have you done in is dead himself."

"Dead?" she asked.

"Fished out of the Thames last evening. Been there several days at least. Must have jumped in soon after his boat disembarked. Unfortunately, the account books were nowhere to be found aboard the vessel. Probably at the bottom of the Thames."

Grace sat down heavily and pressed her fingers to her temples. The relief was so great, she could hardly believe it. "You're certain he was the one?"

"Must have been," Trent assured her. "His pockets contained a waterlogged announcement of your betrothal and the names and directions of three people. One man named was the one who murdered Madame Latrice and would have killed you. The other hired man, the one who shot Caine, will be found soon since we have his name. The woman has already been arrested for entering Hadley House with the intention of poisoning Caine soon after he was shot."

"What! Why did no one tell me of that?" Grace demanded.

Trent soothed her with a placating gesture. "Because you had enough to deal with tending Caine. The woman was never anywhere near successful in the endeavor."

Grace groaned, burying her face in her hands for a moment, fully realizing the horrid determination of the one who wished them dead. She fought to calm herself. They were saying this man was dead now. Drowned. Surely it was over.

"Well, I suppose those names are proof enough for anyone," she said, turning to Neville, whom she had quite ignored until now. "And you are innocent, sir. I am so glad of it."

"You had me taken up so quickly when I arrived here, you nearly convinced *me* of my guilt," Neville replied with a grin.

Trent came over to sit beside Grace and took her hand. "Now all you have to worry about is the wedding. Anything we can do to help with preparations? I am, after all, the best man."

Neville groaned. "Or so he would have you believe. All I've heard the entire ride is how lucky Caine is and how he doesn't deserve you."

Grace laughed. "He's a wretch! And I do apologize for my mistake in thinking you were the villain of the piece. I was too overset by Caine's wound to give you my regrets after you were freed. I suppose I should have listened to what you had to say instead of having you tossed into the root cellar."

He grimaced. "Not a pleasant place to languish, I admit, but at least I wouldn't have starved. My wife might take longer to forgive you, though. She was quite upset that you didn't recognize me as the upstanding fellow she believes me to be."

"You are married, sir? Would I know her?"

"Perhaps as Miranda Williams when she was a girl, or later as Lady Ludmore. She was Baron Ludmore's widow. We were wed a bit over month ago in a very quiet ceremony, since it is her second marriage and she was hardly a year out of mourning."

"I don't believe I've met her, but congratulations to you, Mr. Morleigh," Grace said. "I do hope she can attend the wedding, too, and I will tender my apology to her in person for treating you so poorly. We should celebrate your nuptials, as well as ours, since your whole family will be here."

"Thank you for the thought, but the day should be yours and Caine's alone. May I offer my sincere best wishes, ma'am?"

"Please call me Grace, now that we are to be cousins," she offered.

"Of course, and I shall be Neville to you. I'm certain you and my Miranda will get on famously."

Grace could well understand his wife's anger. "I shall see she forgives me, then. And I must thank you profusely for your part in the investigation and finding someone to help."

"We have not uncovered all thus far," Trent said. "We still suspect that Wardfelton has done wrong by you and your inheritance. Without the account books, however, it will be difficult to prove."

Neville said, "He is still under investigation."

She waved her hand to dismiss the worry. "I am free of his wardship and that's the important thing to me."

Trent got up and helped himself to the bottle on the sideboard. He returned with a glass of brandy for both her and Neville. He went back and retrieved a glass for himself. "Shall we toast?"

Grace raised her glass. "To new friendships. My heartfelt thanks to you both."

She sipped, then set down her glass. "Now to get you two settled. Please make yourselves at home here and ring if there is anything you want." She pulled the bell cord and had Mrs. Bowden show them to their quarters.

They left her happier than she had been in days, just knowing the threat was over and that

Caine would be here tomorrow. Their wedding would commence the morning after.

Back in London, Caine dismissed Neville's enquiry agent and sent a footman to the Hadley stables to ready his mount. He was glad he'd sent Trent and Neville on ahead. Guards had probably been reassigned to other duties. Everyone at Wildenhurst would be unaware that danger to Grace still existed.

It was already late in the day and he should hurry. Though his favorite bay was a goer, Caine knew it was impossible to run at top speed for long, certainly not for eighteen miles on a dark road, risking injury to horse and rider.

Caine had to travel much slower than he wished and, even so, arrived exhausted late in the night. He approached the stables. No one rushed out to meet him, so he knew it was as he feared. The guard had relaxed, probably at Trent's suggestion.

Caine woke a stable lad and ordered him to care for the bay, then took a lantern and went to the back entrance of Wildenhurst. The door was not locked. He entered the kitchens, which were dark and deserted in the middle of the night.

He sat down on a bench to take off his muddy boots, then blew out his lantern and left it on the table. No point in rousing the entire household before he notified Trent, Neville and Grace of the still-existing threat—that Sorensen was not the culprit, or at least not the only one. Also interesting was the fact that Wardfelton had shaken surveillance.

Caine decided to go to Grace first so she wouldn't be frightened if she was awakened by the outdoor commotion of Mr. Harrell's getting the guards back on duty. More important than that, he had to make certain she was all right. It had been entirely too easy for him to enter the house without anyone the wiser.

He knew Wildenhurst so well he had no need of a light to find his way upstairs to the bed-rooms. He also knew that Grace slept in the north end, in the room adjacent to the one in which he had recovered from the fever.

Caine treaded silently through the upper corridor until he arrived at her door. Then he paused. How should he wake her? Gently call her name from across the room or go in quietly and wake her with touch?

Touch, he decided, would be less likely to startle her. He opened the door, stepped inside and turned to close it.

The blow felled him immediately.

Chapter Fourteen

"Grace!"

She had raised the brass lamp to strike again when she heard him groan her name. Weak moonlight from the window revealed only shapes, but she recognized his voice immediately.

"Caine?" She dropped her makeshift weapon and knelt beside him, her hands on his shoulder. "What were you thinking, sneaking into my room? I almost killed you!"

Caine reached up to feel the damage to the back of his head. She could swear she heard him laugh.

"What is wrong with you?" she demanded. "Have I addled your wits?"

Caine slipped his arms around her and crushed her to him so that she was sprawled across his lap. "More than you know. We could have used you in battle against the French."

She brushed the back of his head with her hands. "Oh no, it's swelling. You'll have a goose egg. I'm so sorry!"

"Nonsense. You did precisely what you should have done. I was a fool to steal up here like a thief in the night, but I wanted to wake you first and explain—"

She kissed him. It began as a way to stop his words. He must have come to tell her he was delaying the wedding again. Why else would he seek her out in the middle of the night for private words?

Then as he responded and the kiss grew fierce, almost desperate, Grace saw her chance. She wanted him and she knew, at the moment at least, that he wanted her, too. With her fingers threaded through his hair, she renewed her assault. Her tongue battled with his. She loved the intimacy of it, the taste of him, the urgency of the need that swept through her.

She moved against him, sinuously inviting closer contact with that part of her needing him most. Slowly, as if in mindless surrender, he lay back on the floor.

Grace stretched above him, fitting her body to his as he embraced her. His eager hands clutched, caressed, explored and tangled in her nightdress. And then she felt his palms hot on her bare flesh, soothing, exciting, claiming.

Grace knew the instant his reason intruded. Caine's hands halted their delicious exploration and he tensed beneath her.

"What's wrong?" she gasped, her mouth only inches from his.

"This!" he hissed through his teeth. "*This* is wrong." He lifted her away from him, yanked her nightdress down over her body and smoothed it with a hand that trembled. He sat up.

She knelt beside him, not touching, sighed with resignation and wished she were capable of cursing out loud. So close, she thought, frustrated to the point of anger.

Nevertheless, in all fairness, she had to grant him credit for self-control. He did have her best interests at heart. It was simply that his idea of best interests and hers did not coincide at the moment. She should not be angry with him. But she was.

It piqued that she had not been able to overcome that iron control of his. "We certainly wouldn't want to make such a dreadful mistake," she snapped. "Anticipating vows that might never take place."

"I was thinking of you, Grace. You know—"

"I can *guess*. No point doing anything until it must be done," she finished, hating the bite in her voice even as she said it. Vanity was a terrible thing and she recognized it right away, though it had lain mostly dormant in her until tonight.

He turned to her, a mere shadow in the darkness of the room, but an ominous presence all the same. "You think I don't want you, Grace?" When she didn't answer, he added, "Well, I do."

"Nicely said, if not meant. So tell me why you've come here in the middle of the night and then leave."

He rose then and reached down to help her up. She pretended not to see his outstretched hand and got up on her own.

"This is not how we should begin, Grace. I never meant to… Well, I was carried away, but there's no excusing it. Are you all right?" He ran his hands up and down her arms as if searching for injuries.

She batted at his hands and turned to go and light the lamp beside her bed. Then she realized it was on the floor where she had dropped it after crashing it over his head. She smelled the bit of fuel that had spilled. Thank goodness it had been nearly empty and that she'd had the presence of mind to remove the glass globe. She found a candle, stuck it in the holder and lit it with a sulphur stick.

"I came to inform you the danger is not over, Grace."

"The solicitor isn't dead?" She whirled around to face him. "They said he was dead!"

"You need not worry about the details," he said gently. "You will be well protected. I'm telling you because I don't want you to be alarmed when you hear Harrell summoning the men to guard you more closely."

Grace hated the tone of his voice. "Tell me everything," she ordered in a firm voice. "I am an adult, Caine, if you will remember."

"I never treat you like a child, Grace."

"You *do!* As if I cannot process what you say or understand the onus of this threat! As if I'm completely without the sense to act on my own if need be!"

"I am trying to spare you worry, Grace." He threw up his hands and glanced heavenward as if for assistance. "You are just like the rest. All tantrums and fits."

"The *rest?*" she demanded, then lowered her voice, realizing this could become quite public if she roused the household. Besides, this *was* nearly a tantrum she was having and if she let it escalate, it would prove his point.

She took a deep breath, striving for calm. "The rest. Well, what sort of women do you frequent, Caine, and why cast their faults upon me? This is to do with that cork-brained Thoren-Snipes henwit, isn't it!"

He made a rude noise that sounded like a

curse. "Does any woman have the presence of mind to sustain a coherent conversation? They inevitably end in tears, recriminations, outrageous changes of topic. Or *sex!*" he exclaimed. "None of which solves a thing!"

Well. "And how many women do you know? Two?"

He huffed, threw up his hands again and shook his head. "I didn't come to you to argue! This is ridiculous."

She marched right up to him, shaking a finger under his nose. "You cannot, in your wildest imagination, credit me with overcoming a highwayman, can you? Or admit that I could have killed you tonight before you realized what was happening?"

She gestured wildly, so upset she feared she might strike him again if her hands weren't busy. "Some trick of fate, some stroke of luck, perhaps, but not Grace Renfair employing her wits and defensive means! Oh, nooo!"

He kissed her. Assuredly to shut her up and she knew it. She almost bit him, but refrained due to the practicality she had so recently boasted. He was bigger, stronger and perfectly able to do her harm. Not that he would, of course, but momentary surrender seemed the better part of valor. And she loved his kisses, even this sort. Especially this sort.

Her bones nearly melted along with her anger,

but she kept the anger cool by hanging on to a thread of pride. He released her mouth and she granted him his goal. She said nothing.

Small concession on her part, she could scarcely form a thought, let alone a word.

"Now then," he rasped, sounding as shaken as she felt. "Since you insist on the adult version of events, here it is. Wardfelton's solicitor was no suicide. He was murdered. I think Wardfelton killed him or had someone do it."

"What of the evidence found in his pockets?"

"Planted there by whoever killed him. He was strangled and there were bruises made there by strong hands. No water in his lungs, so he was dead before he entered the Thames. The coroner discovered this when he performed the autopsy. This was done only last evening."

"After Gavin and Neville left London?" Grace guessed.

"Yes. The enquiry agent, that fellow Neville hired, learned of it. He came and told me. He also said that your uncle has not been seen by the man set to surveil him since last evening. So there you have it, Grace. The whole sordid tale."

Grace nodded as she drew in a shuddering breath, determined to behave reasonably. As if her body was not on fire for Caine still. As if she had her self-touted wits under control.

His findings were serious and discussing them certainly deserved more urgency than solidifying their betrothal by seducing him. That seemed a lost cause anyway. Caine had a mind of his own.

She probably should thank him for full honesty, but she still resented the tardiness of it. "So it is my uncle's doing, all of it," she snapped, fisting her hands together in front of her to keep them still.

"I believe so. I reinstituted your guards as soon as I arrived. I had no problem gaining entrance tonight, to the house or to your room. If I had been the culprit and you had been sleeping..."

She went to the bed and sat down, patting the mattress beside her to show she was granting him a modicum of forgiveness. Her temper had cooled. The excitement of her terror, subsequent arousal and their confrontation were now dwindling. Grace felt rather hollow at the moment.

He sat, but left a good deal of space between them, indicating he would not repeat what he considered a great mistake. Fine. Now she must find a way to help evaluate the problem or he would continue to believe she was a featherbrain given to fits.

"All right. We know that my uncle is probably behind these attacks and obviously determined to prevent our marriage. Do you think he will give up once it is a fait accompli? If it ever becomes that?"

Caine sighed and she could imagine his expression of determined tolerance as he answered. "I think it is developing the marriage contract that he dreads. His solicitor is dead, the account books missing and probably at the bottom of the river. By all rights, he should feel safe now."

"But we cannot count on that," she guessed.

"Best not. My next logical step would be to approach your uncle again and demand terms this time. It is usually the bride's family that insists upon those, for her protection. I shall ask for your dower funds. If he refuses to produce your father's will or evidence that you have nothing, that indicates his guilt as far as I'm concerned."

"I've told you and he's told you that I have nothing to settle. That could well be true."

Caine shrugged. "Then what motive could he have to stop the wedding? He has to know that I will, as your husband, have the legal right to investigate your holdings at any time after the ceremony."

"You wish to delay it again," she guessed.

"What I am saying is that we cannot rely on the marriage itself to remove what he might see as the threat. In fact, it increases it. Yet, I find it hard to believe he would commit murder over several thousand pounds of misused funds. That, I can't figure."

"Assuming there were funds to misuse," she reminded him again.

"I believe there were. But if so, why did he not simply replace the money? The scandal would be minor, given the offense and he could easily lay blame at the solicitor's door, whether it was true or not." He got up and began to pace. "It makes so little sense!"

"He might be financially strapped and unable to make it right," she suggested.

"You think so? He owns the valuable town house and his country estate must contain treasures he could sell, even if the land and house are entailed."

Grace tried to recall what her uncle might possess that would be worth selling. "The paintings, statuary and much of the furniture were gone when I arrived. He said he planned to refurbish, that everything there had been old and outdated. Yet he bought nothing new to replace anything while I was there."

"Selling off. See, that's telling." Caine shook his finger as he paced and considered.

Grace racked her memory. "The books," she murmured, running a hand through her hair and twisting it into a coil. "Most of the books were gone, as well. There were some newer ones left, but not many. The old ones, some priceless first editions that Father had pointed out to me in the two years we lived there, were no longer in the library."

Caine had stopped pacing to listen. "But the town house is not entailed. He could have sold or mortgaged that to cover a theft."

Grace shrugged and shook her head. "We might be misreading his motive altogether. Perhaps it's simple hatred. He suddenly seemed determined to drive me to suicide long before I met you."

She watched Caine's face harden the moment she said that. He looked fierce enough to kill. "When was this?"

"Ever since his regard for me changed, he's been at it one way or another. For months after I came, we got on well. I think I told you that."

"Yes, go on. Every detail you can recall."

Grace shrugged a shoulder. "He was never affectionate or eager to have me there, but he acted cordial enough. He allowed me to supervise the household staff, to act as hostess whenever he entertained and occasionally asked my opinion on inconsequential matters. Then, overnight, he changed."

"How so? Did he…hurt you?" Caine demanded. "I want the truth, Grace."

"You believe I would lie to you about it?"

He stalked over and sat down heavily on her bed again, rubbing his face with his hand. "No, of course not. This upsets me, that's all. I want to throttle the man and he's not here. I never meant to direct any anger at you. So he didn't hurt you?"

"No. He confined me to the house, to my room for the most part. He only allowed walks in the garden. Supervised walks. And he seemed particularly concerned about halting any correspondence. I was cut off from the world. There were veiled threats of poison. I became afraid to eat."

Caine shifted restlessly. "You were so thin."

"I was required to join him for supper. Meager fare, that. I ate only what I saw him eat. He would glare at me down the table, sometimes add an evil smile and trail one finger along the edge of his knife. I suppose that was meant to interfere with my digestion."

"I'm sure it did," Caine said, his voice tight with fury. "Why on earth did you stay, Grace? Why not run?"

"I did, twice, even though I had nowhere to go and no means to get there if I had. He had me brought back and informed me yet again that he had the legal right to do as he would with me. Such is the law."

"And a bad one that needs to be remedied!" Caine exclaimed.

She confirmed that with a nod. "As it is now, a woman cannot go running off on her own unless she intends to take to the streets. I am reluctant to admit it, but I became desperate enough to do that." She paused. "Without proper training, references or recommendation for employment, none of which I had, acceptance or ruination are the only choices for a female. Unless she seeks the protection of another man, one with honorable intentions. Such as you," she added.

"I was your only means of escape. Small wonder you agreed so readily to marry a perfect stranger."

Grace couldn't deny it. "A *perfect* stranger, yes," she said with a smile. He either missed or ignored her small jest.

"I don't like the laws regarding women any more than you do and once I have a say in the House of Lords, my first order of business will be to take up this issue. But for now, I need a full understanding of your ordeal. So when the rumors went round that you might be dead, he produced you at that late season ball to prove you were not."

She made a face, thinking of her uncle's orders that evening. "Thank God he did. I was near the end of my patience with that man. I might have done *him* harm."

Caine laughed without humor. "I daresay you might." He reached over and took her hand. "I will resolve this." He sighed wearily. "But you should not have to marry to escape him, Grace.

Once this is over, you will be free. I'll see to that."

She snatched her hand from his. "You offer it so often, it must be *you* who wishes freedom. I have stated time and again and have shown you clearly how willing I am. Now I am losing patience with *you!*"

He reared back his head. "Should I be afraid?" She heard the smile in his voice.

"Perhaps you should. I never meant to embroil you in this sort of fix." Grace felt the sting of tears and looked away from him.

"We'll sort this out, I promise. The main thing is to keep you safe until we do."

He was so kind, she felt the need to weep. But she would not. He already saw her as a weakling, failing to stand up to her uncle and falling in a faint after the proposal. Little question as to why he felt he must coddle her as he did. And very likely why he wanted to set her aside.

"I am stronger than you think!" she declared as she lifted her chin and faced him squarely.

"Have you any idea how exquisite you are?"

Grace simply stared at him, wondering what had prompted that.

"I'll wake Trent and my cousin now," he said. "Where are they?"

"The green and blue rooms just down the hall," she murmured, holding his gaze.

"I will see you in the morning. Try to sleep

again." He rose, walked over and picked up the lamp, replacing it on the table beside its glass globe.

The candle beside it flickered. The flame caused shadows to dance on his rugged features, highlighting the scars, giving him a saturnine appearance.

"Devilishly lucky for me you didn't bring the highwayman's pistol to bed with you," he said.

She swallowed hard, imagining what might have happened if she had.

He turned as he reached the door and opened it. "I promise never to underestimate you again, Grace. And I admire you more than you will ever know."

She stared at the door as it closed behind him. *He thought her exquisite? He admired her?* Well, then.

Chapter Fifteen

⁂

Caine felt so proud of Grace. What a resilient spirit she had, what a practical nature and inner strength. He remembered the waif of the ugly yellow dress and how she had sparred with him even then. And now she could add beauty and good health to that self-confident nature. She was damned amazing and full of fire.

If she had intrigued him that first night, he now found himself absolutely fascinated. He was either in love or in lust with her, perhaps both, and he certainly had never bargained for either.

Trent and Neville joined him in the library, interrupting his ruminations. He had wakened them a good deal more carefully than he had done with Grace.

Gingerly, he touched the aching knot on the back of his head. If one small woman could inflict that much damage with a lamp, he could only imagine how those two would have reacted to their doors opening quietly in the middle of the night.

"You have a headache?" Trent asked as he flopped down in a chair beside the grate. He had thrown on his clothes, shirt open at the neck, not having bothered with either neckcloth or coat at such an hour.

"Nothing significant," Caine replied. Damned if he would relate what Grace had done to him. He would never hear the end of it.

Neville wore a dressing gown over his trousers, quite the fashion plate. He raked Caine with an assessing gaze. "There's blood on his shirtfront," he remarked to Trent. "Been fighting, coz?"

"A small accident. Now to the purpose of my coming," Caine said, determined to change the topic. He immediately began relating what he knew of the solicitor's death in much the same brief fashion that he had with Grace. He included his own conclusions as well as hers.

"So you've already spoken with Grace tonight," Trent said.

"He has," Grace announced, sweeping into the room. "I hope you gentlemen won't mind if I join you."

They all stood immediately. Trent straightened his shirt and ran a hand through his tousled hair. Neville smiled and bowed.

She, too, wore a dressing gown, one of dark green silk trimmed with gold gimp. She had pinned up her hair in a casual way that flattered her features enormously.

Caine tried without success to banish the candlelit vision of her earlier, hair mussed, slumberous blue eyes at half-mast, her breath coming in fits and starts after he kissed her. His hands tingled with the memory of the silken pliancy of her body beneath that modest nightrail. Even the subtle scent of her stirred him so he could hardly think straight.

He shook his head to clear it. The woman played havoc with his senses without even trying. Now was not the time to have his faculties disturbed. Lives were at stake. Did she know what a distraction she was?

"You should be abed," he told her, but tried to couch it in the form of a suggestion instead of a command.

"So should we all, but circumstances demand we settle on a plan, don't you think?" She went to the carved oak cabinet, opened it and removed a decanter of brandy and four glasses. "Shall we?"

Trent went to assist. "You see? This is why I love your lady, Caine. She keeps spirits in every room! And best of all, she's so eager to share. Allow me to pour, Sweeting."

"My, my," Neville said with a lighthearted chuckle. "You do like to live dangerously, Trent." He accepted the glass, swirled his brandy and took a sip. "I recall from childhood how jealous Caine was of his toys."

Grace raised her chin and looked down her small, straight nose at Neville. "A greater danger is to those who consider me a *toy,* sir."

Caine smiled and held his tongue. No reason to upbraid Trent for flirting. The man would cut his own throat before betraying a friend. And there was certainly no need to chastise Neville. Grace had taken care of that.

"So, what shall we do about Wardfelton?" Trent asked.

Caine set down his glass. "The men are assembling and remanning their posts. If Wardfelton comes here or sends anyone, they will be apprehended and dealt with."

Neville gave a wordless sound of approval. "I'll leave for Town tomorrow. It's time to approach the banks, twist a few arms and dig more deeply into Wardfelton's finances. This business of Sorensen's murder leaves little doubt the earl is our man. We must find him."

Caine agreed. "Trent, will you be going, too?"

"I'll stay. There's still the wedding," he said. "Or do you intend to postpone it yet again?"

Grace preempted quickly before Caine could answer. "Yes, we must delay it, perhaps indefinitely. Caine believes it will do nothing to change my uncle's plans to be rid of one or the other of us."

"Indefinitely?" Caine asked.

Her nod was defiant. And resolute. Her expression was pensive as she regarded the three of them in turn, settling last on Caine.

Obviously she had been rethinking their earlier conversation about freedom, Caine decided. Though he had suggested it himself, her belated agreement struck him like another bullet. With this strike, there was no delay in the pain.

His heart sank as he thought of not having her. Ever. And knowing he had caused this himself made it worse. Could she really have changed her mind so completely in less than an hour? He picked up his glass, tossed back the brandy in one draught and winced at the burn.

"Well, I'm off to bed," Neville said with another slight bow to Grace. He left in haste.

Grace followed him out of the library without another word. Caine watched through the open doorway as she glided to the stairs and started up.

"Rather downcast, isn't she?" Trent remarked. "She has to be worried Wardfelton will strike again soon." He poured himself another shot of brandy. "As we all are. Or is it further delay on the marriage that bothers her?"

"I honestly don't know," Caine admitted. "This has become so much more complicated than I expected. She's more complicated, too. Certainly not the same girl I proposed to at the ball."

"Not biddable, not retiring and definitely not weak-minded," Trent agreed. "Not ugly, either, though she never really filled that requirement."

Caine shook his head. "No, yet her appearance has changed so drastically, it stuns me every time I look at her. She's so lovely now her health has improved, she could have her choice of men."

"So why stick with you, eh?"

Caine scoffed. "I'm not the man I used to be, my friend. I only wish I had known her then."

"Ah well, truth to tell, you weren't all that pretty before the scars, old friend. You only thought you were. Women are attracted to confidence, y'see. You did, and still do, have that in abundance."

"Grace has never minded my scars, not even at first. They are not the problem. I simply believe she should have a say in her future and not have to accept me as a husband just because she promised in order to save herself."

Trent glanced at the doorway as if he could still see Grace. "She has nothing but her good looks at present. Perhaps with a dowry, she'd have excellent prospects, but whatever her uncle had of hers is likely gone. As it stands now, you are probably her best bet. Were I you, I'd close this deal while you have the chance. You'll never do better."

Caine laughed wryly. "Trust you to lift my self-esteem."

"You want her. You know you do," Trent said.

"As I said, I'd like to be fair to her. Conscience demands I *must* be fair."

"Fair? Life's never *fair,* Caine." Trent sighed. "Not being a widow of means, she must belong to some man. Better you than the man who wants her dead, or some other man we don't know."

"Yes, but I wonder how we would get on once she realizes I have no intention of doing the social whirl each season with house parties interspersed? She has missed that, losing her fiancé when she was so young, being companion to his mother in their grief, then suffering virtual imprisonment by Wardfelton. She has had hardly any social life and she'll surely want that now."

"Only natural she should, and she deserves it," Trent agreed.

"I know that. I just wonder how am I to provide that if I'm to do the earldom justice? I have more work than I can handle and haven't even inherited yet. Imagine how that will increase

once I must sit in the Lords and help govern. You
and I have talked of this before. There seems no
solution, so we might as well let it be."

Even as he said the words, Caine realized that
other nobles managed to juggle duty and social
obligations well enough. He would not be right-
ing all the wrongs in government by himself.
And who would he be governing for anyway if
not the people of Britain, the families, his own
included? Grace in particular.

"Best call off the wedding, then," Trent said
with a smile. "Shall I take her off your hands?"

"Oh, stop." Caine glared at him. "You push
me too far, Trent. Why do you do that?"

He toasted Caine with his empty glass. "Just
driving home a point. You want her. You don't
want anyone else to have her. So do her justice,
for your sake and hers."

"I never thought to do otherwise, however
this goes."

Trent set down the glass with a thunk. "Remember that your cousin is not the wastrel your
uncle painted him. Don't marry Grace and
Neville can be responsible for the earl's wealth
and investments. All you'd have then is the
title, the entailed manse and the Lords to con-
tend with. Tons of free time to do your *duty* to
the country. And to miss what you might have
had with Grace." He looked unusually serious.
"But if you do give her up, I will step in. That,

my friend, is no joke. Jilt her and, I swear, it will happen."

"Jilting her never occurred to me and you know it. Go to bed," Caine ordered, impatient to end the discussion. "And stop coveting Grace. Unless she throws me over of her own accord, she will be mine."

He wasn't really angry with Trent and they both knew it. The man did have a way of resetting Caine's priorities and that was his sole intention. Wasn't it? He had not been smiling with that last warning.

The very idea of Trent wooing Grace for real disturbed him to the core, even though he was certain that would never happen. Fairly certain.

Trent might not stoop to that, but some man would step in sooner or later if she broke the betrothal. Grace would be obliged to find a husband quickly to avoid her former situation with Wardfelton. Unless they found evidence against him, she would have to go back to her uncle or marry someone.

Was she considering crying off after all? Perhaps the argument they'd had convinced her she should. She hadn't seemed to mind the delay of the wedding just now and, in fact, had agreed to it all too readily.

The word *indefinitely* disturbed him no end. He had to know exactly what she meant by that, and there was no way to find out unless he asked her to explain it. Now he could demand that explanation in private.

Caine hurried to the stairs, hoping she hadn't fallen asleep yet.

This time, he knocked.

Grace heard the rap on her door and knew it had to be Caine again. "Come," she said just loudly enough for him to hear. She was sitting in the chair beside her window, looking out at the moon-shadowed stables. Figures came and went as she watched.

"The men are assembling and arming to return to their guard posts," she said as Caine joined her. "There are so many, seeing them all at once."

"Every one that we and Harrell could muster."

"I've been thinking." She looked up at him. "You must be wishing you had never spoken to me that night at Cavanaugh's."

He blinked as if she had surprised him. "You can't believe that, surely. Is this why you seemed so eager for another postponement when Trent asked about it?"

She looked back out the window. "I don't believe this marriage will ever happen, Caine. Perhaps it shouldn't."

"So you've thought about what I said earlier, about your having a choice."

She stood and faced him. "No, it's because I

have made my feelings for you all too clear and still you draw away. I am not what you want."

When he would have spoken, she silenced him with a gesture. "Please make no declarations of concern for me, of your duty or keeping to your word as a gentleman. That insults me, Caine. You are honorable and we both know that. But I am not what you want in a wife."

"You are *all* that I want!" he protested, his words soft, yet adamant.

"No. Your voices carried and I stopped to listen, Caine. You were right in what you said to Trent. It's true I would require more of you than you could ever give."

"I would give you everything I have," he declared.

"Except your constant presence in my life, eventually your love and children." She wrapped her arms around her middle to still the trembling. "You must think me an ingrate to want so much after all you've already done on my behalf. I'm not, Caine. I feel enormously grateful to you."

He ran a hand through his hair and began to pace. "Gratitude is not what I want from you, Grace. That is the problem!"

"Your offer of marriage is what brought us together and gave me relief from a situation I could not control. How could I not thank you with all my heart? Because of all that I owe you

in that regard, I have to let you go. You must find
someone who suits you better."

"*You* suit me," he argued, moving closer. "No
one else."

Grace put out her palms and backed away.
"Please leave my room, Caine. Enough has been
said."

If he came any nearer, she knew she could not
resist throwing herself into his arms and pleading for him to care. He did not and never would.
"Please go," she added, turning away.

Grace stood very still long after she heard
the door close. A numbness had come over her,
as if all life had drained away and left only a
shell. Though she stared out the window, she
saw nothing through the haze of tears.

"I don't want to leave," he said in a harsh
whisper. "Not with you thinking as you do, that
I don't care for you or want to marry you. I
know what I said, but I was only trying to be
fair." She heard his groan of frustration. "I *do*
want you. But can't you understand what guilt I
would carry, how miserable we *both* would be if
you went through with this only because I was
your only alternative? I don't want to be that, for
you to see me that way, as a relief from danger.
I would always be that for you, marriage or no.
Just do not choose me for that reason!"

She whirled around and saw him standing,
back against the door. His look of distress moved

her more than a declaration of love might have done. A long silence drew out as they regarded one another.

Finally, she broke it. "I know there is desire between us. You could stay tonight for that alone and I wouldn't deny you. But you would see that as my repaying you for protection."

He said nothing, which was an answer in itself.

Grace sighed and pressed her fingers to her forehead, wishing she could rub away the memory of his embrace, that last heated kiss, his words to Trent, and think clearly.

"Anything I give to you at the moment, you will take as gratitude, Caine. And whatever you offer me, I would see as your way to keep me under your protection because you feel obliged to do it. Maybe both of us would be right."

"No, you would be very wrong," he said softly.

Her need to believe him was so fierce it frightened her. Yet he had not asked if he would be wrong in thinking her merely grateful. No matter what she said now, there was no way she could convince him of what she really felt for him.

"Could…could you leave me to think about it?" she asked. "Please, just for the rest of the night. We can settle things in the morning, one way or the other."

"Just for the night, then," he agreed finally. He crossed the room, took her hands and held them to his lips. His gaze held hers as he said, "Duty and fairness be damned, Grace. No matter what I've said, I do want to marry you if you want it, too."

He slowly released her hands, bowed ever so slightly and left as she had asked.

Exhausted as she was, sleep was out of the question. She tried for over an hour to shut out the worries, but Caine's final words echoed in her head and would not leave her alone. He did want to marry her despite what he'd said earlier. Could he mean it?

Grace left the bed and donned her wrapper. Perhaps a glass of milk with honey would help, she thought. With that in mind, she lit a candle, exited her room as quietly as possible and started downstairs.

The house was incredibly silent after the night's activities, all the servants long abed. She noted the comfortable, somewhat faded grandeur of the place. She loved every inch of it and hoped it would remain her home. Hers and Caine's. How could she ever make him see that she wanted him as a man, not a bulwark between her and disaster?

The cavernous kitchen was redolent of cinnamon, nutmeg and lingering wood smoke. She opened the cooling chest where perishables were kept and was about to lift out the container of milk when a noise alerted her. She paused, turning toward the back door. With the blast of night air, her candle had whooshed out. One of the guards, surely.

She waited. Perhaps whoever opened the door hadn't seen her. It wouldn't do to surprise him, armed as he surely was. But what if it was not a guard?

The room was totally dark and she sensed someone moving near the door. Prudence was the better part of valor. Grace sank in a crouch behind the cooling box and remained still. There were no further sounds.

She stayed where she was until her legs began to cramp from the uncomfortable position. Then she stood there in the dark, listening intently. Nothing.

The guard must have opened the door to check that all was well in the kitchen and then retreated, closing it again. She felt around until she found the candle, lighted it and looked around. Nothing appeared to have been disturbed. No one was in the room with her.

She abandoned the idea of having milk and hurried back upstairs. The incident, which was probably nothing significant, had shaken her more than she realized. Should she tell Caine?

The clock in the atrium bonged softly. Three o'clock. He would be asleep. Grace felt a strong compulsion to wake him. She admitted the sound in the kitchen only provided an excuse. Maybe she had imagined it for that very reason.

After all their arguing about the marriage, she could not deny how much she wanted to marry Caine. Somehow, even given the doubts he had, she would make things work.

When she reached his room, she didn't stop to knock. She entered in a swirl of silk wrapper and shut the door behind her. "Caine!" she exclaimed softly. He had already rolled from the bed, weapon in hand to meet an intruder.

"Grace?" He lowered the pistol. Moonlight haloed his form as he stood between her and his window. "What is it?"

"Morning's too far away," she whispered as she rushed to him and threw herself into his arms.

He closed around her, enveloping her with his strength and maleness, banishing any doubts she had about what she was doing. He was naked! Grace ran her hands over his back, loving the smoothness of his skin, the way his muscles hardened and flexed beneath her fingers. She drew in a deep breath, reveling in the compelling scent unique to him with its hints of bay rum, leather and Caine himself.

"This is your *yes!* At last, thank God." He groaned as he took her mouth in a wild and wondrous kiss. Grace answered his passion, so stirred by his obvious relief, she could hardly think. He wanted her here, he really did.

His hand slid between them, working loose the tie of her wrapper. She moved a handbreadth to allow that as she sought another angle and renewed the kiss. It went on and on, mouths seeking, finding, increasing hunger and answering demand.

Seconds later, she felt his naked warmth with only the sheer fabric of thin nightrail between their bodies. A moment more, and he had raked it up above her breasts and they were skin to skin. She moved against him, fitting closer, seeking.

He cupped her hips and lifted her. Grace locked her legs around him as he carried her to his bed and followed her down. His hands were everywhere at once, caressing, fondling, clutching and soothing. Yet not soothing at all. Inciting.

She heard encouraging sounds emerge from her own throat with no prompting from her mind, eager sounds that matched his own wordless entreaties.

His mouth found her breast and she almost cried out with pleasure. He murmured something, his words lost, their sounds and the whisper of his breath vibrating through her as he turned attention to the other. Sensations she had never felt rushed through her body, a liquid heat searing her veins.

He rose above her and entered her without a pause, a swift, determined exclamation to the sentence of her determined assault. The momentary glance of pain gave way to a heavenly invasion of pure pleasure.

He stilled inside her, his breath audible and unsteady. "Grace, I—"

"Love me," she whispered. A demand. A desperate wish. A prayer.

Bracing on his elbows, their lower bodies joined, he peered down at her. She wished she could see his eyes, his expression in the darkness, but he remained a silent, featureless silhouette above her. Her conqueror and her conquered. Grace closed her eyes and uttered a deep groan of encouragement.

He sighed once, a ragged exhalation, and then began to move. The exquisite friction, igniting something new within her, began to ebb and flow. She matched his rhythm, glorying in every thrust she met. Her senses ruled, eclipsing thought and reason and possible consequence. This, this was everything. This, now.

He lowered himself onto her fully and she welcomed the weight. Strong fingers spread beneath her hips and held her fast as he rose and thrust time and again in an escalating cadence she tried to equal and exceed. Reaching for something...

She gasped his name, breathed in his essence, clutched at the strength in his hard muscled arms, his back and lower still.

"Give!" he ground out in a harsh whisper. She gave and took, surrendered herself and claimed him at once and forever. The feelings were so overpowering, she cried out, reaching a pinnacle she had never dreamed existed.

He groaned again as he thrust harder, filling her completely. His body seemed to melt into her, as if they were one. When they stilled, exhausted and sated, Grace released a soul-deep sigh.

She did not want to move ever again, just wanted to lie and savor the euphoria. Never had she known this exquisite feeling was possible. Never would she give him up.

His lips brushed her cheek as he moved to her side. "Oh, Grace," he whispered, his words almost inaudible. "What have I done?"

"Whatever it was," she whispered breathlessly, "I hope you can do it again."

She felt the lazy rumble of what might have been a laugh, but emerged as another groan. A wry sound. No mistaking that.

"You deserved more care, but I was carried away, still half asleep," he muttered. "I am sorry, Grace."

It was her turn to laugh, weakly but with true amusement. "You are *not* sorry." With a concerted effort, she reached up to her neck and raked her nightdress down over her nakedness. "And neither am I."

"Are you all right?" he asked, brushing her tumbled hair off her shoulder and dropping a kiss there. "How do you feel?"

"Better than I can ever remember," she replied softly and sincerely. "And you?"

"Delirious. This settles it, you know," he said, sounding rather smug. And rather satisfied. "We will marry in the morning. No delay, indefinite or otherwise."

"No, Caine. We cannot."

Chapter Sixteen

Grace leaned into him, loving the way his strong arms surrounded her and held her close, as if she were precious to him. She turned her lips to his chest, just to taste him, to inhale his scent more keenly, to brand him as hers. "We can't marry tomorrow. Cook will need to rally her staff and work half a night to prepare a wedding breakfast."

"Hang Cook." He slid a hand to her breast and caressed her through the silk.

"It is early morning now and tomorrow is too soon. The day after, then," Grace suggested. "Will that suit?"

"And waste two perfectly good nights of married life?" he asked, continuing the caresses, becoming more determined.

Grace grinned and trailed the backs of her

nails down his arm, a languid gesture, a loving touch. "So this will be a nightly thing, you think?"

"Unless you bar your door and even then, I think so." His palm traveled to her hip as he pushed her back on the bed. "Perhaps an *hourly* thing."

"My, my," Grace said with a happy laugh. "How greed becomes you!"

He kissed the tip of her nose as his hand soothed her comfortingly. "It was your first time. You should rest and recover."

Grace ran a finger down the side of his face and smiled into the darkness. "If I did as I *should,* I would never have come here in the first place."

"You chose me freely, didn't you, Grace?" he asked, a hint of worry lingering in his voice. "I hope you're certain you want this marriage… that you want *me?*"

Grace blew out a gust of frustration and rolled her eyes. "If you think *this* was merely a gesture of thanks, perhaps not."

He rolled away from her and locked his hands behind his head. "Even if it was, there's no retreat possible for you now."

"Or for *you,* either!" Grace climbed off his bed and swept up her discarded wrapper. She tugged it on and tied the sash with a determined tug.

"Grace!" he exclaimed as he sat up. "Come back here!"

"You are the most *pigheaded* man! It's a wonder I love you at all!" She yanked open the door. "Do not come after me, you hear?" The slam probably woke the house.

And he did not come. She had halfway hoped he would. Fitfully, she passed the remainder of the night, wondering what the morning would bring. And, more crucial to their future, all of the mornings after that.

The next day dawned with a deluge. The pouring rain would force everyone to remain indoors, Caine thought as he dressed. He was filled with both anticipation and trepidation at seeing Grace. Would she still be angry?

The thought he had clung to all night was that Grace actually said she loved him. She'd not uttered it in the context he would have chosen to hear, instead coupling it with his being pigheaded, but she'd said it all the same.

He had to smile every time he thought of that. The words had slipped out in the midst of her fury, which made them all the more believable. He admitted he might not have taken her admission as truth if she had declared it in the midst of passion.

And what passion it had been. How eagerly she had welcomed his kisses, his hands explor-

ing her body, making her his own at last. The
memory of her smooth, creamy skin and the
taste of her, her little cries of delight aroused
him even now.

He tucked the sapphire parure in his coat
pocket. Jewels should go well with an apology.
He had planned the set as a morning gift anyway. This particular morning would probably
seem more significant to her than the one after
their wedding night. It certainly was significant
to him.

"Where might I find my little lady?" he asked
Mrs. Oliver as he stopped her on the stairs.

"In the morning room with his lordship," she
said, eyeing him keenly as if she knew he had
taken Grace's innocence in the early-morning
hours.

His own guilt made him imagine that, he decided. "Lord Trent is up?" Surprising. It was not
yet nine and Trent was a late sleeper.

"No, sir, Lord Hadley. He's up and about.
Much improved! See for yourself."

Caine took the stairs two at a time. When he
entered the morning room, his uncle sat on the
divan. Grace had her ear to his chest. "What's
this?" he asked, curious as to how they had gotten so close that his uncle would offer her a comforting embrace. And a greater question was
why she might need one.

Grace sat up, beaming. "His heart! Come and listen! The foxglove has worked its magic!"

Caine approached them and stood, hands on his hips. "Foxglove? What are you talking about?"

"Gracie cured me, that's what!" his uncle exclaimed. He tapped his chest. "Sound as a sovereign!"

Caine frowned. "Foxglove, Grace? That's poison!"

"Not in a small tincture," she informed him. "It regulates the heartbeat. Too fast, it slows it, and too sluggish, speeds it. It has a steadying and strengthening effect either way." She smiled at Hadley. "Dr. Ackers has been taking great care, though, according to Dr. Withering's writings. A week on and a week off in dosing."

His uncle laughed. "She and Ackers have done you out of a quick fortune, boy. I ain't all that ready to cock up my toes now!"

"Glad to hear it," Caine muttered, distracted by the very sight of his uncle. His color looked as near normal as could be, his eyes much clearer. Except for his arrival at Wildenhurst, this was the first time since returning from the war that Caine had seen the man in other than nightgown and banyan. Dressed in trousers and morning coat, he was every inch the earl. "You look… splendid, sir."

"Neckcloth's not right, but I feel like a new

man." He lay a steady hand against Grace's face and gave it a fond pat. Then he got up. "Off to the kitchens. I'm not waiting for breakfast. Cook will have biscuits, won't she, Gracie? And coffee on the brew?"

"No coffee, mind," Grace warned. "Milk or weak tea, sir."

The earl knocked Caine on the shoulder playfully with his fist as he passed by.

Caine was too amazed to speak. He stared at Grace, who sat, one arm propped on the back of the divan. However did he manage to underestimate the woman when he strove not to with every breath he took? She kept adding dimensions he couldn't even begin to imagine.

"Come, sit," she offered, glancing at the cushion beside her that the earl had just vacated. "Immediately on arriving here, I wrote to Dr. Ackers about Father's patients and how well it worked for them. He and the earl agreed the risk was worth it."

"He's well! I can't believe it!"

"No, not precisely *well,*" Grace said, covering one of his hands with hers. "But he has more time with us now, I hope. Dr. Ackers says his heart is still damaged and will fail him eventually, but at least he will feel better in the time he has left."

"Ackers left for London today. I wonder if that was wise."

Grace squeezed his hands. "You mustn't worry. He had to see to his own family and promised to return in two days, three at most. I know exactly what must be done in his absence. I hope you trust me. Uncle Hadley does."

"Of course I do. And *Uncle Hadley,* is it?" Caine smiled, happy that they were getting on so well as that. "What of my aunt? Has she been well?" he asked.

Grace shrugged. "She always seems a bit sad, Caine, despite the earl's improvement. Do you think she misses city life already?"

He looked at Grace for a full minute without answering, unsure whether he should confide in her and, if so, how to begin. "She likes to shop. Uncle used to take her out daily and she would come home with some small thing or another."

"Every woman enjoys that."

"I suppose so." He smiled as he toyed absently with the ring he wore, twisting it round and round on his finger. "She'd want a pair of gloves or a few lengths of ribbon, such as that. Sometimes she would sit for the rest of the day, admiring whatever it was he bought for her. The next morning it would lie forgotten and she would ask to go out again."

Grace said nothing, just waited for him to go on.

"She's a child, Grace. No one ever told me why she's the way she is, whether it was a fever, an accident or simply the way she was born. Maybe no one knows. She was taught to write and read a bit somewhere along the way, but has trouble with numbers."

"Well, that's not so remarkable. Many women aren't taught that much," Grace said.

Caine went on. "She's quiet as a rule and her manners are usually so nice, people rarely notice how different she is or if they do, merely think her eccentric." He pursed his lips for a moment, then gave a nod. "But you noticed."

"Yes," she admitted. "Your uncle seems very fond of her and quite protective. One can see how much they care for each other in every exchange between them."

Caine nodded in total agreement. "He married her just as she is now over thirty-five years ago when she was twenty." He gave Grace a meaningful look. "They never had children."

Grace obviously grasped what he meant, that the Hadley marriage was and always had been platonic. He could see in her eyes that she understood.

"The earl must love her very much indeed," she said. "A remarkable man, that uncle of yours. I hope he lives forever."

"Yes, so does he. He worries dreadfully about what will happen to her when he's gone. I can't count the times I've had to promise him I would care for her as if she were my mother."

"Of course you will! I could shop with her," Grace offered eagerly. "We could go into the village today if she wants!"

"Not now," Caine said. "Even with guards along, it might not be safe. But I appreciate the generous offer, Grace, and so will Uncle Hadley when I tell him."

"I have years of experience as a lady's companion, so whenever she needs company to entertain her, I will do what I can. I've read to her from a novel I found here, but she doesn't appear to listen. All she does is embroider, hour upon hour. Is there anything else you can think of that I might do to make her happier than she is while they're here?"

He smiled and took her hand. "Just be who you are, Grace. I think that will suffice."

"I hope she realizes, at least in some small way, just how fortunate she is to have married your uncle."

"I hope so, too. There's no way to thank you enough for doing what you've already done for them."

"Some things are done with no thought of a return, Caine. But if you like, consider our debts to each other evenly paid. You saved me and I've saved the uncle you love. Now we can dispense with all talk of gratitude, can we not?"

Caine nodded as he took her hands and looked into her eyes. "I need to apologize, Grace. Forgive me for doubting your motive in coming to me last night. It was just so hard to believe you would actually…well…choose *me*."

"You still don't believe it," she said with a soft laugh. "But you will come to, I promise. Marry me, Caine, and try not to think too much."

He raised an eyebrow. "Because it makes me pigheaded?"

She nodded and made a face.

Caine reached into his pocket and drew out the jeweler's box. "Your morning gift."

Her eyes widened as he opened it for her and she saw the stones. "Oh, my! This comes a bit early!"

"So did the consummation," he reminded her in a whisper, grinning as she lifted the necklace and held it to the light.

"Oh, Caine, it's beautiful! How lovely this will look with my wedding gown!" She kissed him full on the lips. "Thank you so much!"

Caine had a sudden epiphany. "You know, Grace, we might have just discovered the secret to a happy union. You do something I can thank you for, I do something requiring your gratitude, on and on throughout life. Gratitude isn't a bad thing at all, is it! Perhaps that's the secret to a good marriage. What do you think?"

She shook her finger under his nose. "You're overthinking again. And talking too much, so hush and kiss me," she ordered.

He laughed out loud. "Thank you, Grace, I think I will!"

"Excuse me! I am interrupting."

Caine released Grace and shot Trent a quelling look. "You are, in fact."

"We're being married the day after tomorrow!" Grace announced, breathlessly.

"None too soon, I'll wager," Trent said, taking a chair without being invited to sit. "Hope the rain stops. *Happy is the bride the sun shines on.*"

Grace stood up and whirled around to peer out the window at the downpour. "It won't matter to me!" she declared. "No one could be happier, rain or shine!"

Caine thought she had never looked more beautiful, face flushed with excitement, modestly covered breasts rising and falling rapidly with arousal. She wore a rose-sprigged muslin gown, her hair pulled up into a braided knot tied with pink ribbons. Her childlike enthusiasm was contagious. He could hardly wait until she was truly his for all the world to know.

Neville joined them just then. "Greetings, all. Any further word from London in the morning post?"

"It hasn't arrived yet," Grace said, her happy mood suddenly diminishing. "By the way, I almost forgot. There was a letter." She fetched it and gave it to Caine. "I don't believe it was written by my uncle," she told him.

He examined it for a minute. "Belinda Thoren-Snipes. She's made some attempt to disguise her handwriting, but I recognize it from the few letters she sent to me. I could jolly well wring her neck for upsetting you, Grace." He tossed the letter down on the table.

Trent promptly picked it up. "At least you have grounds for libel if you can prove she wrote it."

"I know she wrote it, but it's not worth pursuing," Caine replied. He took Grace's hands in his and drew her to him.

"I'll handle the matter for you if you like," Neville offered.

"Forget it, please!" Grace insisted. "Let's not give it any consequence." Caine felt the chill in her hands and pressed them between his to warm them.

"Wise to dismiss it altogether," Trent agreed, frowning at Neville with a slight shake of his head. "Forget everything but having a wedding to anticipate, Grace."

"Quite right. Mr. Harrell will keep the guard up, so there's no need to worry, is there?" she said.

Her smile returned, but Caine thought it looked a bit forced. He wished he could get her alone and really reassure her that all would be well.

"Yes, everything seems well in hand," Trent said with assurance. "Besides, no self-respecting assassin would be lurking about in this down-pour anyway. Weather's fit only for ducks!"

Caine deftly changed the topic, regaling his friend and cousin with the news of Hadley's improvement, then assigning them tasks as his groomsmen.

Breakfast was announced later in the morning and the day crawled by with maddening slowness for Caine. He could not concentrate on cards or billiards or conversation. The thought of one more day like it wore on his nerves.

When they retired for the night and headed up the stairs, he caught Grace's arm and whispered in her ear. "My room or yours?"

"Neither!" she exclaimed. "We must wait."

"Why?" he demanded, frowning down at her.

"Just because," she whispered back with a teasing glint in her eyes. "So I might enjoy your impatience. It's very flattering."

"A streak of cruelty," he grumbled. "See, I *knew* you weren't perfect."

Her merry laughter assuaged his disappointment, so he said good-night, kissed her soundly and left her at her door, hoping that kiss rendered her as frustrated as he felt. This night and one more. Then she would be his forever.

Later that night, Caine woke to a soft knock on his door. "What?" he muttered in a loud grunt. He opened one eye and squinted at the window. Still dark. Who would be waking him before dawn? Grace, of course, he thought as he came fully alert. She'd said no to him earlier, but she must have changed her mind. He rolled out of bed and grabbed his breeches, hoping he wouldn't need them for long.

He opened the door slowly, fully expecting to see her impish face grinning up at him. No one was there. His bare foot landed on a slick surface different from the plush turkey carpet. He bent down and picked up a folded paper that had been pushed under his door.

He lighted his lamp and opened the note. What was this, a dare?

"Meet me in the root cellar. There is something you need to see. Yours, G."

An odd place to meet. Surely she didn't mean to have a tryst there, the little minx, not when there were perfectly comfortable beds available.

He hurriedly dragged on a shirt and pushed his feet into his slippers. Whatever her reason for summoning him, why not simply wait until he answered her knock so they could go downstairs together if there really was something to see there?

What if someone else had left the note? He went over to the lamp and examined it again. He couldn't be certain, but the handwriting looked like Grace's, her feminine flowing hand that he had seen when she had written to him in London.

Someone could have forced her write it, but how in the world could anyone have gotten past the bevy of guards they had stationed around the property? Harrell had even added several more. The rain, of course, might have prevented them patrolling as they should. He listened, then glanced at the window. The rain had stopped.

Best be prepared for trickery. He checked his pistol's load and carried it with him.

Without lamp or candle to light the familiar route, Caine quickly made his way down to the kitchens. He followed the narrow stairway that tunneled from the very end of the ground-floor kitchens to the cellar's storage chamber beneath it.

The thick oak door stood half open and weak candlelight spilled from the interior. Softly, he approached the portal, listening for movement inside.

He peered in. A bundled form in the corner moved, and he heard her muffled shriek! "Grace!" He cocked his pistol and rushed in.

The last thing he heard as he fell was her tortured moan.

Chapter Seventeen

 ∞∞∞

Grace wept as she watched Wardfelton bind Caine's motionless wrists and ankles with the same narrow, pliable rope he had used for hers. When he had finished, her uncle was breathing hard. "Perfect. Now to you again," he said, crouching beside her where she sat and reaching to remove the gag from her mouth. "If you scream, I will cut his throat," he promised.

"Wh-what do you want?" she rasped, terrified that he would kill them both. She glanced at Caine, but he had not moved.

"I want to know who else knows what you know."

"About what?" she asked, truly puzzled.

He scoffed. "You know very well what I mean! I'm sure you've told your future *husband* what you overheard. Who else?" he demanded.

"What I overheard *when?* Please tell me what you mean!"

"That night with Sorenson in my library, of course. What else would I mean?" He glared at her. "I saw you just outside the door that evening. You gave me that look of yours when we came out. You heard us and you meant to use it against me. I could see it in your greedy little eyes, planning blackmail. Well, I didn't give you a chance for that, did I!"

Grace struggled to breathe normally and make sense of it all. "For goodness' sake, Uncle, you were both speaking French! I don't know two words of the language, only its nasal sound! Did you forget I was never sent to school? Father taught me all I know. I only had Latin."

Wardfelton stared at her, wide-eyed with surprise. Then he narrowed his gaze. "That's impossible. All girls are taught French!"

"No, it's true!" she insisted. "As for the look you saw, I was upset that you ignored the summons to dinner twice! Everything had gone cold. When I came to see what was the matter, Sorenson was still there. You were always so furious with Cook when dinner was so much as a minute late!"

"Good God," her uncle groaned. He remained silent for several moments, apparently thinking about the situation. "Well, no matter now, even if what you say is true. This has gone too far."

"Please let us go. Neither of us knows anything damaging about you, Uncle. Please."

He glared at her. "You know I hired someone to kill you." He waggled his knife in Caine's direction. "And him. Bloody fools couldn't do the simplest of jobs I paid for. Now I have to…"

"But you don't need to do this, Uncle. You could just leave us here and go away." Again, she looked at Caine. He was moving a bit, coming to, she supposed, and almost hoped not.

Wardfelton scoffed, dragging her attention back to him. "Go away, Grace? Where?"

For a moment, he simply looked at her, much in the way he had before he had turned against her and treated her so bad. "It's unfortunate how matters have turned out if you really didn't know. I quite liked you at first." He made a wry face. "But I didn't mind disposing of James and your mother. Meddling fools brought it on themselves."

"Mother and Father?" Grace asked in a horrified whisper. "You *killed* them?" She shook her head, unable to believe it. "But it was cholera. Everyone said it was cholera!"

He nodded. "Convenient, that epidemic. No one examines a cholera victim all that closely, now do they? No, James found out, you see, and promised to expose me. And he had told that mother of yours."

Grace was weeping openly now, grieving for

her parents, as well as for Caine and herself. They had no chance of survival. He would cut their throats before she could get free to stop him. But he surprised her yet again as he stood up and went to the door.

She saw him glance up at the slit of a window. The thick, narrow panes, barely above ground, allowed a bit of light into the cellar in the daytime and provided ventilation when necessary. Unfortunately, she knew without looking that the window was ten feet up and too narrow to provide an avenue of escape even if it could be reached.

"Goodbye, Grace," he said, and stepped outside the door. She heard the key turn in the lock.

Caine's unexpected roll toward her surprised Grace. "You're conscious! Thank God!"

"We have to hurry, Grace," he muttered. "Your fingers are smaller to work the rope. Turn your back to mine and see if you can untie me. Not a minute to lose."

"Why hurry? He has locked us in." She began to work the bonds on her own wrists.

"No, but we can move that cache of gunpowder he intends to explode."

"What?" She looked up to see a hole in the glass with a narrow ropelike fuse running to a wooden cask that sat on a top shelf above the baskets of apples. Now she worked frantically at the ropes on her wrists and was free in less than a minute.

Caine still wrestled with his. She crawled over to him. "Be still, I'll do it."

He grunted in surprise. "How the hell did you get free?"

She worked at his bonds. "Childhood trick. Obviously, my uncle never played pirates with the local hellions the way I did. One quickly learns how to *let* someone tie them up! Clasp hands together, separate and expand the wrists as much as possible, wriggle around and cry a lot. Usually works, especially for girls."

He tossed the cords she'd untied and began working at the ones on his ankles. "Wonders never cease around you."

"Well, they might if we tarry." She rushed over and studied the shelving.

He jumped up and followed. "The sideboards are sturdy, but those slats won't support me. Besides none of these are bolted to the wall," Caine said, feeling the thickness of the slats. "And if *you* try, it could tumble forward. That keg's iron bands striking the flagstone could cause it to explode."

"What do we do?" she asked. "Wait, I know! Prop against the wall next to the shelves and crouch down. I'll climb your body."

He didn't argue, just did as she said. "Have a care you don't fall," he warned as she braced a foot on his leg and climbed until her feet were on his shoulders.

She held on to his head with one hand and balanced herself against the wall with the other as he straightened slowly. "Can your bad shoulder take my weight when I stand?" she asked, and felt him shift to aid the attempt.

"Go," he said, grasping her ankles.

"I'm going to stand now," she gasped. "If I can manage."

"Keep one hand on the wall, other on the shelves for balance, but don't pull on them."

She rose slowly and carefully. He felt the slight jerk as she yanked the fuse from the cask of powder and heaved a sigh of relief. "Done."

"Move the fuse well away from it," Caine said. "Are you steady up there?"

"So far. Are you steady down there?" she gasped.

"Did I mention that I love you?" he asked, tightening his grip on her ankles.

"Hush. You'll make my knees weak. Is this fuse far enough over?"

"I can't see a thing with your gown over my head. Ready to dismount?"

"How should we do this? Getting down might be harder than getting up, I think!"

"Walk your hands down the wall and lower yourself to a crouch if you can. There. Now, slide one foot at the time until you straddle my neck."

The skirt of her nightrail completely covered his head and her bare thighs surrounded his neck. "This feels rather wicked."

"Not a position I favor at the moment." Grunting with the effort, he squatted low so that she could reach the floor and helped her off. Then he whirled her around and grabbed her to him, raining desperate kisses all over her face until he settled on her mouth for a passionate kiss that seemed all too brief.

Breathless, he broke the kiss and groaned. "Is there anything you *cannot* do?"

She sighed, nuzzling his neck. "Well, I can't pick locks. When the powder doesn't explode soon after he lights the fuse, he might come back to finish us off."

"I'll be ready for him this time. I can take his knife," Caine assured her.

"Yes, but he has your pistol."

"Damn." He leaned against the wall under the window and drew her into a hug as he looked around the cellar. "We need to get out of here."

Grace thought about her uncle's actions. "You know, he could have cut our throats and had done with it. I thought he planned to, but he didn't. That would have been much more reliable than blowing us up, don't you think? I mean, suppose the powder was too damp or the fuse proved faulty? He hired others to do murder until they failed him. Maybe he lacks the fortitude for killing face-to-face."

"What of his strangling Sorensen?"

"Hired, I expect."

"Then there's your parents," Caine reminded her. "He confessed to that."

"Poison, most likely. No wounds visible. Again, he was probably removed from it."

Caine was not convinced. "Perhaps you're right, but if he leaves us alive, he knows we will talk. So he'll come back in—"

"Or set fire to the manor!" Grace guessed.

"Oh, God, it just occurred to me..." Caine's face changed, his expression one of horror. "Something quicker and more to the point than fire. If he brought in one cask of powder, there could be more. We have to get out of here *now*."

Caine approached the shelves on the far end of the room away from the gunpowder shelf and rapidly began taking down the baskets and slatted boxes containing victuals. "Stack these against the wall over there so the floor's clear in front of the shelves," he ordered.

Grace obeyed without question, talking as she worked. "He could say it's our word against his. We have no proof. How do you think he got the gunpowder down here in the first place?" she asked, huffing with exertion as she hefted a box of turnips.

"Delivered it himself. Harrell would have thought nothing of it if Wardfelton arrived dressed as a deliveryman. Harrell had ordered some. Providing the guards with ammunition, as well as supplying it for the autumn hunt Harrell mentioned would require three or four casks of powder, the very reasons we need to vacate this room in a hurry."

"There's more powder?" Grace asked, glancing up at the one barrel on the shelf. "Out there? With him?"

"Very probably." He motioned for her to stand back against the far wall. "Shield the candle. I'm going to tip this and hope it falls apart with the crash. We need a battering ram. Stand clear."

He braced a foot against the wall, gave the shelving a tug and it fell. Grace winced at the clatter. She watched as he pried apart the boards. "There!" he said, lifting one of the long and sturdy side pieces. "The interior walls are not so thick, just partitions really. Mortar's old and crumbly."

"You hope," Grace muttered.

"I pray," he admitted. "Shield the candle." He gripped the board, backed against the outside wall and ran across the room. The board bounced and knocked him backward. Three times, he ran at it, striking the same place with the makeshift battering ram.

"I think it's giving way!" Grace exclaimed.

He hit it again and once more. One stone fell through to the other side. She cheered. Relentlessly, he banged the board at the surrounding stones. In moments, he had an opening a good two feet across and almost that high.

He paused for a few seconds and they heard a loud thump. Both looked up at the window. A barrel rested against it. *LMN WORKS* was stenciled on the side next to the pane, plainly visible in the steady candlelight.

"Go, Grace! Squeeze through to the wine room and go up the stairs. Get to the other end of the house and, for God's sake, hurry. Shout *fire* and wake everyone as you go. Get everyone to the far end and out through the conservatory. Count heads and make them stay together."

She grasped his arm as he lifted her through the hole. "But you—"

"Will be right behind you. A few more knocks and I can get through. Hurry now. Most of the men who sleep below will be out on guard but I'll check below stairs on my way to the stairs at the far end. Go on now. *Run!*"

Grace hit the floor of the wine cellar, felt her way to the stair there and ran through the pitch-dark kitchens. "Fire!" she screamed the instant she reached the vestibule. She lifted her gown and tore up to the first-floor bedrooms. "Wake up! Fire in the house! Everyone, go north side! Servants' stairs! Hurry!"

Neville emerged with a lamp just before she reached his door. "Fire?"

"Gunpowder! Root cellar! Wardfelton!" she gasped. "Help me get the others out the north end."

"Caine?"

"Waking those left in the cellar quarters." She hoped.

"Go on out," he said with a not-so-gentle shove. "Trent and I will clear the house."

The earl shuffled toward them, the countess huddled close. "Come!" Grace said, taking the earl's other arm. "We must hurry."

"Where are we going?" Lady Hadley demanded. "It's still dark."

"To the end of the hall and down the servants' stairs," Grace replied, trying to sound calm when she could hardly get her breath. "Mind you don't trip on your gown, Lord Hadley."

"I smell no smoke! Nose is as good as ever," the earl declared, lifting his head and sniffing loudly. "Where's this fire, gel?"

"In the cellar, sir. Let's move along now."

Several of the maids, including Jane, rushed by them. "To the conservatory and out!" Grace called to them. "Jane! Keep everyone together on the terrace!"

Judd approached at a trot, his nightcap askew, lamp in hand. The tweenies flew by, catching up to Jane and the others. "I let Mrs. Oliver and

Mrs. Bowden out through the library door," Judd informed her. He had Mrs. Bowden's large ring of household keys in his hand.

"Good. Anyone else on the ground floor?"

"No, my lady. Nor upstairs. Should we form up with buckets? I'll fetch Mr. Harrell and the lads."

"Leave it for now. Give me the keys and your light." They had reached the servants' stairs. "Go down with Lord and Lady Hadley. I'll be there directly."

Grace could not leave without knowing Caine was safely out of the root cellar. What if the other stones had not come loose? What if he were trapped there when her uncle blew it up? She turned and ran, the keys banging against her wrist.

She had just reached the kitchens when the world erupted.

"Where the devil is she?" Caine demanded, plowing through the crowd gathered on the terrace just as dawn was breaking. "Grace!"

He saw Judd. "Have you seen her? Did she come out earlier?"

"No, sir. She took the keys from me upstairs," Judd told him. "She went back down the main hall. Perhaps she went out the library door where Mrs. Oliver and Mrs. Bowden were. I told her they were there."

"Oh, God," Caine muttered, closing his eyes against what he already knew. She had gone back for him. The root cellar would be demolished, probably the entire southeast corner of the manor, including the kitchen.

He had been halfway through the lower level when it blew, relieved that he and the servants he'd awakened down there escaped injury and were only shaken. Now he might have lost her.

Might have lost Grace. He grabbed a lantern from one of the footmen, reentered the house and took the hallway at a run.

"Caine, wait!" he heard Neville shout behind him.

"Grace is still in here!" he shouted back.

"We're with you," Trent called.

"Go back outside!" he ordered. "The walls might not be stable at the other end."

But he knew they would not go back and they did not. He ran on. Dust still filled the air as he reached the back of the vestibule. The kitchen area was in ruin, windows shattered, debris everywhere. He saw her then, covered in dust, lying in a heap, nightdress up to her knees and her bare feet curled together like a sleeping child's.

"Oh, Grace," he whispered, kneeling beside her still form. He lifted her gently and held her against his chest.

Trent fell beside him. "Is she…"

"No!" Caine shouted, rising with Grace in his arms. "Trent, get the doctor!" He saw Neville standing there, mouth agape. "You! Find Ward-felton and bring him here. I mean to kill that son of a bitch!"

Neville and Trent ran out the maw that had once been the kitchen door and dashed to the stables.

Caine carried Grace out of the rubble and down the hallway to the stairs. There, he trudged up to her room, kicked open her door and laid her on the bed. She had not moved.

Mrs. Oliver appeared. "Is she…"

"She breathes, but God only knows for how long," he murmured, brushing the hair out of her eyes with a trembling and dust-stained finger. "Fetch water and cloths to bathe her. And a fresh gown. Trent's gone for the doctor."

"I'll see to it, sir," she said softly, and disappeared.

"Grace?" he whispered, leaning close to her ear. "Grace, can you hear me?"

Nothing. Not a twitch of an eyelid or any movement at all.

Caine took her limp hand in his and held it, two fingers on the pulse at her wrist. The vein was hard to locate and the beat seemed slow, almost not there at all. "Don't leave me," he whispered. "Please."

Chapter Eighteen

Mrs. Oliver nudged Caine's shoulder. "Jane's bringing water. Let's try a vinegarette, sir. That might bring her around."

He moved to let her closer. "Do it."

She waved the small bottle just beneath Grace's nose and gained a weak cough.

"Enough," Caine said, moving Oliver's arm to the side. "It might hurt her to cough if anything's broken."

"Or it could help clear her lungs if she's breathed in too much dust," Mrs. Oliver said. "Have you felt her head? Maybe she was just knocked out."

He ran a careful hand over Grace's head, examining it inch by inch with his fingers. "Nothing there that I can feel," he said. He continued, testing her shoulders and arms.

Mrs. Oliver stopped him when he reached her ribs. "Best allow me, sir," she said firmly, and took over.

Caine watched as the older woman did a hasty examination of Grace's form, right down to the toes.

"I don't believe anything's broken unless it's the neck or back," she told him.

"Oh, God," Caine groaned, covering his face with his hand.

"Now, now, sir. Not likely that's the case, is it? Hardly a mark on her, save a few scrapes. Not that we can see anyway. I need to undress her and be sure."

Caine shook his head, but he didn't know what damage the blast might have caused her. The only explosion he had ever witnessed was that of the shell that nearly blinded him. Not the same thing at all. Grace had no visible wounds other than abrasions on her arms, probably from climbing through that small hole in the root-cellar wall.

Jane arrived with a basin of water and the other things he'd asked for. She set them down and went to Grace's wardrobe for a gown.

"If you'd leave us to it now, sir, we'll see to her," Mrs. Oliver said. "We'll take every care," she added, laying a hand on his arm.

"No. I'll stay," he declared.

"Sir, we'll have to undress her. It's not proper,

your not being her husband yet and all." Her kind eyes met his. "Think of *her.*"

He could not think of anything else. "Just outside the door, then," he said reluctantly. "If you find any hidden hurt she suffered, come and tell me."

"Straightaway. Without fail," Mrs. Oliver promised.

Caine leaned against the wall in the hallway, waiting. After a quarter hour, Mr. Harrell approached, hat in hand. "Sir, the search is on for Lord Wardfelton. Mr. Neville said we should fan out and take any strangers into custody, since none of us would recognize the man but him."

"Oh, you'll know him, I expect. No doubt he's the one who delivered the gunpowder."

Harrell's eyes widened. "That Mr. Trueblood? I thought it strange you would request a barrel put in the root cellar. He said you wanted it there for house use and it would be safe to do if it was kept well away from sparks. The rest he put in the outbuilding with the tools as usual."

Harrell covered his face with a hand and groaned. "Sir, he asked for work. Said he was home from the war. Said he needed something more steady than delivery work."

"So you hired him." Caine barely held his anger in check as Harrell nodded. "Well, it's done. We did need more guards and how could you know? So, did he actually work, other than bringing the powder?"

"He patrolled like the others."

"So I thought. And had the opportunity to roll all the barrels next to the house after we disabled his fuse on that one he had planted inside."

Harrell swallowed hard and ducked his head. "I'm sorry, sir. He had paperwork from LMN factory where we usually order."

"Where everyone in the south of England usually orders. Go, join the hunt and run him to ground, Harrell. I mean to kill him."

"Sir? Best haul him in to the London authorities, don't you think? He is a noble."

"Noble, hell. He's a blackguard who needs to die," Caine declared. "And I'll kill him even if I hang for it."

Harrell shrugged and offered a grim smile. "Aye, well, I doubt it'll come to that. Accidents happen all the time, don't they, sir. I'd swear to it."

"Go on, then. He'll be harder to track if he reaches the city."

Caine paced, impatience mounting, waiting to see Grace again, waiting for the doctor to come, waiting for Neville and the men to find Wardfelton. He should be *doing* something. But what?

Judd came up. "We've begun the cleanup, sir, now that it's light enough to see well. Perhaps you and the family will want to return to London until we've repaired what can be fixed."

Caine sighed. "Lady Grace shouldn't be moved, so of course I'll be staying."

"How is she, sir? Everyone will want to know." His concern touched Caine. Grace had made herself a part of Wildenhurst. The staff doted on her.

"As soon as I know myself, I will send word. In the meantime, have Lord and Lady Hadley's things readied and the carriage prepared for travel. They need to be away by midmorning."

"Right away, sir. What of Lord Trent and Mr. Neville? Shall I pack for them?"

"No. I expect they will stay, at least for today. Have someone bring food from the village until we can arrange a makeshift kitchen. Perhaps the fireplace in the drawing room will serve since it's the largest. Salvage what you can, but take care. The whole south end might collapse without its support."

"What of sleeping arrangements for the night, sir?"

"The master suite won't be safe, but that will be unoccupied anyway with the Hadleys gone. The upstairs maids will have to sleep elsewhere, too, perhaps the north end of the attic."

There was so much to do, so many things to see to, and all Caine could do was worry about Grace's survival. "You and Mrs. Bowden take charge of the household. Arrange it anyway that's convenient for operation. Use your own judgment and only come to me if there's a crisis."

"Yes, sir. Not to worry."

Not to worry? When he could be losing all that was dear to him? The woman he loved and couldn't live without?

He began to pace again, running his fingers through his hair, pressing his temples, trying to banish the pounding ache in his head. Nothing could fix the ache in his heart except Grace regaining consciousness and assuring him she would be well.

How had he ever believed he could let her go? Why had he ever thought she would be a drain on his time and an impediment to his proper service as earl? Now he doubted he would amount to anything at all without her.

She had done more in organizing Wildenhurst than anyone in his memory. She had saved his uncle's life. And helped save Caine's and her own in that cellar. She had restored his own faith in women, surrendered her innocence without a whimper and, most surprising of all, had made him able to laugh again.

He felt the tears on his cheeks and dashed them away. Hell, she made him cry, too. Made him feel again, and dwell on something other than his anger and vanity. Grace was all that her name implied.

"God save her," he whispered. "Please."

Trent came dashing down the hall from the main stairs. "The doctor's coming up. Hadley insisted on sending a rider to London for Dr. Ackers, as well. How is she?"

Caine shrugged. "Oliver and young Jane are seeing to her injuries where I may not." He swayed and Trent steadied him.

"Are you hurt, Caine?" he asked. "What's wrong?"

Caine shook his head and sniffed. "Fighting despair is all. She has to make it through this, Gavin, or I might not."

"Look at me, Caine!" Trent demanded. "Listen to me now. Grace is going to be all right. She's the strongest woman we've ever met and you know that."

"You love her, too," Caine guessed.

Trent slapped his shoulder. "Of course I love her, you idiot! Everyone loves her but that lunatic Wardfelton. Grace is my friend, same as you are."

Caine nodded. "Any sign of the lunatic? I look forward to choking the life out of him."

"No one has seen him, but he can't hide for long. Neville finally confided something to me today that you should probably know. He's worked for the War Office for several years.

Clandestine assignments, some abroad and some in England. He has suspicions concerning Wardfelton that have nothing to do with this."

Caine snapped to attention. "Perhaps they do have to do with it. Grace once overheard Wardfelton and Sorensen speaking together in French. He thought she understood them. That's why he wanted to kill her. And me, because he was afraid she'd confided in me, or would do after we were married. He must have been spying for the French."

"Neville thinks it's more likely he was a sympathizer or financier. He says Wardfelton's inheritance has dwindled to nothing and he has no acquisitions to show for it. Could be gambling, I suppose, but Neville doesn't think so."

"Grace told me he had sold off things of value from the country seat," Caine added.

"Yes, and he tried to sell the town house, too, but Neville's man has uncovered records showing that it was left to Grace by her father and he couldn't dispose of it."

Caine's eyes met Trent's as they came to the same conclusion. "Unless she was dead!" they exclaimed in unison.

"And still unmarried, so he would have it as her next of kin," Caine added. "This explains so much. The war's over and he's destitute with the possibility of being exposed for treason as long as she's alive."

Trent blew out a sigh. "God, speak of motive for murder!"

"He won't live to be tried for it. I mean to kill him," Caine said with cold determination.

"Not if I find him first," Trent said with a succinct nod. "And I'm off to do just that. Sorry you can't come, old boy. Give Grace my regards." He grinned as he backed a few steps down the hall. "And tell her I love her when she wakes, will you?"

"Go to hell," Caine said, but he smiled.

"Sir?" Jane said, standing in the doorway to Grace's room. "You may come in now."

Caine immediately dismissed Trent and Wardfelton from his mind and rushed to Grace's bedside. He swallowed a groan. She looked… lifeless. Pale and unmoving, laid out in a clean gown with her hands by her sides. Afraid to breathe, he picked up one of her hands and pressed his fingers to her wrist as he had done earlier. There! A slow, steady pulse.

The doctor arrived within the half hour, Dr. Samuels, the same fellow who had treated Caine's gunshot wound here at Wildenhurst. Caine did not dislike the man, but nor did he trust him completely. His smile was too obsequious and his manner annoying.

"Good day, Captain," he said by way of greeting as he set down his bag.

"Not thus far," Caine replied. "Thank you for

coming." He stood. "The women have examined her and there are no open wounds. Her knees, one shoulder and one hip are bruised, probably as she fell. The scratches on her arms were acquired earlier, not in the explosion. She has been unconscious since we found her a quarter hour after the blast."

The doctor leaned over Grace and pried open one eyelid, then both. He raked back her hair and checked her ears. He ran his fingers through her hair, pressing at certain points as Caine watched.

Then he straightened. "I believe she has sustained an injury to the brain, sir. I saw this in the war as you might have done yourself. There are signs the brain is swelling within her skull or loose blood is collecting there."

Caine had never felt such fear in his life, even when he thought he would die himself. "Will… will she live?"

The doctor glanced at Grace and back at Caine. "I can relieve the pressure. That will give her a chance."

"A *chance*? How much of a chance?" Caine demanded.

Samuels shrugged a shoulder. "I'm given to believe one out of four survive the procedure."

"*You are given to believe?* What procedure?" Caine watched as the doctor opened his medical case. He took out a vise of some sort. "What is that? It's not…"

"Yes, trepanning instruments."

Caine was already shaking his head. "You are not boring a hole in her head! Are you mad?"

"Sir, it is the only way!"

It took every restraint Caine possessed to refrain from tossing the man out the window. "You can't be positive her brain is swelling," he said, trying to sound reasonable. He looked down at the apparatus. "This looks brand-new. You haven't done this before, have you? Even if I were convinced this was necessary, I wouldn't allow a novice to do it!"

Samuels wore an expression of studied tolerance. "Sir, I have studied, apprenticed and practiced surgery on the battlefield. Be assured I know what I'm about."

Caine almost lost his reason. "You are *about* to be shown the door, Mr. Samuels. We don't require your services."

"She will probably die, then," Samuels warned, his expression dark.

"If so, it will be without another hole in her head," Caine declared. "Leave."

Samuels tossed in the instrument, snapped his bag shut and stalked to the door. "I shall send you the bill for my trouble."

Caine collapsed in the chair and rested his head on the bed beside Grace. Mrs. Oliver lay a hand on his shoulder and he looked up at her.

"Have I done wrong to refuse that?" he whispered.

She shook her head and smiled. "No, sir. The earl's physician will come soon. Our lady trusts him. He knew her da."

The hours crept by as Caine stood watch over Grace, alternately praying she would recover and cursing Wardfelton's murderous soul.

Grace struggled through the darkness, a viscous mass enveloped her, hampered her breathing, obstructed her limbs as she fought her way. One goal pushed her efforts. She had to find Caine. To save him.

The grayness swirled into shapes that moved and slowly, menacingly, features formed out of it. Wardfelton's smirking grin taunted her. His eyes promised a slow, smothering death. Grace tried to scream but her throat was so dry, her tongue so thick. She cried out for Caine, to warn him.

Dr. Ackers arrived at eight o'clock in the evening.

"She moved a little," Caine informed him as the physician entered Grace's room. "Tried to speak, I think."

Ackers went straight to the bedside and did exactly what Samuels had done that morning.

Caine's patience almost snapped. Did no one know what to do for her?

The doctor moved away after his cursory assessment and spoke to Caine. "There's little to be done other than wait. Dr. Samuels is still downstairs, convinced that relieving the pressure is the thing to do." He held up a hand to silence Caine when he started to protest. "I agree with you, sir. It's too dangerous. At times, these surgeons are a bit too eager to ply their trade. As it stands, she probably has an even chance to come around on her own when the swelling subsides. Her chances are reduced by half again if we proceed with surgery."

Caine breathed a sigh so deep it made him dizzy. "What can we do for her?"

"Cold compresses on the face, head and neck. Moving her limbs occasionally to encourage blood flow into them, away from the brain."

"Yes! That makes sense!" Caine felt vastly relieved at having something positive to do. And to have Ackers's agreement that he had not condemned Grace, but had done the best thing after all.

"The women can do what needs doing." Ackers beckoned to Mrs. Oliver and Jane, then continued to Caine, "My advice to you is to leave her for a while. Have some nourishment and rest. You aren't long out of a sickbed yourself."

"She might call for me. I need to be here," Caine argued.

"Then we shall find you on the instant," the doctor promised. "Go now and do as I say."

Caine crossed to Grace again and kissed her forehead. With a last lingering look at her, he left the room.

Others were depending on him, he knew, but he could scarcely think of anything but her. If she died, he feared nothing else would matter anyway.

Trent met him at the foot of the main stairs. "We have everything sorted down here. How is Grace?"

Caine shook his head, unable to answer. He clung to the fact that she had moved, slight as the stirring had been, it gave him hope. And her lips had opened, twitched a little. "I can't leave her for long," he told Trent. "How goes the search?"

"Neville's taken it to London. Harrell and I will commence here in the county at first light. God only knows where he went, but we will find him, Caine."

He found he couldn't discuss Wardfelton any longer or his blast of anger would erupt full force and convince everyone he was mad. Instead, he tried to concentrate on a lesser concern. "The house," he said as he surveyed the vestibule. "I think half must be brought down and rebuilt."

Trent took his arm. "But not tonight. Come

with me. Mrs. Bowden has a good stew and decent ale, everything's set up in the drawing room."

Caine went, noting absently that the doors to the damaged portion of the house had been closed and everything in the immediate area had been dusted. The floors shone. One would never guess from this vantage that nearly half the ground floor of the house lay in ruin with the floors over it highly unstable.

His entire life might lie in ruin if Grace lost hers. But if she recovered, as she must do, she would be furious if he had done nothing in the meantime but brace himself for grief. If their conditions were reversed, she would be taking charge, issuing orders and doing her duty. Hadn't she done precisely that when he lay abed with the gunshot?

He forced down a hearty bowl of venison stew, emptied a tankard of stout and went to compose a letter to a London architect he knew who had engineering experience. There at the desk in the library, he fell sound asleep.

"Wake up, sir!"

Caine stirred, catching himself as he nearly fell from his chair. Someone was shaking his shoulder. "What?" he mumbled just as full awareness hit. "Is it Grace?"

"Yes, sir."

Chapter Nineteen

"Mrs. Oliver shouted down just now for me to get you," Judd added in a rush. "Lady Grace called your name!"

"Thank God," Caine whispered. "Dr. Ackers is there?" he asked, hurrying out ahead of Judd.

"All night, sir. It's almost six now."

Caine dashed up the stairs and down the hall. He burst into the room and hurried to her side. She looked the same as before, not wide awake as he had hoped. He leaned over her, took her hand and kissed her lips, a brief touch only. "Grace? I'm here, love."

She moved her head and issued a sound, not quite a word. Her eyes opened slightly.

"You're back with me, aren't you! You came back," he murmured, brushing her brow with fingers that shook. "All will be well now. You will be well."

Her lips stretched into a weak smile and she spoke his name, a mere breath, but the most precious sound he'd ever heard.

She lapsed into sleep again, but he knew she would live. He kept her hand in his as he sank into the chair beside her bed, pressed his face into the edge of her pillow and wept soundlessly into the soft linen.

Grace woke hours later as the small mantel clock chimed ten. She remembered waking before or perhaps had only dreamed that. Caine had been hovering beside her, coaxing her awake, his hand holding hers, chafing it, warming it. She moved her fingers and realized he held it yet. When she turned her head on the pillow, his hair brushed her face. He was sitting in the chair beside the bed, leaned over so that his head rested next to hers.

She glanced around the room and noticed nothing had changed. Thank God the manor still stood and they had, by some stroke of good luck, avoided catastrophe. She figured she must have fallen and hit her head as she rushed to see if he had made it out of the cellar.

"Caine?" she whispered.

He raised his head immediately. "Do you hurt? Can I get you anything?" His free hand gingerly brushed her hair back, then cradled the side of her face. "God, I worried you would never wake fully! You've been in and out four times now. Does your head ache?"

"I fell. But I don't quite remember falling." She closed her eyes and tried again to think of what had happened. "Clumsy of me."

"It's all right, darling. You shouldn't worry about anything."

She swallowed hard. "The rain wet the powder then? Everyone's safe?"

"Everyone else is fine."

"My uncle?" she asked.

"Gone. You need not think of him ever again."

She sighed. "You…you have killed him then?"

Caine shook his head. "No, not yet."

She closed her eyes again as she heard the intent in his tone. They had no proof of her uncle's misdeeds and Caine would be arrested if he dealt out justice on his own. "You mustn't. I don't want you to."

"I know, love. I know you don't. Rest easy and it'll all work out in the end. You've had a terrible injury."

Her eyes flew open. "Do you believe I will die of it? You sound as if you do!"

He smiled. "Absolutely not. You will live to a ripe old age and bear us a few hellions just like yourself."

Grace tried to nod, but it hurt. "They might have to be bastards. I think fate is against this marriage of ours."

He patted her face gently. "We'll tie the knot as soon as you're able to stand upright without the headache. I promise."

"Tomorrow, then," she muttered as she drifted back to sleep.

Tomorrow did not work out. When Grace woke again, it was to overhear Mrs. Bowden and Jane discussing the damages to the kitchen wing and bemoaning the fact that the house would never be the same.

Grace was livid. Why hadn't Caine told her the explosion had happened? Damn the man for his coddling and cooing to her how everything was all right.

"Where is he?" she demanded in the strongest voice she could manage. The servants gasped and rushed to her side, but there was no calming her. Her home was ruined and no one had seen fit to tell her?

Her anger had cooled somewhat by the time Caine answered her summons, but she still resented his keeping her in the dark. "Why was I not told?" she demanded. "I want to see for myself how severely the house is damaged."

He sat on the edge of the bed and took her hands in his. "Of course you will, but later, when you feel a bit steadier. Not to worry, all can be repaired. I have someone working on the plans already."

She pressed him for details, but he ignored

that and cleverly guided her into a discussion of wedding plans. Grace allowed it, but only because she tired too quickly to sustain an argument.

Two days later, Grace was chafing at her confinement to bed. Dr. Ackers had insisted she rest until he gave her leave to resume her normal activities.

Caine kept her company most hours of the day and evening, letting her best him at cards, showing off his expertise at chess, teasing her with riddles and sharing stories of his childhood.

He acted as if everything was settled between them, almost as if they had been married for ages and well past the first bloom of passion.

She recalled how he had said he loved her when she was standing on his shoulders next to the barrel of gunpowder. Was that a momentary expostulation because she could climb like a monkey and had ripped out that fuse? Hardly the most enviable of circumstances to hear such a thing.

Caine never asked even once whether she loved him. Did he take that for granted? Well, she had told him only that once in the heat of anger. He must say it first and mean it before she would admit it again. But perhaps he really didn't love her, in which case, she shouldn't admit it at all.

Caine was totally unlike himself since the explosion. This playfulness of his, while endearing in its probable intent, now made her wonder if his brain had been affected by events, as well. She was bored, restless and also a bit annoyed by what seemed very like condescension of his part.

"We really should discuss what happened," she said, suddenly too impatient with him to avoid crossing swords. "Why do you always refuse?"

"I merely change the topic." He tapped her on the nose. "Because you need to dwell on happy things until you're well again. And there is nothing you can do that isn't being done to right matters. Wildenhurst is already under repair."

He traced the side of her face with his finger, peering at it as if to check for undiscovered damage.

She batted his hand away. "You know very well I mean we should speak of my uncle and what he's done, not of the house. What have you heard? Is there any news of him?"

"The search is still on. That's all I know."

He reached into his pocket and drew out a length of string. "Cat's cradle. Ever played that?" He began looping the string around his fingers. "Pull this one."

Grace groaned and closed her eyes. "You are impossible."

Chapter Twenty

Neville arrived at Wildenhurst that afternoon. Grace and Caine were having tea off trays in her chamber when Judd announced him.

"Come in, cousin," Grace said as she held out a hand. "Thank goodness for your company. This man is driving me to distraction!"

"My current goal in life," Caine admitted. "Hello, Neville."

Neville bowed over Grace's hand as he laid his other on Caine's shoulder. "I see you're both in fine form today. So happy to see you smiling, Grace."

After a few more pleasantries, he gave Caine a meaningful look and inclined his head toward the door. "You and I have a bit of business to discuss, if Grace will excuse us."

"If it concerns the incident with my uncle, I

wish you would include me," Grace said. "I'm quite well now, except for an occasional spell of dizziness and I promise not to swoon. Caine tells me nothing."

Neville looked to Caine for permission.

"Knowing nothing is definitely more trying than hearing the facts," she prompted. "I imagine the very worst."

Caine nodded with obvious reluctance.

"Very well. Wardfelton must have gone directly back to the town house," Neville told them. She could almost hear him grit his teeth. "He was there when I arrived to question his staff. They all swear he was there that entire night. When I accused him of setting the charges, he laughed."

"He denies it?" Grace asked, astounded. "How can he deny it?"

"That's no matter," Caine said. "Harrell can identify him as the one who delivered the gunpowder, the very one who put a barrel of it in the root cellar. We have him dead to rights."

Neville disagreed. "He has six employees who will vouch for his presence there in London at the time. You have only the one."

"What of his sympathies with the French? How did he answer that?" Caine asked.

"Unmentioned, because I have no proof whatsoever and it would have alerted him there is an investigation underway. When I said that you two would bring charges of attempted murder and testify against him in a court, he very patiently explained that you both have good cause to ruin him. That you, Caine, had threatened him with precisely that. And that you, Grace, strongly resented his assuming your father's title and having care of you because you are willful to the extreme. He cites your plan to marry a total stranger without his consent. And he further swore that you promised to slander him in the worst possible ways."

"What lies!" she cried.

"Of course they are, but a magistrate might not view them as such. He's quite persuasive. And he is an earl."

Caine smiled without humor. "He will never see a court. I vowed that from the beginning."

"You can't kill him, Caine," Neville warned. "I can't let you do that. You would hang."

"But he will be dead first."

"No!" Grace exclaimed, grabbing Caine's arm. "Listen to me. He dares not make another attempt. He cannot, without everyone knowing, now that he's been accused. You have to let it go, Caine."

Caine had grown calm. Deathly calm as he spoke. "Wardfelton is responsible for at least four deaths, including your parents', Grace. And he would have murdered both of us and possibly half this household. He is without conscience and was abominably cruel to you. How can I possibly let that go?"

"He must be stopped," Neville agreed. "Men convinced they are above the law will dare anything. But as it stands now, the law won't touch him. I can't prove his treason and you can't prove murder or even his attempt at it." Neville thought for a moment, then held up a finger. "We must let him hang himself."

"Get him alone. I have rope," Caine said, shifting restlessly, obviously eager to get on with it.

"No, no, that's not what I meant," Neville said with a half smile. "But I'm almost certain that if Wardfelton believes he's gotten away with everything, he'll want to gloat to someone. A man such as he will *need* to. His old cohort Sorenson is dead. Who will he boast to then?"

"Neville's right," Grace said, nodding. "That's exactly how he is. He won't be able to stand not crowing about his cleverness." She looked to Neville. "But to whom would he go? He hasn't any friends, or any acquaintances who would not be horrified by his actions."

"Precisely," Neville agreed. "It would have to be someone whom he knows could do absolutely nothing about it."

"Grace," guessed Caine immediately.

"Me?" she scoffed, crossing her arms over her chest. "He wouldn't dare show his face to me now. Not with all the protection I have about me. He would be mad to try."

"He *is* mad, Grace," Neville said. "Caine is right. It will be you he wants to taunt, to dare you to speak ill of him afterward and he will probably leave you with a threat for good measure."

"Only, he will never leave," Caine promised.

"Oh, stop it, Caine," Grace said. "Go on, Trent."

"We shall let him confess his cleverness to Grace, and there will be hidden witnesses," Neville said. "Reliable ones, with the authority to arrest him."

Caine took Grace's hand in his and gave it a fond squeeze. "I hate to put you in the position of bait, but I believe he will come eventually whether we do this or not. At least we can be in control of the meeting instead of having him spring a surprise visit in the middle of the night as he did before."

Neville added, "He won't be coming to kill you now that he thinks the threat of your accusation is over, Grace, so the danger to you is slight."

"It had better be nonexistent," Caine corrected. "So when should we do this and how do we get him to come when we want?"

Neville smiled. "Simple enough. Invite him to your wedding."

* * *

The Plan, as they now termed it, necessitated yet another delay in the wedding. Two weeks wait ensued so that invitations could be sent, received and replied to, and arrangements for three times as many guests could be made.

The Plan, in order to justify Wardfelton's invitation, required a larger guest list. Twenty or thirty at least would be included, many of them friends and peers of the Hadleys, other neighbors near Wildenhurst. Also attending would be the several gentlemen of Neville's acquaintance, one from the War Office. Caine wondered whether Wildenhurst would be too small to accommodate everyone.

Structural repairs on the cellar had been hastened and the kitchens were shored up, making the upper floors secure. Everything save a few minor surface fixes had been done. He had hired a bevy of workmen out of London who excelled in construction. The repairs and everything else had progressed so smoothly it worried Caine. He had grown so used to crisis on top of crisis, he kept wondering what catastrophe might happen next. The feeling left him on edge.

Now, on the day before the wedding, Caine wondered if the ceremony would really happen or if some other unexpected calamity would prevent it. But perhaps it was only frustration that plagued him. He wanted Grace so desperately and she had become as elusive as the holy grail.

Though she seemed well enough for anything now, Grace had not come to him again in the night. Mrs. Oliver had taken to sleeping in Grace's dressing room with the door left open. She insisted on doing that in the event Grace had a relapse.

All parties involved knew that was not the case. Mrs. Oliver had obviously guessed that he and Grace had anticipated their vows at some point and made it her business to see it did not happen again, at least not before it should.

Grace's injury had demoted her to Little Miss again, he supposed. Grace found all of this highly amusing, judging by her expression when he made the slightest suggestion that they needed to be alone.

"Patience, *love*," she would say and look at him as though he should reply to that in some way.

He thought he might go mad with the waiting and sorely needed more distraction if he was to endure.

The afternoon delivery of the mare he had purchased from a local trader proved a welcome interruption of his libidinous musings. The anticipation of giving Grace a gift lightened his mood considerably.

The roan was a beauty. He gave her a pat and

handed the reins to the groom. "Walk her around to the stables and make her shine, Jacky. Put on Lady Grace's new saddle, too."

He could hardly wait to present the mare to Grace, to see the pleasure on her face and to watch her ride. He imagined her flying across the meadows, wind in her hair, exultation on her face and in every line of her strong, slender body. Yes, just thinking of that expression of flying free she would wear, so like the one...

He shook himself sharply and whipped his mind back to the matter at hand. His gift to her.

While he searched for her in the house, Caine thought back to the first night they had met. He had promised her diamonds and she would have those in her ring. She had opted for a mare and new sidesaddle instead of the curricle and matched pair.

He had promised her freedom, too. He would give her more choices than most women had, but he doubted he could leave her alone for very long at the time. She didn't seem to want free of him anyway.

"Grace?" he called as he entered the kitchens, the last place he'd thought to look, of course.

"In here," he heard her answer. "The still room."

He entered and saw her, covered chin to knee in a large white apron and wearing gloves as she plied a mortar and pestle. "Stirring up spices?"

he asked. "Put it away and come with me. I have a surprise!"

She looked up from her task. "Will it wait a few moments? This has to be completed before I leave it or it will dry out."

Caine leaned against the wall to watch. "Of course. No hurry." Her efficiency impressed him. No wasted effort, no dithering, no pause to question her actions. "You seem to be doing everything yourself," he commented. "Should I hire more help?"

She worked the pestle as she glanced up. "No. Some things I prefer doing myself. Besides, we have taken on so many new people to serve as guards, more hiring would cut into estate profits. As it is, those are minimal at best."

"Are they?" How would she know about profits? "Harrell has complained to you?"

Her hands stilled. "Not at all. We discussed ways to economize, of course, once I studied the finances and began keeping the records."

Caine straightened, frowning. This was his fault. He hadn't had a chance yet to examine the Wildenhurst books. Straightening out Hadley Grange's affairs and dealing with Town expenses had consumed so much of his time and effort. He had assumed that Harrell had things in hand here. "Grace, I never meant you to burden yourself with that sort of thing."

"You said I might do what I would with the

place, and Mr. Harrell has been in a strut since I came, what with managing the guards' schedules, as well as seeing to the crops and tenants. Not to worry, my maths are quite adequate."

"I don't doubt it, but this is too much of an imposition."

"Nonsense." She tossed him a smile as she began bottling the substance she had mixed. "I enjoyed keeping my father's records and did a fair job of it. This is not so different. Only, on a larger scale. It's interesting to me, far more so than sewing, doing little watercolors, playing a pianoforte and the like." Her grimace at that list was endearing. "Mother despaired of me, but Father approved."

"What a delightful daughter you must have been!" Caine said with a chuckle. "Well, I approve of you, too, as you shall soon see."

She began clearing the table and called to one of the scullery maids to wash up. When she had discarded her gloves and apron, she blew a strand of hair from her eyes and raked another behind her ear. "Now then, you have a surprise you say?"

Caine offered his arm. "Indeed. I keep my promises."

And she exceeded hers. Perhaps having a wife might be a deal more advantageous than he once thought. A small weight lifted off his shoulders and he guided her to the stables with a spring in his step.

"Close your eyes!" he ordered her, and gave Jacky and the other grooms a jerk of his head to dismiss them. The boys scurried out, grinning at one another like little jackasses.

He led Grace to the mare that was tethered to a support post between the rows of stalls. The little mount's coat gleamed in the sunlight that streamed through the open doors. The groom had braided a portion of mane and secured it with a ribbon. *Nice touch, Jacky Boy,* he thought with a smile.

"Now, Grace, meet your newest friend, Sienna," he said.

Grace opened her eyes and the look on her face was priceless. In speechless wonder, she reached out and touched the mare. "For me?"

"All yours," he assured her with a grin.

Grace burst into tears, threw her arms around his neck and wept like a child.

Caine was unused to weeping women and hardly knew what to do. Grace never cried! He had done something really wrong. This had to cease! "Please don't!" He patted her back, held her head to his chest until she stopped. "I'm sorry, I thought you would like her," he muttered.

She grasped his face with her hands and kissed him soundly. When she released his lips, she whispered, "I *love* her and you are the *dearest* man!"

Caine's heart swelled as he kissed her back. Nothing wrong, then. Everything right. She tasted of cinnamon, nutmeg and tears, smelled of the spices and all that was Grace and felt as slender and pliable as a willow in his hands. *Everything* right.

A loud equine snuffle intruded on his entirely impossible hope of a quick roll in the hay. Taking his future wife to a hayloft and having his way with her was hardly the thing. Still, it was a worthy fantasy for all that. He released her with a half laugh of regret. "I suppose you'll want to ride?"

She laughed with him, not even attempting to deny her own arousal. It was so evident in her pinkened cheeks, the way her pupils nearly eclipsed the blue of her eyes and the rapid rise and fall of her breath. "I suppose I *should* want to."

He slid one palm over her breast. "We could go inside."

"The house is bursting with people," she replied.

He kissed her neck and whispered, "The accounting office will be deserted. And I should examine your figures."

She laughed low in her throat and pushed closer to him. "A *singular* figure is what you have in mind to examine...and it definitely could stand your attention."

She linked the fingers of one hand with his and gave the mare an absent pat with the other as they wandered out of the stables.

"I have this overwhelming urge to race you inside," he muttered to her as he nodded in passing to Jacky and the lads. They were punching each other and hiding grins behind hands.

"Tempting to rush, but that would draw attention," she replied. But her steps hastened a little even as she said it.

Caine delighted in her frank desire, her playful nature and her unabashed straightforwardness. He even appreciated her eye for propriety, no matter how inconvenient and totally useless it was at the moment. He knew *his* desire was evident to anyone who cared to look in his direction, but perhaps in her relative innocence, she was unaware of that.

They entered the house through the kitchen door and almost made it to the main corridor when Neville intercepted them. "We have an idea you'll want to hear," he announced. "Come in the library. Trent's waiting."

The library. Adjacent to the accounts office. Caine rolled his eyes and groaned as Grace squeezed his hand and murmured, "Patience. One more night."

One more lonely night to endure and she

would be his. The thought of that almost eclipsed his worry about the confrontation with Wardfelton. That remained in mind, however, and would until it was over.

Grace had taken to Neville's sly maneuverings like the proverbial duck to water. The four of them had spent a number of evenings secluded in the Wildenhurst library already, working out the details. Her suggestions proved exceedingly helpful, he admitted. Neville declared she should have been a spy herself, delighting her no end.

This was the last day of it. Tomorrow The Plan would either work or it wouldn't. Caine's nerves were so frayed, he could scarcely think. Grace excused herself, leaving it to them, but was gone only a few moments.

"Look!" she said, sweeping back into the library. She waved the paper she held and plunked it down on the desk. "At last, the expected missive from Uncle Wardfelton. Just as we first thought, he insists on coming. He left it late, though, didn't he! I'd almost given up on him."

Caine couldn't cheer her success as Trent and Neville were doing. They had decided that the invitations should be made by the Hadleys in London, so that Wardfelton's might seem to be a mistake. He had sent an acceptance, of course, unable to resist coming.

Grace had mailed a terse note explaining Aunt Hadley's mistake and warning him not to come, that he was not wanted here, which of course insured that he would.

Caine continued to protest about the risk involved. The closer it came to time, the more he dreaded it. "Neville, I want your men in place by the time we return from the church. There must be absolutely no chance that Grace will be alone with him, even for a moment."

"Not to worry. They want Wardfelton as much as we do, certainly enough to suffer confinement behind the false panels."

"And you, Grace," Caine said, hoping the gravity of his words impressed on her further the need for caution, "Keep the table between you at all times. Never let him near you."

Grace smiled and laid her hand on his arm. "We have been through this time and again. Nothing will go wrong." She gave him a comforting pat and headed out of the room. "Now, if you will excuse me, gentlemen, I have a final fitting on my wedding gown. I will see you all at supper."

Caine tried to imagine the worst that could happen, so he could prepare for it, but it seemed there was no detail left unresolved. "He might not reveal anything that could be used against him. What if he suspects a trap?"

"Then we are no worse off than before," Trent said. "We will try something else."

Neville agreed. "Yes, there's the investigation into his spending habits. Something could turn up yet. But, knowing Wardfelton, I do believe this will work. Grace knows exactly what she must do."

"She must be kept safe," Caine insisted. "Even if it means revealing everything before he's caught. Even if he goes free, laughing at our efforts. Grace must not be hurt again."

Neville sighed and reached for the brandy decanter. "Bridegroom's nerves," he stated as he winked at Trent. "You need a drink." He poured one and sat back. "Caine, leave this to us and enjoy your wedding. Tomorrow should be the happiest of your life thus far, eh? A quarter hour of it to rid England of a traitor and rid yourselves of an enemy is a small concession. The interruption will be over before you know it."

Trent raised his glass in a toast. "Just think how the excitement of it all will add to your wedding night. Grace will be over the moon, flushed with success, ready to celebrate!"

"And your relief will only add to the fervor," Neville added with a laugh.

Caine shot each of them a dark look. "You are both entirely too cavalier. And do stop drinking!" He slammed out of the room, more worried than ever. He knew Neville was right about the nerves, doubly on edge now. Two potentially life-changing events expected in one day were enough to ravel any man's constitution.

* * *

Grace slept quite late the morning of her wedding day. Sun streamed through her window and lay across her bed like a blessing as she drank the chocolate Jane brought her and nibbled on a toast point. Her calmness surprised her a little. She figured it was probably due to the two cups of valerian tea Mrs. Oliver had provided the night before.

Mrs. Bowden peeped into the room. "Good wishes from the staff, Lady Grace! Lord and Lady Hadley have arrived already and Mr. Neville's wife and the doctor have come with them."

"Thank you, Mrs. Bowden. I hope all is in order for the breakfast?"

The woman beamed. "La, you should see! The kitchens are like a hive of bees! They've worked half the night. It'll be grand." She gave a little wave and disappeared, closing the door behind her.

Jane was laying out Grace's wedding clothes, a wistful look on her face as she smoothed out the gown of pale blue taffeta topped with lace-trimmed sarcenet. It was very simply cut, but Grace thought that only added to its elegance.

"We did all right by it even without a proper dressmaker, don't you think?" Grace asked as she slid out of bed. She had not sewn a stitch on the gown itself, for that would have been bad luck, but she had supervised it closely.

She had a moment's thought of that long-ago time when she had dreamed of her future wedding at sixteen. This was real and happening today, though, not a young girl's grand fantasy of some fairy-tale affair. Her hopes and dreams now centered more on her future with Caine, not with fancy trappings or even the ceremony itself. She loved him beyond all reason.

"It's the loveliest frock ever," Jane replied with a misty expression.

Grace bathed quickly and Jane helped her on with the fancy clocked stockings, pantalettes, filmy chemise and brief corset.

All the while, Grace kept watch on the mantel clock. It bonged once at half ten. "A bit over an hour until we leave for the church. Best start on my hair now. Are the irons ready?"

Jane wound and heated the straight locks into curls and caught them up in a crown, surrounding them with a delicate edging of lace. She carefully added the sapphire combs so that they showed to best advantage. "There! More princesslike than a cap or bonnet!"

"I like it. You are a wonder, Janie." Grace peered into her mirror, daubed a bit of rose salve on her lips and smacked them together. She splashed on a bit of scent, pinched her cheeks for color and grinned up at Jane. "Will I do?"

Jane laughed merrily. "Not in your underpinnings! Time for the gown."

Mrs. Oliver hurried in, all aflutter, just as Jane finished buttoning. The housekeeper stood, hands clasped beneath her double chin, and watched as Jane fastened the sapphire necklace Caine had given Grace. "Oh, my lady, you look so *beautiful!* The carriage awaits. The captain's gone down to the church with the menfolk."

Grace gave her a hug. "You look wonderful, Mrs. Oliver. And doesn't Jane look pretty? What would I do without you two?"

"Very well, I should think, but we should go now. Hurry, Jane, and bring her flowers there." She bustled them out like a mother hen. "We shall go along first, Jane, then our little bride and the family will arrive with the church full, waiting to see her. This will be the nicest wedding ever had at Wildenhurst!"

Grace deliberately did not dwell on her uncle at the moment. She was determined he would not impose on this day any more than necessary. For the next hour, she would think only of becoming Caine's wife. The wait had seemed so long, the fear that it would never happen, so great. Now that the time had come, she felt like singing a hallelujah chorus to the world.

Repressing her longing for him and denying him what he desired of her these past weeks was the hardest thing she had ever done. Yesterday in the stables, she had given up trying. If Neville and Trent had not turned up, Grace thought she might have given a rather good account of herself in the accounts room. The thought made her laugh to herself. Caine's disappointment had mirrored her own, but it had worked out for the best, after all. Tonight would be the more perfect for it.

She was no longer an innocent, but she certainly did not regret going to him that night. If not for that, she would now be overset with worry about their wedding night and how it might go between them. As it was, she knew very well how things would progress and could hardly wait. With an entire day to get through, however, she mustn't let herself focus on that just yet.

The open carriage bumped along the drive and onto the road at a snail's pace to avoid throwing up dust. The Hadleys accompanied her, as did Neville's wife, Miranda. She was a lovely lady, and although they'd only just met, Grace hoped they would be friends. Neville had become one in short order. She prompted Miranda to describe their wedding and subsequent travels on the honeymoon as they rode to the church.

She noticed the earl gazing on her with appreciation while Lady Hadley remained her usual quiet self and stared out at the passing scenery. It was a pleasant ride and helped to calm Grace.

That calm ended too soon. When they arrived at the church, everyone was already inside. Except Wardfelton, who stood just outside the door. Waiting.

Chapter Twenty-One

Grace worked to conceal her panic as the Hadleys exited the carriage first.

Neville's wife grasped Grace's hand and whispered. "I shall stay between you. Chin up and smile."

Grace allowed the footmen to assist her down after Miranda. They walked to the church arm in arm as if they were close companions. Neville must have related The Plan and Wardfelton's significance to his wife.

Wardfelton opened the door for the Hadleys and watched them go inside. Then he turned to Grace. "You look rather washed out this morning, niece. Aren't you well?" He offered her arm, which she ignored.

"I feel wonderful," she replied. "Please step aside."

"I mean to escort you in, my dear. What is an uncle for but to give you away in the absence of your *father?*"

She stifled the urge to kick him, but only just. So the taunts had begun already. Why couldn't he have waited until afterward to bait her this way? She felt Miranda squeeze her arm in support.

They entered the vestibule and Wardfelton grasped her other arm, his fingers digging into her flesh. "Go on ahead of us, my lady," he ordered Miranda. "Let's do this properly or *not at all.*"

It was a threat and he was serious. Grace nodded to Miranda. "Go. I shall be fine." If her uncle did the least thing more than walk her down that aisle, Grace meant to scream down the church and claw out his eyes, even if it ruined the wedding and foiled their plan. The men would be on him within seconds. She was not afraid, she kept repeating to herself. He could do nothing to her here in front of so many witnesses. And he would be oh so sorry for this trick later.

Everyone stood as she marched to the altar. Caine frowned darkly at her unexpected escort and started toward them. Grace shook her head and he stopped, hands fisted at his sides. Damn Wardfelton, he was doing everything he could to spoil this for her. She held Caine's gaze and smiled defiantly.

There was no way she could conceal her deep breath of relief when her uncle deposited her at Caine's side and stepped a few feet away.

The ceremony became a blur, her responses instinctive, until Caine slipped the ring onto her finger and peered down at her, deep concern in his eyes. She swallowed and squeezed his hand to reassure him she was all right.

Thank goodness she had not even heard the vicar question whether anyone had objections. If she had, she might have expected Wardfelton to speak up. But now the words resounded that she had waited far too long to hear spoken.

"By the Grace of God and the Church of England, I pronounce you husband and wife together. What God has joined, let no man put asunder."

Indeed, that would be her constant prayer all day.

And then Caine was kissing her. Hungrily, desperately, as if they might never kiss again. She shuddered at the thought that they might not, even as she responded to Caine in kind.

Applause followed as they strode quickly down the aisle to the church doors. Guests had spilled out and were tossing flowers and rice as Caine rushed her to the waiting carriage and lifted her in. He climbed up beside her, tossed a handful of coins to the well-wishers, signaled the driver and they were off to the manor.

He threw his arms around her and held her close. "God help me, I thought I might kill him right there at the altar," he gasped. "Are you all right, Grace?"

"I will be if you cease cracking my ribs. Nothing he could do will spoil this day for me, Caine. Tell me you feel the same."

"I do, I swear. How did he get his hands on you? Guards were all along the way here. Where was Uncle Hadley?"

Grace sighed, pushing away a little so she could breathe. "It was so neatly done, and at the church door. I expect the earl hadn't time to think how to avoid it. Miranda tried her best." She shrugged. "It turned out well enough in the end. He did give me to you without a scene."

Caine picked up his hat, which had fallen off onto the carriage seat. "Ah well, we shall have to do vows again. I scarcely recall a word of what I promised you." His smile was wry as he met her eyes.

Grace appreciated his attempt to conceal his anger and concern. "Neither do I. Perhaps it's that way for all brides and grooms. Well, at least we know the gist of it." She stretched out her arm and looked at her wedding ring for the first time, a gold band set with five sparkling stones.

"I did promise you diamonds," he reminded

her. "Though, the sapphires suit you perfectly." He touched the gems of her necklace. "I suppose I should have thought to buy you pearls for the wedding. More appropriate and sedate."

Grace laughed. "Pearls are boring little things."

"Which you never are, so I forgive myself." He settled her against him and sighed. "So it's done. Here we are, wed at last. Hard to believe after so much going on to prevent it."

He would believe it soon enough, Grace decided, smiling to herself. In a few hours time, perhaps not that long, they would have nothing left to distract them from a future together, a future as shiny and as full of fire as her new diamonds.

Mrs. Bowden, Cook and the staff had outdone themselves. Grace had never seen such an array of food as was presented at the wedding breakfast. She counted at least thirty guests in attendance and likely missed a few with all the milling around. Most were strangers to Grace, friends and peers of the Hadleys.

Tables had been set about the drawing room, as well as two buffets laden with food. Musicians played softly so as not to interfere with conversations. Huge arrangements of roses scented the air and added festive color.

Grace refused to let the imminent confron-

tation with Wardfelton detract from her immediate happiness and pride in her new home and
the Wildenhurst people who had made it all possible.

Once the meal concluded, toasts had been
made and cake had been served, the event took
on the attitude of a ball. Tables were being
cleared for dancing. The musicians began playing and the day wore on. Grace stayed on edge,
her only comfort Caine's nearness. She wanted
Wardfelton gone so she could enjoy what was
left of the day.

Finally, Neville caught her eye and gave an
almost imperceptible nod. She nudged Caine.
"Time to ignore me. Go."

He clutched her hand. "Take care, Grace.
Promise?"

"I shall."

"I love you," he whispered, then left her side.

Why in Heaven's name couldn't the man declare that when she wasn't poised on the edge of
some cliff? Grace threw up a hand and blinked
with frustration as he walked away to join Trent
and Neville. She let herself appear annoyed, as
indeed she was.

That was precisely when she saw Wardfelton across the room, smirking. Her cue to proceed, she figured. She began to weave her way
through the crowd of guests until she reached
the vestibule. It was deserted at the moment. As

planned, even Judd was not hanging about. The south end of the house was closed off to guests, including the morning room they had prepared for the confrontation.

She glanced back and saw her uncle heading in her direction. A moment longer and he would be able to see exactly where she was going. Grace waited, then went into the morning room across the vestibule's corridor from the drawing-room doorway.

She closed the door, crossed the room and waited. "I'm here," she said in a low voice, alerting the men behind the false wall panels constructed for this purpose alone. That had taken two full days, but they looked perfectly normal, as if they had been there since the room was first built. "If you hear me well, knock twice and hurry." The knocks came. She knew that Caine and Neville would be just outside the windows in the event of trouble. She should be perfectly safe.

One deep breath, followed by another and another before she heard the door latch click open.

"You have deserted your guests," her uncle said, an amused reprimand.

"I felt stifled, but now I find it even more so in here," she retorted.

"Grace, Grace, you were once such a delightful girl, quite likeable, and I was glad to have you around. So industrious, so helpful."

"You tried to kill me!"

He laughed. "I could have, at any time, you know. I kept hoping you would relieve me of that necessity."

"I hate you!" The angry exclamation had slipped out. Grace knew she needed to make him confess, not leave in a huff. She took a deep breath and clenched her eyes to regain her composure.

"Oh, Grace. And here I came to do my duty," he said as he pulled a cigar from his pocket. "And to warn you not to persist in your wild accusations." He proceeded to light the cigar and puff on it, pausing only to add, "I will ruin your life and Morleigh's if you do."

"Ha! You'll be found out soon enough. Caine is going to the gunpowder company. They will remember that you were the one who ordered it and took delivery. That will *soundly* implicate you in the plot to destroy us." She moved around the table as he tried to approach her.

"They won't recognize me, Grace. People see only what they expect to see," he said with an evil grin. "I went there in disguise. With an eye patch. A private jest, you see. A former soldier who needed the job. He gave me work." Wardfelton laughed. "And so did your Mr. Harrell here. As a guard. Imagine that."

"You think you're so clever, don't you? Mr. Sorensen obviously thought himself so, too.

Well, neither of you were." She shot him a sly look and repeated the words she had looked up and memorized. Her own idea, an added prod. *"Ceci va exactement comme vous avez prévu? Peut-être ma mémoire est meilleure maintenant."*

His expression of shock was worth memorizing every word in the French language, not only the few she had committed. Grace smiled, eyebrows raised, awaiting his response.

For a long moment, he remained silent. When he did speak, his words were calm. "So you *were* taught. Not very well, Grace. Your French is atrocious."

"A bit lacking, perhaps, but you may be assured that I comprehend far better than I speak it," she lied.

"I suppose this is meant to let me know you did overhear us that evening. To answer your poorly phrased question, yes, things are going exactly as planned with only a few minor diversions. And your memory of it is of no consequence at all. I warn you, repeating what you heard between Sorenson and me will gain you nothing. No one will believe it," he snapped. *"No one."*

"That you are a spy? That you committed treason? Oh, I believe some will listen to me!"

He tossed down the cigar and moved around

the table toward her, but Grace moved, too, keeping her distance.

"I was never a spy," he said, clearing his throat, straightening his sleeves and staring down his long straight nose. "The funds I provided the French were only for insurance."

She pursed her lips and trailed one finger along the tabletop, as if pondering what he said. "Insurance against what, pray tell?"

"In the beginning, I believed that revolution here was imminent. The unrest, the rabble siding with the citizens of France against the nobles posed a credible threat. My inheritance was new then. I merely sought a way to keep what was mine if it ever happened."

"So Sorensen collected it from you for the French," Grace said, willing him to admit everything in detail.

He glared to one side, as if remembering the arrangement, perhaps justifying his actions to himself. "Soren Sennelier promised me I would lose nothing after the revolution reached England if I supported Bonaparte beforehand. He nearly beggared me, the bloody fool."

"Sennelier? So your Mr. Sorensen was a Frenchman," Grace said, waiting for him to elaborate.

He scoffed. "Yes, but I never *spied,* Grace. The very thought is ridiculous. Say as much and you'll be laughed out of London. I am a peer of the realm and I would never *spy!*"

"You gave the Corsican financial support that aided his cause," she argued. "That sounds very much like treason to me. What happened when the war ended? Did you refuse to pay when the man blackmailed you? Is that why you killed him?"

He puffed out his chest, indignant. "I did not kill him!"

"Hired it done, did you? And that gunpowder for Caine and me would have provided you distance. What about my parents, *Uncle?* Your own brother and sister-in-law? Did you distance yourself from that death scene, as well? With poison, perhaps?"

The very thought of it incensed Grace. "Haven't you enough evil in you to murder face-to-face?" She felt such hatred for him at that moment, such livid anger, she cared nothing about proximity. She saw a trace of regret flicker in his eyes. "How could you kill your own *brother?*" she demanded.

He looked away from her as he moved around the table. "He should never have threatened me." His eyes met hers again. "And neither should you!"

She was close enough to strike him, so she did. She dealt him a resounding slap that numbed her hand.

Wall panels flew open and three men emerged, two armed with pistols. Grace yelped as Wardfelton grabbed and turned her back against him. The arm on her neck choked off her breath. "Back away or I will kill her!"

And they did! Grace clawed at his arm to no avail as the three men watched, tensed to interfere, but not moving. "Help!" she cried, struggling.

He was too strong, nearly lifting her right off the floor by his grip on her neck. She cursed the temper that had led her to carelessness. Caine would be furious with her!

Wardfelton was dragging her near the windows. "Open one!" he demanded of the man standing closest to them, the one unarmed official.

Grace could not let the traitorous murderer get away and she certainly didn't mean to let him take her with him. Why didn't the men overpower him? He only had an arm around her neck!

She fought, trying her best to twist away or reach behind her and hurt him somehow. Nothing she did broke his stranglehold. Next thing she knew, he had backed through the open floor-length window and dragged her with him.

She didn't know how he planned to leave with her. Or maybe she did. Teams were tethered to graze at the side of the house, out of their traces for the duration of the celebration. Break her neck, take one horse, scatter the others and he could get away!

"Nooo!" She screamed and kicked backward, hitting his knee. His hold loosened as he cursed her and she bit down hard through his sleeve. The moment his arm jerked, Grace dropped to the ground and scrambled away.

She looked back in time to see Caine plant him a facer worthy of a boxing champion. She winced as Wardfelton stumbled backward and fell against a window left closed, smashing the panes with his head.

Caine rushed to her and helped her up. "Are you daft, woman?" Furious. Just as she had known he would be. He must have come out the front to watch through the windows and would have seen how she disobeyed, letting Wardfelton get too close.

"I went a little mad, yes!" She looked down, extremely put out with herself at her lapse of caution.

Her shoulders drooped as she exhaled sharply. The danger was past but she was a wreck. Shaking with relief, yet angry that the entire day was spoiled. She flapped her arms once in frustration and brushed a hand over her grass-stained gown. "I've ruined it."

"To hell with the dress, Grace! You nearly got yourself killed!" Caine shook visibly, huffing like an angry bull about to charge. "God, when he raised that knife…"

"Knife?" Grace squeaked. "There was a knife?"

Caine caught her as she swayed. "Steady on, Grace. This isn't over yet."

Grace leaned against him, holding fast to the front of his coat for a moment. Then she straightened and glanced over at Neville, who was kneeling beside Wardfelton. "How is he?"

Neville shook his head. "Neck's severed." Others, including Trent were spilling out the front door to see what had caused the commotion

Explanations must be made. Caine and his family must not suffer the scandal of having a traitor in his wife's family. She refused to let Wardfelton's perfidy ruin them.

She ran to Neville and leaned close. "Bury this, Neville. Do not let Caine's family suffer for it."

Pretending hysterics, she rushed back and grasped Caine's arm, muttering swiftly so that none but he could hear, "Clear everyone away as soon as may be. No one must remark the window was broken inward instead of outward." She pushed away from him, waving her arm in distress as she cried out, "My poor uncle has fallen through the glass! Hurry! Someone fetch the doctor!"

Grace hoped Neville had the presence of mind to remove the knife from her uncle's hand before anyone happened to see it. "A distraction," she ordered Caine. "Remember Cavanaugh's?"

Hand to her head, Grace collapsed against him with a loud, tortured moan. He grabbed her up in his arms and met the gathering crowd with her in his arms, pushing through as he exclaimed in a loud voice, "Please, men, get the ladies back inside! It's a bloody sight they shouldn't see! She's fainted from it! I need help!"

The guests trailed him en masse, hurrying to keep up, concerned for the bride, murmuring sympathy, offering suggestions. Caine carried her into the drawing room, laid her on the divan there and knelt beside her. "Someone, smelling salts, please!"

Grace suffered the sharp smell as he shoved the bottle under her nose. Her sneeze wrecked her attempt to revive with any dignity. She peered up at Caine and sobbed. "Uncle should not have had so much to drink," she moaned. "I was too late to save him!"

"There, there, dearest," Caine said, brushing her hair from her forehead and laying a kiss on it. "You cannot blame yourself!"

"No, no, gel!" the earl piped up. "Tippling even before the wedding, he was, and after, too! Hardly ate a bite to soak it up! Damned shame, that, but what can be done?" He began pontificating to the others about the evils of drink, drawing much of the attention away from Caine and Grace. The countess stood by the earl, nodding.

Ten minutes later, Trent strode in. "There was nothing to be done for him," he announced. "I am very sorry, Lady Grace, but your uncle is dead."

Grace buried her face in Caine's vest since no tears would come. Damn Wardfelton. Even in death he had almost ruined her life. She would don no black for that man, no matter what society might expect of her.

Caine stroked her hair. "It is over now, sweetheart," he crooned. "Let me take you upstairs to recover."

"Yes, let's put the poor child to bed. I'll bring up something to help her sleep," Mrs. Oliver declared.

Caine lifted Grace again and spoke to the guests in a sorrowful tone, "Thank all of you for coming today to share our joy. I regret such a tragedy marks the occasion for all of us. Please have care on your way home."

It was a kind dismissal, Grace thought. And necessary. Caine took her to her room and Trent followed them up, closing the door behind him.

"Trent! Get out of here!" Caine ordered. "This is the first chance I've had to kiss my bride since the ceremony."

He laughed. "Kiss her, then, but hurry. You haven't time to...do anything else...much. The earl insists we meet him in the master suite's sitting room within the hour, and I wanted to give you my gift before I have to leave." He handed over two wrapped parcels. He waited. "Well?"

Grace tore off the paper wrapping of hers. Trent had captured Caine at his worst, unshaven, hair tousled, the old eye patch turned up on his forehead. He wore an expression of absolute ennui. It was a perfect likeness, yet so totally unlike the Caine she knew, Grace couldn't control her laughter.

Caine rolled his eyes at the sight, but he laughed with her. Trent preened at their responses as he pointed to the parcel Caine held.

Caine ripped the paper off and his laughter died. He looked at the picture for several moments, then at Trent and nodded, obviously pleased. "Now *that* is Grace. A labor of love, wasn't it?"

"For you both," Trent said.

Grace tipped the picture so that she could see. "But it's not funny!" she said, surprised at the way Trent had portrayed her. "Why, I look so...I don't know...sort of windblown and transported! *This* is how the two of you see me?" Perhaps how they *wished* she appeared.

"Exactly the way you look when you ride," Caine said, nodding.

Grace grinned. "Then I might decide to *live* on a horse! Thank you!" She gave Trent a quick hug and kissed his cheek.

Trent cleared his throat. "On that pretty note, I believe I shall make my exit. See you in a quarter hour. Earl's orders."

Grace barely had time to tend Caine's fist, repair her hair and brush off her gown. And have that kiss. She could barely tear herself away when Caine ended it.

"We have to go," he said, "and say good-night to everyone. Then I want you all to myself."

All the guests had already departed Wildenhurst, except for the Hadleys, Dr. Ackers, Trent, Neville and his wife. The three men who had come at Neville's behest had taken Wardfelton's body away to London. Mrs. Oliver kept the staff busy in the kitchens preparing a light supper.

Everyone who remained now repaired to the master chamber's sitting room as the earl requested. Grace thought it an odd place to gather, but figured his lordship must be too exhausted from the day's events to meet downstairs.

Hadley took charge once they had all assembled. "This will be brief and to the point," he declared. "We will put what has happened with Wardfelton behind us now. Life is too short to dwell on unhappy doings."

No one objected to that— Least of all, Grace.

She smiled her thanks to the earl, who looked very like a king holding court.

He smiled back at her as he continued, "I suppose each of you knows that, according to Dr. Ackers, Grace has saved my life, or at least prolonged and improved it. Also, Caine has had the goodness to keep me informed of everything despite my frailties. I thank you, my boy, for your continued deference to the title and for your trust. My wedding gift to you both is joint title to Wildenhurst."

He handed Caine the deed. Grace curtsied as Caine bowed and thanked him.

"Neville," the earl said in a strong, sonorous voice, "you and your Miranda shall have the hunting box in Northumberland, since you loved it so as a little lad. Refurbishments were begun when you married and now have been completed."

He handed Neville the documents for that. "Apologies for my lies to your cousin concerning your character. I had to do something to get him hopping after that Thoren-Snipes debacle." He grunted a rusty laugh. "If not pushed to wed, I feared he might give up on women altogether."

"Never the smallest chance of that, sir," Trent drawled, "but I grant you, he might not have married."

"All is forgiven, sir," Neville assured the earl. "Miranda and I thank you for the gift."

"Now, briefly back to this business with Wardfelton," the earl said to Neville. "Buried now, is it? I hope maybe you might prevent a scandal?"

"Not a single rumor will emerge," Neville promised. "I was assured today by my colleague from the War Office that the Regent will be most grateful if treason by one of his nobles is never brought to light." His questioning gaze went to Dr. Ackers, the only one among them who might expose the truth.

Ackers nodded. "The earl of Wardfelton bled out from a glass cut through his jugular vein after stumbling through a window. There was liquor on his breath when I examined the body. An accidental death with no indication of foul play that I could ascertain."

The earl smiled and slapped Ackers on the back. "Fine then, that concludes the business of the day. Everyone who is hungry should repair to the dining room, partake as hastily as possible and be off to London!"

"It will be full dark before you reach Town!" Grace said quickly. "Surely you'll wait until morning!"

Hadley was nearly to the door, leading the way. "Not possible, gel. The master's bed here is no longer mine to occupy. Besides, I am still earl and have matters in London long neglected. Come along, Bewley dear, mustn't dawdle, eh!"

The countess did delay, though, stopping beside Grace. "She was a fool, wasn't she? You know, the pretty one?"

"Quite right, ma'am, indeed she was," Grace replied.

"I thought so," the countess said in her odd, pensive way. "Here." She handed Grace a small piece of embroidery still stretched in its little frame, then followed everyone else out of the room.

Grace looked down at the gift so off-handedly presented. A ring of jagged and mismatched roses surrounded Grace's name. The letters were crooked and oddly worked, but the fact that the countess had done this just for her brought tears to Grace's eyes.

Caine was looking at it, too. "Not the most beautiful thing in the world, is it?" he commented when they were alone.

"Perhaps not on the surface," Grace replied, holding the piece to her chest and loving it. "But beyond that…"

"So, Mrs. Morleigh, are you hungry?" Caine asked, still standing with his arm around her.

"For once, food is the last thing on my mind," she replied, her heart full of happiness, anticipation rushing through her like a wildfire.

"Then perhaps it's time for bed," he suggested, sliding his arms around her and drawing her close.

She cut her gaze to his teasing one. "Don't you think we should wait for darkness to fall?"

He grinned, swept her off her feet and into the adjacent master's chamber, kicking the door shut behind him. "I think we've waited quite long enough."

Grace laughed as he tossed her onto the massive bed and followed her down. His mouth was hot as it found hers, his body insistent as he pressed her into the counterpane. He finally relented, breathless as he rose to his knees and tugged off his coat.

Grace watched with fascination as he undressed. Nothing meticulous or methodical about it, thank goodness. She reached up and toyed with the buttons on the flap of his trousers, undoing them one by one while he dispensed with his waistcoat. He yanked his shirt over his head as she reached the last button.

"Now you," he growled as he flipped her over and unbuttoned her gown. His impatience delighted her, fueled her eagerness as they wrestled her out of her clothes.

He kissed her again, thoroughly. And unexpectedly released her. Grace watched as he ran a hand through his hair and laughed a little.

"Better give me a minute to marshal my senses, or this will be too swiftly done," he advised as he lay down beside her, holding her more gently against him.

Grace looked into his eyes. She touched the scars that surrounded them with her finger. "I treasure every line of these marks. Without them, I would not have you. You do know that I love you, Caine? That I chose you freely that first night I came to you? It had nothing to do with gratitude."

"I hope that's true," he murmured, kissing her finger as it traced his lips. "For there's no going back, ever."

"There never was any question of that," she admitted. "Not since you first asked me to dance."

He kissed her again, tenderly, sweetly as his hand slid over her body. "We'll dance often, then. A ball every week if you want. Fox hunts, house parties, whatever you wish." He nipped her earlobe.

"But the time involved in all that, Caine. What of your work, your duties and dealings for the earl? I know your worries about that and I refuse to be an impediment."

He pulled her on top of him and framed her face with his palms. "You are no impediment, Grace. You're a part of me, the very best part. You remind me to live life and take it as it comes, good or ill, instead of driving myself mad trying to impose order on everyone and everything. You keep me sane, even as you drive me mad."

She moved sinuously beneath him, sliding her arms around his waist. "Then say you love me when I'm not poised to die, would you please?"

He leaned to press his lips to hers for just an instant. "I do love you, Grace. I think from the first time I saw those eyes of yours speaking to me from across Cavanaugh's ballroom."

He wore a serious look as he softly repeated words once spoken so loudly for all to hear. *"You've quite stolen my heart and I cannot live without you.* I said it then, Grace. But I *know* that I mean it now."

"And I simply cannot wait to be your wife," she said, echoing her own words of that fateful night in a slow, suggestive tone. "It's not a done thing yet, you know."

So, in the earl's enormous bed covered with a deep yellow canopy, they made it so.

Epilogue

April 1816, London

"She's making up for lost seasons," Caine remarked, nodding to Grace from across the room as he watched his uncle Hadley lead her sedately in a quadrille. "Danced every dance. I had to call in reinforcements."

Trent smiled and pointed with his glass of champagne. "The most beautiful of the lot, as it turned out. Not exactly what you once asked me to find for you."

"Not in any respect." Caine laughed. He did that often these days and with excellent reason.

"Oh, my, would you look there?" Trent said, keeping his voice low. "Miss Thoren-Snipes herself, pirouetting so grandly under the hand of Lord Logan. What an absolutely off-putting sight!" He made a face and shuddered.

Caine followed the direction of Trent's gaze. "Off-putting? That's ill said of you, man." He remembered when the very people around them were probably saying the same of him. "The fellow can't help being old and wrinkled."

"Oh, not Logan." Trent shook his head. "I meant *her*." He grinned at Caine. "Watch when she turns around."

Caine looked, squinting to focus better. The couple danced closer and Belinda made the turn. "My God, what is that on her bare back? Looks like a terrible boil or something. Two of them, in fact!"

"Pustules, yes." Trent sighed sorrowfully. "Too bad they aren't real."

"Look genuine to me," Caine observed.

"Hmm. Amazing what a half-baked sculptor can fashion with globs of soft rosin, a bit of paint and rabbit-skin glue, isn't it?"

"I daresay you have missed your calling." Caine drew his mouth to one side and considered. "Must have been damned hard to apply."

"Had to dance with her twice," Trent admitted. "Ruined my left glove." He polished off his champagne and reached for another as a servant passed by with a tray. "But I do love the waltz."

Trent would never grow up, Caine thought with a chuckle, just as the music dwindled and

Uncle Hadley brought Grace back to him. Trent made his bow and reached for her hand. "May I?"

Her cheeks were flushed with pleasure and she was a bit breathless, cooling herself with the new silk fan that perfectly matched her dress of azure blue. Her eyes sparkled like the sapphires she wore and the beautifully tortured curls danced as she shook her head. "That has to be my last turn for a while! Sorry, Trent."

"She's danced quite enough for tonight. In fact, we should be leaving soon," Caine declared, laying down the law with a look directed at Trent, his uncle and Grace.

"Will you let this bounder order you about that way?" Trent demanded of her. "What a bully he's become!"

"Well, we must forgive and indulge him, you see. After all, the man is…" she said, pausing for a second before whispering the rest, "in an *interesting way.*"

Trent's mouth dropped open as his gaze shot from her to Caine, to Hadley and back again to Grace. "You don't say!"

Caine grinned ear to ear as she leaned forward, fan open to shield her next whisper as she confided to them, "He's to become a father."

Trent and his uncle whooped, disturbing the crowd around them as they slapped him on the back and kissed Grace's hands.

Caine decided he rather enjoyed these social

events again, but would be even happier when they could return to Wildenhurst.

Fortunately, he would not need to worry about taking up the mantle of lord anytime soon. The earl seemed hale enough to last a good while.

Grace had been a godsend, putting in order the Hadley finances and numerous other tasks Caine had thought so overwhelming when faced with them alone. How could he ever have thought she would be a hindrance?

Each day when he looked into his mirror to shave, his scars were still there, unchanged. But he saw a new man who bore them, thanks to her, a very happy man full of hopes, dreams and plans. Ironically, Grace's appearance was so different, no one recognized her as the sad wallflower of almost a year ago. And yet, she was the same inside herself, a force to be reckoned with and a joy to all who knew her.

He wished with all his might that she now carried a tiny Grace within her, because the world, and especially he, would be exceedingly glad to have two such marvels. However, an heir would be perfectly acceptable this time around.

They said their good-nights at twelve, left the ball and strolled the short distance to Hadley House, arm in arm. "Uncle and Aunt Hadley won't be home until the wee hours," he said. "What shall we do with ourselves?" He had ideas.

She squeezed his arm with both hands and peered up at him, her expression very serious. "You have a mad craving for strawberries, don't you, my darling?"

"Strawberries." He nodded. "Mmm-hmm. And perhaps some cream?"

"I knew it. I could sense it," she said, nodding emphatically, hurrying him along. "I'll order a tray sent up for us the moment we get there. For the life of me, I don't know how we shall get you through these next six months with all these unusual cravings of yours." She clicked her tongue and shook her head.

Caine smiled, loving her so dearly he ached with it, an ache she sensed and soothed quite often. She was the one with a taste for the strawberries, of course. And the oranges out of season. And cucumber slices with jam. He winced and wondered if he could hide his portion under the pillows next time they were required.

All he ever really craved was Grace.

* * * * *